THROUGH THE HEADLIGHTS
AN AUTO-BIOGRAPHY

♦

Peter & Gwenny —

Maybe your car is more astute
than you suspected!

Mike

THROUGH THE HEADLIGHTS
AN AUTO-BIOGRAPHY

Michael L. Oliver

First Henway Publishing
paperback edition November 2011

ISBN: 978-0-615-52785-7

Designed by Steve Mitchell

Published in the United States of America
by Henway Publishing, Napa Valley California

Manufactured in the United States of America

THROUGH THE HEADLIGHTS
AN AUTO-BIOGRAPHY

Michael L. Oliver

HENWAY
PUBLISHING
NAPA VALLEY, CALIFORNIA

*To everybody who
has had a conversation
with a car, especially those
who are partial to a stick shift.
You know who you are.*

TABLE OF CONTENTS

Chapter 1:   Dust, snow, idiots and a long life   1

Chapter 2:   Surviving teenage drivers   17

Chapter 3:   All American with a bermuda bell   33

Chapter 4:   Convoy   49

Chapter 5:   Semaphores in the wind   61

Chapter 6:   Chicken feathers and a sticky pinion   79

Chapter 7:   Weird wiring   91

Chapter 8:   Roads well traveled   107

Chapter 9:   Reclining seats and another baby   125

Chapter 10:   Feisty survivor   143

Chapter 11:   Elegant but doomed   173

Chapter 12:   Life in the slow lane   187

Chapter 13:   Not exactly a Ferrari   203

Chapter 14:   New beginnings   221

Chapter 15:   Pursuing the ultimate image   241

Chapter 16:   Pesky American speed limits   263

Chapter 17:   Wisdom   283

Epilogue   305

FOREWORD

Back in the dark ages of the 1950s I knew I must get a car. It didn't much matter what kind of a car. Cool would have been nice, but I would have settled for anything with internal combustion and wheels. Although I had logged many miles on my bike by then, no self-respecting boy with a new driver's license would deign to be seen on a lowly two-wheeled vehicle with seating for one and no engine. Nope. I had to get a car. A car meant freedom. Independence. Adventure. A crucial rite (and right!) of passage. It was my destiny and my obsession. That beautiful Model A Ford with more than its fair share of dents, its rusty bumpers, a gazillion miles on the odometer, a leaky crankcase and a broken heater was the first of many cars in my life. While other people turned up their noses at the fume emissions from its leaky carburetor, I smelled a manly cologne. I've owned quite a few vehicles since that first one and I'm fairly certain there will be more in my future. I've loved some of them, tolerated others and hated a few, but all had a presence and their own distinct influence on my life.

I don't pretend to be a gearhead. I'm confident I could take an engine apart but I'm not too sure I could put it back together without a few puzzling leftover parts. I don't know a lot of technical stuff and I don't have a skilled mechanic's appreciation of a finely designed engine. Nor am I in a position to buy a warehouse and stock it with classics displayed on a spotless floor to make other guys jealous. That's not to say, though, that

I don't recognize quality or that I can't hear a car when it's trying to tell me something.

On occasion I find myself reflecting on all the cars I've driven through the years, beginning with my first love, that '31 Model A. And as I relive those old memories I sometimes wonder what, if that ancient Ford could talk, it would say about me. Would it like me as much as I liked it? Would it be annoyed that I never fixed its heater? Would it resent the stupid teenage antics and abuse I subjected it to? And what opinions about me might its successors have formed? These questions led to the creation of Leroy, the book's central character and common denominator for a diverse group of cars, experiences and observations.

Rational people think of cars as mindless, inanimate machines that are built of metal, plastic, rubber and glass in factories. But who hasn't at one time or another spoken to his or her car? And who among us hasn't named at least one of our cars? As we live with our cars they develop their own personalities, quirks and needs which they make known to us. Indeed, they definitely communicate in their own way. If we take the time to listen, we will hear them. And for all we know they're a lot more insightful about us than we are about ourselves.

Chapter 1

DUST, SNOW, IDIOTS
AND A LONG LIFE

My owner over the past three years was Mr. Guiglini, the local butcher. He wasn't much of a mechanic, but he did keep me running with the help of a pretty handy guy named Harvey who owned the gas station across the street. Cars can tell if somebody who works on us is any good or not and I reckoned Harvey was no worse than most and a lot better than some. He knew where my lube points was, what kind of oil I was partial to, how tight to make my fan belt and how to gap a spark plug. He replaced a lot of my baling wire with proper nuts and bolts and metal straps, and my brakes, carburetor, plugs and points was all new, rebuilt or adjusted. My tires was still used recaps. It didn't really matter, though, since I'm not likely to go for a long road trip, much as I'd like to. I don't recollect ever having new tires and I can only imagine how good they must feel: tubes not covered with patches, no boots or plugs, and deep tread that holds me on the road a whole lot better than them shiners do.

It was 1956 and I found myself in a place called Chester, a small lumber town up north in California's Sierra Nevada Mountains. By then I wasn't sure how many more miles I had left in me. I was just plumb tuckered out and crotchety.

I was built in 1931, after the Great Depression had settled in. That was the same year that the Empire State Building was built and the Star Spangled Banner became our National Anthem. This also was the last year us Model A's was built. I was affordable and there ain't nothing fancy about me. I'm of simple design and function. I don't have no radio. I do have a heater, although it don't work worth a tinker's damn. I suffered through them hard years like everbody else did, with bad gas, recycled oil, recaps and baling wire. Just when I thought times was about to get better, our country was in the midst of World War II, so my dreams of unlimited gas, new oil and real rubber on my tires stayed on hold. It didn't make no never mind, though. I wasn't no worse off than any other car, just getting a little old and dinged up.

Something most people don't know about cars is that we have memories. We can generally recollect our original owners, how much we cost when we was new and how much we was last sold for. Most of the in-between transactions just blew out of my exhaust pipe. Rather than trying to do all that remembering of the past, I decided a while back that it would be a whole lot easier just to be like a dog and live in the here and now. That ain't all bad, since cars often have things happen to them that is better forgotten, lest they shut down permanently to avoid it.

I don't recollect exactly where I was first bought, although it was someplace in Oklahoma and it was for $750. The first few years of my life wasn't bad. I was on a hardscrabble farm with a family of four who didn't do much other than work, eat, sleep and go to church. It was dusty there and I mostly sat because my owner couldn't afford much gas. It wasn't a bad life all in all, but we left it behind after a dry year that cost the family their entire crop. Everything they could carry was piled on my roof and tied to my fenders and into a right pitiful little two-wheeled trailer, and we set out for a long trip west. We ended up a couple weeks later in southern California. I met a mess of other cars pretty much like me — dirty, dented, overloaded and pretty much held together with tape, chewin' gum and rusty wire. My owners, like the others, lived in community camps and tried to eke out their living by picking fruit. It was a tough time since there was a lot more pickers than there was fruit. It was a sad time as well. None of the cars, myself included, had much to smile about. We was all overworked and underserviced. On them days when the family could get work, I'd be drove to some orchard to spend my day in the hot sun while they picked oranges, peaches, prunes or whatever was being harvested just then. When there wasn't no work, which was most days, I would either sit in the camp or be drove to another one where things didn't seem no more promising.

One good thing was that I got to see a lot of country and meet a lot of other cars. The ones from California used to make fun of our accents. When we spoke they could tell we was Okie cars. I didn't find it funny at all and I didn't even bother coming up with any smart comebacks. They wasn't worth it. Them cars from out of state, though, was mostly decent. As I got to know them I learned that my situation wasn't no worse than theirs and that made me feel a might better.

I'd been in California for a couple of years when my owner flat run out of money and had to sell me. After that I went through a whole passel of different owners, some nice, some not, and all poor as church mice on welfare. I reckoned that my life was destined to be what I was going through so I tried to make peace with it. I vowed to leave the bad memories behind if I could, aim my radiator cap at the present and get through it. As a result, what I can remember most about my life is just my last couple of years. It ain't brain damage. I've got a good memory. It's just short.

For now my life was with Mr. Guiglini. He had hired Leroy, a teenager, to work in his shop after school. He let Leroy drive me to make deliveries to the local restaurants. He was too young to drive legal but nobody worried too much about that back then, especially in small towns with only one policeman who had better things to do than hassle kids. I have to say it was a fairly iffy relationship at first with Leroy. He told Mr. Guiglini he knew how to drive. It was plain as the grill on my hood to me that he hadn't never drove no stick shift before me. Talk about painful! That kid had the goldangdest huge clodhoppers and no concept of how to make me start off without coughing, lurching, stalling, and causing way too much grinding pain in my gearbox for a car my age. The first time he took me on a delivery he jammed his size 11 boot on the clutch, stomped on my gas pedal and released the clutch way before I was ready. So I killed my engine to catch my breath. He started me up again, went through the same routine, and so did I. After the third time it started to sink into his zit-covered noggin that I was more likely to respond to a gentle touch; that if he let my clutch out gradual and pressed my gas pedal gradual, we might reach an understanding. I suppose kids have to learn by doing, but I sure would have been happier if Leroy had done his doing on some other poor car.

To his credit, Leroy was a fast learner for a teenaged human male. After that first painful experience he worked hard to become one with his machine, and I was able to trust him a little more. And then it snowed. It snowed for three days without letup. I hadn't been drove since it started and my roof and hood was feeling pretty heavy, with almost three feet of the stuff piled on me.

Leroy had to make a delivery to Larry's Greasy Spoon Cafe that evening. The snowplows had done their jobs, but us cars, especially the ones with bald tires, get nervous on roads that are covered with snow and ice, and when that first good storm of the winter hit Chester, I could tell that he was every bit as scared as I was, like some car going downhill at 60 when the lug nuts start to loosen. We both knew he had never drove on a slick road and we both was praying to our respective Gods, his somewhere up in the sky and mine in Michigan. Leroy used his arms to scrape the snow off of me which I appreciated. The added weight was OK as long as I was sitting still but it would have been pointless and a strain on my little four cylinder engine to cart it all over town. When he set down I could tell by the way his leg was shaking and by his stranglehold on my steering wheel that this was going to be a memorable experience at best, and right possibly, a disaster.

He backed me out of my parking spot and as we pulled onto the deserted Main Street I made a note to myself how grateful I was that Mr. Guiglini sent his delivery boy out when most people was off the roads and at home eating their suppers. We started out smooth enough, but we both was pretty dang tense. The snow that had covered the road had been plowed into the middle, creating a ten-foot high mountain of snow bank, broken only at the intersections. Once we was heading down the street I could feel Leroy relax his grip as he gained confidence — and speed. Sure as shootin', when he tried to turn left at the first intersection he was going too fast. My bald tires and his overcorrecting put us into a uncontrolled spin, rotating us in two wildly careening circles until I came to a sudden jarring halt up against the snow bank. Whew! Both Leroy and I was sweating bullets and had also dodged one, as there didn't appear to be no physical damage to either of us, and I didn't flip over.

Leroy took a few minutes to compose himself, furtively looking around to see if anybody had witnessed his dumb performance behind the wheel. One of many flaws with teenage boys is that they tend to worry about their consarned image when they ought to be worried about their mortality. He breathed a deep sigh of relief once he was able to reassure himself that we was both unscathed and more important, that nobody had witnessed our near-death experience. He started me again, backed me away from the snow bank which was left with a distinct imprint of my right side running board and fenders, and we continued our mission to Larry's Greasy Spoon, slow, cautious, and with Leroy a little bit wiser.

By the time he returned to Mr. Guiglini's shop, Leroy had managed to justify the episode and let himself off the hook completely by blaming the whole thing on my recaps. If I knew he was going to pin the rap on me I would of given him a pretty dang exciting ride back to the shop, but I didn't know his intentions until we was already there. For the record, I eventually got even with him but I don't want to get ahead of myself. When Mr. Guiglini asked him how the delivery went, Leroy said it was fine but if not for his exceptional skill as a driver, my bald tires could have caused a serious accident. He briefly mentioned that there was a minor skid into a snow bank and reckoned it would be a good idea to replace my tires. I can't say I disagreed — what car doesn't appreciate a new set of tires?! — but dagnabbit, I didn't appreciate his rationale or his skewed reporting of the facts.

As he walked around me with a cursory examination, Mr. Guiglini couldn't help but notice that, even though I didn't have no new dents or scratches, my right side running board and fenders was caked with a lot more snow than the left side was, and it was clear that I done had more than a "minor skid", but possibly remembering that he was once a kid himself, he didn't point out the obvious to Leroy. He agreed that I was overdue for some new tires, but added that he was about to buy a new car anyhow, and didn't want to make any further investments in me before he sold me. Of all the nerve! I give him years of loyal service, never missing a single delivery hauling raw meat all over town, and that's the appreciation I get! I was tempted to blow a gasket right then and there or at least flood myself the next time he tried to start me so he could walk home through the snow and maybe freeze to death.

I could feel it in my tie rods that the mention of my impending sale got Leroy's interest up. He had never owned a car (as I said earlier, he wasn't even driving legal) and like all red-blooded

American teenage boys, that was his second most frequent fantasy. The first most frequent one is something I never really understood other than the fact that it might be less expensive at the outset but a lot more costly in the long run.

Leroy asked Mr. Guiglini how much he wanted for me, and Mr. Guiglini told him that since he was a good kid (hah!) and I needed new tires, he'd let me go for fifty dollars. I thought that was a fair price compared to what I had been sold for all them other times over the years. I had to confess that in addition to the tire issue, I was getting pretty old, my parts was worn, I couldn't keep up with them big chrome-clad tail finned V8s people was driving now. Most cars of my generation had long ago been crushed or junked so I had to remind myself that I was beating the odds just by being able to start. So on balance, I reckoned that $50 was a realistic price for me and I had no squawk coming. Leroy agreed, but was suffering from another chronic teenage condition: he was broke.

He told Mr. Guiglini that he would like to buy me, and asked if he could work off the debt in the shop by having $10 per week withheld from his pay. That represented half his income but it would leave Leroy with enough to keep me in gas. Mr. Guiglini agreed to the deal, but he pointed out that since he was too young to own a car, Leroy's father would have to agree to hold my title.

Because Leroy was still attending high school and could only work part-time, I didn't see him for a couple of days. One afternoon he showed up and loaded up my rumble seat with his deliveries. We set off and I sensed a newfound respect on his part. Before stomping on the starter he pulled out my choke, moved the spark lever to retard my ignition timing and set the throttle lever to make sure I would idle smooth. He was careful to reset the spark and let my engine warm up proper, not to grind my gears or pop my clutch, and most important in light of our most recent trip, to proceed with exceptional caution down the slick road to the Greasy Spoon. To my considerable relief and benefit

I figured he must be maturing. We returned to the shop where he parked me, and after work I was surprised to have him get in and start me up again. Was we making two deliveries tonight? We drove away in the opposite direction from town though, and before long he come to a stop and parked me in front of a house. The driveway already had a car in it, so I had to be left on the street. Leroy went into the house and I went into my patient wait mode, which was a good thing, since he didn't come out until morning.

He seemed to be full of energy as he attacked the driveway with a snow shovel, clearing the way for the other car to make it to the street. Then he cleaned off the walkway to the house as well. When I saw him loading up his arms with fireplace wood from the pile it struck me as very out of character that not only was he doing chores that teenagers avoid like chickens avoid coyotes but also that he was actually whistling while he worked. That's when it dawned on me that he must have persuaded his father to keep my pink slip in return for some hard labor, that I had yet another new owner, and that my days of hauling meat had come to an end. The unknown was what I was going to be used for next, but that wasn't no new experience for me, given my long life.

That afternoon Leroy shoveled out a space beside the driveway, started me up and moved me off the street. I felt a whole bunch safer and was appreciative of his concern. In the evening it commenced to snow again, and this time it didn't stop for almost a week. People was shoveling it from their walks, their driveways and even their roofs, and the snow plows was blocking the driveways as fast as people could make their way to the street. It was a huge snow, and when it was done it was eight foot deep! I was completely buried and couldn't see or hear nothing. Actually, I found it plumb cozy and I had no objection to waiting there until Leroy could dig me out.

I'm not sure how long I sat there. After a few days I felt my battery weakening and I slowly dropped off to a dreamless sleep, remaining there until I was jarred awake with a freshly charged battery. I looked around and saw that most of the snow was gone and signs of spring was emerging. Trees was budding, the ice had melted into sloppy puddles, the roads was dry. I figured I must of been sleeping for two or three months. My oil felt thick and was all settled in the bottom of my crankcase in a big glop, but my gas tasted like it was still OK. Leroy must of took my battery to have it charged because I was suddenly feeling pretty frisky. He got in, turned the key, flipped up the spark advance, pulled out my choke and stomped on the starter, but I wasn't ready. At my age we need a little more time to get going after a long nap. He kept grinding my starter though, so I flooded my engine to get him to stop. Leroy was insistent. It wasn't long before my battery was again dead and I returned to a blissful sleep.

I was rousted without warning and I could feel that my battery had been once again charged. This time, Leroy was a bit more patient. He went through the same procedure as before, but when I didn't start right away he waited a few minutes. He tried again and I felt myself about to fire up, but with a raspy cough and a hearty pop from my tailpipe, I gave it up. Leroy seemed to understand how difficult this was for me so he let me rest for another few minutes while he poured some gas directly into my carburetor. That felt great — probably like a stiff shot of moonshine would be to a human, and when he stepped on the starter again I done sprang into action. I was belching blue smoke from my pipe but as my engine warmed up the oil began circulating around my pistons, by cracky, I was ready for action.

"Action" is an exaggeration, since it consisted of backing me out, driving me around the block and re-parking me. I guess Leroy needed reassurance that I was ready, even if he wasn't. It probably had something to do with the fact that he still didn't have no license yet, or insurance. His dad wasn't as lackadaisical as Mr. Guiglini so Leroy had to resign himself to minimal driving for the next two months until he turned 16. I'm sure time dragged by for him as slow as me trying to reach the top of a steep grade, but I was perfectly content to go back to sleep. So I did.

When I once more was aroused from my dreamless slumber, it was warm. The snow was completely gone and them trees and flowers was in full bloom. I felt Leroy's presence in my cab, and I could tell he was hankering to take me for a spin. I wasn't nearly as enthusiastic as he was but I resigned myself to doing my job and after a couple of coughs and sputters for effect, I let my engine come to life. A few minutes later I was delighted to find myself at Harvey's garage, having some new tires mounted! Well, not new as in never used, but new as in freshly recapped. That was good enough, as I doubted Leroy would be taking me on the kind of trek that would require an expensive new set.

The next day Leroy drove me to school. I was well along in years and had seen just about everything a car sees in a life, but still I felt myself sharing his pride as he showed me off to his buddies. Everybody wanted to take me for a spin and I was plumb grateful that Leroy refused to let anybody else drive me. Training one teen how to handle my complex mechanics was difficult; training another half dozen was far beyond my patience if not my capacity!

There was another Model A parked next to me and while Leroy and the rest of the guys went to class, we introduced ourselves. He was a little older than me, a 1929, but we had the same engines. I was a little envious of him. He was a four-door sedan, painted with a flat primer accented with bold yellow lightning bolts on his sides that matched his yellow spokes. My exterior was right smart drab by comparison. I had a rumble seat that worked sometimes but he had a full back seat. He didn't gloat. Like me, he had done been around the block a few times and our differences was not important to him. Besides, we had more similarities than differences, given our age, our maker and our life experiences. He said he was owned by a teen as well, a guy named James, and that James had done his paint by hand. That was fairly obvious to me, but I let it pass. I asked him if he had been drove all winter or put to sleep like I had. He said he had spent the entire time slipping and sliding all over Chester, and that he had seen me around but had never had a chance to get acquainted until we happened to be parked together that day.

I asked the '29 what it was like being owned by a teenage boy and he said there was some good things and some not so good things. On the upside, he got a lot of attention to his engine, radiator, brakes, tires and lube points, in addition to having that unique paint job. He felt truly appreciated. However, James, being a male teen, pushed his limits farther than he thought they should be pushed. Somehow, James failed to recognize that he was an old car with old car needs, which emphatically did not include clutch popping and seeing how fast he could go from zero to sixty — about a minute if the road is flat; never if it's an uphill grade. The spring on his clutch was so wore out that James had tied a rope to the pedal to pull it back out when he shifted. It didn't work too good but it was better than nothing. On balance, he felt like I did: we accept our fate and as long as our owner keeps us fueled and tuned, we do what he asks to the best of our ability. That's what us Model A's do.

Leroy and I fell into a routine for the next couple of months until school was out for the summer. He'd drive me to school, park me there for the day, and after school we'd go to Mr. Guiglini's for work a couple or three days per week. Ever chance he got we would cruise up and down Main Street, from one end of Chester to the other, making U-turns and repeating our route until something more interesting attracted him like another guy driving the same circuit or a group of teenage girls which I could feel made him tense, a condition he tried to hide by slouching in my seat, hanging his scrawny arm out my window and pointedly ignoring them. Him, them, and even me for that matter, knew it was all a big act. He'd also stop at the Frosty-Freeze, the drug store soda fountain and the building with a sign saying it was a recreation center but everbody called the pool hall. All us cars who was owned by teenagers got to know each other since we all seemed to end up at the same place more often than not. I liked some of them, particularly the old guys who had more in common with me than the upstarts. There was one brand new 1955 Plymouth that lorded over us with his shiny red fins but we mostly ignored him. He was new and fast, but hadn't been around long enough to earn any credibility. He would smugly offer to race us. Big deal. He was 25 years younger than I was and he had twice the number of cylinders as I have, for criminy sakes! That wouldn't exactly have made for a close match. I didn't even acknowledge his presence. It would have been beneath my dignity.

I was made to suffer through one race, though. Leroy and James was driving around with no particular goal, and for some reason concluded it would be fun to take James' '29 and me out on one of the nearby logging roads and put us through our paces. Jumpin' Jehoshaphat! They lined us up so our radiators was even and when Leroy shouted "GO!" our clutches was popped, our gas pedals was mashed to the floor, and away we flew, or rather lurched, as fast as we could which wasn't very. I reached a top speed of 48 MPH, which was way too fast for that road and my nerves. I don't know who won and neither of us cared, although James and Leroy seemed to, as they argued loudly about cheating, finish lines and road hogging. All I remember is being totally blinded by thick, choking dust from the washboarded, potholed dirt road and feeling a lot more stress on my moving parts that I should have at my age. That was my first, and what I prayed would be my last ever drag race. My transmission gears didn't stop hurting for a week.

Leroy did some other stuff that I thought wasn't too smart. One day him and James was driving me around. We was down at the end of the runway of the little airport in Chester where there was a dirt road. Leroy told James he thought it would be fun to flip some brodies. I didn't know what a brody was until I felt him speed up and then suddenly slam on my brakes and cramp my steering wheel to the left. Naturally, I skidded and spun around, nearly toppling over on the process. I couldn't hardly believe what was happening to me! He done it again, three or four times before they got chewed out pretty good when the manager of the airport came a-stormin' out in his pickup. He yelled at Leroy to stop my engine, which he did. Then he told them boys that they was stirring up so much dust that the airplanes couldn't land or take off. I had to admit that it looked an awful lot like Oklahoma that year I left in the middle of a dry wind. He let them go with a stern warning not to come back to the airport again, and as far as I can reckon they didn't, at least not in me.

On another occasion Leroy drove me into a pasture at the edge of town. Him and James was going fishing and they decided to drive as close to the creek as they could so they wouldn't have to walk so far. Well, that was just dumb because any fool could see that the grass was damp, which meant the ground probably was too. We hadn't gone ten yards into that dang swamp when I was up to my axles in mud with my back wheels spinning but not going anywhere. They ended up not doing any fishing at all that day because it took them two hours to get me unstuck. They'd get enough limbs from the ground around the nearby trees to stick under my rear tires, and then Leroy would carefully back me up until I got to the end of the wood, at which point I'd sink again. So they'd repeat the process again and again, gradually working me back to dry land. I was a mess of mud by the time we got out of there, and so was they.

I guess the stuff Leroy did to me was typical of teenage boys, who aren't known for thinking things through very good before acting. But one day that poor old '29 got treated even worse than me. I didn't see it happen, but he had a real bad afternoon at the high school parking lot. There was a passel of boys in him, and James wanted to see if he could do a sharp turn without tipping over if everybody leaned to the opposite side. They did, and it worked. Then he had them all lean into the turn and naturally the poor car turned over on his side, with all them stupid boys piled on top of one another inside. They all managed to climb out and tip the '29 back up proper, but he had some new dents and some serious scratches on his lightening bolts.

————————————

Leroy had an older brother, John, who was getting some schoolin' at the college down in Chico. John had an ugly, banged up 1937 Plymouth who I had become acquainted with that summer. He (the Plymouth) seemed nice enough, although not very outgoing. We'd sit there, side by each, at night and he would just stare off into the distance with his oddly focused headlights and not say anything. I was intrigued but I also had enough respect for him to leave him alone with his thoughts. During the days John would take him and Leroy would take me, and our paths wouldn't cross again until evening so I had no idea how he spent his waking hours.

One day late in the summer, John drove up in a new (at least new for him) car, a 1950 Ford which could of been my grandson if we was humans. I have to confess that he was a pretty slick looking car with his sun visor, fender skirts and all that shiny chrome. I wondered what was going to become of John's Plymouth, but not for long. He replaced me! John gave the Plymouth to Leroy, so Leroy apparently decided I was expendable because over the next few days a half dozen guys in his social group came over to look me over, kick my tires and take me for short drives. It was plain as day that my tires was fine so I didn't understand that infernal kicking. All in all, it was not a good way to spend time, with all them teenage boys trying to be manly and prove how they could drive a vintage stick shift like myself, but mostly grinding my gears down to nubs. Cripes! Hadn't they never heard of double-clutching?!

My relationship with Leroy came to an end a few days later when he sold me for $60. I once again headed off to an unknown future, feeling somewhat smug that Leroy sold me for ten dollars more than he paid for me. As I drove away with my new owner

I looked back at Leroy through my rear-view mirror for the last time, and I think both of us was a little sad. We actually had grown to like each other. He done taught me to lighten up and enjoy life a little, and I done taught him how to drive. Fair trade.

Chapter 2

SURVIVING TEENAGE DRIVERS

I t was 1956 and I was in Chester. I was sharing parking space with a Model A Ford but I didn't see much of him. Both of us were gone during the day and at night I was so depressed and exhausted that I didn't feel like socializing, so I chose to go within myself and contemplate my bad fortune and what the future might hold for me. I wasn't optimistic. I had not enjoyed a good life and I had no reason to believe that better things were in store for me.

Late in the summer, my owner, John left me parked while he drove off with his father. He returned a few hours later in a car I'd never met. He was a pretty streamlined looking 1950 Ford, with a sleek design (compared to me anyhow), an impressive chrome exterior sun visor over the windshield, fender skirts and white wall tires. I soon found out that the Ford would go to college with John instead of me. I can't say I was sad at that prospect given my experience with John during his freshman year there, and I could only hope that the Ford wouldn't suffer the same maltreatment. Now I was curious as to what would happen to me. Cars don't waste emotional energy worrying about things we can't control, but we do wonder.

I didn't have to wait very long. I learned the very next day that John's brother, Leroy, was now my owner. Some of his friends came by and looked me over, offering suggestions as to how to fix me up. To be honest I didn't think any of them would be capable of improving my looks and as it turned out, I was right. Teenage boys all seem to think they are capable of a lot more than they really are, and they normally use lack of funds as the excuse for inaction. Leroy's friends also examined the Model A in detail and after some negotiating, one of them handed a wad of cash to Leroy and then drove him away. I had a hunch the Model A had been sold and I was once again proven to be correct. I regret now having been so selfish and inconsiderate when we were parked together and not talking more. After all, he was older than I am and deserved respect for that alone. I resolved at that point to go forward with a more positive attitude. It was a good thing, too, because I was about to cover some interesting terrain.

Franklin Roosevelt began his second term as President in 1937, the year I was built. That was the same year the Golden Gate Bridge opened, gas cost a dime a gallon and Amelia Earhardt disappeared somewhere in the Pacific. I'm surprised I got built at all, given the labor unrest that year. Unemployment stood at 14%, and the United Auto Workers unionized the company that created me.

I retailed originally for $680. I was a proud, powerful car when I was built, with a straight six cylinder engine, four doors, plush front and back bench seats, optional radio and heater, and a dramatic, modern design.

My first owner treated me with care but when he was drafted into the Army at the outset of World War II he sold me to an uneducated, uncouth 4-F wretch who had no respect for me or for my needs. He didn't lube, oil or tune me up until I would quit altogether in protest. He let trash pile up in my back seat — old newspapers, hamburger wrappers, beer bottles, discarded clothing and the like. It not only was ugly, it caused me to have a disgusting interior odor that even I couldn't stand, and I don't even have a nose.

I was in San Francisco during those awful years and that can be hard for a car, straining every piston to get up the hills and overheating the brakes going down. Add to this the shock absorber-jarring pothole-filled roads and the salt air eating my paint and you'll get an idea of what I was up against. My owner had pretty much destroyed me and was about to park me for good when a 16-year old boy offered to buy me for $100 in 1954. Most cars my age and style were worth a lot more than that insulting amount, but I was pretty much done for, so I swallowed what was left of my pride and was relieved when the deal was made. Unless he was going to cut me up for scrap metal I figured I wouldn't be any worse off than I was with the jerk that sold me.

––––––––––––––

My new owner's name was Robbie. He lived out in the Sunset area of San Francisco with his single mom. From my first day with Robbie I knew I was in for an adventure because he was an undisciplined, testosterone-charged boy who loved a good con almost as much as he hated school. He was a fast talker and a convincing braggart until people (and I) got to know him and could see through his swagger. My first drive home from my old owner's house was nothing short of harrowing as we dodged in and out of traffic, cutting off other cars, busses, trolleys and bicycles, and very nearly running down several pedestrians as we careened through the City as fast as my engine could take us. If cars could sweat I would have been soaking wet under my fender wells! But we have no choice. We have to go where our driver takes us, at the speed he dictates and that's what I did with Robbie, hoping my tires and brakes, not to mention my grill, would survive the trip. To my great relief we made it safely to his house and I expelled a sizable backfire of relief when he turned off my engine.

As I sat in the driveway acclimating to my new surroundings and my new owner, I couldn't help but hear the raised voices of Robbie and his mother arguing about me. It was obvious even to an inanimate car like myself that there was considerable stress in that home. She accused him of throwing his life away by cutting school and wasting what little money he had on junk cars. Robbie argued that school was useless and he needed me in order to get a job because he was fed up with being a low life and wanted to be a somebody. His mom told him that she was at the end of her rope and until he was 18, she was going to send him to his grandmother's in Chester to get him away from the City's temptations and bad influences. Finally, Robbie reluctantly agreed to go and complete his last year of school in Chester as long as he could take me with him. That seemed OK with me. I had never heard of Chester but I figured it couldn't be any worse than San Francisco.

Robbie spent the next day cleaning my interior and trunk. I have to say it was a huge relief to get rid of all that accumulated trash. He filled an entire garbage can! As his reward, he managed to find almost three dollars in coins under my seat and I felt that he was fully justified in keeping it. Then he vacuumed me and I felt several pounds lighter with all that dust, dirt, gravel and bits and those pieces of unknown materials sucked from my floor, ceiling and upholstery. He washed my exterior, and while I did appreciate the gesture, it didn't improve my looks much. I was a pretty sorry looking automobile. Most of my original paint was gone, replaced by irregular splotches of rust, primer, grease, scratches and random brushed-over paint of various colors. The final touch was getting my windows washed and my dashboard dusted and cleaned with Windex. By the time Robbie was done with me I was so deeply appreciative of his efforts that I had completely forgiven him for our initial hair raising ride together.

Early the next day I was loaded up with Robbie's belongings that barely filled my trunk. By 9 a.m. we were ready to go. Robbie got behind my wheel, laid his open map on my seat beside him, pulled out my choke, pumped my accelerator a couple of times and stepped on my starter. I was almost as excited as he was. There's something about a road trip that males and cars understand — getting out of the crowded city, watching the white lines and telephone poles speed by, and heading for an unknown destination. This is usually lost on females and not worth explaining because it's all so intangible.

Our first stop was the gas station, where the attendant filled my tank, checked my oil (a quart low), my radiator and tires, and washed my windows (didn't need it). Robbie paid him the $4.35 and off we went. To his credit and my relief, he was more mellow than he was on our first ride. It was almost as if he wanted to savor every moment of his newfound freedom and relish the journey which was just fine by me. As long as he continued to treat me with respect, I resolved to deliver him safely to Chester. I did about six hours later.

Both Robbie and I felt like aliens. We'd never seen such a small town, with no traffic, no stoplights, no noise, no busses, and pretty much no nothing. We were at a higher altitude than we were used to, and I could feel that my carburetor needed an adjustment. None of the houses had numbers and the layout of the streets was not the logical grid we were used to. We pulled into a gas station to ask for directions to his grandmother's house. The attendant was friendly and eager to help, and even knew his grandmother and how to get there. I was taken aback and even a little suspicious at this open, unguarded behavior, which was not what we were accustomed to in the City. But Robbie decided to trust the guy and five minutes later we were at our new home.

The next morning I sat parked while Robbie and his grand-mother drove off in her car. I hadn't yet been introduced to him as he had been parked in the garage. He seemed nice enough as we made headlight contact when they were leaving the driveway. He was much newer than I am and although I was a little embar-rassed at my exterior, he didn't seem to pass judgment on me, which was nice but not what I expected.

Robbie was officially enrolled as a senior in Chester High School and the following day he drove me there and left me in the park-ing lot with a bunch of other cars. I was relieved to see that most of them were not unlike me, in that we all had a lot of miles on us and our bodies showed a lot of wear and tear — except for one 1955 Plymouth with an attitude that the other cars didn't appre-ciate. Since he was a fellow Plymouth I didn't want to be too harsh on him but he was hard to like with his shiny red paint and his ostentatious fins. When I gave him the secret Plymouth code word he surprised me by laughing and calling me an old geezer. Well, same make or not, that did it for me. I've been around too long to put up with a smart-ass so I ignored him from then on. The other cars were OK though, and before long I was one of the crowd.

When the school year came to an end, Robbie decided to spend the summer in Chester and in the fall he returned to San Fran-cisco to find a job. He sold me for $50 to his friend, John, who was on his way to college. I never saw Robbie again and I've often wondered if he became a somebody.

This began my exhausting year as the car of a college freshman who spent a lot more time in me than in the classroom. Once again, my back seat filled up with discarded beer cans and ham-burger wrappers and I began to experience depressing flashbacks. By the end of the school year when we returned to Chester, I was feeling my age and I was tired and discouraged about what the Detroit gods had destined for me.

I was dirty with more dents and scratches than I had last year, my right headlight was out of adjustment, pointing up at the trees rather than down the road, and my driver's side door had to be held closed by a red bandanna tied to the door post. That worked OK, although I was concerned about how I would keep my interior warm and dry in the winter since my window couldn't be raised all the way up with that bandanna in the way.

And now John's younger brother Leroy was my owner. I was worried that Leroy, as a young driver, would be challenged by my sophisticated three-on-the-floor transmission. When we went for our first drive, though, I was impressed at his ability to coordinate the accelerator, clutch and gear shift, going from first to second to high with minimal grinding and lurching. By the time he had repeated the process a couple of times he had it down, much to my relief. Then I remembered that he had been driving the Model A, and it made perfect sense that if he could work that primitive system he certainly should be able to work mine.

Typical of new car owners, Leroy spent our first day attending to my hygiene. Despite his effort, I still was not attractive when he was done, but at least I was clean once again, and I smelled a lot better. That evening we went for a drive, going aimlessly from one end of Chester to the other. It was pretty boring if you ask me but at least it was not stressful and I was able to relax. We pulled into the Frosty Freeze next to Leroy's former Model A, and while Leroy talked with his friends I tried to make amends with the Ford, who thankfully harbored no ill feelings about my earlier snubbing of him.

On that first evening at the Frosty Freeze, Leroy persuaded one of the local girls to take a spin. She eyed me suspiciously as he opened my passenger side door, giving me some hope that perhaps he was actually a gentleman. The girl, whose name was Katy, was a real cutie and I found it oddly pleasurable when she settled into my front seat. We slid back into the routine of cruising from one end of town to the other. Katy fiddled with my radio knobs to find a station that wasn't full of static like they all seemed to be in remote Chester, while Leroy focused on shifting my gears without grinding me and embarrassing himself. As for me, I put a huge effort into my radio to please Katy and I managed to find a station that had just the right kind of '50s pop tunes and came in clearly. I also decided to turn off my right headlight so we wouldn't look like we were searching for night hawks.

One advantage of Chester as far as the teenage population was concerned, was that it was surrounded by those logging roads, which allowed for a high degree of privacy. Well, Leroy, who clearly had rehearsed his route, turned me off the highway and onto one of them. Suddenly we were all alone. The only sounds were my engine and radio, and the only scenes were what I was lighting up with my single headlight. Leroy came to a stop and cut my engine. I don't think I had ever seen anything this dark! He and Katy made self-conscious small talk as he slowly inched his arm across the back of my seat. I can't say I blame him for being attracted to Katy. He was encouraged when she didn't recoil in horror as he tentatively dropped his arm across her shoulder and pulled her toward him. It got uncomfortably quiet then, as they stopped talking and I could sense that this could get out of control pretty fast, given the hormones that were bouncing off my ceiling and door panels. I wasn't sure what to do, or even if it was my responsibility, but I was saved from having to decide when Leroy got himself tangled up in my gearshift and destroyed the mood. What a doofus. In a last ditch effort to have his way with Katy, he suggested they get into my back seat which was free of encumbrances, but she told him that wouldn't be a good idea. He gave her some half-hearted arguments, but he was new at this and not very smooth, and it was apparent he had gone as far as he was going to on this night. It was probably just as well although I don't believe he thought so at the time. He started me up and we returned to the Frosty Freeze. He did get some consolation when his pals razzed him about the lipstick on his face and he chose to remain silent about the details, letting them draw their own, hopefully incorrect conclusions. On other nights we returned to that logging road, sometimes with Katy, sometimes with other girls. He even managed to get one or two of them into my back seat but he was never able to close the deal, whatever it was. I didn't fully understand his obsession. All I can say for sure is that there were a few times when my windows got pretty steamed up.

———————————

One fine summer day, Leroy and his friend J.C. were whiling away an afternoon, driving around with no particular goal. On a whim, Leroy abruptly turned us left off the highway onto one of the many unpaved roads surrounding Chester. I was too old to be equipped with signal lights and the rules then were for the driver to use arm signals before turning. He wasn't paying attention and as he turned, another car of approximately my vintage was passing us. It careened off the road and came to a very sudden halt on a low stump, catching his right rear bumper on my left front fender in the process, leaving me with an unattractive and dramatic eight inch tear. Leroy and J.C. piled out of me and ran over to the other car. The driver was uninjured but I could sense that all three of them were shaken by the experience. Meanwhile, that poor other car was sitting uncomfortably on the stump awaiting their attention. They were able to use a jack and as much brute force as they could muster to free it from the stump, and after a short but effective lecture about safe driving and shaking hands with Leroy and J.C., the other car and his driver continued on their way. I was worried that the incident might be reported but both parties were at fault, really, and some things are better left with no further action. Except for my torn fender.

Toward the end of the summer J.C. and Leroy were once again driving me around and they parked me near a meadow when they spotted some other friends nearby. These guys had their .22

rifles with them and were spending their afternoon plinking at cans, pinecones and chipmunks. One of them must have taken me for a target of opportunity. I saw all four looking at me from the distance, which was maybe fifty yards. There was evidently some discussion and then one of the rifle packers raised his weapon and shot right at me!! Fortunately, it was a small caliber bullet. It made a clean little hole in my driver's side door, although it had lost too much velocity to break my window so the harm was minimal. Still, I was just furious that Leroy would disrespect me so much that he would allow somebody to shoot me. I was so upset I drained my battery, which served him right. The other guys had some jumper cables with which they connected their beat up old 1949 Chevy pickup's battery to mine. I'm sure that if that truck had a neck it would have been as red as theirs, with its gun rack, heavy duty bumper and a bed filled with old tires and rusty, dented rims and other useless junk. Because my battery was dead I didn't have to communicate with it, though. Before long we were back on the road but my distrust in Leroy was growing.

That distrust was justified, too, because a few days later I was put through another humiliating episode. In Chester there was a railroad track that led from the lumber mill, across the highway and out of town to a junction some fifteen miles away. I had heard Leroy mention that it was used only once daily during the week to transport boxcars and flat cars of lumber from the mill to the junction. It was a Saturday, and Leroy and another friend, James, came up with a brilliant (to them) idea of seeing if I could travel on the track. Before I could protest I found myself parked on an uninhabited crossing with my tires resting on the tracks. They then let most of the air out of my tires to give me a better grip and away we went. I had to work at it and I was scared and angry, but I had no choice but to keep my wheels on the track or get high centered or mired down far from the road. We drove out of town and continued on to the next crossing, two miles down the track. At that point Leroy and James had satisfied their curiosity and need for amusement, so Leroy steered me off the track and back onto the road. The only satisfaction I got from this abuse was watching them struggle to manually pump up my tires again so we could all get back to Chester. I swore that day that if I were ever sold to another teenager I would simply stop running forever and take my chances at the junkyard.

Things calmed down when school started again and I could breathe a sigh of relief to be left in the parking lot with the other cars. I didn't even get upset when I had to spend a day next to that snooty '55 Plymouth who bragged and preened incessantly. I just ignored him and went to sleep, dreaming fitfully of flying through the air like a clay pigeon and being shot to smithereens.

It was a short respite. In the autumn, many people in Chester hunt deer. Leroy, like his friends, would often spend a couple of hours before or after school at this strange activity. Normally, he would park me and traipse off through the woods looking for a likely spot to sit and wait for his prey, and that was fine with me because I enjoyed biding my time in the quiet of the trees, away from the distractions of Chester. One Saturday before dawn in October, Leroy, J.C. and James climbed into me and we set out for another morning of deer hunting. Rather than parking me as usual, Leroy pulled onto a logging road and stopped. The other two guys got out and sat on my two front fenders, rifles loaded and ready. Leroy started down the road and I felt like a very slow, wingless fighter plane. I had a hunch this was not a legal way to hunt. The road was fairly rough and they had trouble staying on my fenders, so after a mile or so Leroy stopped and they dismounted. I don't think there was any chance they would have been able to bag a deer from there and they were lucky they didn't bag each other. That helped confirm my opinion that teenagers are not the smartest humans.

———————————

As winter approached that year, 1956, I wasn't feeling 100%. I had a chronic cough, I was belching blue smoke from my tail pipe and I had an embarrassing oil leak under my valve cover. Leroy took note of my failing health and I found myself parked in an actual garage at his house. That was my first experience with a garage, and I have to say that if there were spas for cars, they would be garages. I felt absolutely decadent spending those cold evenings sheltered from the elements and when it began snowing my joy was tenfold. Despite my new living situation, my maladies had not been addressed. My morale was higher, but my health was not good. Out of uncharacteristic consideration, Leroy began walking to school or finding rides, leaving me parked.

One Saturday morning he came into the garage and opened the right side of my hood, exposing most of my engine. I had a glimmer of optimism that he was going to fix whatever it was that was ailing me and I was hoping it was a minor adjustment, like tweaking my carb or cleaning my plugs. To Leroy's credit, he tried both of these approaches and he also adjusted the gap on my points. But none of this did much good. Next, he unbolted my valve cover and I'm sure it was easy to see that I had a sizable tear in my gasket that could have been repaired for probably a dollar.

However, Leroy didn't stop there. I don't know if he had read a repair manual about me or if he was just curious, because I felt a socket wrench on one of the bolts holding my cylinder head on. It had never been removed and was quite snug, but he gave a mighty yank and it broke loose. He removed this one along with the others, and actually lifted my head off, exposing my cylinders and pistons. I was pretty nervous because this is major surgery and I didn't have any confidence that he was a certified mechanic. In fact, I was absolutely positive he wasn't, but I had to resign myself and place my engine in his trust.

He set my head to the side and covered my pistons with an old bed sheet, presumably to keep out the dirt, and then he called it a day. Here I was, completely disabled and at his mercy, and he just leaves. I didn't see him for a week. At that point, I figured I'd had my last trip on a road. On the upside, that garage would have been a nice place to end my days — a whole lot more comfortable than, say, a head-on collision.

But the next weekend he came back, removed the sheet and wiped away all the accumulated oil and grime. Using a fine piece of wet/dry emery paper, he scraped off the rust from my piston walls. I was in no position to know if that was a smart thing to do but I will say it felt pretty good. It sort of tickled, and when he was finished he used a vacuum hose to remove the debris. That afternoon, he put a new gasket on me and replaced my head. I don't know much about mechanics but I'm pretty sure he was supposed to use a torque wrench to make sure the pressure on my bolts was evenly distributed. At least that's what I'd heard from other cars who had undergone valve jobs. Leroy didn't have a torque wrench though, and he simply tightened all my bolts with an end wrench, pulling all of them as tightly as he could. When he was through with that, he replaced my damaged manifold gasket too, and put my cover back on.

After he had me put back together and added some oil, he got in, turned the key, pulled out my choke and mashed down my starter. To the amazement of both of us, I started! I don't know who was more surprised. He quickly opened the garage door so my fumes wouldn't put him to sleep and then returned to me, racing my engine. I have to say that although I wasn't running perfectly, I felt a lot better than I had for weeks, and I was eager to get back on the road. Leroy backed me out and took me for a short test drive, which to the great relief to both of us, I passed. He drove me to school on Monday and when we came home he parked me outside. That confirmed to me that I had recovered, but I sure did miss that cozy garage.

The remainder of the winter we drove back and forth to school, cruised Main Street and parked at the Frosty Freeze on weekend evenings. Because the logging roads were buried in snow we didn't venture out on any of them.

As winter wound down, Leroy got an after-school job at Harvey's Shell Station where he pumped gas, cleaned windshields and checked oil and water levels of customers' cars. He also learned how to administer lube jobs, change oil, clean spark plugs and balance wheels. Harvey was a patient teacher. When school was out and Leroy had graduated, he was able to work full time in that summer of 1957 as he eagerly awaited the start of college. Because he didn't have a lot of free time we had settled into what was, at least for me, a comfortable routine. I spent most of my time parked either at his house or at Harvey's, giving me plenty of opportunity to reflect on my life. I found that while I missed the hustle-bustle of city driving, I'd made a happy transition to rural living and was at peace with it. But I was curious and maybe a little apprehensive about what my future held as Leroy headed off to college. Would I go with him? Would I be put up on blocks while I waited for him to come home? Would I be sold? I thought of myself as too young and vibrant to be sent to a junk-yard.

The answer came like a bolt out of the blue. Leroy had driven us home for lunch and I heard him and his father in a discussion with raised voices; never a good sign. When we returned to Harvey's, I heard Leroy tell him that his dad had received my insurance bill and had concluded that the premium was more than I was worth. I don't know much about money but that seemed a bit harsh to me. Regardless of Leroy's feelings or mine, I was to be sold, and the quicker the better. That very afternoon Leroy let me go for $15 to a guy who needed a car to get back and forth to his job at the lumber mill. He took the money, signed a paper, and I was driven away to begin a new phase.

On balance, my life with Leroy was mostly positive in spite of the foolhardy stunts he pulled. We had grown close through some fun and some not-so-fun adventures. He did repair my engine, but he never did do anything about that bandanna that held my door shut, my torn fender or my unfocused headlight. Like all cars who are bought, traded, stolen or sold, I did not know what the future had in store for me but I was grateful for my short but exciting time with Leroy.

Chapter 3

ALL AMERICAN WITH A BERMUDA BELL

Leroy and I were both guarded the first time we met. He didn't comment on my appearance other than to utter, "Doesn't look too bad for a car that old." Humph. He then settled in behind the wheel and hit my starter. As we backed out of the driveway and eased down the road I allowed myself a brief sigh of relief, quickly realizing as cars innately can, that he had some experience with the stick shift and was actually pretty adept. I figured this to be a positive omen and was grateful that my clutch and transmission did not appear to be in any immediate peril in spite of his huge feet.

We drove around Chester for a while over a different route than I was accustomed to. We went up Main Street to the end of town, made a U-turn, came down Main Street to the other end of town, made another U-turn and then pulled in to the Frosty Freeze parking lot. I had passed the Frosty Freeze my entire life but didn't know what it was, although there always seemed to be a goodly number of mostly vintage cars full of teenagers parked there. I was parked next to the one exception, which was a highly polished red 1955 Plymouth whom I instantly disliked. He looked at my modest rear fenders with disdain, insinuating that some cars don't need fins like his because they are too slow to need any stabilizing. Personally, I thought his were tasteless and ostentatious. But I sensed that this gleaming hulk was more interested in his ego than an intelligent discourse so I pointedly ignored him and pretended to doze until Leroy returned.

When we returned to Leroy's house later that afternoon there was a Ford sedan of my age in the driveway. We pulled up behind it and parked, leaving me with a view of his rear-end. Cars are not as offended by that as people seem to be. As evening fell and the night wore on, we became acquainted, telling each other our history and even revealing attitudes and, although personal, our mechanical quirks. For a '50 Ford, he was easy to talk to. My earlier experiences with his cousins had convinced me that most of them had a superiority complex. I think it was because one of them had played Robert Mitchum's getaway car in the movie "Thunder Road" in which he starred as a bootlegger who always managed to outrun the revenuers in his Ford, its trunk filled with freshly distilled white lightning. The whole thing wasn't even real life. It was a movie, and those other '49 and '50 Fords hadn't earned their bragging rights as far as I was concerned, so I largely ignored them. I'll acknowledge that I was envious of his sleek lines and striking chrome windshield visor. I supposed if we had been 1957 haircuts instead of 1950 cars, he would have been a slick ducktail and I a boring flattop. Oh well.

It turned out that the Ford belonged to Leroy's brother, John. They had spent the last year at college together and he was more than happy to have the summer months to recover from the wild adventures he had been subjected to, with way too much drinking, parking in the dark and heavy breathing with a succession of girls, and racing with other cars on country roads. The conversation made me nervous as I wondered if the same fate awaited me. That life didn't sound like anything I would want to participate in. I was about to find out.

————————————

I'm a 1950 Chevrolet. I wasn't fancy when I was new, and I'm still not. I was designed and engineered to be an unpretentious, reliable car and I've done my best to live up to those American values. The U.S. was recovering from the Great Depression and World War II, and the country had settled into gradually improving prosperity until the Korean War broke out the year I was built. Then President Harry Truman authorized the development of the Hydrogen Bomb and Senator Joe McCarthy started his Communist witch-hunt. These events, in addition to the struggle of the United Auto Workers to unionize General Motors, made me wonder if I really wanted to come off that assembly line and deal with the messes humans always seem to get themselves into. But I had no choice, so I gritted my grillwork and determined that I would survive as best as I could and to do what was expected of me.

By 1959 I'd had lots of drivers but only two owners. I don't know if that makes me special, but I think that stability has been a good thing. I was purchased for $1,450 by my first owner, Alvin Godfrey, the general manager of the lumber mill in Chester. Technically, the mill owned me but for my first three years I was driven almost exclusively by Mr. Godfrey and I was broadly considered to be his. He was a portly man. Frankly, during the first few months my driver's seat had trouble supporting his considerable bulk but rather than resist, I made some Zen-like adjustments to accommodate him by relaxing and developing a comfortable sag. That practical adaptation enabled me to cope. To his credit, Mr. Godfrey was a conservative driver who never took unnecessary risks with me, and he made sure I was serviced as recommended in my manual. We did spend quite a bit of time on unpaved roads, choking on a lot more dust than either of us liked but he always had me washed and vacuumed when we returned to the mill. Frankly, I was usually a lot cleaner than most of the other cars in Chester, probably because Mr. Godfrey maintained me at company expense. That was fine with me.

I was a well-equipped car, with a three-speed manual shift on the column, a factory installed radio, a heater and durable upholstery. I also sported some elegant fender skirts that other cars would ogle enviously when they thought I wasn't looking. Although I was proud of them, I am a modest automobile with no desire to be flashy — taste and reliability are ever so much more important to me than gaudy excesses. I couldn't wear my skirts in the wintertime, since I often had to have chains attached to my rear wheels. I didn't care much for chains. They were uncomfortable and noisy, and they made for a pretty rough ride, but at least they improved my odds of staying on the road. It was always a relief to have them removed in the spring and to have my fender skirts reinstalled. As soon as the chains were hung up in Mr. Godfrey's garage I felt a happy optimism as I anticipated the impending warm weather. I did my best in the winter, but I wasn't designed to be anything close to a snowmobile. I had met a few of those, as well as several four-wheel drive pickup trucks and one Dodge Power Wagon in particular. I will confess that they were very good at control in ice and snow, but to be honest, they had limited intelligence. All they were interested in talking about was how tough they were and how they could go anywhere. On balance, I believe I was a far better machine, especially in the summer.

Another unique feature I boasted was a two-way radio that Mr. Godfrey had added. It was attached to the floor in the center of the front passenger compartment and I had a little hook attached to my dashboard on which the microphone was stowed when not in use. A small antenna was installed on my trunk lid. Although this radio did nothing for my innate beauty, I must say that I spent many happy hours eavesdropping on other shortwave conversations. The most interesting were the ones involving the local deputy sheriff when he did his tour of Chester on Thursdays. Chester didn't have much crime and most people didn't even lock their houses or even remove the keys from the ignitions of us cars. That made the chatter on my radio more entertaining than serious, but it was at least something to listen to, like the time Mr. Godfrey got the message that two men at the mill got into a noisy altercation because one had discovered that his wife was having a dalliance with the other one. I wasn't sure what a dalliance was but it was apparent that men don't like their wives to have them.

All things considered, and especially when I compared my life to other cars in Chester, I had it pretty good. Sure, there was the cigar smoke that filled my passenger compartment which was particularly noxious during the winter, and in the summer there were those frequent rides down dusty roads with Mr. Godfrey bouncing heavily on my seat over every pothole. But these annoyances were more than compensated for by my regular maintenance and the fact that I was allowed to sleep in a garage every night — a rare treat for a Chester car.

Mr. Godfrey and I parted ways in 1954. He "upgraded" to a new sedan. I take offense at that term, but that's what they called it. To my way of thinking, just because something is new doesn't necessarily mean it's an upgrade. Is trading an old Bentley for a new Plymouth an upgrade? Is moving from an old stately mansion to a new duplex an upgrade? I'll confess to being sensitive but that term just got under my primer after the unwavering loyalty I had given to Mr. Godfrey. I honestly did my very best and never once did I fail to start for him. Upgrade indeed.

I had no time to wallow in self-pity or worry for very long about what would become of me because it was immediately revealed to me that I was now the "company car" for other managers to use as needed. It was essential to be quick on my tires and adjust to the many drivers who now were operating me, for as one might imagine, no two drove alike. At first I was bitter that Mr. Godfrey had deserted me and our comfortable relationship, but being the practical and accommodating model I am, I resolved to make the best of my new situation and before long I found myself actually enjoying the variety of drivers and their destinations. Nobody mentioned to Mr. Godfrey that my front seat was quietly replaced. What worked well for him became a problem for other drivers, who had trouble seeing over my steering wheel after sinking into "Alvin's Well". Also, my interior was sprayed, vacuumed and wiped down in an effort to get rid of the cigar odor. I wasn't impressed with the fumigation efforts, as most of my drivers were smokers anyhow, and evidently figured that cigarettes smelled better than cigars. To each his own, I guess. Personally, I find the smell of exhaust more pleasing than either of those.

I was on a first-come, first-served basis, so whoever got to my keys first was my driver. Mr. Godfrey never expressed any appreciation about me for this, but I think that my popularity made his staff come to work earlier in hopes of beating their competitors to my key ring. Some of my drivers were careful and some were maniacs. Some took me to places around town and the mill and others out on the dusty logging roads. All liked to take me to lunch and soon I was a regular at Larry's Greasy Spoon, where I would doze or chat with other cars while we waited.

My life was still OK, but in addition to having to adapt to multiple drivers there were some other changes. My two-way radio had been removed and I missed surreptitiously listening to others' conversations. I now had a small rubber plug on my trunk to cover the hole that had been exposed when the antenna was removed. I also didn't receive the same degree of attention to my exterior. Whoever drove me was responsible for making sure I was clean at the end of the day, but some guys were more conscientious than others. As I spoke with other cars and reflected on my life, I had to admit that I had enjoyed a pretty good first few years. Like my experience with Mr. Godfrey, I soon fell into a routine with my new role, always looking for the bright side and never complaining. That is the Chevrolet way.

I had settled into a comfortable routine for the next few years as my odometer clocked upwards of 70,000 miles. Although that seemed like a lot to me, I was quickly informed by other cars who had traveled far and wide that had I lived a more typical life I would be well over 100,000 miles at this ripe age of seven years. It was true that I had not seen many roads outside of the Chester environs other than a rare trip to a neighboring town, and they were certainly nothing to get excited about. I had heard of stoplights and four-lane highways but had never actually seen either. I doubted if I ever would.

My life took another swerve late that summer of 1957 when I was surplused to one of the managers at the mill. Like "upgrade" I find "surplus" to be an offensive term. I preferred to consider myself purchased to be put to a more productive use. Semantics aside, I was driven to a residence and parked in the driveway. That was the beginning of my relationship with Leroy. As I mentioned, at the outset we were wary of each other. I am always self-conscious when people examine my body in detail, peer under my hood and explore my trunk. It's just plain invasive of my personal space. But after that initial uneasy first meeting, things worked out between us and soon we had grown comfortable with each other.

A couple of weeks after he took ownership of me, Leroy filled my trunk and back seat with clothing, his hi-fi, a well-used baseball glove, some books and binders and a few other necessities a young man might need. Yes, I was off to college. He filled me with gas, and then we embarked for places unknown and a new phase in my life.

It took just two hours to reach the college town of Chico. I could tell that Leroy enjoyed the trip, which was likely his first solo journey outside the city limits of Chester. I, too, settled back and enjoyed the moment. It was a sunny, warm day. My windows were open and the breeze blowing into my passenger compartment was filled with the aromas of fresh trees, flowers, grass and occasionally, exhaust from other cars we encountered. The drive was a heady experience and I began to think I might have a pleasant future in Chico.

Leroy parked in a lot filled with many other cars — some old, some new, some sporty, and some beat up. I was nondescript enough to fit in nicely. After he unpacked me, he left me alone, giving me the opportunity to get acquainted with my new lot-mates. I learned that this was a dorm parking lot but none of the other cars knew what exactly a dorm was, other than a place where all of our owners were living. It was a new word for me. I was disappointed to see that there was no garage at the dorm but I could see that we were all in the same situation, which made me feel a little better.

I didn't see Leroy for two days but I didn't mind. We cars enjoy an occasional rest as long as it's not so long as to make our batteries drain or fluids leak (always embarrassing!) or tires go flat. When he clambered into my passenger compartment that evening there were three other guys with him. They were all laughing and wisecracking so I gathered Leroy had some new friends. I was pleased to be going somewhere, and eagerly anticipating a chance to explore Chico.

Our first stop was a drive-in restaurant called the Toot 'n Tell 'em. A young woman wearing a t-shirt, tight shorts and roller skates came to Leroy's window, handed in four menus, and was subjected to some obnoxious remarks that probably were meant to be flirtatious but came off to me (and I suspect, her) as stupid bravado. She rolled her eyes, popped her gum and didn't look directly at any of them, which indicated to me that this was not a new experience for her.

Leroy and his new pals downed their burgers and shakes, and to my relief, the lady in the roller skates took away the papers, cups and straws, so while I now smelled like a grease pit, at least I didn't look like one. We spent the next couple of hours driving around Chico getting acquainted with the geography. We eventually came across a large public park that I would get to know intimately over the next couple of years as Leroy settled into college life and the many intriguing activities it has to offer in addition to lectures and homework, especially after dark with a fellow student of the female persuasion on my front (and on rare occasions, back) seat with him.

We Chevrolets prefer regimen so as with my previous owners, I quickly settled into a routine with Leroy at college. Not that it was dull by any means! In addition to the ventures in the dark park with his girlfriends, we had a number of exciting events together, usually after he had filled his own tank with beer. It looked sort of like the gas he put into my tank, but he reacted a lot differently than I do when my tank is filled. He would wobble, laugh uncontrollably at things that I didn't think were particularly funny, loudly sing off-key and drive me with a lot less good judgment.

I had way too many close calls. I was parked on somebody's lawn, I was zoomed down Chico's residential streets at double the speed limit and I once ended up in a pasture where my engine died. Actually, I was the one who intentionally stalled myself to save Leroy from himself and from doing any serious damage. I refused to cooperate when he repeatedly tried to start me, so he gave up and walked home, leaving me in the pasture, but only after administering a disrespectful kick to my left-rear tire. The next morning he returned with a friend who had agreed to tow me, except when Leroy got behind my wheel I started right up on the first try. It may have been a mystery to him, but not to me. As I reflect back, I'm amazed at how Leroy avoided arrest or I avoided serious bodywork, but miraculously, we both did.

———————

In early June 1958 Leroy once again packed his worldly possessions in me and we returned to Chester. He had managed to pass all of his courses, which surprised me, but then I wasn't with him all the time. My contact with him during the school year was mostly in the evenings and weekends when he was not likely to be on his most academically serious behavior. For the summer he had managed to get his old job back at Harvey's Shell Station, so I spent most days parked there napping, watching other cars drive by and getting reacquainted with my old friends.

I was taken aback when that flashy '55 Plymouth I had met the previous summer pulled in to the station. He didn't look so good. For one thing, his design, while radically different when he was built, had not aged well and was now seriously dated. His fins now just looked big, ungainly and well, dumb. He was also sporting quite a few new dents and scratches I hadn't seen before, and he was in serious need of a wash and wax. I said hello, hoping he wouldn't remember how dismissive I'd been at our first meeting at the Frosty Freeze. He acted like he vaguely remembered me, but like most flashy cars, he probably didn't. As his tank was being filled I learned that he had been wrecked during the winter when his driver spun him out of control and into a tree. He was never the same. His frame had been bent and the new paint didn't match the original. Then he was sold to an uncaring and abusive new owner. It was sad, yet predictable (as comeuppances are), to see the resigned dullness in his once bright headlights.

Most of the cars that thought of themselves as cool in the mid to late 1950s mostly had powerful gas-sucking V8 engines and dual exhausts. They could emit an impressive rumble, conveying the message, like rutting stags, that they were ready to race and win. By now, I was well into my maturity and even though I was powered by a comparatively wimpy straight six that wasn't going to win any trophies getting from zero to sixty, I was reliable and economical. I was perfectly satisfied being who I was, and was comfortable in my own sheet metal. Leroy, though, had other wishes. He couldn't afford to replace my engine with one of those obnoxious monsters, yet he wanted to be as hip as he could on a small budget. He compromised by removing my factory muffler, which was about shot anyway, and replacing it with something called a "Smitty." It made me louder than I wanted to be but not as loud as a Hollywood Glasspac would have been. I didn't think it was at all appropriate and I hoped he would come to his senses.

Yet Leroy was 19 years old, and coming to his senses was more likely an event for the distant future than for the present. He not only put that silly Smitty on my underside, but he installed curb-finders, port-a-walls on my tires and a necking knob on my steering wheel, and hung a huge set of fuzzy dice on my rear-view mirror. I guess these feeble efforts at cool were the extent of his financial wherewithal.

About a week later he drove me up the grade leading out of Chester. Then we turned around and started back down the hill. When we got up to about sixty, he turned off my ignition and then turned it back on again, causing me to involuntarily emit a huge, embarrassing backfire. I couldn't believe how thoughtless that was! It was obvious from his laughter that he didn't seem to care that I almost blew off that brand new muffler. He sped up to sixty again. This time he put in my clutch and shifted me down into second gear. When he released the clutch I felt a painful grinding and I let out a noisy, long whine. Leroy immediately put me into neutral, but the damage had been done. Second gear was no longer an option for me. He managed to get me into low and we limped home. I subsequently learned when I overheard him explain the experience to a friend, that he simply wanted to hear that Smitty roar. His tactic failed and I hated that muffler even more now than I had when he bolted it on. It set Leroy back $40 to have my clutch plate replaced and it served him right.

Another incident that summer made me wonder about Leroy's state of mind. One warm Saturday morning he opened my driver's side door, removed my floor mat and began drilling a hole in my floorboard, to the left of my clutch. He drilled two or three more, as I wondered what was in store for me. He then put some bolts through the holes and crawled on his back under me. He was holding a shiny object in his hands. After some wiggling around and a few angry words, he managed to attach the thing to the bolts and tighten everything down. I was totally chagrined when he climbed into the driver's seat and mashed his foot down on a plunger extending through my floorboard. As he pushed it, there was a loud "ding-dong!" in response. It was startling and I was absolutely humiliated. He seemed to be very amused but I was not in the least. He drove me through town a few times, ding-donging as we passed some of his acquaintances, laughing hysterically. I noticed people staring at us, which I suppose was the whole point. But I was just plain ashamed because this addition was so un-Chevrolet. I was greatly relieved when the bell stopped operating after a few months.

When we returned to Chico in the fall for another school year we did not park at the dorm. Leroy was living in a different place. It was a large Victorian house full of young men. There were about twenty of us cars in the lot. I struck up a conversation with one and learned that this was something called a fraternity house. I had never heard of this term, but I soon came to realize what it was: A bunch of young guys who dress a lot alike, sing the same songs over and over, have meetings and drink a lot of beer from a large metal keg. These guys called themselves Gamma Alpha Rho, which sounded Greek to me and it turned out that it really was. At first I thought it was all pretty stupid but as I got to know the other cars and their owners I found myself, like Leroy, liking them, forming bonds, and getting into the fraternal spirit.

There were those noisy parties on the weekends and a lot of other activities during the week. However, there was also enforced study time most weeknights. That routine and peer pressure worked a positive change for Leroy, who showed substantial academic improvement compared to his freshman year. I could sense that he was gradually beginning to mature and consider his future, and I was most encouraged. By the time we returned to Chester the following summer he had evolved from gangly teenager to marginally self-assured young man. I modestly hoped that the combination of my loyal service and dignified mien had contributed to the improvement.

That summer was pleasant. Leroy had a job at the mill so I spent my days in the familiar surroundings of the mill parking lot, renewing old acquaintances. After work and on the weekends we would cruise around Chester and Lake Almanor, usually accompanied by one or two of Leroy's friends, James and J.C. Judging from their conversations, the objective always was to find some girls. I don't know why but it doesn't really matter because they never found any who were willing to accompany them.

One weekend James and Leroy tossed their sleeping bags and a change of clothing into my trunk and we headed east, ending up a few hours later at Lake Tahoe where they did meet some girls. I learned during our trip there that there was some kind of family connection to James. They parked me by the lake and spent the afternoon riding around in a boat. They also rode behind the boat, attached by a rope and standing on boards. It made no sense to me. Why would anybody do that when they could be riding in comfort in the boat itself? Humans are odd at times. In the evening, the parents of the girls took them away, so Leroy and James were once again without company. It didn't seem to deter them from enjoying their brief adventure, though. They ended up sleeping at the edge of a campground. Leroy correctly figured that if they arrived late, remained quiet and departed early they could avoid paying, which they did.

———————

As summer came to an end I expected that Leroy and I would return to Chico but that did not happen. I found myself parked in the garage of his parents' house in Chester. Leroy jacked me up and placed blocks under my axles, drained my oil and disconnected my battery. At that point I immediately went into a dreamless sleep. When I awoke, winter had come so I knew I had been idle for several months. Leroy had reconnected my battery, lowered me to the floor and filled my crankcase. Although I was a little groggy and stiff, he was able to start my engine, and I emitted an impressive cloud of blue smoke when he did so. I warmed up quickly, however, and was soon ready to take up where we had left off, wondering where Leroy had been and why I had not been with him.

As time passed I gleaned from bits and pieces of overheard conversations that he had been to Europe. I was disappointed that I had not accompanied him. I'd always wanted to see a foreign country. But I gathered it was a long drive to get there. I suppose Leroy did not have confidence I could reach it, although I did. We had returned to Chico and the routine of university life until early summer, when we headed up again to Chester.

I had learned by now, my ninth year, that nothing is forever. At more than 150,000 miles, my odometer was running high and some of my parts were worn and nearing the end of their useful lives. I was sad but I understood, albeit reluctantly, that it was time for Leroy and me to part ways. Chevrolets are known for their willingness to accept reality and adapt to whatever life's highway brings them. Our relationship ended in August 1960 when we returned to Chico and he parked me at a used car lot instead of the familiar fraternity house. I think Leroy was a little sad, too, because he smiled at me and gave me an affectionate pat on my hood before he drove away in an odd looking little car with a distinct German accent, who I believe called himself a "FolksFagen" or something like that.

Over the next few years I was sold several times. Each sale brought a little less money than the one before, and each new owner seemed to be a little less smart and caring as the one before. Eventually I ended up in an overgrown back yard on blocks, surrounded by weeds, broken down appliances and beer cans.

I'm not road-worthy now, although I believe and hope that somebody will rescue me and return me to my former glory, or at least let me do what I was engineered to do. Some of my parts are beyond repair, such as my condenser and generator and that rusty bell, but I think most of the others, including my pistons, still have potential. My life has been good. My owners, at least the early ones, were decent. I was well maintained and I never was wrecked. And with the exception of a few questionable episodes, my time with Leroy was positive. I have no regrets. I will continue to wait patiently for my final outcome and will accept whatever that might be. That is the Chevrolet way.

Chapter 4

CONVOY

Seven of us were sold all together at The Volkswagen Commercial Vehicles Transporter (VWN) factory in Hanover, West Germany. It was August 1959. The first Chancellor of the Federal Republic of Germany, Herr Konrad Adenauer, had been in office for ten years by then. Dwight Eisenhower had served six years as President of the United States. Fidel Castro and his band of rebels overthrew Fulgencio Batista in Cuba and Señor Castro became the Prime Minister there. Alaska and Hawaii became the 49th and 50th states in the USA. Sadly, it also was the year that Buddy Holly, Richie Valens and The Big Bopper died in an airplane crash.

Our official purchaser was a university located in a place called Chico, California, in the USA. Our MSRP was 8,775 German Marks, or approximately $2,100 when converted but I am fairly certain we were bought for a substantial discount, given that we were a fleet and also that we were being sold to a school. It was a sunny late summer afternoon. We were resting in a neat, evenly spaced row in the factory parking lot when five of our sedan cousins appeared and disgorged 14 young men and one older squat and balding man who seemed to be in charge. He was greeted by several important looking, smiling factory officials and escorted inside while the younger men kicked our tires, looked at our engines, opened and closed our doors and sat in us. I could understand everything but the tire kicking. What did they expect from that?

Before long the older man reappeared, stuffing papers into an untidy portfolio and calling for the young men to gather around him. He issued our ignition keys and assigned two drivers to each of us. Mine were called Leroy and Wayne.

We VW Busses are not designed to lean into the wind and zoom down the Autobahn at break-neck speeds. Nein, we are functional, reliable, roomy, practical people's busses with a capacity for nine passengers (unless they have eaten too many sausages or too much schlag over the years) and a four-cylinder engine with a maximum of 36 horsepower. Our four-speed floor shift gets plenty of workouts navigating the rugged, mountainous terrain of Europe. We don't delude ourselves that we can keep up with our fellow countrymen, the Porsches, Audis and BMWs. But they can't carry as many people or as much cargo. We all make our unique contributions to the happiness of the German people and in this case, non-German people, who purchase us.

As we left the factory I was second in line in the convoy. I had never been driven before so the whole experience was very exciting. My engine was not quite as powerful as the others (my number three valve was lacking compression), and one by one they passed me until I was last in line and lagging well behind the rest of the convoy. I felt OK and my engine seemed to be running fine, so it clearly was not a warranty problem, yet I had trouble keeping up with the other six. I figured that if I couldn't be the leader of the convoy I would be its tail because the thought of being in the middle made me claustrophobic. I was philosophical about it. One of us had to be the slowest, so why not me? As it turned out on subsequent days, what could have been a lemon turned into Schnapps. Because we were always well behind, Leroy and Wayne would often make unscheduled stops so my passengers could take photos, stretch their legs and do something they called "P". So I got to see a lot of the countryside and get plenty of rest along the way. We were always last to arrive at our destination but nobody cared much as long as we eventually got there.

As the sun was beginning to set after our drive from the factory, we arrived in Amsterdam, which is in another country entirely, called Holland. It was easy to tell we were no longer in Germany because things were not as orderly and also it was very difficult to avoid running over an annoying bicycle. There were thousands of them jockeying for space on the city roads, enjoying the same right of way that we cars have. I was miffed that a pesky bicycle would presume to have the same rights to use a paved road that I have. The caravan had paused to wait for me and as I approached we all continued down the road, eventually stopping at a large parking lot. We were all parked there and locked up. The drivers left on foot and we didn't see them for a couple of days.

When they returned it was with a large group of people, mostly young women. There were just enough men to handle the driving and enough women to fill our seats. Leroy and Wayne occupied my front seat and three women plus a professor and his wife, also a professor as it turned out, filled the passenger seats. The rest of the busses had similar loads. As our convoy left the parking lot, Leroy waited until we were the last bus, as he and I both knew that we eventually would be in any case, so why make everybody pass us on the road?

Cars, like people, can learn a lot by listening and we're generally better at it because we don't talk. For example, that day I learned that we were going to Haarlem to see a museum and then to a cheese market in a place called Ijsselmeer. I was interested in neither art nor cheese, so I whiled away my time viewing the countryside and listening to my passengers. I felt the side trips over the next two days were productive in that my passengers, drivers and I got to know each other better. I had learned by now that they were here as part of their education, and that they were required to attend lectures when we were not on the road, and to do all the things expected of students like taking notes, studying, writing papers, and passing examinations. The older people turned out to be the teachers.

I did wonder why it was only the men who did the driving. Since nobody brought the issue up, I didn't get the answer. I guess it was a cultural thing. The men seemed to truly enjoy driving me and the women seemed perfectly satisfied to sit in the back and talk incessantly. Their happiness behind the wheel aside, I was picking up clues that both Leroy and Wayne were having trouble adjusting. They complained to each other about how much they disliked some of the professors, how hard it was to find a quiet place to study, how boring the museums were, how bad the food at the hotel was, and how depressed they were. I wanted to advise them to wake up and smell the exhaust but that is not my job.

At the beginning of our second week together, all of us busses were moved to the front of a small hotel, taking up an embarrassingly large share of the parking spaces. Each of our occupants' two metal suitcases were secured with rope to our roof luggage racks by our drivers. Then everybody piled in and off we went, causing heads to turn as we lumbered down the narrow cobblestone streets, leaving Amsterdam behind us. Soon we were back in West Germany and it was almost like homecoming for me. I had left my birth country before learning the language but I was nevertheless drawn to it. We stopped that first night in Bonn after a long day replete with wonderful German sights and smells. Leroy and Wayne were in better spirits now that we were on a road trip.

The next night found us in Heidelberg after a raucous day that started in Koblenz, on the Rhine River. Our passengers all got out, leaving each bus with only a single driver. Everybody else boarded a ferryboat while our drivers took us to another town well down the river, called Bingen. When the boat arrived in the late afternoon and people re-boarded us, many of them seemed to be out of sorts. They were singing off key, talking loudly and unclearly, and were not very steady on their feet. As it turned out, there was plenty of good German beer on the boat and having no particular reason not to, they had taken full advantage of it. Leroy drove me into Heidelberg. We made two stops along the way so the women could engage in that "P" thing and also in something they called "barfing", which I did not understand because air-cooled cars don't do that. I suppose a car with a plugged radiator might barf, which if so, reinforces to me the superiority of our rear engine design. We eventually arrived safely at our hotel and by the next morning everybody seemed to be fine, although some were complaining of headaches as we continued our journey through my beautiful homeland.

We enjoyed a pleasant journey through the German countryside as we headed for Munich. The closer we got to the city, the more traffic we encountered and by late afternoon we had slowed to a crawl. My engine strained under the heavy load and the constant shifting, but as a Volkswagen bus there was no question that I had a job to do and that I would give it my very best. A beautiful Mercedes Benz 220S passed me and I couldn't help but admire his classic lines and smooth demeanor. We exchanged glances and he moved on, passing all of us busses with ease as he skillfully avoided the oncoming traffic.

We stopped in Munich for two nights and I was disappointed to learn that we busses would be parked the whole time. It did not seem fair that a proud Volkswagen would sit in a German parking lot when there was so much to see in his homeland. There was nothing we could do about it, however, so we accepted our fate, hoping that we would at least take the scenic route out of town when it was time to move on. My senses were filled with all things German, from lederhosen to cuckoo clocks as we struck out on the open road once again. I heard Wayne mention to Leroy that the day's destination was Bad Vöslau. I'd never heard of it but I figured they knew where they were going.

Bad Vöslau turned out to be a nearly deserted, downtrodden little town about 50 kilometers from Vienna, in Austria. We parked at what appeared to be the only hotel in town and after our roof racks were unloaded I struck up a conversation with the VW Beetle parked in back of me since I was, as usual, the last in line. He belonged to an employee of the hotel. I told him who we were and in exchange he provided some insight. He explained that Bad Vöslau had been a popular spa but had fallen into disrepair during World War II. After the war the town was occupied by the Soviet Army until 1955. When they departed they took with them most things of value, such as plumbing, furniture, even drainage pipes. Now, four years later, the town was slowly recovering but it was nowhere near its former glory. The Beetle said he had heard that the locals were happy to host the students from the USA, not only for the money they would contribute to the economy, but just as much for the diversion from the quiet boredom.

We remained in Bad Vöslau for a whole month. We busses spent most of our time parked, dozing and refining our German and English while our passengers attended classes in the hotel. We did take a few trips, mostly to museums and operas in Vienna. I noticed that Leroy once again was feeling depressed. He complained to Wayne about his grades, his relationship with his girlfriend, his professors, his cold room at the hotel, the food and, it seemed to me, anything else he could find to be unhappy about. To be honest I soon grew tired of his self-pity so I focused on the road, the scenery and the conversations among the other passengers. Leroy seemed to be happy only when we were traveling.

I did have one frightening experience when returning to Bad Vöslau after the group had attended an opera performance. As my passengers climbed in I heard them laughing as they recollected how Leroy and another driver had sold their tickets for a handsome profit in front of the opera house. Rather than attend the show they opted for less structured entertainment at a nearby bar and enjoyed several glasses of Austrian beer. The effects on Leroy were obvious as he began the drive out of Vienna. About halfway to Bad Vöslau we came upon traffic cones in the middle of the two-lane road. Work was not being done that night, but the cones had been left in place. The driver in front of me began weaving between them as if on a slalom course and Leroy followed suit. Both of them were having great fun but I was petrified, as was the other bus. We are not designed for abrupt turns and I was feeling dangerously unstable. The antics came to an end after the final cone and by that time my passengers were as frightened as I was. Fortunately, we made it safely to our hotel. The next morning Leroy apologized to his passengers and asked if any of them would be willing to share notes on the opera he had missed. He did not apologize to me. I suppose he could not have known how upset I was.

I witnessed a memorable experience a few days later when we took a field trip to the Austria-Hungary border. As we arrived, we saw a woman and her father being reunited after having been apart for ten years. She was living in the USA, and he in Hungary. I spoke with the Beetle she had arrived in, and learned that his visit to the West would be limited to two weeks. He would then be required to return to Hungary. I found that to be both perplexing and moving. It caused me to wonder how people could be so mean to each other that they would force a family to live apart. It also reinforced to me that in spite of the many good qualities I had observed in humans, sometimes there are distinct advantages to being a car.

Toward the end of October the weather had definitely turned cold in Bad Vöslau. When I heard some of the complaints from other cars nearby I was struck by two thoughts: German cars accept whatever challenges are presented and they do not complain — we do our job; and my air-cooled engine was a blessing because I did not have to be concerned about water in my system turning to ice and doing internal damage. I wished I could imbue Leroy, to whom I had become attached despite his immaturity and tendency toward self-pity, with my positive attitude which let me accept my lot in life and do my best to deal with whatever comes my way.

Our stay in Bad Vöslau came to an end a few days later. Our passengers brought out all their luggage and our drivers once again secured it to our roof racks. By late morning we were on the road again and as usual, we were the tail of the seven-bus snake. As the day progressed the others eventually disappeared from view. Thankfully, Leroy and Wayne had a map so nobody was concerned about being separated. Best of all, Leroy was in a good mood for a change, confirming to me that he was happiest while behind my wheel and not in a classroom.

Our road adventure lasted a week, taking us to Salzburg, Innsbruck, Zurich, Geneva, and through some striking mountains the passengers referred to as Alps. They awed me with their majesty but also seriously challenged my capabilities as a humble and committed transporter of people. With seven people and all their luggage, my poor little 36 horsepower engine was strained to its maximum capability. I also noticed that most of the women had more possessions now than they did when we began our odyssey, adding to my burden. Leroy and Wayne did their best to pick up speed on the downhills in order to get a good start on the inevitable uphills. By the time we reached the crest I was normally in second gear and sometimes even in low.

We came to a stop at a little town called Brig. It was very cold and snowy. We busses were loaded onto flat cars that were attached to each other and ultimately to a very large, smoky diesel engine. The wheels of this thing I heard referred to as a train were metal, resting on rails also made of metal. I didn't see any-body kicking those tires. I was apprehensive, as were we all, but we saw a lot of other cars parked similarly and that gave us some comfort. It turned out to be a good thing. The engine started up and we slowly lurched forward, picked up speed and suddenly found ourselves in a dark tunnel. When we emerged, the sun was shining, it was warm and people were speaking an unfamiliar language. A man rode past us on a bicycle, singing at the top of his lungs. I couldn't understand the words, but I could sense that he was on key, happy and most important, warm.

As we were driven off the flat cars I learned that we had just come through a big hole in the Alps called the Simplon Pass. As I looked back I was grateful for that train ride through a tunnel as a welcome alternative to negotiating that steep mountain range.

Soon we were back in formation and on the road, ending up in Venice where we stayed for two days. We were parked outside of the town. I learned from a nearby Fiat that Venice had no streets, and that people had to walk everywhere or ride in boats. Although a Beetle had told me once that we float, it was fine with me not to test the theory. After Venice we stopped in Florence for three weeks where Leroy was once again in a sour mood, so I assumed our passengers were back into their school routine.

Winter had set in and we busses sat huddled in a big parking lot. Our silence was broken every few days as we carried our passengers on day trips around northern Italy, but mostly it was just quiet and brisk. Leroy and Wayne complained about their cold room but by now I had begun to tune out their negative feelings, telling myself not to bother paying attention to my drivers until we were again on a road trip and their moods were better.

One morning we went through our by now familiar routine of having our roof racks loaded and the passengers piling in for departure to another city. To my disappointment, this trip lasted only a single day. When we arrived in Rome that evening we were once again parked, this time for a one-month stay broken up by day trips to Naples, Pompeii, Paestum, the Amalfi coast and even a boat trip to the Isle of Capri. I did not get to see it, as cars were not allowed on the small boat, but it looked pretty from the distance. This is a downside of being a car but not a serious one when weighed against the many upsides.

My concern for Leroy and Wayne's depressed moods was growing. I discussed it with the other busses and they confirmed that their passengers, too, were in a sour mood. We compared the bits of information we had picked up because it did not make sense to us that young people traveling around together, experiencing new cultures, seeing things of great historical significance and broadening their education would have anything to complain about. Nevertheless, their tempers were short, anxiety was high and they were becoming downright surly. We eventually decided that unlike the straightforward problems that we cars may encounter, there was not one simple answer to explain the mood of our passengers. We concluded that they were not accustomed to extended living in close group situations, and that many were homesick because something called Christmas was approaching, although I could not see it. And their studies were rigorous because this trip was a first and therefore had to meet a high standard if it was to be repeated by future groups. When we took into account all these factors and added the cold weather and poorly heated rooms, we began to understand why morale was low. Perhaps more seasoned adults would have made a better adjustment, but most of these people were only around twenty years old. That is quite old for a car but quite young for a human being.

On a rainy, chilly morning toward the end of December, we left Rome behind us with our noses pointed north. Our destination was Barcelona. Morale remained low. Christmas had been a lonely, introspective experience for our passengers, most of whom had never been away from home for that holiday. As we continued on, spirits seemed to improve and by the time we reached sunny, warm France there was a noticeable cheering up.

We spent a night in Carcassonne where I learned a few French words from some Peugeots and Citroens, who expressed heavily accented envy at the experience we busses were having.

The next day we cruised around a scenic place called the Riviera (I thought that would be a great name for a car), stopping in Monte Carlo (also not a bad name for a car) for a few hours. Leroy was miffed at being refused entrance to the casino without a tie while the women were all passed right through. Then it was on to Nimes for the night, and the next day to Barcelona.

There we once again spent most of our time parked, except for occasional side trips. Leroy and Wayne returned to their collective depressed state, which by now was getting tiresome. I wasn't sure how much more they (or I) could stand. After three weeks in Barcelona my question was answered when I saw both of them getting into another van with their luggage. I guess they left the group, because I never saw them again. I hoped they would find a better life wherever it was they were headed. As for me, I had a new driver to get used to. I was justifiably nervous because some other men had left as well, and there was no alternative but to allow the women to take on the driving role. It worked out fine, although both we and our new drivers had to adapt. I was being driven by another man, Fred, along with Lil, a woman. Fred was more aggressive behind my wheel, much like Leroy and Wayne had been, while Lil was more cautious and, I might add, considerate of my welfare. Her feet were about half the size of Leroy's, and as she quickly managed to negotiate my pedals with skill, we were both able to relax.

We ultimately ended up in Calais where we were unloaded, and our passengers boarded a ferry for England. We busses were shipped back to Germany and sold, all going our separate ways but with happy memories in common. I thought about Leroy over the years because although he had his problems, he was a likable enough guy with potential that I hoped he would ultimately realize. I'm betting he did.

Chapter 5

SEMAPHORES IN THE WIND

Life in the car lot was not good. I'd been there for two weeks and I just sat there, day after day, listening to other cars around me complain about how unfairly they had been treated and how ungrateful their owners had been. They were an unhappy bunch and it was depressing. Volkswagens never complain. We are not built that way. With the carping and the random tire kicking, hood raising, test driving and very personal and intrusive examinations, it added up to a period of resigning myself to whatever life had in store for me and resolving to make the best of it.

One Saturday in August 1960, after having been on display for two weeks, I was test driven by a college student. I was apprehensive because of what I had heard from other cars owned by these kinds of drivers. So I coughed, sputtered and jerked a little bit in order to discourage him, hoping I would end up with somebody like my previous owner, Professor Sloan. But it was not to be. All my acting worked against me. It ended up driving my price down so far that the guy could afford me after trading in his 1950 Chevrolet. I didn't have much time to talk with the Chevrolet while the deal was being made, and the combination of his hearing loss and my accent made it hard for him to understand my questions. About all I learned was that my new owner was named Leroy and that most of the time he was a good driver but not always, especially when he had a lot of beer in his tank.

Leroy drove me off the lot after patting the Chevrolet on his hood, which I thought was a very considerate thing to do and a good omen. Not every owner bonds with his car and it appeared that this Leroy guy was one who might do that. Cars all appreciate being appreciated. It's a two way street. I vowed right then that if he would be good to me I would return the favor and be as reliable and trusty as I was engineered to be.

I'm a 1955 Volkswagen sedan. I was constructed in a place called Wolfsburg, in West Germany, which is a very long way from where I am now. 1955 was the year that my home country joined NATO. Also, Disneyland opened in Anaheim, and the first McDonald's hamburgers were served. Elvis Presley was in his prime. Neither the country of my roots, West Germany, nor the country of my residence, the USA, was at war.

I was first sold after I was shipped to California, to a man who lived in Chico, a college town. I liked it there because it was flat. When we went for drives to the mountains I had to work hard to climb the hills, as my engine has only 36 horsepower. But I am German and I do not complain. There were not very many of us in this country back then because most Americans preferred big, powerful cars and I was anything but that. To my credit, I get very good mileage — 28 MPG — which was about twice what the big American cars could muster, plus I have a four-speed, floor mounted manual shift. People also thought I was funny looking. I am relatively small with a dramatic slope to my nose and my engine is in the back where it should be. My passenger compartment can hold four people if they are young or short. I have turn signals that are different from the ones on cars made in the USA. Mine are semaphores, mounted on the outside of the doorposts and when my driver activates them they pop up. They work fine, but if we are going fast they don't retract very well because the wind keeps them up and the driver has to reach outside and push them back down. That's fine during the summer but not very convenient when it is cold or raining.

People and other cars used to gawk at me because I was different. They called me a "bug" or a "beetle" and I was not amused. I think I am much more handsome than any bug or beetle I have ever seen, especially the ones smashed on my windshield. If my name is to be shortened I prefer "VW". My owner, Professor Sloan, though, was proud of me and was quick to defend me when others made fun of my appearance. He would point out that I was the design of the future, with my aerodynamic look and rear engine that was air-cooled. I was not plush, but I was reliable and easy to maintain. Professor Sloan took good care of me, making sure I was in the garage every night and that I was serviced and washed regularly. I considered myself fortunate to be owned by him and I did my best to meet his expectations. My MSRP was just under $1,800 when I was new. As a college professor he didn't make too much money like actors and athletes do, so I was bought because I was affordable and also economical.

I had a good life. I was driven carefully, mostly between school and home. When I talked with other cars I realized how lucky I was not to be owned by a student. They would tell me stories about being raced, being filled with way more passengers than they were designed for, being driven by drunks and being parked in dark places, resulting in their windows being steamed up at night.

Professor Sloan and his wife had no children when they bought me but within three years their family had grown to four. Between all the people and the extra equipment needed to cart babies around, it was obvious I was being outgrown. I wanted to make them happy but I could not stretch to be any bigger than I was made. So while it was a disappointment, it was not a surprise when I found myself on a used car lot in the summer of 1959, watching with a tear in my headlight as Professor Sloan drove away in an ugly but roomy new Ford.

My new home with Leroy was a parking lot at a fraternity house. I could tell right away that it was more active than Professor Sloan's garage, and I quickly learned that my garage days were over as I spent all my parking time out of doors with the other fraternity cars. Most of them were pretty reasonable and friendly toward me. I was the only German car around. A few of them made fun of my accent, and pretty much all of them thought I was odd looking. I could sense it. And when they learned that I had only 36 horsepower it caused a few headlights to rise. Some of them teased me with questions like why I bother to have more than a low gear with such a wimpy engine, and why my back seat was only roomy enough for people with no arms or legs. Then, when they found that my engine was in the rear I was teased that when my front hood was raised it was revealed that my engine had been stolen, but that was OK because I had a spare one in my trunk. Very funny.

All of us got to know each other I gradually gained acceptance by demonstrating that we Germans can actually have a sense of humor and take a little teasing. Mostly, however, I knew that my main job was to work and that is what I set out to do. Whenever Leroy would turn my key I would start my engine immediately. I gave him good mileage, my radio came in clearly, my lights always worked and my semaphores never failed, except when we were exceeding 50 MPH and Leroy would have to stick his arm out the window and push them back down. Another unique feature of mine is that I had no gasoline gauge. We early Volkswagens were equipped instead with a lever on our floor that would be turned when we ran out of gas, allowing access to our reserve tank and an additional 25 miles in which to find a gas station. This did not present a serious problem to most VW drivers, but in my experience, and based on conversations I had with my peers, college students were often short of funds for gas and were unable to top off our tanks as frequently as they might. It was not uncommon to see one of us parked on the side of the road awaiting a fuel can. The worst part was when other cars would drive by and shout insults at us and ridicule us for being gauge-free. Naturally, they would invariably toss in insults about our unconventional appearance and compact stature but we were above allowing those remarks to get under our paint.

Leroy was a good driver. He understood manual shifting and he never ground my gears, finely honed skills for which I was very grateful. Speeding was not really an issue, since it was hard to do with my engine, which got us from zero to sixty in about 45 seconds, and back to fifty, then forty, then thirty in a hurry if there was an uphill slope ahead. We did have some frightening moments when he and his pals drank beer on Saturday nights. He was not quite as careful then, and we did some ill advised speeding around town, running stop signs, driving on the wrong side of the road and parking on lawns and sidewalks. I found that behavior to be quite embarrassing and beneath my dignity but I had no control when Leroy was behind my wheel. All I could do was try not to crash into anything and that was challenge enough.

On one of those Saturday nights when Leroy was not around, his fraternity brothers physically picked me up and deposited me on the front porch of the house. They thought it was highly amusing, but I did not, nor did I care for all the laughing and stares of people as they passed by. I had never felt so disrespected! When Leroy came home he immediately checked me for damage, which I appreciated. Then he got into my passenger compartment and started me up. This worried me, as a crowd gathered outside the house and on the sidewalk. As I said, Leroy was skillful when he needed to be. He very carefully moved me back and forth in that limited space, gradually turning me until my nose was pointed straight ahead, toward the street. Then he started forward, alarming me to no small degree. My front wheels dropped over the top step and he braked, giving both of us a chance to recover. Before I had a chance to put myself into reverse and get back up to the porch, he cut my engine and I was helpless. Then he released the brake and I thumped down to the next step. I didn't care for the angle, as my rear end was still on the porch and my transmission was within less than an inch of contact with the stair. He released the brake again, causing my front to go down another step and my rear to come off the porch onto the top step, and miraculously, my transmission did not make contact. Leroy and I were gaining confidence by now, and I was beginning to think that we might survive this ordeal after all. A few more bumper-jarring thumps, and we were finally on the sidewalk, surrounded by cheering people. It was a huge relief and the attention was gratifying, although I had to wonder if these college people didn't have something better to do.

Leroy and I had made a few trips to another town called Chester. It was up in the mountains so it was quite a chore for me to get us there. Usually, he would toss a bag of dirty laundry on my back seat so the trip up never smelled quite as good as the trip back to Chico. I didn't complain, of course. Our first couple of trips were actually quite pleasant. I had never been to that part of the country or any part of the country other than Chico, for that matter. So it was interesting to see the different kinds of trees and bushes and the absence of houses and people. Because Chester was at a higher altitude, I had some trouble with my carburetor, which was not adjusted for that elevation. But I got us there and back anyway.

There was one scary trip for Christmas vacation. Leroy loaded me up with the usual bag of dirty clothes and some books (which he never removed from my back seat until we returned to Chico, two weeks later). When we set off it had begun to rain but that was no problem, as I was used to it and my wiper blades were in good shape. As the road climbed higher and higher the rain was replaced by something I had never seen before. It was white, blinding and slick. I was extremely apprehensive. Leroy seemed to sense my anxiety, and he slowed down and drove me very carefully, but the road was soon covered with the stuff and I was having trouble getting a grip with my tires. He found a wide spot and pulled over, where I breathed a huge sigh of relief. Then I felt him jacking up my rear end. I knew my tires were not flat, so I was puzzled. Then he wrapped some uncomfortable metal chains around my tires, fastened them in place and lowered the jack.

I didn't know what was going on, but those things really dug uncomfortably into my tires. Leroy was not helping our situation one bit. But as he started me up and we drove back onto the road I felt like I had more control. It was noisy and bumpy but at least we were no longer slipping and sliding so I decided to go along with him and not shut down my engine in protest as I had been considering. It was a chilly, frame-jarring trip. We Volkswagens do not boast a sophisticated heating system but if our knob is turned fully on, we eventually are able to warm our passenger compartment. I knew Leroy was impatient but I was doing the best I could, and besides, my focus was on keeping us on the road, not the creature comforts.

After three hours of slow driving we made it to Chester. I was looking forward to drying off and warming up in the garage but my space had already been taken by a 1950 Ford so I had to stay in the driveway for the night. By morning I was completely covered by the white stuff. It was dark in my passenger compartment and I didn't even realize it was daytime until Leroy brushed my windshield and windows. He then got behind the wheel and started me up after almost completely draining my battery. I was cold, my battery was weak and all I wanted was to thaw out; however, I did my best and soon my engine was warm and I could feel my battery recharging. Leroy backed me out and we started clickity clacking down the street. I was amazed that I could see nothing except large white expanses and piles. There were no lawns or bushes or flowers. Parked cars were buried and houses were barely visible. It was as if we had never been to Chester before, so foreign was the landscape. We drove to the end of town, made a U-turn and went to the other end, where we made another U-turn, and then we pulled into the Frosty Freeze and parked next to a sad, beat up dull red 1955 Plymouth on its last tires. I tried to strike up a conversation with him but other than telling me that the white blanket was called snow and those things on my tires were called chains, I learned little about him. He had lived in Chester his entire life, which was a happy time until he crashed into a tree, and after that it was never the same. He cautioned me to be very careful or the same fate might befall me. Given his sad state, I vowed to do just that.

When we returned to the house the Ford was not there so Leroy parked me in the garage. It was heaven! I just let the snow melt from me and drip on the floor. I normally prefer things to be tidy but I didn't care about the floor or anything else right then. All I wanted to do was get warm and dry, which I did, as Leroy left me there all night. I heard the Ford grousing outside but I ignored it. First come, first served.

I had grown accustomed to snow by the time Leroy had to return to school, but I must say I was happy to be back in Chico where I was free of those awful chains and the only stuff that gathered on my roof was rain.

———

It was spring, 1960. I knew by this point in my life that the college would shut down for Easter like it did over Christmas, and most of the students would go away for a week. People seem to need a lot more time off than cars do. I was wondering if we would be returning to Chester and was soon disabused of that idea. Leroy and two of his fraternity brothers, Lucky and Thunder, piled into me early Saturday morning after tossing their duffels and sleeping bags onto my roof rack and cinching them down, and wrestling two cases of Olympia beer into my back seat, along with a box of various kinds of beans which I later heard them refer to as chili, porken and musical fruit. My passenger compartment was filled to the max with Leroy (six feet four inches tall) and Lucky (six feet two inches tall) in the front and Thunder (six feet four inches tall) in the back. Thunder had to lay sideways with his feet resting on the beer cases. I could feel that he was not very comfortable.

I did not know where we were going. We left Chico and headed out of town, eventually connecting with Highway 101. I had never been there, but I had heard other cars mention it so I knew we were going south because there was an ocean to our right. We drove all day, stopping every couple of hours so the people could stretch their legs and trade places. Nobody wanted to be in the cramped back seat nor were they willing to sacrifice the beer, so they took turns. The full load also slowed me down a lot and it took every one of my 36 horses to get up any little rise in the road that we encountered. I did pretty well going downhill though. We ended up that first evening in Pismo Beach. After finding a spot to camp, Leroy and his pals, who now were referring to themselves as "Los Tres Borrachos", emptied some of the beer into their tanks. An hour later they piled in to my passenger compartment again. I was relieved that it was just a quick drive to a restaurant instead of another marathon like we had just completed. A short time later they emerged from the restaurant and when they re-boarded me I heard some clanking noise coming from Thunder's pockets as if he had broken a piston. It turned out to be purloined cutlery. He explained to Leroy and Lucky that he had to do it for the good of Los Tres Borrachos because they could not afford to eat in restaurants every night and they would need utensils for the musical fruit. That made perfect sense to me. I don't eat human food but if I did I would hope to have tools to do it with.

We returned to our campsite where they refilled their tanks and as the sun set over the ocean, we all watched it, temporarily lost in our private thoughts. I don't know what theirs were but mine were mostly about fresh oil, new tires and wondering whatever became of Professor Sloan and his family. I missed them but I also had to confess that I was having an intriguing adventure with Los Tres Borrachos.

Just after daybreak the next morning we were packed and on our way again, continuing south and seeing places I had never seen before. We came to a place called Los Angeles and I was flabbergasted! There was so much traffic on such wide roads going so fast! We stayed in the far right lane and cars whizzed by us in three other lanes. Some of the other cars would greet us as they passed, but most of them seemed to be kind of snooty, especially the Porsches, which disappointed me since they knew I was a cousin. I guess they were ashamed of the family connection or just too self-important to care.

We pressed on through Los Angeles but even after we were beyond the city, the traffic didn't thin out very much. I had never seen so many cars and people crammed into one place and while I enjoy the smell of fresh exhaust, it was too much of a good thing there. Lucky complained about smog and as he explained what it was I realized that my headlights were watering and I couldn't see nearly as far ahead as I could in Chico. I was grateful that we were only visiting and would not have to live there full time because it seemed to be dangerous, fast, callous and hot. Some of the other cars were quite attractive, though, and Los Tres Borrachos seemed to think some of the drivers were also, as they made several graphic observations about some of them. It struck me that Professor Sloan never talked like that.

By late afternoon we had to downshift to a crawl as we got into a slow line to cross a bridge. When we crept over it and got to the other side it was a different world entirely. We were in a noisy, colorful place called Tijuana. I had to be extra careful not to run over anybody and not to end up with a dented fender as the streets were crowded with people who were not obeying pedestrian laws, and the other cars were just as undisciplined, parking on the wrong side of the road, speeding, honking their horns, and generally just being uncivilized. As far as I was concerned, we couldn't get away from there quick enough, but Los Tres Borrachos parked me and took a walk to look things over. I was thankful they emptied my roof rack into my passenger compartment and locked my doors because I was seeing some unsavory types lurking around and I didn't want to be stolen or burglarized. They were gone for an hour or so and I was unharmed, probably because of my humble appearance. Had I been a fancy, shiny car like my Porsche cousins I'm sure I would have not been as fortunate, so there is an upside to being old, small, dirty and boxy.

When my roof rack was repacked we left Tijuana behind us. I was happy about that but apprehensive about what was in store for us. As we drove, my three passengers shared a bottle of a beverage called tequila that made them laugh and sing, and Leroy was not at his best behind my wheel. We narrowly missed an oncoming truck on the narrow, pothole filled road and as it passed, it glared at me as if it were my fault. As dusk was falling we pulled into another town that was quieter than Tijuana, although not very prosperous looking. Lucky kept talking about finding some langosta for dinner, but first they needed to find a place to stay because even I knew it would not be safe to sleep outside tonight. They found a run-down motel that was no worse than any of the other establishments in town (the name of the town turned out to be Ensenada). They unloaded my roof rack and took their stuff inside, leaving me outdoors and more than a little nervous. I tried to strike up a conversation with a dusty old Pontiac nearby, but I couldn't speak whatever it was he was speaking, which was neither English nor German.

Los Tres Borrachos struck out on foot to explore Ensenada and try to find some of that langosta Lucky was yapping on about. They returned an hour later, still hungry, so I guess they didn't have any luck. Leroy suggested they return to the room and dine on porken beans and Olympia, which they did after locking me up for the night.

We set out the next morning, and I again did my best to avoid the many potholes as we headed slowly east, ending up that afternoon in a town called Tecate. Los Tres Borrachos once again removed their belongings from my roof rack and locked them in my passenger compartment before going into a building with a bright neon sign that repeatedly flashed "Club Vera Cruz", so I figured that was the name of the place. They were gone for quite a long time and when they returned that evening it was obvious that their tanks were all filled to the brim with tequila. They had a new man with them whose name was Haysoos, which for some reason Thunder thought was a good omen. We gave Haysoos a ride to something called a casa, where he thanked us and staggered through the door.

As we wove unsteadily away from Tecate, Los Tres Borrachos recounted their evening and all I could think of was that I was very happy not to have participated. They had come upon a birthday party where a tequila bottle was being passed around for everybody to share, which they did. When it was empty, they bought another one. When that one was empty they decided it was time to leave, as they were sensing some hostility toward gringos, which I gathered is what they were in the eyes of the people who lived there. So Leroy continued to drive aimlessly while Lucky and Thunder recounted the adventure they had found hilarious. I was not amused. Gradually, they quieted down and eventually we came to a stop by a little house with a man who asked Leroy some questions about where he was from, where he had been, where he was going and did he have any alcohol in me. Leroy answered as best he could, although his words did not come out as clearly as normal. When he was asked about the alcohol, he said he did not think we had any, as all of those bottles in the back seat and on the floor seemed to be empty. The man said we could go ahead, so we drove on. The road got immediately better, but Leroy pulled to the side of the road to rest. As they drifted off to sleep they snored loudly and made other odd noises that I attributed to the musical fruit. Los Tres Borrachos stayed there until awakened by the hot sun beating down on them. They did not know where we were, nor did I. It was hot, sandy, and treeless and the area was dotted with strange looking growths with spines sticking out of them.

They figured the logical thing to do was drive on until they found a town in which they could get their bearings. As they discussed the previous night's journey, none of them had any recollection of the man who had stopped them, which added to their confusion as to where we were. Before long I was happy to see that we had found a gas station because my tank was getting dangerously low. The man who filled me told them we were in Canyon City, Arizona. We had never heard of that place and I could tell that none of us wanted to stick around, so Leroy asked the gas station man what direction it was to Santa Barbara. He pointed his finger to the northwest, and off we went.

We didn't make it all the way to Santa Barbara that day because we stopped at a place called Laguna Beach. We had returned to the ocean and the land of nicer roads, so I was feeling more comfortable than I had over the past two days. Los Tres Borrachos decided to camp out, saving their limited funds for food and beer, which by now was gone. There were no campgrounds to be found, however, and they ended up sleeping that night on an embankment filled with ice plant.

The following morning they concluded that before continuing to Santa Barbara they needed to find a place to bathe (even I was beginning to notice, and odors normally don't offend me at all). They parked near a public beach and one at a time, changed into swimming suits in my passenger compartment, which I must say was not the most pleasant experience I had ever had. I had a good view of the ocean and I watched them as they walked down the beach and went into the water. When they returned after an hour or so they smelled much cleaner and they put on different clothes. All of us felt a lot better about that.

We drove around Laguna Beach and found that it was full of college students so they decided to stay another day. They tried to strike up conversations with a number of young women but they were either rejected outright or ignored. That was understandable even to me, given their indecorous appearance and demeanor. As night fell the streets of Laguna were crowded with hundreds of young people, most of whom were drinking large quantities of beer, as were Los Tres Borrachos. We drove around with no particular goal other than to find even more people and women who would not be too afraid or disgusted to have a conversation. Somebody mentioned Balboa Island as the place to be, so we went in search of it. By this time, my passengers had consumed quite of bit of beer and Thunder had discovered a half-full bottle of tequila behind my back seat, which they promptly drank. Leroy managed to find the freeway, but as we drove up, then down, then up, then down, looking for the exit for Balboa, nobody could focus enough to read the overhead signs on the freeway. Leroy arbitrarily concluded that it would be best to find a place to spend the night. He took an exit and as luck would have it, meandered our way to the beach, where we parked near the ocean. Los Tres Borrachos resigned themselves to their fate and called it a night after a dinner of cold chili beans and warm beer. Everybody, including me, had plenty of gas.

We all awoke to mist-filtered sunshine and cool ocean breezes, refreshed and ready to press on to Santa Barbara. My passengers were not exactly sure what their mission was, but they were willing to grasp at any goal by this time. Leroy knew a lady there who he wanted to get to know better. She lived with her parents, so Thunder and Lucky were happy to go along for, if nothing else, the outside chance of something to eat besides musical fruit. We arrived mid-afternoon and Leroy called Carol, his lady friend. To his delight, she invited all of us to her home. It was a nice, clean house and I was extremely pleased and hopeful when I spotted another Volkswagen in the driveway.

I saw another woman who must have been Carol's mother looking at us through a curtain inside the house. She looked apprehensive. I introduced myself to the other VW there, who seemed pleased to have one of his own kind to talk with. He told me he belonged to Carol. I was envious of his life. He spent most of his time on a campus, being driven by a female and being kept clean and odorized. He, however, said his life was fairly boring and he would love to trade places with me and to experience the adventure I was having. We agreed that the gas is always higher octane on the other side of the center divide.

Meanwhile, Los Tres Borrachos accompanied Carol into her house, coming out a few minutes later and following her to the back yard. Her car told me there is a guesthouse there, along with a pool so I figured things were looking pretty good for them if not me. But to my grateful surprise later that afternoon, Leroy and Carol took a hose to me, along with a bucket of warm, soapy water and before long I was a shiny, happy car. Judging from his frequent stares at Carol, I think maybe Leroy's motivation was the skimpy bikini she wore but I didn't care one way or the other what it took to get him to wash me.

Late in the afternoon two more young ladies showed up, presumably friends of Carol's. Amazingly enough, both were driving Volkswagens! I couldn't see the back yard from where I was parked so I can't share the details of the rest of the afternoon and evening. I did smell barbecue smoke and heard lots of animated conversation. I'm sure I was every bit as relieved as they were that Los Tres Borrachos were getting to eat something besides musical fruit. I was perfectly satisfied to chat with my new soul mates before the two late arrivals were driven away well after midnight. All in all, I think everybody was happy, or at least a lot happier than when we woke up on that Arizona desert.

That was a nice end to a memorable vacation and the next morning we headed back to Chico. Los Tres Borrachos all were in good moods as they discussed the previous night. I don't know exactly what put them into such good moods but whatever it was, I hoped they could find more of it.

_____

The remainder of the school year was short and uneventful. We returned to Chester for the summer, where Leroy got a temporary job in the lumber mill. I didn't mind spending my days in the employee parking lot and, in fact, I got to know quite a few of the local cars. Some of them looked askance at me, as I was the only Volkswagen there, but as we got used to each other I was more accepted. When I told any of them that my design, with my air cooled engine and 28 MPG fuel consumption, was futuristic some of them just smirked while others honked out loud. Sometimes cars, like people, resist change and deny that it is occurring even when it is under their noses or hood ornaments, as the case may be.

After work, Leroy and I would while away our evenings driving around and stopping in at the Frosty Freeze. On the weekends Leroy would take us to nearby Lake Almanor for swimming, water skiing and ogling girls, although I had no interest in any of those activities. I was happy to sit beneath the trees and sleep. All in all, it was a pleasant summer that ended too soon. Before I knew it we were back in Chico for another school year.

Leroy did drive me down to Santa Barbara a couple of times to visit Carol. Within a few months they agreed that the distance was too great to have a meaningful relationship. That was fine by me because it was not an easy trip to make. So we remained in Chico and I honestly cannot recall anything about that school year that is worth remembering except for Leroy meeting and spending a lot of time with another young woman named Diana. They would stop by the Toot 'n Tell 'em in the evenings after study hours were over, and then head to the park where it was dark and quiet. I saw a few other cars there from time to time and they were quiet as well.

I guess Leroy and Diana grew closer than I thought. The following summer they got married so I was back in a family situation like I had been with Professor Sloan. I found myself looking forward to sleeping in a garage again and not spending my nights in the fraternity parking lot where the other cars all smelled like beer and human sweat. When we did return to school, Leroy and Diana lived in an apartment and I still had to sleep outside on the street. I was disappointed but what could I do? So I accepted my lot, as Volkswagens do.

Two things of note happened to me by the end of that year, 1961. First, I was pleasantly surprised when Leroy had me painted. My color had faded and I had quite a few scratches, and the new paint — a dignified, dark red, came as a welcome change. I was exactly the same color as the maroon on a 1955 Cadillac, only I was much smaller. Still, I thought I looked pretty spiffy. The second thing was when I was taken to a muffler shop where Leroy's friend worked. I had developed a hole and was louder than either Leroy or I thought I should be. When his friend replaced my muffler, he added a second tail pipe, so I ended up with what appeared to be dual exhausts like I had seen on many other Volkswagens but never on one of my vintage. They thought it looked pretty good and so did I. And I sure did sound a lot better.

My time with Leroy came to an abrupt end late that summer. He and a friend he called Eggman had spent the afternoon filling their tanks with beer. I was parked next to a 1952 MG, which turned out to be Eggman's car. We could overhear Leroy and Eggman as they sat in yard chairs with their beer. Eggman was admiring my new good looks and Leroy was admiring the MG. By the time the beer was gone they had agreed to trade us straight across and suddenly my life with Leroy was over. I was hurt to be traded for an older British model, but once again I reminded myself that I am a Volkswagen, and Volkswagens follow orders.

Chapter 6
CHICKEN FEATHERS AND A STICKY PINION

On balance, I did not particularly care for my life with Eggman due to his cavalier behavior, his recklessness, his negligence of my chassis and cabriolet roof, and his using me to deliver eggs. Furthermore, his impressive collection of unpaid speeding citations implied to me a very real risk of impoundment. Indeed, I began seriously to long for a life more befitting of my stature.

My wish was fulfilled in the spring of 1962. The circumstances were not promising, as Eggman and another man he referred to as Leroy spent an afternoon drinking beer on rickety lawn chairs in Eggman's overgrown and untidy Chico garden. Leroy owned a 1955 Volkswagen with whom I had chatted from time to time and whom I found to be a bit stuffy and Germanic, but basically decent. Well, by the end of that afternoon, with neither Eggman nor Leroy very stable on his feet, the respective ownership of the VW and I had been traded evenly. I was moderately insulted to be considered a peer to a Volkswagen Beetle, knowing in my heart that I was a far superior automobile in appearance (that thing was downright homely) in horsepower and ability to bring joy to my driver. How in the world could anybody revel in driving a Volkswagen?

———————

But I digress. My life started before Eggman or Leroy ever set eyes on me. I emigrated from Great Britain in 1952. I was built in an Abingdon factory specifically for use in the Colonies, or as those who live here prefer to call them, the United States. Nevertheless, I fancy myself British to my core and ever so much more tasteful and proper than my American counterparts. In my home country that year, our beloved King George VI died and his daughter, Elizabeth was proclaimed Queen of England. In my adopted country, Dwight Eisenhower was elected President. Other noteworthy events that year were the development of the polio vaccine, the invention of the transistor radio and the detonation of the first hydrogen bomb which, in my opinion, is not much to be proud about after all is said and done.

I was advertised as an MG TD Midget, a term to which I still take offense. I may be compact, but I am most decidedly not a midget. My name stems from the fact that my earliest ancestor was built in Cecil Kimber's Morris Garage 1922. I suppose I could have been named CK, Kimber or Cecil, but I do believe MG has a nicer ring to it. I boast 52 horsepower, 44% more than my German counterpart, the homely Volkswagen. I confess that I drop an occasional spot of oil on the macadam, that my miles per gallon of petrol are on the low side, that I have no power steering or power brakes — or even a heater or a de-mister for my windscreen for that matter — but I most definitely have some positive offsetting features. In particular, my lines are handsome and perfectly proportioned. My dramatic bonnet is beautifully complemented by my abbreviated boot providing a long, streamlined demeanor that is anything but diminutive and certainly not "midget" in the least. My drivers always look quite sporty whilst perched behind my substantial steering wheel. As we proceed down the street people frequently stop and look at us with envious expressions.

When I was new my retail price in American dollars was a very reasonable $2,150. I consider that a bargain, quite beneath my own perceived worth and certainly adequate to offset the minor annoyance my pinion gear might cause when it fails properly to engage with my flywheel upon starting, thereby compelling the driver to put me in gear and push me forward to unlock the mechanism. And I agree that I can be noisy and drafty, but if this bothers somebody they simply do not belong in a sports car.

My first owner in America was a wealthy gentleman with an elegant estate in a small, tony village called Hillsborough, a bit south of San Francisco. He paid cash for me and put his daughter Sally's name on the title. As the three of us drove off the car lot we were all quite happy: Sally because she had a brand new automobile of her very own; me because I was embarking on my life; and Sally's father because he was able to give his daughter a wonderful gift as a reward for her excellent scholastic performance. Although she had just celebrated her sixteenth birthday and was granted her driving licence, in many ways Sally was mature beyond her years. She was exceptionally well mannered and clean, she showed admirable respect for her parents, and — here's the rub — she was cautious to a fault when operating me. Whilst I consider her demeanor to be refined and exemplary in so many ways, there was a part of me that pined for her to go wild, to take me out onto the open road and put me through my paces and let the wind blow through her meticulously coiffured hair. But neither of us once got the opportunity, even when a boyfriend pleaded to have a turn behind my wheel. I so wanted her to relent! But she was not prone to relent, either by letting a boyfriend drive me or any other activity that was against her firmly grounded, dare I say staid, principles. So my first two years, until Sally graduated from high school as the class valedictorian, were safe and secure, but quite honestly, rather boring. I knew myself to be an exceptional, exotic cabriolet automobile with a four-speed gearstick, keen to serve but also to explore, and to be a little reckless now and again and put those gears to a test.

Sally was most certainly a proper young lady who was quite careful to avoid any pranging of my body, but on the other hand, she didn't know the difference between a spanner and a grease nipple. I lived with constant anxiety that we would be stranded on a dark road somewhere and she would have no inkling of what to do. For as sleek and racy as I am, I can tend to be mechanically temperamental. She drove me extremely carefully — almost timidly. Even after enrolling in the university Sally continued to be proper to the core and it was a rather dull four years. She demonstrated no interest in speed and whenever a gentleman friend asked to drive me she consistently refused, which was a major disappointment to me. I believe she was intimidated by her father, for whenever she drove me home he would walk around me, inspect me for any dings, kick my tyres and compliment her on the nice care she was providing for me. I believe Sally was terrified, actually, and that she was more aptly suited to a used Chevrolet. I mean no offense to my Colonial counterparts; it is simply a fact that we Brits are built for speed, sport and scenic country roads, whereas American cars are comparatively gigantic, heavy steel and chrome behemoths that lumber down the wide motorways, taking more than their share of space and preventing me from overtaking them unless we are on a dual carriageway. I shall admit, however, that they can be more reliable and judging from the appearance of many of them, less sensitive to dents than I might be.

———————

Upon Sally's graduation I was advertised for sale. She had been offered a position in another part of the country and concluded I would not be appropriate for a cross-country drive (if only she knew how desperately I wanted to experience one!), nor did I offer adequate storage capacity for the belongings she would be taking with her. She was correct in that assessment as I was designed for people who revel in the driving experience, not to serve as a substitute for a bloody articulated lorry.

Being offered for sale is a degrading yet oddly hopeful experience. Degrading because perfect strangers would poke and prod, raise my bonnet to examine my engine, sit in my passenger compartment, activate my hooter and, if their interest was deemed to be sincere, take me for a test drive. It was the first time in four years that anybody but Sally had driven me or even sat behind my wheel, and it was both disconcerting and humiliating. I'd only ever known Sally's bum in my driver's seat — I was accustomed to its weight and shape. And now there were new ones in all shapes, sizes and hefts. In addition, I was suddenly being driven by various prospective owners, all of whom used differing techniques and none of whom had similar skills when it came to clutching, shifting, accelerating and braking. I consoled myself that this was temporary and was thankful that I was not a rental automobile, driven thusly for the remainder of my life.

After suffering through five days of close inspection, pawing and gear grinding, Sally's father came to an agreement with a young man and I was sold for $950. I did not overhear his name but I came to know him as Eggman. I decided to refer to him as such until somebody chose to address him by a more traditional name. It really makes no difference to a car what his owner may call himself.

Eggman, like Sally, was a university student although significantly less devoted to his studies and, as far as I could discern, in no apparent rush to graduate. He drove me to a town called Chico where he lived with three other flat mates in a run down place with no car park and a most disreputable garden. I very quickly learned that I was facing a radically different lifestyle than that to which I had become accustomed. I learned as well that one should be wary of what one wishes for, as Eggman was not the least bit shy about pushing me to my limits whether within the confines of Chico or upon the open road. I did my utmost to accommodate his demands as evidenced by the plethora of speeding citations Eggman accumulated. I found myself remembering with fondness the calm, predictable life I had experienced with Sally.

I soon learnt the genesis of my new owner's sobriquet. He was employed part time by a nearby poultry farm and his job was to deliver eggs to various retail establishments in Chico. Usually he accomplished his duties with the aid of a small lorry provided by the poultry farmer. But on occasion he had to use me, much to my chagrin. This was far beneath my dignity and I began to protest by freezing my pinion gear, thus necessitating that he bump start me. We MG TDs have a reputation for stubbornly locking our pinion gears but until then I had kept mine working properly. However, after intentionally locking it a few times for Eggman, it became a habit with me and a straightforward way to discourage maltreatment and on occasion, simply as an act of recalcitrance. I attribute this to Eggman's disrespect more than I do to my British engineering and assembly.

On the day of my trade to Leroy in exchange for his VW, I was ready to move on from my life with Eggman. I wished the VW well and advised him to freeze his pinion gear from time to time when Eggman's attitude required an adjustment. Then I turned my attention to my new owner, Leroy, allowing myself a faint hope that my life was about to improve.

Like Eggman, Leroy was a university student, but I detected no other similarities between the two of them other than enjoying beer. Eggman had no desire to graduate; Leroy was keen to get school over with and move on with his life; Eggman was a committed bachelor; Leroy was newly married to a woman named Diana who seemed nice and certainly classier than the string of women parading through Eggman's flat. Leroy kept me clean and lubricated, and despite some exceptionally large feet, drove me with a surprising degree of finesse and care. I do not like to be thought of as a midget, but I am a compact car and Leroy was a tall man. He had difficulty squeezing behind my steering wheel, and when he managed to do so, his knees rubbed against it. He solved the problem by taking me to a shop to have the tracks on my driver's side seat repositioned as far toward the rear as they would go. This minor outpatient surgery provided enough additional space for him to drive more comfortably, but just barely. We both adapted.

By the time I came to Leroy my cabriolet roof was in desperate need of repair due to several winters of being parked outside in the rain and elements. Therefore, I was quite pleased one Saturday morning when Leroy and a friend approached me with a box containing a replacement roof. Removing my original tattered roof was the easy part. Installing the new one presented a challenge, for neither Leroy nor I wanted any wrinkles when the task was completed. They worked at it most of the day, tacking it a bit at a time, stretching and tacking some more and when almost finished, removing the tacks because the canvas was either off-centre or wrinkled. At the end of a long, frustrating day they called it done, after many more tack holes than they had anticipated. I had to confess that I looked quite nice, so at least in my opinion the effort was a good investment.

Although I tried to will it otherwise, my pinion gear continued to stick. It had become ingrained, I suppose, and I was powerless to stop it after having done it so often with Eggman. I felt bad for Leroy, and especially Diana when I would freeze up. It felt much like a seizure must have felt to humans — involuntary, unpredictable and chronic. When Leroy was operating me he would put me in gear and get out, and then rock me to and fro, which normally solved the problem. When Diana drove me, though, she always had to ask for help. Fortunately, she was attractive and never had difficulty finding a young man or two to help out. A mechanic advised Leroy that I needed a new pinion gear and very likely, a replacement flywheel. I could have told him my flywheel was just fine but it was moot anyway since Leroy did not have the funds for any repairs at all.

Leroy drove me with much more respect than Eggman, but my life still lacked the élan I believe the car gods had intended for me. Most of my trips were local — shopping, commuting to Leroy's part time job, parking at a place called the Toot 'n Tell 'em, and occasional scenic but short rides on the weekends. We never ventured in excess of fifty miles from Chico, with one memorable exception. That was a trip to a place called Chester.

It was a warm, late springtime Saturday. Leroy secured a bag onto my rack with a bungee cord. Then he unlatched and folded my roof back, and he and Diana settled in. I was so excited that I was distracted enough not to freeze my pinion and I started right up. We departed Chico a few minutes later and began a gradual and steady climb uphill. I had never been taken up a mountain before. The trees looked and smelled different from what I had been accustomed to, and I noted that my carburetor mixture was a bit off as the air thinned but it did not seriously affect my performance. It was a true joy to be on the open road with no traffic to speak of, and as Leroy shifted my gears I realized that I was at last, at nine years of age, being permitted to show my stuff. It was a day that I could only describe as invigorating. I hoped Leroy and Diana noticed how responsive and smooth I was.

At about teatime we arrived in Chester, a small town with one High Street and what appeared to be a smaller population than Chico had. We parked in the driveway of a house and Leroy removed the bag from my rack, leaving me to look around at the strange surroundings whilst he and Diana went in. They returned a few hours later and when Leroy attempted to start me this time, my bloody pinion gear froze again and he had to get out and rock me. I felt badly for him but I was powerless. He seemed to retain his good spirits when my engine started, and he and Diana started down the road, turning onto the High Street. We went to one end of town where Leroy performed a U-turn and then we went to the other end of town and repeated the maneuver. He pulled into a place called the Frosty-Freeze and parked. After they went inside I struck up a conversation with the car next to me, a handsome, if overly large in my opinion, blue and white two-toned 1957

Chevrolet. He told me Chester is in the mountains (as if I had not already discerned that tidbit) and the primary industry entailed removing trees from the ground and sawing them into pieces. The Chevrolet also told me snow covers the ground during the winter. I did not want to show my ignorance by asking what snow is, so I simply nodded, hoping an explanation would be forthcoming. It was not but I suppose it didn't really matter. I gleaned that snow was cold and slippery and I was appreciative that I did not have to live in it. I unquestionably am more of a warm-weather car.

When Leroy and Diana emerged from the Frosty-Freeze and attempted to start my engine, I again froze. This time as he got out to rock me I heard Leroy curse, which only made me more stubborn. His usual technique did not work this time, and he had to enlist the assistance of some other men who had emerged from the Frosty-Freeze. With him behind the wheel and two others pushing, Leroy managed to bump start me. As his helpers climbed into pickup trucks, one of them made what I took to be a derogatory comment about college boys and their sissy cars. Humph. I may not be dented, have a half-tonne storage capacity or a gun rack in my rear window, but I am not a sissy. Those louts deserved no further consideration in my view but they did put Leroy into a fowl mood and he cursed them — and me — all the way back to where he and Diana were staying.

After this incident I was more than ready to return to Chico the following morning and I showed my appreciation by managing to start instantly. I had no regrets about leaving tiny Chester, with its pickup trucks and their cheeky drivers. This clearly was not the sort of village that could appreciate an MG.

————————————

Another memorable but far less than pleasant experience I recall was the rainy evening Diana's mother popped in for a visit. She was driving a huge, obnoxious Cadillac that took up an excessive amount of space and had an attitude to match. It was overbearing and neither interesting nor worldly, but I refrained from pointing out his flaws because I doubted that my opinion would be either welcomed or valued by this giant hulk of an inefficient, rumbling machine. A short time later they all emerged from the flat, got in to the Cadillac and drove away. When they returned a few hours later, Diana was driving and her mother was nowhere to be seen. Leroy disembarked and I overheard him say to Diana that her mother would be fine in the back seat until she sobered up, and that he would be right behind them. He got behind my wheel. Because it was storming I attempted valiantly to start my engine on the first try and, to his great relief I did so. We pulled onto the road, following Diana in that fat car.

I should point out that we TD models were not equipped with windows in our doors like most cars. Rather, we were supplied with side curtains through which our driver and passenger might see out, at least when they were new and the weather was not inclement. My curtains were in place that evening, but because they were not new and it was most inclement, the visibility was indeed quite limited. The lack of circulating air also caused my windscreen to fog up and it was necessary that Leroy constantly wipe it with a cloth. We followed Diana through the storm for thirty miles, where she parked in a driveway and we pulled in behind her. Leroy got out and he and Diana struggled to retrieve her mother from the back seat. She was quite unsteady and both of them had to support her as they led her through the rain into the house. They emerged a few minutes later, hurried to me, got in, and as luck would have it, I failed to start and Leroy shouted those epithets again. They both got out. Diana then sat behind the wheel and Leroy pushed me until my pinion gear was no longer jammed. I was embarrassed but helpless and I vowed to make the return trip to Chico as pleasant as possible for them. However, through no fault of my own, our return trip was as unpleasant as the first half and by the time we returned home both Leroy and Diana were quite unhappy and uncomfortable in their damp clothing. The mood was made even more negative with the words they were having about her mother, Leroy calling her a drunk and his wife defending her. All in all, it was a most unpleasant episode.

Great Britain. That country is not as warm as many other places in the world, and spots like Chico in particular, which can get very hot in the summer time. As such, I am not equipped with a mechanical air conditioning feature. Whilst my engineers had designed my top to be easily retracted in warm weather it is obvious that none of them had ever visited Chico or envisioned one of their creations living there. In the midst of the summer my interior was stifling with my top in place, and the heat from the sun was unbearable with it down. There was no escaping the discomfort. All we could do was stay off the road as much as possible during the day and hope for an early autumn.

Leroy graduated from the university at the beginning of the summer and obtained a job in a lumberyard. We settled into an uneventful routine of driving to work Monday through Friday, or sometimes he let Diana use me during the day and pick him up in the evening. On weekend evenings I was typically parked with other cars I knew whilst Leroy and Diana visited with their friends. The Volkswagen for which I had been traded told me he missed the care and respect Leroy had shown him and that he was not all that happy with Eggman. I could not help but notice that he had a few dents and was dirty, and that his back seat was covered with chicken feathers.

In August I heard Leroy and Diana discussing a move to a place called Texas. Leroy had been accepted for military service in the United States Air Force and he was required to report for training. As was the case when Sally had owned me, I was now deemed too small to suit their needs. Diana was going to accompany Leroy and they would require a larger car to accommodate their limited belongings. So shortly I found myself once again being poked, prodded and inspected by potential buyers. The last I heard of Leroy he was explaining to my new owner that my pinion gear had just begun "acting up" and might need "a little work". A little work indeed!

Chapter 7
WEIRD WIRING

Leroy and I began our relationship on a positive note. Before he bought me in 1962 my previous owner, George, had taken me in for tune-up so I was feeling a little better than normal and I was relieved to find that Leroy understood how to use a stick shift. He drove me to what I learned was his home, another rundown university rental apartment much like the one where George lived. He brought out his wife, Diana, and a large dog with hair in its eyes, making it difficult to tell if it was coming or going. They loaded the dog whom they called Tiger into my back seat — a new and disconcerting experience for me — and away we went for our first drive together, Leroy behind the wheel, Diana playing with my radio and Tiger with her shaggy head sticking out of my rear window, tongue hanging out and wind blowing through her hair. It was a good beginning, aside from a few involuntary coughs and jerks from me. Leroy assured Diana he could make some adjustments to take care of that problem but I knew better.

I'm a 1958 Ford two-door sedan with a three-speed column shift and a transplanted V8 engine that is too big for my body, which was designed for a more modest six cylinders. 1958 wasn't particularly groundbreaking, at least for us Fords, who continued to improve each year. We expected that of ourselves. Egypt and Syria joined the United Arab Republic in 1958 but that didn't do much good in calming down the political scene in that part of the world. It made me happy I was a Ford, not a camel. President Eisenhower was leading the U.S.A., and his counterpart in the Soviet Union was Premier Nikita Khrushchev. War hero Charles De Gaulle was the President of France. One very positive and dramatic event was the U.S. Supreme Court's ordering the integration of schools in Little Rock, Arkansas. Some other occurrences of note were the launching of the first U.S. satellite, the introduction of jet plane transport across the Atlantic by BOAC, and the induction of Elvis Presley into the Army. The teenage girls sobbed when they saw his new haircut.

I don't know much about my beginnings because when my engine was replaced my wiring didn't get put back together right. Most of the connections were made correctly, but a few were not, which led to memory loss and some erratic behavior. My headlights would often go dark for no reason; my fan belt slipped and wobbled on my generator, which weakened my battery; my coil and distributor were out of whack; and I had memory lapses — or did I just say that?

My first two years are pretty much a blank. It was as if my life began in 1960 in a place called Chico. My earliest recollection is being driven by George, a college student who, to his credit, took good care of me despite knowing next to nothing about car engines. Perhaps that is why he bought me in the first place, for anybody who was marginally qualified as a mechanic would likely have avoided taking on the challenge I presented. It's not that I have a poor self-image; in fact, I believe I'm quite good looking and on those days when my engine was operating as it is supposed to, my getup and go were impressive. I was quick off the mark and could get to 60 in 11 seconds. Those two extra cylinders provided an impressive extra kick although they took their toll on my average miles per gallon.

The problem was that I didn't feel very chipper most days. I was moody, depressed and suffered constantly from non-specific anxiety because of my flawed innards. Given a choice, I would have preferred not being driven at all and being parked permanently under a large shade tree (with no birds living in it) with my battery removed and surrendering to a deep, dreamless slumber.

But cars are designed and built to be driven, not to sleep under trees. So I vowed to do my best. George was a careful driver, using me to get to his part time job, and on the weekends to get to his girlfriend Rosie's home, which was 30 miles south of Chico. Getting to and from work wasn't difficult. There were evenings when my headlights wouldn't work until their wires were jiggled, and my generator didn't always charge my battery. I also had a bit of a drinking problem with oil and my crankcase required frequent attention. The minor annoyances aside, the only real stress I experienced was when we traveled to Rosie's house. I enjoyed the feel of the open road and I looked forward to Friday afternoons. As stimulating as those trips were, they exacted a toll. I would overheat, my plugs would foul, causing me to misfire, and I would belch embarrassing clouds of blue smoke from my tail pipes.

The beginning of the end of my relationship with George began one warm summer evening when he was visiting Rosie. They had been to a movie and afterward had driven me to a dark spot by a canal where I was parked and my engine and lights shut off. The radio, however, was left on. I felt my battery fading rapidly, and within an hour it was dead and I was fast asleep. When I awoke we were back at Rosie's house, attached with a chain to her father's pickup truck. I asked him what was going on and he just rolled his headlights and told me that I needed to get some real wiring. As if that were news. When I wouldn't start, George and Rosie walked to town and telephoned her father to come and rescue me. Nobody was happy about this, especially Rosie's father whose beer and baseball game on the radio had been interrupted. Rosie had to explain why we were parked by that canal, pretty much pinning the blame on George, who then had to endure the ice-cold stare of Rosie's father as if he had actually committed the sin he had been hoping to commit but had been stymied by my exigencies.

A jump-start with the assistance of that smug pickup brought my engine back to life. After a brief and uncomfortable good-bye George and I headed home to Chico, both hoping upon hope to make it all the way with no further difficulties, but neither of us was very confident. We were both depressed. George was berating himself for parking me by an isolated canal and probably losing his girlfriend forever because of his shortsightedness. I was just plain worn out and anxious about getting us home, swearing to myself that if George ever tried that stunt in the future I would simply refuse to start, rather than go through that humiliation again. Meanwhile, George nursed me along, paying attention to every little odd sound I made (and I made a few just to keep him on his toes) and coaxing me to keep going. We breathed a collective sigh of relief when he pulled up in front of his apartment and cut the engine. It had been a very long day.

———————

The remainder of George's school year was uneventful. He drove me as little as possible, which was just fine with me. Early in the summer as I was napping in my favorite spot under a big sycamore tree in front of George's apartment, I felt a sharp kick to my left front tire. Jarred awake, I saw that George was looking me over with another guy who was the tire kicker with a formidable pair of size 14 shoes: Leroy. Like most cars I had spoken with in my life, I don't know what it is about us that makes people want to kick our tires. I suppose it's possible that this is how males react when they want to check us out but don't know what to check or how to check it. Any fool could see that my tires were fine, and to Leroy's ultimate misfortune they were what he based his decision upon when he offered by buy me.

I heard Leroy explain to George that he had graduated and rather than be drafted into the Army where he would squander his hard-earned education digging ditches and being shot at, he had applied for Officers Training School in the Air Force. He was to report to a place called Texas in two months. He said he and his wife owned an MG TD (I had seen it around town, frequently being pushed), and that it would be too small for the trip with him, his wife, their dog and their stuff. He promised George to buy me as soon as his MG was sold. So now, in addition to my chronic health issues, I had something new to fret about: What kind of a driver would Leroy be? Would he maintain me with appropriate lube and oil changes? Would he be inclined to attend to my electrical idiosyncrasies?

Within a couple of weeks I was about to get all the answers. Leroy came to George's apartment and paid him $750, signed some papers, and drove me away. I looked back and saw George taking one last look at me. I thought I detected wistfulness in his eyes, but they might well have been tears of joy.

———————

Leroy had a friend named Lucky. They had taken a road trip together a few years earlier and they often reminisced about it. Listening to the details, I had to wonder why. It certainly did not sound like an adventure I would have enjoyed. Lucky was pretty handy with a wrench and was known to be happy to work for beer. After putting a case on ice, Leroy invited him over and asked him to bring along his tools. It was a bright, warm Saturday morning. First, Lucky took me for a drive around the block to get a feel for my engine, brakes and transmission. I was as cooperative as I could be, but when we returned he told Leroy he detected some problems. I wondered if he was referring to the same ones I had detected so often.

They raised my hood, and unlike Leroy, Lucky seemed to know what he was looking for. He removed my plugs that were incorrectly gapped and damp with unburned fuel. After cleaning and reinstalling them, he removed all eight of my spark plug wires. I could tell I wasn't going anywhere for a while. He sent Leroy to the auto parts store on his bike to buy a new set, and while he was gone, Lucky adjusted the gap in my distributor points. He also tried to trace my wiring but after mumbling something about weird schematics, he gave up and sat in the shade with a beer. Leroy returned with the new plug wires, which they installed, and then Lucky started my engine. I was pleased, as I'm sure they were, that I sounded really good. They took me out of town and tested their handiwork on the highway. I performed nicely, with good acceleration and an impressive, smooth roar in my twin pipes. I agreed with Leroy that Lucky had earned his beer, and the two of them almost finished the case as the afternoon warmed up and wore on. Lucky took the last remaining six cans home with him as dusk approached, tossing them into his back seat before driving away, lurching and weaving from one side of the road to the other. I don't know if he made it.

I was running better now but I couldn't shake the cobwebs from my memory. I continued to have lapses, forgetting details like when I was last filled up or what that dog's name was who left so much hair on my back seat and slobbered on my rear windows. As for the distant past, it was still a total blank. In an occasional lucid moment I deduced that my problem was not related to anything mechanical — Lucky had done his very best. No, it was that wiring job. It didn't make sense that my headlights would work only sporadically, or that my gauges would suddenly either stop or peg all the way to the right for no reason, or that my generator, despite a new fan belt, just didn't feel right. Leroy didn't have enough money to have me rewired, which probably would have cost more than he paid for me in the first place so we both resolved to live with it.

———————

It was mid-morning in early August. Chico had endured an un-usually warm summer and everybody was moving slowly and doing everything possible to stay cool. I was not driven much because I had no air conditioner and the breeze through my win-dows was uncomfortably warm even at 60 MPH. So I spent most of my time parked under a tree which was, unfortunately, the home to many inconsiderate birds. Leroy approached me with a bucket of water and a garden hose and proceeded to give me a thorough wash. It was nothing short of ecstasy having all that nasty bird poop washed off, and the cool rinse was bracing and refreshing. Then he washed all my windows and even vacuumed me! I felt like a new car.

It cooled down a little that evening. Leroy and Diana got in, and to my happy surprise, Tiger was not with them. We drove around aimlessly, going by some of their old haunts, and we parked at the Toot 'n Tell 'em where they ordered some cold drinks and walked around chatting with friends. Everybody seemed to be in a good mood and it was a pleasant evening.

Early the next morning, Leroy and Diana filled my trunk and back seat with all kinds of stuff — suitcases, a stereo, boxes of dishes and even an ironing board that extended from my rear window over the back of the front seat. I was filled to capacity and when they loaded Tiger and themselves in as well, I felt as if my tires would burst. I had no idea what the future had in store for me but I did sense that my days of sleeping under that tree had likely come to an end.

We worked our way out of Chico to Highway 99, and headed south. The day quickly turned warm and all my windows and vents were open. Leroy's back was sweating on my seat and Tiger was slobbering all over the place in the back. So much for yes-terday's clean-up effort. By evening, after traveling nearly 500 miles, we reached Los Angeles. I had heard of this city from other cars but had never actually seen it. All of the reports were right: cars were all over the place, zooming down four-lane roads. The air was brown with exhaust and between the pollution and the heat I was having trouble keeping my engine running properly. I started to cough and miss a little. We were all road weary by the time Leroy found an affordable motel. It was close to the freeway and not fancy at all, but we were so relieved to call it a day that they didn't care about a big room and I didn't care about the absence of a garage or even a carport. After sundown when the heat began to let up, Leroy removed all of my spark plugs, cleaned them and reinstalled them. I appreciated that and I vowed to do my best not to let him down if we had another long drive the next day.

The next morning I was feeling better. It was still early when Leroy, Diana and that mutt piled in but it was nice to get going before the heat of the day settled in. We turned east onto Route 66. I had heard a lot about this road, and even a song played about it on my radio, but I had never been there. I didn't see what everybody was so excited about. It was just a hot drive with lots of cacti, rundown roadside diners and gas stations, and not a lot of water or trees. Another near-500 miles got us to a place called Flagstaff. It was a lot cooler here, so that was a big relief. However, we were at 7,000 feet elevation. The day before it was the heat that made me run rough. Today it was the thin air. When Leroy stepped on my accelerator I would sputter and then slowly pick up speed, but it was obvious that I was struggling. I was relieved, as usual, when he pulled into the parking lot of another motel and turned off my engine and I immediately went soundly to sleep.

On day three we covered 325 miles and stopped for the night in Albuquerque. I felt a little better not only because we didn't go as far, but also because it was still cool. I found it a little easier to get air into my carburetor here. Leroy did notice that my battery charge gauge showed that the generator was not doing its job. He tightened the belt before calling it a night and I was confident that would solve the problem, even if only temporarily. Once again I slept soundly, too exhausted to be the least concerned about all the accumulated road dust and smashed bugs on my lights, grill and windshield. As I drifted off I thought this would be an exciting adventure if I felt better but in my condition it was all work and I was just hoping to hang on.

We left Route 66 the next morning and turned south on US Highway 87. I had no regrets about trying a different road. I had listened to other cars who had experienced cross-country trips rave about Route 66 but my impression of it was that it was a dying highway. Many former businesses — coffee shops, motels, and gas stations — were boarded up, the traffic was thin and the pavement was in need of repair. We had come upon one run-down, uninviting hovel that was open, advertising live Gila monsters and snakes. I wondered why anybody would ever want to visit such a place, not to mention own one. Fortunately, we passed it by. I spent a lot of time that day looking down and trying to avoid potholes. I was thankful to leave that awful road and to give Route 87 a try.

Soon we were in the state of Texas. The road was a lot better and people were driving fast. Leroy, correctly sensing that I was in no mood to race, didn't push me beyond 70. The highlight of the day was when he stopped at a seedy gas station in some sparsely populated, windswept, dry, unwelcoming town to fill me up. The owner didn't offer to check under my hood or even to clean my windshield, which was almost entirely covered with dead bugs. Leroy asked him for a rag so he could check my oil, and for some water. The guy handed him a paper towel and pointed his finger at a bucket with a filthy sponge floating in it. After Leroy paid him he walked away without so much as a thank you, mumbling under his breath about "them damn uppity Californians". Diana, meanwhile, had taken Tiger for a walk and I noted with some gratification that the dog finally did something useful: it left a sizable deposit at the doorway of the gas station office. Diana quickly loaded up the dog and told Leroy to get out of there quick, which he did. Aside from that minor bit of entertainment, it was a long, but stress-free day with my radio tuned to nothing but country music stations, which was about all it could receive in that area.

After covering 400 miles we were in a little place called Big Spring. I didn't see any sign of water so I wondered if its name had anything to do with those things all cars have under them to smooth out the ride, and if so, why anybody would name a town after an auto part. As I pondered that question, Leroy and Diana left me in the motel parking lot. I hadn't been running great but I was OK and Leroy didn't do any maintenance on me that night.

We reached our destination the next afternoon. San Antonio was busy, hot and humid. We ended up at a housing area near an Air Force Base where Leroy was going to attend Officers Training School. They parked me in front of one of the nondescript brick buildings and unloaded me. It was quite a relief to be rid of all that excess weight and I was able to relax. In fact, I relaxed so much that one of my tires went flat. I couldn't help it and I didn't care. All I wanted to do was shut myself down and sleep and that's exactly what I did as I quietly dripped a little oil on the ground and let my springs, hoses, wires and metal cool down and relax after that marathon drive of 2,000 miles in five days. That may not seem like much for a new car with new parts diving on Interstate Highways, but for this old rewired and tired '58 Ford it was a monumental stretch.

———————————

I don't know how long I slept. It could have been a day or a month. When I did awaken I felt a little better, although I was a bit stiff in the ball joints and tie rods and feeling the need for a tune up, or at the very least an oil change. There were several other cars parked around me. I could tell from the license plates that we all were from different states. I introduced myself to a very fancy Corvette and for a racy new car he was unusually civil.

He was from a place called Bahstin in Massachusetts and I had a little trouble understanding him at first when he talked about the other "cahs" in the "pahking" lot. The Oldsmobile to my right was from South Dakota and behind me was another Ford — a newer '59 — from Louisiana, and he was almost impossible to understand with that lazy French accent and terms like "mo' betta", "picayune" and "voodoo". He said he was from N'awlins. There were others of all makes and models from places far and wide, all here for the same reason: We had just carried our own-ers and their wives to this housing development, where the wives would live for three months while their husbands completed their training.

Leroy didn't have time to get me in for a service, although he did manage to have my flat tire repaired. He and Diana spent the day settling into their apartment and getting acquainted with the other new residents. Early the next morning a bus came by and about twenty guys including Leroy said goodbye to their wives, climbed on board, and were driven away. We cars were left sitting in the lot, wondering what our roles would be, and some (at least I) hoping this would mean a three-month vacation.

I pretty much got my wish. I didn't see Leroy for six weeks and during that time Diana didn't drive me much. When the wives needed to run errands they would carpool, and with no air con-ditioning I wasn't the first choice. On a Friday afternoon, Leroy and the rest of the husbands came home for a weekend. Diana drove me to the Air Base to pick him up, and when he got into the car he looked and acted a lot different. His head was almost bald, he was very tanned and it was obvious that he had been get-ting some exercise because he was very fit, with more muscle and less fat than he had when I last saw him. What really stood out to me was that he seemed to have matured and had become a more serious man. There wasn't much joking around. He was also tired, I think, because Leroy, as well as the rest of the guys just went straight to their apartments on that Friday evening and nobody came out until late Saturday morning. A few couples got together for a BBQ that evening and by Sunday afternoon all the guys had been delivered back to the Air Base. That was the last I saw of Leroy for another six weeks.

Summer was over and I was enjoying the crisp mornings and mellow days. I had settled in to a sedentary life that was much more in tune with my idiosyncrasies. As far as I was concerned, it could have continued forever. As cars age we develop a certain amount of wisdom. One thing I had learned is that until the day I go to the junkyard, things will evolve and nothing will be forever. This was driven home to me (no pun intended) when Leroy came back to the apartment in a new uniform with shiny gold bars on his shoulders and an odd looking hat with an oversized eyeshade. I correctly assumed that his training had been completed. He and Diana spent the next day packing and loading me up so I knew we were about to head out. I just didn't know where to, or if I was up to it. At sunup the next morning we hit the road. I wasn't mentally prepared for that early start and didn't even have time to say goodbye to the other cars in the lot. Sometimes it seems as if humans don't even realize that cars have feelings.

We headed north and kept going and going and going, pausing only for brief rests, dog draining, food for them and gas and oil for me. It was raining, which was fine because that meant no bugs and no overheating, and no dog slobbering out the window. After 425 miles we pulled into a motel in Oklahoma City in the early evening. I was worn out but functional and I think Leroy and Diana felt the same. I don't know if the dog was ever functional though. The next day was a repeat, continuing north in the rain another 375 miles to Lincoln, Nebraska. I was beginning to feel some aches and pains by then. Something was bothering my coil, which made me cough and sputter again. I was hoping it was nothing more serious than rain seeping in and decided not to worry about it, and opted to call it a night after Leroy and Diana checked into their motel. There's something about rain on a metal roof — even if it's your own — that makes a snooze more cozy.

The next day found us exploring Lincoln, which boasted that "O" Street is "the longest Main Street in the world". I guess this was because the main east-west road ran through the middle of town and extended across the whole state with barely any curves. I suppose every town wants something to brag about, but that seemed like they were grasping at something. To the credit of whoever came up with the name of that city, at least it was in honor of a whole car instead of just a part like that little place in Texas.

Anyway, Leroy and Diana had to find a place to live. They found an apartment that afternoon but we returned to the motel that evening, since their furniture shipment could not be delivered for another week. They both seemed distracted and ill at ease. I think it was because they were both native Californians and neither had been to Nebraska before. Leroy was displeased about the smoking ban in movie theaters and no beer sold on Sundays. It didn't bother me one way or the other as long as I could get my gas and oil whenever I needed it.

They settled in to their new apartment the next weekend and it was a relief to once again get all that stuff out of my trunk and back seat, especially the ironing board and the dog. I was hoping Leroy would vacuum my back seat and he must have sensed my message because he did.

I don't know anything about Leroy's job. He drove me to an Air Force base every morning and left me parked there. It struck me that he always wore the same outfit, and that everybody pretty much dressed alike. I asked a few other cars if they thought it was odd. Some did, others didn't notice or seem to care, and a few told me that was the way things should be in an orderly world. Curiously, all the cars with that attitude were exactly the same dark blue color and they all had US Government license plates.

I continued to feel out of sorts. My coil never did completely recover and my generator was acting up again. The chronic wiring issues weren't getting any better either. I was feeling more and more as if my days were numbered and caring less and less about it. I had never been so exhausted. I was becoming more forgetful, sometimes waking up in the night wondering where I was and not remembering how I got there. I got fleeting images but I had no coherent memory. I believe that both Leroy and I felt it was about time to consign me to the junkyard. One might think I would have dreaded such a fate, but in truth I thought it might well be for the best. I did have some serious flaws, although many of my parts were perfectly functional. But the reality was that even though my odometer was approaching just 100,000 miles, I was definitely in my twilight years.

We were soon experiencing the most miserable weather I had ever witnessed. It was constantly snowing and the freezing wind blew incessantly from the north. I was having more and more trouble getting my engine to kick over in the mornings and I had developed a chronic cough that I couldn't shake. One morning I just couldn't manage it. I had never felt so terrible. I just wanted to go into a permanent sleep and although I tried my best to do my job, I failed. My battery died and this time Leroy didn't bother to recharge it. He had me towed to a junkyard where the owner gave him $50 for me. I was just a little over five years old and too young to die, but dying is something that neither cars nor people can dictate.

Some of my parts now reside in a number of cars in the area. To be sure, my old wiring harness is gone for good. But my block is on a local mechanic's second car, my generator on another, my dual carbs on a teenager's project, my radio in a redneck's pickup and my manifold covers are on a Ford on a farm near Omaha. Don't be sad for me. I had a full life and my organs are giving life to others now. Although my physical being may be dispersed, my soul is intact. And I can't begin to express how relieved I was to be rid of that weird wiring job and that worthless dog.

Through The Headlights

Chapter 8
ROADS WELL TRAVELED

I remained on the used car lot of the Buick dealer for a week, which judging from the appearance of and conversations with other cars around me, was a relatively short time. I was happy to get away from that depressing environment, especially because I am not a Buick. Yet I was apprehensive of what might be in store when I found myself with a new owner.

His name was Leroy. Like my previous owner, Fred, he was a USAF officer living in Lincoln, Nebraska. Leroy evidently had no car to trade in for me. A friend had driven him to the Buick dealer and after looking me over and taking me for a test drive, he bought me for $2,000 and drove me away. We both were cautious. I was relieved that this Leroy fellow seemed familiar with manual transmissions and had no trouble shifting me smoothly. Yet I reserved judgment; a driver's ability to use a clutch is no basis for a long-term relationship.

Leroy parked me in the driveway of a large brick home. I could tell from the number of mailboxes on the porch that it had been converted into apartments. He went in and returned in a few minutes with a woman he called Diana, who turned out to be his wife. They got in and he started me up and backed out to the street. We drove aimlessly around Lincoln, both Leroy and I still being cautious. Clearly, Diana liked me. I could tell by the way she eyed my interior and experimented with my heater, radio, glove box and ashtray. But she told Leroy that I was much too fancy for their Second Lieutenant budget and that she felt I was unaffordable. He reassured her that although the payments of $47 per month would be a stretch they could handle it. He argued they would be OK if they were careful, and since they needed a car, why not me? I sensed that he was trying to reassure himself as much as Diana and that told me we were beginning to bond.

And bond we did! Leroy and I developed a strong mutual respect and rapport. He never once abused my engine, he always tried to park where those big General Motors doors couldn't ding my sides, he kept me serviced and clean and he treated me to a new set of tires. I learned to trust him. I could even feel Diana's affection after it became apparent that they would be able to keep up my payments.

I may not be handsome in the eyes of those who see beauty as sleek lines, tail fins and understated, horizontal radiators, but technically I am nothing short of sterling. I am a finely engineered luxury class four-door 1959 Mercedes-Benz 220S sedan. My six-cylinder in-line engine provides an efficient 105 horsepower that allows me to reach 100 miles per hour with no strain whatsoever. My manual shift, mounted on the column, boasts four forward gears. And I have a quiet dignity about me enhanced by my fine, lumbar-supportive leather seats, real walnut dashboard and bold, yet graceful fenders.

My hood ornament, the Benz logo, is a clean, three-pointed star designed by Gottlieb Daimler to show the ability of his motors for land, air and sea-usage. It was first seen on a Daimler in 1909, and was combined with the Benz laurel wreath in 1926 to signify the union of the two firms. I am a product of the world's oldest automobile manufacturer, and being of German design and manufacture I am unquestionably reliable. Each of my four doors closes with a firm click. My seams are even with no gaps or tight spots, unlike those seen on those mass-produced American cars.

As I listened to my radio I concluded 1959 was eventful, even though I did not understand what most of the news stories meant. Apparently, some important things occurred that year. Presidents Richard Nixon and Nikita Khrushchev argued in a kitchen about the relative advantages of communism and capitalism; Explorer 6 took the first pictures of Earth from outer space; Xerox introduced its first commercial copier; the Dalai Lama fled Tibet and obtained political asylum in India; and the first known human with HIV died in the Congo.

I was originally purchased in Stuttgart for the equivalent of $4,500, by Fred, a USAF Captain and pilot stationed at Ramstein Air Base. Fred and his wife, Katie, were very proud of me and treated me with respect except when we were on the Autobahn. Fred had a heavy foot and although I certainly was able to do all that was asked of me, I was not always confident that he was capable of maintaining control at high speeds. I sometimes wondered if he was taking my hood ornament a little too seriously and thought I could fly. I obviously lacked wings. We were never involved in any accidents, so perhaps my anxiety was misplaced.

My life with Fred and Katie gave me nothing to complain about and indeed, much for which to be grateful. When they had a few days to themselves they often would toss their luggage into my ample trunk and we would embark on an adventure. We eventually explored most of West Germany, much of Switzerland and Austria and even a little bit of France and Belgium. The roads were smooth and fast and except for the cities, the vistas were dramatic and beautiful. I would never confess this to another German car but I enjoyed the countryside of Switzerland and Austria more than my native land. The green, snowcapped Alps offered winding roads that I relished because they let me test my mettle.

When I saw other cars and trucks with their dents and scratches, loaded to capacity and crawling along the road, I was deeply appreciative of my privileged life. While they were put to work I was on a constant vacation. This was really driven home to me one afternoon when we were near Munich and we passed a convoy of seven Volkswagen busses. Their roof racks were piled high with identical cheap looking metal suitcases and each bus contained seven people. All were struggling to keep up with the traffic flow with one lagging far behind the others. I knew they were doing their best because they were German, but I could tell they knew as I shot past them that it was a simple and fortunate luck of the draw that I was created as a Mercedes-Benz and not as a workhorse VW bus.

On one occasion, when we visited Berlin I was astonished to find that an imposing wall had been erected to separate the Western and Eastern sectors. On prior visits we had not been permitted to cross into the Eastern sector but this huge, ugly wall was new and darkly foreboding. I did not know if the wall was to keep the Easterners in or the Westerners out. I learned from conversations between Fred and Katie that we were not allowed to cross because the U.S. and Russia were engaged in a cold war. It seemed warm enough to me and pretty stupid to restrict access. However, part of me was glad because when I looked through the gate at Checkpoint Charlie I saw that the cars on the other side were cheap, tired and dull-headlighted. If I had to be confined to one side I was grateful it was the Western sector.

After two years of travels with Fred and Katie I knew most of the towns in West Germany and the bordering areas. I had settled into a comfortable life; perhaps too comfortable, actually. I felt a growing complacency. My tires were getting a little round on the edges, my blinkers were lethargic, my fuel filter was a feeling gummy and I found that I was just as happy biding my time parked as I was carting around my passengers. I was beginning to think I needed a change of venue – some different routes and new experiences. As fate would have it, I soon got much more than I bargained for when, in the autumn of 1961, Fred got his orders to return to the USA.

When I heard him and Katie discussing their impending transfer I felt every emotion from optimism to dread. Would I be sold, and if so to whom, and would I be treated with the same deference? Would I accompany them to a new, strange land? Would I be donated to charity? Or would I simply be abandoned? I spent some restless nights trying to sort out things over which I had no control and eventually, to protect my own sanity, I resigned myself to whatever the car gods of Stuttgart had in store for me. My belief in this higher power comforted me.

It wasn't long before I saw what they had in mind. One morning I realized Fred was driving me to Hamburg. He parked me in a lot at what I later learned was a shipping port, locked me and walked away. That was the last I saw of him for almost a month. I spoke with the other cars there, who were just as confused as I was. None of us knew why we were there and none of us had seen our owners since we were parked. We were powerless to do anything, of course, so we sat there and awaited our collective fate. After a week of waiting and wondering, I was unlocked with the rest of the other cars and a stranger started me up and drove me to a dock where some straps were attached to my undercarriage. Suddenly I found myself hoisted into the air and positioned over a large ship. That was a new experience for me and I was not at all happy about it. Despite Gottlieb's ambitions, motorcars are not designed to fly. It was a few minutes that seemed like an eternity before I was lowered onto the deck of the ship and driven into a big room with a hundred or so other cars. I was parked and locked once again and something was placed under my wheels to keep me from moving. After the big room was filled, the door was closed and we were shrouded in close, total darkness. I couldn't even see the rear bumper in front of me, just a few inches away from my grill.

Resigning myself once again to my situation, I chose to go into a deep slumber, assuming someone would awaken me when it was time. The last thing I heard before nodding off were two indignant, arrogant Maseratis expressing their outrage at being confined thus with cars of such lesser worth. Hearing them whine, I was happy to be of stoic German stock.

I do not know how long I had been sleeping when a bright light suddenly flooded the big room. We all were awakened with a start and had little time to regain our bearings before being driven down a ramp and into another parking lot. I saw a sign that said something about New Jersey. I didn't know where that was but it didn't feel at all like Germany. In a few days I was driven up another ramp on the back of a large truck and secured in place, along with seven other cars. As soon as we were loaded, the truck pulled out and we began a three-day trip.

The truck lumbered along what we learned was an Interstate highway. I was encouraged to see that the signs indicated that they were U.S. routes, so I was hopeful that I was on my way to be reunited with Fred and Katie. We made two stops, and one car each was unloaded at each one. At the third stop I was driven off the truck in Lincoln, Nebraska. Within a couple of hours I was relieved to see Fred appear. He walked around me, inspecting me for damage, signed a paper, took the keys from another man and drove me away.

As with any expatriate, it took me some time to adapt to my new surroundings. I slowly grew accustomed to being different from my American counterparts. I knew I was superior in design and appearance, but I did not make an issue of it. The huge Pontiac GTO next door was unjustifiably proud, I thought. He burst forth with a menacing roar when his owner started his engine. I don't know whom he was trying to intimidate, but if it was I, he was wasting his time. I wrote him off as a vain, oversized, heavily chromed, mass-produced monster that undoubtedly would develop rattles and engine problems before his odometer registered 75,000 miles.

Most of the other cars I encountered were civil enough. I did my best to shrug off the occasional comment I overheard from some of the less sensitive ones about foreign cars trying to take over the country, thereby putting all the native Fords and Chevys out of work. Personally, I felt there was room for all of us and that we all could learn something from each other if we would allow ourselves to. I focused on my job to serve as reliable transportation for Fred and Katie. It struck me that if the Fords and Chevys had that same attitude they would not be so concerned about losing their jobs.

I must say that I missed the breathtaking countryside of Germany. Nebraska was just plain flat and uninteresting unless you like corn, which I am sure I would not unless it tasted like gasoline. (Who was I to know that one day ethanol would be considered a replacement for my familiar diet?) Even when we took a leisure trip we were surrounded by the flat sameness of that corn-covered land. I knew that an Alp was out of the question, but I would have loved to see even a small mountain. Fred never took me to one.

As the months passed in Lincoln, I felt our relationship changing. Fred was still nice enough, but I sensed that he no longer felt the joy of driving me that he had when I was new. He seemed distant and I no longer heard him boast about me to his friends. I wondered if it was something about my performance or appearance, neither of which I had any control over. I was disappointed but not all that surprised when he drove me to the Buick dealer in November 1962 and left me behind as he drove off in a new Buick. A Buick?! I was heartbroken to be shunted aside and forgotten, and doubly so when I saw what he had replaced me with. I wasn't sure I could ever trust another owner not to do the same thing, in spite of my unwavering loyalty.

But when I was repurchased in December 1962 I resolved to give my new owner, Leroy, a chance. To his great credit it was not long before I developed a comfort level with him that allowed me to relax and actually relish our time together and think about the possibility of a happy future with him and Diana.

———————————

Our first year together was not particularly adventurous other than one trip across the country to California. It took us three days and I loved getting out on the open road again. When we got to Colorado and I saw the Rocky Mountains I was almost beside myself with joy. What a treat it was to show my power and cornering skills as we negotiated those hills. They weren't Alps but they weren't bad.

We crossed Utah after descending the west side of the Rockies. It seemed strange to me. I heard Leroy and Diana talking about how it was impossible to get a beer there, which explained my uneasiness and confirmed my perception. I was created in a country that prides itself on its fine beer and consumes a goodly amount of it. It was difficult for me to grasp that there was actually a place where it was not available. I was relieved when we crossed the border into Nevada. That relief was short-lived, though, as I looked out at the endless straight road extending to the horizon with no sign of a curve and very little vegetation. That turned into a very long, boring day until we reached California, some 400 miles later.

I liked much of what I saw in California. There was diversity to the landscape that was lacking in Nebraska: hills, trees, curves in the road, water. Leroy's mood improved too. We arrived at a town called Chester, where he parked me for what turned out to be the whole night. I wasn't used to the high altitude there, but my engine had no trouble making the adjustment. I slept more soundly that night than I had for months.

I was awakened the next morning when Leroy got in and started me up. He drove me to the end of the little town, but instead of continuing on, he did a U-turn and drove to the other end of town where he repeated the drill. The route didn't make sense to me but at least I was getting a good look at the area. We pulled in to a place with a Frosty Freeze sign on the roof, where he parked me and went inside. I was next to a very old car. I introduced myself, accepting the distinct possibility that he may be too tired to chat, but he proved to be more gracious than one might expect from a vintage car. He told me he was a 1931 Model A Ford who had lived in Chester for almost as long as he could remember, although he admitted his memory was fading. He had gone through a series of owners, mostly teenagers who had him as their first car. He said that Leroy looked familiar but he couldn't be absolutely sure if their paths had crossed. In fact, he said he couldn't be too sure of anything anymore.

The Model A had come to California during the Great Depression, which I learned was not a big dent, but rather a time when people did not have very much money. He vaguely recalled being driven from Oklahoma. Although he had suffered the fate of being a training car for a series of teenage boys, he described his life in Chester as good. He knew his way around, was comfortable with the roads and traffic and felt that he was treated well by his many owners, who demonstrated varying degrees of driving skill. He told me he spent a great deal of time dozing at the Frosty Freeze and the high school parking lot. I liked the old guy and hoped to myself that I could enjoy as long a life. I felt I had many more adventures in me before settling down like he had but I didn't want to rub his radiator cap in it. I told him I was originally from Germany, and he said he'd never heard of it, asking if it was anywhere near Detroit. I told him Germany was a little farther away than Detroit.

When Leroy emerged from the Frosty Freeze he took a long look at the Model A. Judging from Leroy's eyes and the Model A's headlights, they seemed to recognize each other. As he was walking around it, a teenage boy came out and opened the driver's side door. Leroy asked him if this was the car that had once belonged to the local butcher, Mr. Guiglini a few years back. The kid said he believed it was, and that it had been through a few owners since then. He added that he was trying to restore it. So far, the engine had not been addressed but he had straightened out most of the dents and applied a fairly decent paint job, which is why Leroy didn't immediately recognize it as the first car he had owned back in 1956. Although the kid was polite enough, he didn't seem as impressed as Leroy was at running into that car after all those years. Neither was the Model A, who had dropped off to sleep again.

We remained in Chester for three days. I soon became quite familiar with it and I began to feel comfortable there despite the quizzical looks that came our way as we drove around. I had the feeling that not too many people or cars who lived there had ever seen a vehicle quite like me. When we left Chester we drove to another town that was new to me. It was called Chico. I learned that Leroy and Diana had ties there from their university days and that they were visiting her parents before returning to Nebraska.

We did not spend as much time driving around Chico as we did when in Chester. We did stop by a drive-in restaurant called The Burger Pit where Leroy lamented the fact that it wasn't the same as the "old days" two years ago, when it was called by the odd name of "Toot 'n Tell 'em". Diana snapped at him to accept the reality that things change. Leroy said he realized that, but it didn't make him miss the old place any less. I was beginning to learn that Diana was the more pragmatic of the two of them while Leroy enjoyed reliving the carefree days of his not so distant youth.

I was not eager to leave California. It was not only the climate and the landscape that spoke to me, but also the progressive and accepting attitude of its residents. It was a refreshing contrast to Nebraska and to be honest, my home country as well. I knew in my chassis that I could get used to this place, although I steeled myself for the possibility that we might never come back.

———————

In the months after we returned to Lincoln I noticed that Diana was gradually putting on weight. It seemed that each time she settled into my front seat it would sink a little further than it did the last time. She also was not as upbeat as she had been. She complained about the cold, Leroy's insensitivity toward her feelings, her clothes not fitting, and the provincial attitudes of Nebraskans. I wondered why, if it was her weight that was making her so unhappy, she did not cut down on her fuel intake? What I did not realize was that Diana was manufacturing a baby and that people are constructed differently than cars are. We are built on an assembly line while humans are built in women. This truly was an enigmatic revelation to me. I had so many questions that I was unable to ask. How are new people designed and engineered? How long does it take to build one? How many people are required? Would not an assembly line be much more efficient, cost-effective and able to ensure consistency from one baby to the next? I never learned the answers. I suppose there are many things cars do not comprehend about people, just as there are many things people do not comprehend about cars.

As the months wore on, Diana continued to add weight and more items to what by now was a long list of complaints. I did my best to ignore them, but short of sticking my tires in my windows there was little I could do to tune her out. It was a great relief to me when, on a late January day, Leroy helped her into the car and she felt lighter. She was carrying a bundle that appeared to be a human, albeit a very small, young one with no hair, teeth or vocabulary. Now that I am older and wiser, I understand Diana was carrying a newly manufactured baby. I was uneasy how it would affect my life. In spite of a certain anxiety, it was a relief to hear Diana say something positive for a change. I was hopeful that her unhappy phase had passed now that she had a new human to look after.

They named the baby Annie. I accepted her into our family, despite the fact that she was extremely demanding and self-centered, and the more attention Leroy and Diana devoted to her – and it was considerable – the less important I felt. Their lives seemed to be completely centered on the little creature. I had to put personal feelings aside and call upon my German heritage to remind me of my proper role, which was to provide safe, reliable transportation and live up to my proud Mercedes-Benz standard of service.

I was amazed how Annie was able to dominate the lives of Leroy and Diana and manipulate them to cater to her every whim. When the family went anywhere in me, my backseat would be filled with Annie's supplies. If it was cold outside, Leroy would start my engine and let it idle until my interior was warm enough for Annie to be comfortable. If Annie was sleeping, my radio would be turned off. Nevertheless, I grew to like her and to understand that when humans are helpless, we need to look after them. It was a maturing experience for me, as well as for Leroy and Diana.

We seldom went for rides anymore just for the fun of it. It got to be a special treat when Leroy would run errands on the weekends with just the two of us, even if it was only to the grocery store or the hardware store or the gas station. If he had a few extra minutes he would take me out on the highway to let my engine work out its kinks. I sensed he had to sneak these diversions into his tightly controlled schedule so I especially appreciated them and I believe Leroy's own battery was recharged with the few minutes of freedom they afforded him.

By now I had resigned myself to living out the rest of my miles in Nebraska. I even tried to convince myself that it was a good thing, with no hills to test me in my declining years, not much traffic or interesting places to go that would chalk up numbers on my odometer. As I sat in the driveway during the sweltering, humid summer or the frame-chilling winter when the freezing wind and snow swept down from the Dakotas, I often let my mind wander to distract me from the elements, if only for a short while. I would hark back to my carefree youth in Germany and to my time in California, but I tried not to dwell on these idle daydreams because I had made a personal commitment to accepting the reality of life in Lincoln.

———————

One truth among many I have learned is that nothing is permanent. Just as a car settles into what he thinks will be life-long stability, the macadam gets yanked from under him. It happened to me in Germany, it happened to most other cars I had spoken with, and now it happened again to me, when Leroy received his orders transferring him to a far away place called Vietnam in the summer of 1965. He would be going there without Diana, Annie or me. He and Diana had just one month to figure out where she would live while he was gone and to get resettled. This was a tense phase for all of us for our own unique reasons: Diana because she would be living as a single parent for a year; Leroy because he would be away from his family and in a combat zone; and me because I had been depending on a predictability that was crumbling before my very headlights.

On the other hand, I was delighted when I learned that Diana would relocate to her hometown of Chico. I was eager to head west and leave Nebraska in my rearview mirror. Once the decision was made, life was a flurry, filled with goodbye parties and packing. Within two short weeks we were bound for California! Leroy and Diana found an apartment in Chico that pleased me because I had a reserved spot in a carport for the first time in my life. It felt absolutely self-indulgent to be parked there, and I easily adapted to my new situation.

Leroy left shortly after Diana and Annie had settled into the apartment. Nobody had mentioned to me how long he would be away, and as the weeks passed I felt a wide range of emotions from hopeful anticipation of a quick return, to resentment, to grief, and ultimately to acceptance. After I had resigned myself to never seeing Leroy again, he returned. A year had passed. I liked Diana well enough during his absence, but I missed the quiet confidence of Leroy at my controls. Although Diana could drive me without running into things, she was not one with the machine the way Leroy was. There was an occasional grinding of the gears or a slip of the clutch, a slamming of my brakes or an unintentional racing of the engine, and even a few embarrassing stalls at stoplights. I did my very best to help her. I might have been happier if she had vacuumed and washed me and emptied my ashtray a bit more frequently.

———————

When Leroy returned, I noticed he had changed. He seemed more mature now, but he also seemed to have lost much of his spontaneity and love of driving me. He was serious, brooding, quick to take issue and generally unpleasant to be around. I don't know anything about Vietnam, but it must have not been in a nice place if it had caused such a downshift in his behavior.

Soon we were preparing to relocate once again, and within two short weeks we left Chico behind. We settled this time at March Air Force Base, near Riverside which also was in California, though far from Chico. I do not know where the river was that we were theoretically beside. Leroy and Diana moved into a duplex near the base, and as I grew acquainted with the neighborhood I realized that everybody living in it was, like Leroy, in the USAF. All the houses looked exactly alike and I wondered why anybody would want to live there. But I had a carport and nothing to complain about, so I overlooked that, and besides, the tidy uniformity of the unremarkable houses appealed to my German values.

Parked next to me in the carport was a 1964 BMW. I had not seen many other German cars since I left the country of my birth and it was nice to be able to talk with one. We whiled away our nights reminiscing about the old country and comparing notes on our travels. I considered myself fortunate to be sharing a carport with a fellow German, and we quickly developed a mutual respect.

We had been settled for six months when I heard Leroy and Diana discussing the fact that he had to leave again, although for a shorter duration than his last absence. He was in better spirits by this time, yet not entirely his former upbeat self. Because his previous absence had impacted his behavior so dramatically, I was naturally concerned that all of the progress he had made would be for naught, and that when he returned from this trip he would again be sad and angry. It was a huge relief to me, therefore, when he loaded his luggage into my trunk and drove me away, just the two of us, heading east. Leroy and I were on a road trip!

We covered a lot of miles over the next four days, traveling all day, alone in our thoughts while the white lines of the Interstate highway zoomed past, one after another in an unending parade from early morning to sundown. We stopped only for fuel, food and occasional stretching during the day, and took our rest at motels when the days ended. It felt wonderful to be on the road and I did my best to run smoothly, as would be expected of any loyal Mercedes-Benz. At the conclusion of a no-nonsense four-day trip we arrived at Maxwell Air Force Base near Montgomery, in Alabama. When Leroy parked me in a lot with other cars with license plates from all over the USA and unloaded his gear, I correctly gathered that we had reached our destination.

Cars learn a lot from talking amongst themselves. By sharing the bits and pieces of information we had picked up, we were able to figure out that we would be here for three months while our owners attended a special school. The Oldsmobile station wagon next to me said his owner, like Leroy, had recently returned from Vietnam and when other cars in the vicinity overheard us they chimed in as well. It turned out that nearly every one of our owners had recently come back from there. They also confirmed that their owners were different when they returned and we all agreed that it must be a terrible place.

I spent most of the next three months sitting idle in the lot with my new acquaintances. None of us was driven much, and that was fine, as the weather was hot and sticky. We were perfectly happy not to be driven and overheat our engines. The Oldsmobile, despite his ugly appearance, turned out to be a gentle giant. He was friendly, unpretentious (justifiably so in my opinion), and easy to talk with. A nearby Corvette had an attitude but then every Corvette I had ever met thought he was more special than he deserved to be. Once he concluded that the rest of us were not impressed with him, he calmed down and was reasonable company.

The Plymouth Valiant was quite stylish but it did not seem to me that he would age well, as I had. He did participate in our conversations to the extent possible with his limited vocabulary and mental capacity. I believe he tried his best. A vintage Ford was there as well. He claimed he had been driven 213,000 miles. I questioned that, at least to myself, because I would be astonished to see any American car go that far. It became more believable when he revealed that he had a recently installed rebuilt engine, along with some other parts, like some mellow twin Hollywood Glaspacs, replacement shocks, a generator and some other minor parts that his owner had located, as coincidence would have it, in Lincoln, Nebraska, at a junkyard from a 1958 Ford that had arrived there from California. We had been in Lincoln at about the same time, although we had not met. Most of his old friends were no longer on the road.

Summer waned and in late October our owners all came out to the lot and loaded us up for our departures. I bade my new friends goodbye as Leroy eased me out of the lot. Once again, we settled into the routine of a road trip. I did not feel very well on the return journey. I had a recurring sharp pain in one of my piston wells and a lack of acceleration that began to concern me. I could tell Leroy noticed it as well. He drove much more conservatively, speeding up gradually and doing his best to minimize the stress on my engine. I appreciated that gesture, as my pain intensified with each subsequent day. We took five days to get home and by then I had no doubt that something was seriously wrong with me. It was good to see Diana and Annie and to rest in my comfortable carport, but by that time it was patently obvious to Leroy and me that I was in need of a skilled mechanic.

The next morning when Leroy attempted to start my engine I could not do it. I had to be towed to a garage where a man clad in greasy coveralls and with dirty fingernails and the smell of cheap cigars about him began an examination of my engine. It was intrusive but he had a deft touch and seemed to know what he was doing. He hooked up various analytical instruments to me and after a great effort and an auxiliary battery, managed to start my engine. I sounded terrible, as I coughed and sputtered and missed, and unburned gasoline was dripping from my tailpipe. The mechanic listened carefully and checked the gauges on his instruments. Mercifully, he shut me down after just a couple of minutes, but it had felt like a painful eternity. He concluded that I had a cracked piston and that a major operation was the only option. The estimate was $1,400 that I knew was well out of Leroy's reach.

Leroy left me at the shop that night after advising the mechanic that he would have to take the problem under advisement. I spent a fairly comfortable night sleeping in the garage, although I was restless and beset with fitful dreams about my future prospects. Would I be repaired or would I be taken to the junkyard? I had heard Leroy and Diana discuss their financial situation many times and I knew that money was tight. I figured odds were poor that I would get my needed repairs, and that depressed me enormously. Oddly enough, I also felt guilty for letting Leroy down after he had treated me so well, and I would have done anything within my power to repair myself. But alas, that was beyond the capability of even a Mercedes-Benz. Once again I had to resign myself to whatever the car gods might have in store for me.

I had made the correct assessment. When Leroy returned to speak with the mechanic the next morning, he told him he was unable to pay for the repairs. The mechanic said he knew of a man who might be interested in buying me for the right price. I figured "right" meant "cheap". The mechanic put Leroy on the phone with the buyer and a deal was struck to sell me for $700. Had I been healthy I would have been gravely insulted, but I was not. I was very ill with dim prospects and I concluded that a low price was preferable to the junkyard.

Leroy and I parted ways that morning. We both were depressed. We had grown quite fond of each other and had a strong mutual respect. I was confident that both of us would cherish the memories of our time together as I acknowledged that nothing is forever, not even a Mercedes-Benz.

Chapter 9
RECLINING SEATS AND ANOTHER BABY

I was shaken from my fitful slumber as my engine was started. My windshield was covered with moisture so I knew it was morning and that I had dozed off. Someone drove me into a large garage and parked, and I was examined from grill to tailpipe. I was treated to a complete tune-up and lube that was long overdue and felt great, and then I was washed and my interior was thoroughly cleaned. I hadn't felt this spiffy since the day I was first driven off the lot by my original owner, Ralph more than a year ago. I began to feel optimistic that my life might be improving. By late afternoon I found myself parked amid several other cars of various origins on a lot festooned with bright plastic triangular flags. We all had signs on our windshields that said things like "Low Mileage," "Clean," "One Owner," "Real Bargain" or "Make Offer." My sign said "Repo," whose meaning by now I had come to understand.

I was parked next to a '62 Dodge who'd had a good life. His owner had been a quiet guy who never missed a payment or a scheduled maintenance. He had low mileage (so the sign on his windshield said), and just a few little dings in his doors, but we all had those, thanks to thoughtless people in parking lots. His owner had decided it was time for a new car and he was a little depressed. He'd done his very best to be reliable and likable, only to be tossed aside. I told him this is the fate of all cars, including the one that had replaced him. We have limited lifetimes in a world of fickle owners with changing tastes. I don't think I cheered him up much though. A teenage boy bought him. The kid had long, unkempt hair, low-slung jeans, a tight t-shirt and a smart alecky look about him. As the Dodge was driven away I wished him well, but I didn't hold out much hope.

During the next week several people looked me over. Some gave me a cursory glance, others peered under my hood, a few took me on a test drive and one idiot kicked my tire. I wish I could have kicked him back. I met Leroy the following day, when he purchased me for $1,675. He was with his wife, Diana, and their two-year old daughter, Annie. It took about an hour to take care of my paperwork. I don't know if that made me important but it was nice to know that something official was required to make me legally owned by somebody new. As Leroy drove me off the lot I heard him comment to Diana that I was no Mercedes, but I wasn't bad. I don't know why he said that because it was obvious I'm not a Mercedes. But if I do say so myself, he was right about one thing: I'm not bad.

We stopped at a nondescript house in a neighborhood where the houses mostly looked alike. In that sense it was like my former surroundings but this one was tidier and the cars were newer. I was parked in a covered carport next to a car who said he was a 1964 BMW. I'd never heard of that make. He had a boxy body and I thought he was a strange looking thing, sort of like an early 1950s Plymouth, only smaller. He told me he was made in a place called Germany, which was a long ways away, across an ocean. The farthest I had ever been was Detroit and I'd never heard of an ocean so I took his word for it. He asked my why I was parked in the Mercedes' place and I told him I didn't know any Mercedes. I explained that I had just been purchased and that I believed this carport to be my new home. The BMW raised his headlights at that, saying he knew the Mercedes had some problems, but he had no idea they were serious enough for him to be replaced by a Rambler. He said that with a derisive tone that implied I was somehow lower class than he or that mysterious Mercedes. I caught myself before blurting out a smart reply, figuring that if I have to live next to this odd looking car with an attitude, I would need to do all I could to make sure we got along. So I just explained to him that we are what we are, and that although I may not be fancy, parts of me are pretty outstanding, like my reclining seats and generous storage space. He seemed unimpressed so I ended the conversation, hoping that with time we would become, if not friends, at least civil.

The year I was built, 1964, was noteworthy. To me, the most significant happening was that I was manufactured, but for humans, some other interesting events were taking place. America was embroiled in a social upheaval. Lyndon Johnson was elected President and he immediately set about creating "The Great Society". I didn't understand all that stuff, but people seemed pretty much polarized on the issues of Civil Rights legislation and something called Medicare. The Surgeon General, who is something like the country's head mechanic, issued a report that said smoking is bad for people because it causes cancer. Cars smoke all the time though, and we don't seem to be bothered much. I guess we're immune to cancer. Teenagers didn't care about politics or cancer. All they wanted to do was buy more records by four mop-headed guys who called themselves Beatles, even though it was obvious they were humans.

I was built by a Detroit automobile manufacturer that no longer exists. My ancestors are the Nash family who founded their car company in 1916. In 1938 we were merged and became the Nash

Kelvinator Corporation, and then we merged again in 1954 with Hudson to become American Motors Corporation, or AMC. We never were the leader of the automobile industry, always striving, yet never overtaking the behemoths GMC, Ford or even Chrysler. But we did earn a respectable reputation for producing dependable (if not particularly stylish) cars. Every brand has a role in transporting American families from point A to point B, and we did so with practicality and economy, without flash, superfluous chrome or garish tail fins.

Typically, our owners were middle class, hard working, tax-paying American couples with a few children. Most had mortgaged homes in modest neighborhoods and lived by firmly planted American values. They were pursuing the American Dream of building for a secure retirement and seeing their offspring enjoy richer lives than they had. I, like all other AMC cars I knew, was in complete accord with these values and we were proud to be making our contributions.

My style is what I'd call sleek and clean. I have a three-speed automatic transmission, an AM radio, and air conditioner and white wall tires. I think I'm not just handsome, but a valuable addition to any family. I'm called a station wagon but I don't know why. I've seen gas stations, bus stations, fire stations and police stations and I can't imagine being named after one. Perhaps we are called wagons because of our ample and easily accessible storage space and seating capacity, and perhaps we were originally used to transport people and luggage to and from train stations. I'll probably never know for certain.

Though it is not well known, we could even enhance the life of a male teenager, who, as a rule, likes to drive a snazzy car to impress his friends. Give a kid a '57 Chevy and he becomes a magnet for the bobbysoxers. This is the goal of every red-blooded American sixteen-year old boy. Well, we AMCs have our own assets to offer. It's not normally discussed in polite circles that our front seats recline completely, creating a roomy bed. We may not have those fancy fins or spinner hubcaps but we can be exceptionally accommodating in other ways.

But I digress. My original owner never reclined my front seats and his children were not yet of an age at which they would be interested in doing so. His name was Ralph. He and his wife Millie lived in Riverside, California. Both were employed — Ralph as a bread truck driver and Millie as a hairdresser. Their two kids were fairly typical, I suppose, which means sticky, sneaky and manipulative. Although Ralph and Millie didn't have any education beyond high school, they were innately smart and hard to fool, so their children didn't get away with very much. All things considered, they seemed to be a solid, well-adjusted, happy family.

They purchased me because I was a good value. My MSRP was $2,100, but Ralph managed to negotiate the salesman down to $2,000 and no charge for my radio. When he drove me home in the fall of 1963, just after my introduction, his neighbor came by to check me out. Ralph showed him my interior and my engine, and then the guy gave my left front tire a hard kick. I have no idea why; I had done nothing to offend him. Maybe he was jealous that Ralph had a better car and he was taking it out on me. It didn't hurt, but I thought it was pretty disrespectful.

I settled into my new life with Ralph and Millie and their kids, who they called Butch and Sissy. Butch was about nine years old, and Millie was seven. They seemed nice enough for kids, but I didn't care for them very much. They were always spilling stuff on my back seat and leaving trash behind. Missy had an annoying habit of kicking the back of my front seat and Butch would frequently smear my windows with his sticky fingers. What is it about pre-teen boys that makes their hands so sticky? I guess every car has to put up with human foibles and on balance my family wasn't too bad. In any case, I didn't have the power to gripe.

My neighborhood was OK but nothing to write home about. The houses were simple and looked pretty much the same except for the colors and the state of the yards. They had two-car garages but most families had just one car that shared the garage with accumulated goods like broken lawnmowers, leaky boats, abandoned furniture and haphazardly stacked boxes filled with long-forgotten items.

The other cars I became acquainted with were an eclectic mix of late model, modest vehicles like me, as well as a good number of older sedans and wagons. There wasn't a single Cadillac — this wasn't a Cadillac kind of neighborhood. Some cars were pretty beat up but most seemed to be in good enough condition, and it was obvious that their owners were doing their best to squeeze another year of two out of them. The 1961 Chevy Biscayne next door wasn't very attractive, having been painted a muted grayish-brown with black wall tires and more rust on his grill that any of us wanted. The guy who had kicked my tires on my first day owned him. The Biscayne said he'd had his own tires kicked many times for reasons that evaded him.

During the week my life was a predictable routine. Every morning at 6:45 Ralph would drive me on the same route to the place where he worked, which was exactly 7.4 miles each way. I was parked in the employee lot with a few other cars until a few minutes past 4:00 p.m., when he would drive me home. Millie had her own routine, but I wasn't part of it. I assume she car-pooled to her job after getting the kids off to school. Some evenings I might be driven to the grocery store. They seldom took full advantage of my capabilities for weekend outings or family trips. My cargo space was used mostly for carrying things home in shopping bags. I had heard from other cars about trips to a place called a beach but I never experienced it with Ralph and Millie. It was a pretty boring life until mid-summer when things began to change.

In July 1966 Ralph suddenly stopped driving me to work. He would stay home all day, not doing much of anything. Millie and the kids kept their normal schedules, while I was left to sit in the driveway all day. I began to be concerned for Ralph, who was growing unhappy and more hostile each day. He didn't smell very good and when he did drive me it was more and more often to a place called a bar. On the way home he would weave me down the road, driving erratically and even running stop signs.

During one of those frightening trips a policeman stopped him. Ralph wasn't very polite to him, and I heard the officer instruct him to get out of my driver's seat and blow into a balloon. He looked pretty silly. I guess the policeman agreed, since he told Ralph to lock me up and get into the black and white car with the annoying red light on its roof. As they were discussing this, I asked the other car what was going on. He told me Ralph was getting arrested for something called DUI. I guessed that wasn't a good thing, since Ralph was protesting pretty loudly as he was helped into the back seat of the policeman's car. As they drove off I was left alone by the side of the road to ponder how I was going to get home.

A few hours later another car pulled up behind me and parked. Millie climbed out, got behind my wheel and, as she drove me home I could tell she was unhappy. She was crying and saying very negative things about Ralph that good manners prevent me from repeating. I just did my job, carrying Millie home and minding my own business, thanking the Detroit gods that I was not a human. After seeing that Sissy and Butch were safely deposited with a neighbor, Millie drove me to a police station. She came out a few minutes later with Ralph, who had never looked unhappier. I was grateful that she refused to let him drive me home. They argued loudly. She yelled at him for getting arrested, for losing his job, for not being a man and for wasting his life. He yelled at her for yelling at him, for not understanding the pressure he was under and for her constant nagging. I was extremely uncomfortable, belching a sigh of relief when I was parked at home and they continued their arguing out of my window-shot.

I hoped that this crisis would spur a change and that things would return to normal, but they didn't. In fact, the stress and strife grew by each day until Ralph and Millie rarely spoke, and the kids avoided their father, fearing he would take out his anger on them. I had about given up hope for any kind of normal, happy life. Then, on a chilly November night, a tow truck pulled up behind me. Its lights were turned off and the driver cut the engine. He got out and was surprisingly quiet as he hooked a cable to my underside. I soon felt myself being pulled up so that my rear wheels were off the ground. The lights in the house suddenly went on and Ralph, clad only in his underwear, came running out, screaming at the driver to leave his car alone. The driver, a husky, no-nonsense guy with some large tattoos and long, greasy hair told Ralph to back off as he withdrew a short metal object from his belt and pointed it at him. Ralph stopped yelling and stayed where he was as the driver climbed into his truck and drove away with me attached.

As we left my familiar neighborhood behind us I asked the tow truck what was going on. He had the same unpleasant personality as his driver as he sneered at me and told me I was a "repo". I begged his pardon and told him that I am a Rambler. He snickered and said I might be a Rambler, but I was now a repossessed one because my owner had missed three payments on me. Soon I was deposited at the lot where I had been purchased and left to ponder my fate as the tow truck's taillights disappeared into the night. I never saw Ralph and Millie again. While my time with them was not particularly happy, they did give me valuable insight into human nature. I am grateful for that and I sincerely hope that they eventually overcame their difficulties. If humans could be more like us cars and accept the challenges they are faced with, I believe they would be more at peace. But they are complex creatures and I doubt they have that capability. I realized I had no control over what might become of me after being parked in that used car lot, so I resolved to make the best of whatever might be in store for me. And a few days later I met Leroy.

My life with Leroy and Diana was a significant improvement compared to my previous lot. They seemed nice and I was driven with care. Leroy kept me clean and made sure I got a lube and oil change every thousand miles and that my oil filter was changed every five thousand, at which point I also was tuned up. The BMW and I settled into a peaceful coexistence in our shared carport, never really warming to each other, but at least being civil. The two-year old, Annie, was active, demanding and noisy, but at least her fingers weren't sticky like Butch's and I was thankful that my windows weren't smeared anymore. I did notice that Diana was putting on weight. Every time she sat down my upholstery would stretch to the maximum and I began to wonder how much more she would pack on, and why she didn't seem to care.

In the early morning hours of July 1967, it was still dark when Leroy and Diana rushed out of the house. Leroy flung my tailgate open, tossed in a suitcase, slammed it shut, got behind the wheel and started my engine. Then he suddenly got out, returned to the house and rushed out again, this time with a squalling Annie in his arms. Diana, huge by this point, struggled into my passenger seat and screamed at Leroy to hurry up. I thought he already was but I guess it wasn't fast enough for her. He quickly deposited Annie in the back seat, settled behind the wheel again, fired up my engine, abruptly shifted me into reverse and backed me into the street, where he put me into drive and stomped on my accelerator. I'd never been so abused by Leroy and I was tempted to stall my engine, but something told me I needed to trust his judgment, as he had always treated me well before. I figured I would find out soon enough what all the urgency was about.

Leroy pulled up in front of a house, put me in neutral and hauled Annie out of my back seat. She started crying again. I think she was as confused as I was. The lights were on, so evidently whoever lived there was expecting us. A teenage girl I recognized as Annie's babysitter opened the door and took Annie from Leroy, who ran back to me without even thanking her. He slammed me into drive and sped away. I have to admit, despite the mistreatment, this was kind of exciting.

Very shortly we were at the Base Hospital, where he parked me, got out and hurried around to help Diana out. They rushed into the hospital without even locking my doors. A few minutes later Leroy returned to grab the suitcase. He closed my tailgate with emphasis (I wanted to tell him that it would work just as well if he closed it gently, but I had a feeling that even if I'd been able to talk, his attention was elsewhere). He dashed back into the hospital. I didn't know why he was so upset and I was thankful Diana was along to calm him down.

The keys were still in my ignition all this time so I spent a few uneasy hours worried that I would be stolen. It wasn't a happy prospect, either. I had talked to a few cars that had been stolen and none of them had anything nice to say about the experience. Three of them had been taken for joy rides by teenage boys and were later recovered and returned to their owners. One of them had suffered serious damage when he ran into a telephone pole. He had been repaired but he said he never felt right again; his frame was bent and he's been told he looks like a crab now when he goes down the road. Another one had been taken to a garage in another town where he had been repainted and had new license plates mounted. Then his serial number was filed off. He was sold for cash a few days later and never saw his legal owners again. He lived in constant fear after that, realizing how vulnerable we cars are to theft if our owners do something careless like leave the keys in our ignition — which is exactly what Leroy had done.

I was greatly relieved when Leroy returned around midday. He looked exhausted and more disheveled than I'd ever seen him. I was surprised to hear him whistling happily when he got behind the wheel because his glee certainly belied his appearance. Diana wasn't with him and I wondered if that was what was making him so cheerful. We drove, more sanely this time, back to the babysitter's house where he retrieved Annie, and then we went home. I recognized another car that was parked in front of the house. We had met previously. He was a stately 1967 Cadillac Seville owned by Diana's mother. I was thankful that Leroy parked me in the carport so I wouldn't have to spend my day listening to the Caddie go on and on about his superior construction, quiet interior, stereo sound system, leather seats, smooth transmission, blah blah blah. I suppose he found me to be in a lower class. I found him to be in a boring and pretentious class.

In the late afternoon Leroy drove me to the hospital again but this time he parked farther away from the entrance and locked my doors. While I was waiting I struck up a conversation with the 1966 Ford station wagon next to me. I figured he would be approachable, as we both were wagons. I was right. We bonded right off the bat, sharing stories about the unique lives wagons lead compared to sedans. As modest utility vehicles we both were proud of our role and he had no problem understanding why I held Diana's mother's Cadillac in disdain. That thing is all show and we are all go. The Ford asked if my owner had a boy or a girl. I replied that she had a two-year old girl. He said that's not what he meant; he was inquiring about the new one. I told him I didn't understand his question so he explained that we were parked in the maternity lot, which is the part of the hospital where babies are manufactured. He had been here a year before so he knew what was going on. I told him I couldn't answer his question but maybe I would find out later.

When Leroy drove me home that evening Diana still wasn't with us. I guessed that if she was manufacturing a baby it was taking more time than it did to manufacture me, which was about an hour. The snooty Cadillac was still preening in front of the house but, thankfully, Leroy pulled into the carport and I was spared his crowing.

The following two days were much the same routine. Leroy drove me to the hospital where I'd remain parked for most of the day until we returned home in the late afternoon. On the fourth day, we parked near the entrance of the hospital. Leroy went inside and a few minutes later emerged with Diana. She was walking gingerly and to her credit she had lost a lot of weight. Leroy was carrying something that he handed to her after she was settled into my seat. I could tell that it was a baby but not what kind. On the way home I heard Diana cooing to it, calling it Johnny, so I figured it was a boy.

Diana's mother stayed for a week so I had to put up with the blathering Cadillac whom I mostly ignored, but for the sake of courtesy I occasionally acknowledged him. I doubt he would have been that polite if I were the visitor. Cadillacs are hard to understand. How could any car who looks that classy be so insensitive? I didn't dwell on it much, though. I was more interested in what was going on with Leroy and Diana. I didn't see much of her. Leroy would drive me to the grocery store and run other brief errands, and sometimes he'd bring Annie along but never Diana. I eventually saw her when she came outside with her mother. Leroy loaded a bag into the Cadillac's trunk and after hugs and goodbyes, the Cadillac gave me one last harrumph as it lumbered smugly down the road and out sight. Good riddance. I took brief satisfaction in noticing that his signal light was flashing, yet they were nowhere near any corners. Only addled or inattentive self-absorbed cars do that.

Johnny was a disappointment. When I came off the assembly line I was a functional, rational, fully developed machine ready to begin my life of service. Johnny, on the other hand, was useless. He couldn't speak, he had no teeth, he couldn't walk and he frequently smelled a little off. I don't think his exhaust system was working properly. I had often thought Annie was of marginal value, but compared to Johnny she was a dream. At least she knew a few words and had a properly working exhaust. As the months passed, though, I could see that Johnny was slowly developing into a human.

I have come to realize that people and cars have entirely different ways of coming into being and living their lives. Humans start slow and take a long time to develop. As babies they are demanding and incoherent. As toddlers they are demanding and noisy. As pre-teens they are demanding and preoccupied with dolls or bugs. As teenagers they are demanding and aloof, preoccupied with the opposite sex and restless. Only when they reach their 20s do they begin to add value. They continue to improve until they reach a point when they shouldn't be driving anymore. Some have the good sense to stop but others stubbornly hang on, insisting they are as good as ever, which any car will tell you they are not. But that's another story. Cars, meanwhile, are fully mature from day one. I guess it's because we don't have to spend our first 20 years developing that we have shorter life spans.

I couldn't possibly imagine thousands of Ramblers in various stages of growth, running around the streets, some tiny with no tires, others with tires, but too small to be seen very well, some with smart-ass attitudes, and some that have matured into what I am today. I suppose if Johnny had any value at all it was to reinforce the big difference between people and cars. I think we cars got the better deal.

In June 1968 a moving van pulled up in front of the house and a crew of men began transferring Leroy and Diana's stuff into it. I sensed that something major was afoot and was feeling apprehensive. I was relieved when, after the van drove away, the whole family was loaded in and we also drove away. Had I known we were leaving for the last time, I would have bid farewell to my carport mate, the BMW, but nobody bothered to mention it to me. We drove northwest for a few hours and stopped in Ventura for the evening. The family checked into a motel and I spent the night enjoying the refreshing ocean breeze. The 1960 Chevy next to me had a terrible paint job, and before the night was over I understood that although a night in the salt air can be refreshing, living by the ocean will take a toll on a car's finish. I hoped Leroy knew that and was planning to live inland.

We continued our journey the next morning and I enjoyed the scenery along Highway 101, with its rolling hills, small towns and farms. I learned that Leroy was no longer in the Air Force, and that we were headed for a town called Sunnyvale, in a place known as the Bay Area. I'd never been there but by this time in my life I had visited many new places so I wasn't particularly concerned. If I could have another carport or better yet, a garage, and if I didn't have to live with that insufferable Cadillac I figured I'd be fine. Leroy and Diana spent two days looking at houses and opted for a modest one in a well-kept neighborhood. And it had the garage I was hoping for so I was a happy wagon. A few days later the moving van appeared and soon Leroy and Diana were moved in, beginning another chapter in their lives. And mine as well.

As we all settled in to our new home we established our new routines. Leroy drove me to work each morning to a place called Applied Semiconductor and left me in the lot all day until we returned home in the evening. Diana stayed home with Annie and Johnny. I sensed a growing unrest when I overheard Diana complaining about being stuck in the house and not having enough money. Leroy argued that he was just starting a new job and that things would be tight for a while, but he did agree to try to find a ride to work with somebody else from time to time so Diana could use me. He made an effort, but it was spotty and Diana remained unhappy. To help make ends meet, Leroy decided to get a part-time job at a department store. He would go there two nights per week and all day on Saturdays. That helped relieve some of the money pressure but it meant that he and I were gone even more. I had lived in a stressful environment before and I didn't like what I was seeing.

After another month passed with no resolution in sight, the whole family was loaded into me and we drove a few blocks to another house with a beat up old Volkswagen convertible parked in front with a "For Sale" sign in his window. He was a 1962, which made me only slightly younger, but he clearly had been abused. While Leroy went into the house, the VW spoke to me. After exchanging the usual courtesies (where we were manufactured, how many miles we have, how long we've been in the area, etc.), I asked him why he was for sale. He said his owners were twin boys who were fun loving but disrespectful. He had been on many risky adventures with them, such as racing, speeding down dirt roads, and seeing how many teenagers could fit into him (13). He had spent many days at the beach that wasn't very far away, sitting idle while his twins surfed. That explained the faded paint and rust spots. He concluded that he was being sold because the twins had worn him out and had decided to buy a new car rather than repair him. In spite of his appearance, he seemed to have a positive attitude. I attributed that to his German roots. All German cars I had met were confident, duty-bound and determined to accept whatever was thrown their way.

Leroy emerged from the house with two young men who looked alike. Both were sloppily dressed with long, unkempt hair and flippant attitudes. I could tell that Leroy didn't like them at all. The three of them had a short conversation about the VW and when Leroy opened his door and climbed in I felt some empathy toward the VW as I pictured myself stuffed with surfboards and teenagers and being driven wildly. That life was just not the one for a Rambler. After a little more discussion, Leroy gave the boys some money and Diana drove me home. Leroy followed us in the VW and parked in the driveway. It began to sink in that I was being supplemented and would now be sharing my duties. I wasn't sure how I felt about that. I had always been the sole car and I was proud of my service. Now I was going to have part of my responsibility transferred to another car (and not even a nice looking one at that). I forced myself to calm down, and in the peaceful darkness of the garage I resolved to trust Leroy, who had never given me reason not to. And in any case, sharing my responsibilities was preferable to spending my future with owners like those twins.

As the VW and I grew accustomed to each other, our roles became defined. Leroy drove him to work now, leaving me at Diana's disposal. It didn't take me long to be satisfied with that arrangement. For one thing, I got to spend a lot more time in the cool garage, being used only for short errands during the week. More important, Diana's disposition was noticeably improved as the tension between her and Leroy abated. He was still gone a lot with his two jobs, but she wasn't trapped in the house anymore.

The VW and I actually became friends. He showed no resentment about my sole use of the garage, and in fact seemed to be pleased that he was owned by Leroy, who understood how to drive a manual floor shift and didn't abuse him. We settled into a very comfortable relationship.

Three years passed. It was now 1971. We had moved again, this time to an older neighborhood on a tree-lined street where Leroy and Diana now owned a home. Leroy was doing well and had shed his part time job. Diana had developed a circle of friends, Annie was in school and Johnny was a hyperactive, happy boy who seemed to be everywhere at once and never holding still. The VW was still part of the family and still ugly, but likable and happy. As for me, well, I was beginning to feel my age. I was seven years old and had 120,000 miles on me. My paint was fading, I had a couple of dents thanks to Diana (why don't females have any depth perception?!) and some of my parts were getting worn. I needed new tires, my brake linings were dangerously thin, I had some rattles, my upholstery had some rips in it, and I was beginning to burn oil, which meant I was in serious need of a valve job.

I knew that unless Leroy addressed some of my mechanical issues I would continue to deteriorate. Our parts are interdependent, and when one thing goes on a car it stresses the others. Good mechanics know the Gestalt of the automobile engine and the need to address the whole, not just the parts. I believe Leroy understood this, and also had come to realize that my life with him was coming to an end. This was confirmed one Saturday afternoon in August when Leroy and Diana drove me to the local Buick dealer and just like that, traded me in. They left me there as they drove away in a 1970 Buick. It was a station wagon like me, but much newer, larger and elegant.

I regretted not being able to say goodbye to my good friend, the VW. And I was sad that I was no longer part of Leroy and Diana's family. All I could do was hope that they would remember me fondly and appreciate my efforts on their behalf. I truly had done my best. As an aside, I should note that in my entire life, my seats never have been fully reclined. I think that just might be a record of some sort for a Rambler.

My stay at the Buick dealer was brief. Within three days I was loaded onto a truck with three other cars (I heard somebody call us "vintage"), and we were deposited at a junkyard, or as we prefer to think of it, a recycle center. I'm no longer drivable. I've been here now for eight months and many of my parts have been removed for use on other cars. I'm OK with that. Better to have parts of me out there performing a service. I know by now that when there are no more useful parts on me, I'll go to the crusher. And I'm OK with that, too. It'll be a quick end and I believe I'll live on after I'm smelted and used for something new, whether it is another car or something entirely different. Sometimes I chuckle to myself when I think how ironic it would be if I came back as part of a Cadillac. Whatever the outcome, I'm proud of my life, I have great memories and I look forward to what my future holds.

Chapter 10
FEISTY SURVIVOR

I was in pretty bad shape by the time Leroy bought me. I would-n't have lasted much longer with my original owners and I could sense immediately that life with Leroy was going to be a whole lot better than it had been so far.

Despite the abuse to which I had been subjected over the course of my life, I did my best to uphold the VW tradition. I'll admit that it wasn't always easy, but my German DNA kicked in when I needed it. In late 1968, long after I had resigned myself to my fate, I felt a jolt of optimism when I found a "For Sale" sign on my windshield. That was on a Friday, and on Saturday morning a man who turned out to be Leroy came to see Mike and Ike, the twins who had owned me for six long, awful years.

His wife, Diana and a couple of little kids, Annie and Johnny, stayed in the other car, a '64 Rambler, while Leroy went to fetch the twins. I introduced myself to the Rambler. We both had some scars, but he had far fewer than I did. After a brief discussion with the twins, Leroy negotiated them down from $900, handed them $600 in cash and he drove me away. I was so happy that I made an extra effort to start up on the first try. I didn't bother to look back as my home for the past six years grew smaller in my mirror. I hoped my memories would do the same.

I don't sprecken der Doitch, you should pardon the American accent. I might be German by birth but I was shipped to California before I had a chance to see the place or talk with any other cars. I guess I'll never be able to run for President because you have to be native born (not to mention human), but other than that I'm as American as anybody here. Well, maybe except for my work ethic. I think we German cars are created with an innate focus, determination and commitment to our owners that is lacking in those fat, lazy, rattling, belching, chrome bejeweled battleships made in Detroit. We come from the country where people can drive as fast as they want on the Autobahn, so I believe we have naturally had to develop the ability to save our drivers from themselves.

The year of my manufacture was 1962. I must point out that I've never been on an Autobahn, nor would any right-thinking German ever take me on one. But from what I can tell, I still was about the best thing to happen in that year of gut-wrenching upheaval. John Kennedy was president of the USA. He looked Khrushchev in the eye and accused him of lying when old Nikita told him Russia didn't have any missile silos in Cuba. JFK won that stare down with the assist of quarantine around Cuba, and Russia backed down. It was a pretty tense time. Not only was the country dealing with what became known as the Cuban Missile Crisis, but on the home front those traditional all-white universities in Alabama and Georgia were being forced to integrate. And then the Supreme Court decreed that prayer in public schools was unconstitutional. To top it off, a famous actress named Marilyn Monroe died at age 36, which seemed to make the whole country sad. Hearing about all of this made me feel blessed to be a humble car. We are pretty much in a constant state of awe when we see what humans do to screw up their lives. They have an odd determination not to just get along. If cars acted like that I'd have been squished by an 18-wheeler the first time I hit the freeway.

But I wasn't. I may be small, but when I was new, I was very good looking with a shiny blue body and a white convertible top. The first time I heard somebody refer to me as a "Beetle" I was offended, but over time I learned to accept that nickname and I've even grown fond of it. I suppose we VWs more nearly resemble a beetle than any other car does. And when I hear people use that term, or the other similar one, "Bug", I note that the words are used with affection. I boast a reliable, air-cooled rear mounted four cylinder 40 HP engine. I've got a four speed manual trannie with a floor-mounted shift and on a good day on a flat surface with enough time I can top out at 72 MPH. I don't like it but I can do it, and although it may not be Autobahn worthy, it's plenty fast enough for any reasonable driver. I normally go down the hill a lot faster than I go up the hill, but that's what all my gears are for.

I was first bought from a VW dealer in San Jose by a guy who seemed preoccupied and more eager to get the deal done than to check out my many assets. He paid full MSRP for me, $2,095 (we convertibles were worth $500 more than our hardtop cousins). I've since learned that only suckers pay full price, and the more I got to know my buyer, the more I realized that he fit tidily into that category.

He drove me home, parked me and went into his house. A few minutes later two teenage boys came racing toward me, whooping, hollering, elbowing, punching and bumping into each other. I cringed while I awaited my fate. After all, I had a total of 6.8 miles on my odometer and was pretty new at being a car. From what I was seeing at this early stage I was having second thoughts and wishing I had been manufactured as a Krups coffee maker, a Grundig radio or some other fine German product.

One of the boys (I couldn't yet tell them apart) yanked my door open and plopped himself in the driver's seat, while the other one piled into the passenger side. The one behind the wheel turned the key and I started my engine for him. He jammed me into low and away we went, way too fast in my opinion. He put my clutch in and I cringed again as he ground his way to second gear. I wanted to shout at him that I'm a precision, well-built machine that doesn't need to be abused to be of use. He shifted into third gear and then almost immediately into fourth. While I was straining as he maxed me out in low, I was now struggling because my RPMs were too low for high. This was not an auspicious start to my life with these guys. I hoped the other one would show more skill but when the he got his turn to drive he wasn't any better than the first one. They spent three hours driving around and taking turns behind the wheel. After the initial hysteria they calmed down and did a better job shifting my gears. It helped that when one would cause my transmission to grind or my entire being to lurch, the other would ridicule. I didn't care for their attitude, but at least their performance gradually improved. I exhaled a grateful sigh of relief when we pulled into their driveway.

The garage door was open and a new Pontiac GTO was parked there. I had observed a few of them from a distance but never up close and I'd certainly never spoken to one. All I could see of him was a massive chrome bumper, a couple of tailpipes and a trunk with a chrome stripe down the middle. It wasn't exactly an attractive view. I wondered what the purpose of the stripe was. After the boys had gone into the house I spoke with the Pontiac. He wasn't particularly friendly as he sat there flexing his tires and puffing out his grill. Since he was facing away from me I told him I was a VW convertible and he said that explained my high little voice. That offended me so I asked him if his voice was low because he was so fat. I knew it was petty, but I had endured a rough day and was fed up. I expected him to release his brake and roll into me, but to my surprise he chortled and told me he admired my spunk. I was grateful for that, since the last thing I needed at that point was more stress on my body.

When I told the GTO that I had been purchased that day he said that portended both good and bad news. The bad news was that the boys were still learning to drive and I would be their classroom. The good news was that he wouldn't have to endure them anymore. He explained that they were twins, meaning they were both born on the same day and looked alike. That didn't seem like a big deal to me. On the day I was built in Wolfsburg, I was just one of 39 to come off the assembly line and we all looked exactly alike except for our colors. The GTO explained that humans are manufactured differently and that identical ones are a rarity. He described the twins, Mike and Ike, as hyperactive, overindulged and mostly unsupervised. Their father had by now pretty much given up trying to influence them, preferring simply to keep the peace and be left alone. He spent long hours at work and when he was home he either locked himself in his office or drank a lot of something called gin. The twins' mother didn't care what they did as long as it didn't interfere with her bridge club, book club, tennis club, shopping and social affairs. In the GTO's opinion, I was purchased for the boys to get them off their father's back.

My second day with Mike and Ike was just like the first. We drove all over the place, stopping at the houses of some of their friends so I could be admired. I didn't mind that so much; cars are proud and appreciate nice things being said about them. I took exception to only two things: One guy thought he was a comedian when he repeated the tired old joke about the missing engine in the front and the extra engine in the back. Another guy, for reasons that escape me, kicked my left front tire. That seemed both pointless and impolite. By the time we returned home I was exhausted and ready for a long nap. About the best I could say for it was that my poor transmission wasn't as traumatized as it had been on my first day.

I got a break the next morning when I was driven to school and parked in the lot filled with other cars whose owners also were students. As the new car in the lot I got some curious stares, heard some snide remarks and was subjected to some teasing, especially from the oafish American pigs. I wasn't going to be pushed around, though, and I gave it right back to them. When a puffed up '55 Olds commented on my diminutive size I looked him in the headlight and asked if he needed six-ply tires to cart around all that useless chrome. When the '57 Chevy asked where the chicks would fit in me I said they'd be sitting up like ladies, not like the bimbos in his back seat. It was brazen of me and I was sweating under my sun visors, but I figured I had to establish my turf right off the bat. The Chevy didn't appreciate my snappy comeback and as he began to release his emergency brake a Ford pickup next to him told him to ease up and give the kid (I assumed that was me) a break. Some others chimed in with their support and the tension abated. Later I apologized to the Chevy for my remark and he said to forget it – that he had it coming. I thought that was classy.

I learned a valuable survival lesson that day: When you're small you have to compensate by being tough or other cars will bully you. I had immediately made it clear that no car would intimidate me and as the days passed, I grew comfortable that I had been accepted. Occasionally I would be parked next to another VW Beetle and we understandably bonded. He was a few years older and I was excited to learn that he had originally been purchased in Germany. His accent made him hard to understand at first but after a few conversations I had an easier time with it. He regaled me with stories of how beautiful Germany is, how proud the cars are and how well we are made compared to those from other countries. (He had no use at all for Fiats and outright disdain for Toyotas.) I assumed I would never visit Germany so I contented myself with absorbing his stories and memories, sometimes dimming my headlights and imagining that I was speeding along the Autobahn or snaking my way up an Alpine road.

Winter was upon us with day after day of rain and wind. The GTO hogged all the space in the garage so I didn't get any shelter from the elements. That didn't bother me, though, as my insulated top was snug and watertight. I was pleased to feel that Mike and Ike's driving techniques were improving, which was important because the roads were slick and the vision often limited. I have to admit that my windshield wipers left a lot to be desired, as they were small and the arms weren't all that strong. Streaking was a constant problem. During one particularly intense downpour Mike or Ike (I still couldn't tell them apart) bent my wiper arms, hoping that would help them hold the blades to the windshield. All that did was soak him through and through, which I felt when he sat back down. The windshield was no better than it had been and now my arms looked unnatural. I was annoyed that he thought he was smarter than the engineer who designed me and the technicians who built me. What gall.

When spring arrived we were ready for it. It was a clear day in early April and before driving to school, the twins lowered my top for the first time. Although the temperature was still chilly, they were eager to make the most of owning a convertible. I didn't mind at all because I had never driven with my top down. It was restorative! As we made our way to school the wind blew out a substantial amount of bits and pieces of accumulated trash and several months of teenage boy odors. It wasn't exactly a thorough cleaning but it still felt pretty great. As I'd hoped, they left my top down while they were in school. I got some curious looks from some of the other cars in the parking lot but by this time they knew that any of their guff would be met with a sharp repost, so they mostly just gawked, some raising a headlight, but nobody openly judging. To be honest, I think they were envious.

For the remainder of the school year my top was down almost all the time, even during a few rainstorms. I figured I could stand it once or twice. I'm sturdy, but no car is designed to withstand torrents of water in his interior on a daily basis. That's what happened, though. By the time the rainy season had ended, some of my upholstery piping was coming loose, a puddle of water had accumulated inside the base of my speedometer glass and mold was developing under my floor mats. The twins didn't seem to notice, or if they did, to care. I was powerless to raise my own top so I had to resign myself to their abuse and hope they would one day begin to act more responsibly.

On a Friday in early June everybody seemed to be in a particularly good mood. I learned from another car in the lot that this was the last day of school and that teenagers always got a little crazy then. How right he was! In the afternoon they all came running out, shouting and carrying on. The twins got in and invited a couple of girls to hop in as well. They did, and in turn, invited a few more. Then suddenly somebody yelled "Car-stuff!" Before I could figure out what was going on, kids were piling into and on top of me in their stupid effort to see how many of them I could accommodate. It turned out to be 13. It cost me a rip in my rear seat, three dings in my left rear fender from some goon's pointy shoe, and a broken rear bumper mount. My tires were nearly flat from the excessive weight and my shocks and springs were dangerously compressed. By the time everybody untangled and got out and off I was furious. This was senseless and unforgivable. Despite my commitment to serve at all times to the best of my ability, I just flat out refused to start. That got Mike and Ike's attention. One said that they may have gone too far with this stunt, and that I was broken. Well, duh. They continued to grind my starter motor until my battery (did I mention that I'm just a six volt?) was dead. In desperation, they enlisted the help of some other guys to push me, working up enough speed to force me to start in second gear when my clutch was popped. I fired up at that point and the twins let out a victory whoop, reinforcing to me once again what little regard they had for my well-being. After they drove me home and parked me I spent the night wondering what I had done to deserve such bozos for owners when every day I saw cars who were treated with dignity and respect. I didn't sleep very well that night.

The next morning dawned warm and sunny. I was still sore from yesterday's idiotic car stuffing. I could tell that my shocks and springs would recover and that my fender, although damaged, would not impact my innards. My bumper, though, was going to require a new mounting bracket, and I didn't have much confidence that the twins would bother. They came out of the garage carrying some long things that they loaded into me. They stretched almost my entire length, from the top of my windshield to beyond my rear bumper and were held in place by bungee cords. The boys got in and to my great credit I started. I doubt they appreciated my effort.

We drove for well over an hour, up a slow mountain road, then down again, into a place called Santa Cruz. We continued south and parked near the ocean where they unloaded their equipment and headed toward the water. I was left there with a few other cars. One said he was a "woodie". I gathered that was because his sides were made out of wood. He was a 1947 Ford and I immediately took to him because he was so mellow and approachable. He explained that our owners were surfing and that the equipment we carried were surfboards. I had learned by then that what makes no sense to cars seems perfectly logical to humans so I simply tried to understand what surfing was all about. It turned out to be uncomplicated, I guess, and much more fun that it looked to me. The twins spent the whole day, paddling out and riding their boards back to the beach. To what end I have no idea, as it seemed pointless.

When they quit surfing all the guys gathered on the beach and started drinking what I found out was beer. As the sun began to set, Mike and Ike returned to me, secured their boards and started the journey home. I could tell that whichever one was behind the wheel didn't have as much control as he should have so I had to overcompensate and missed much of the scenery on the way home while I focused on the road. We made it home safely, thanks to me.

The next day was a repeat, as were most days during the summer until school started again. I had no choice but to resign myself to the routine. The more I got to know the twins the less respect I had for them. They were spoiled and self-indulged, and obviously had nothing else on their minds except immediate gratification. My dents and dings began to accumulate thanks to their carelessness, and I developed more rips in my upholstery. I had lost a hubcap, my rear bumper was still sagging, my antenna was bent and the salt air was beginning to eat away at my paint. I was only a year old but I looked like I'd traveled a hard road for at least five.

My life over the next two years was essentially the same — languishing in the parking lot during the school year and trekking to the beach all summer. A lot of kids found other things to do, like part time jobs, but Mike and Ike had no money problems with parents who simply wanted to keep the peace at any price. The German in me was highly indignant and disappointed in them. I was hoping that when they matured and graduated from high school they would go on to college and make something of themselves, but they did not. They set on a course to waste their lives with surfing and partying and staying rent-free with their parents.

Because they had so little regard for my condition, I continued to deteriorate. I had some unsightly rust spots, several more dents, stained and filthy upholstery, and a cracked windshield. My driver's side window mechanism was broken, so to keep it closed they propped a stick on the sill at the bottom and jammed it under the chrome window frame at the top. I was having trouble with my starter motor as well. With increasing frequency nothing happened when the key was turned, but rather than take me into a shop to fix the problem, one of the twins would push me while the other would pop my clutch in second gear when I was up to 5 miles per hour or so. It was degrading and I kept my lights focused on the ground as I heard other nearby cars chuckling.

The neglect and abuse continued until the twins decided to unload me. Then came that morning in the autumn of 1968 when I found my windshield covered with the "For Sale" sign. It was the first day in a long, long time that I felt any hope for my future and I was sure that any buyer would be an improvement.

Leroy and his family lived in a more modest home than I had come from, but in a clean neighborhood. I was hopeful about my new situation. The first thing Leroy did was take me to a mechanic who gave me a long overdue tune-up and repaired the wiring to my starter. I was still unsightly but my innards felt almost brand new by the end of that refreshing spa session.

The following day he drove me to a place called Applied Semiconductor and left me in the lot among hundreds of other cars. Predictably, an oafish, fat, dull-witted Dodge made a joke at my expense, asking me if I had been assembled from a bunch of used spare parts. I'd been the butt of so many insulting comments by now that I hardly even heard them anymore, but because I was probably going to be spending a lot of time in that lot, I figured I'd better establish my turf right off the bat. So I looked over the Dodge and asked him if he needed some diapers for that oil leak. It was evident that he did not think anybody had noticed it but my headlights were low enough to the ground to spot the seepage from his pan. He wasn't the quickest car at the mental drag strip. He just sputtered and looked away, pretending to track a bird that was circling above him while the other cars guffawed and sniggered at him. I asked if any other cars had a comment and there was a long pregnant pause. Then an old Ford pickup announced that he had met me before, a long time ago in the high school parking lot, and that I was not a car to be messed with. He asked me if I remembered him and I did recall his coming to my support, although six years had passed. I thanked him and he introduced me to a few other cars, who seemed to accept his word that I was a lot tougher and deserved more respect than my little beat up body would lead one to believe.

Leroy and I soon fell into a comfortable routine and I was a lot more grateful than he could have imagined after those years with the idiot twins. I had it pretty good now. I didn't mind sleeping outside, I didn't mind spending my days in a lot, and I didn't mind not going to the beach. As a bonus, Leroy was a skillful driver who had an accomplished touch with my floor shift despite his rather large feet, and respect for my clutch mechanism. Leroy's behavior just drove it home to me how awful my first six years had been. His neighbors and some of his coworkers would raise their eyebrows or make impolite remarks about my appearance. Leroy had a couple of pat responses that I didn't fully understand but did appreciate because they sure seemed to work. Sometimes he would say, "To know this Bug is to love it and if you can't grok that you do not deserve a ride," and the other times he'd respond with "My daddy always said ugly women make more loyal wives." I really appreciated his defending me.

Weekends were often a fun adventure when Leroy put my top down and the family piled in for a cruise for a picnic or a petting zoo, a drive down a country road or just around the neighborhood. Annie and Johnny in my back seat were noisy and sticky, but that didn't bother anybody, not even me. I did sometimes feel guilty about having all the fun while the Rambler stayed behind in the garage. He didn't seem to mind, though, as he was beginning to age and would tire easily. We had reached a tacit agreement on our mutual roles with Leroy and Diana and we both were quite satisfied. Those were happy days.

I had heard Leroy tell Diana that he wanted to give me a makeover — get rid of my dents, repair my bumper and window and have me painted. Her reaction made me believe that was not likely ever to happen. She told him his priorities were screwed up, and then cited a list of the many needs that overshadowed his selfish desire to squander money on me. I didn't agree, but then I was hardly objective. I wanted a makeover more than anything in the world. I wanted other people and cars to stop staring at me and making unkind remarks behind my tailpipe. I wanted to be admired as the proud German I was. Diana made some valid points, however, and it surprised me that I caught on faster than Leroy did. The kids needed shoes, she needed some new clothes, and the grocery bill was always a stretch. The house payment, utilities and car expenses ate up most of their cash. I think it wasn't her message that got under Leroy's skin, so much as the hostile, shrill way she delivered it. Every time Leroy broached the subject it had the same result, which was hard to listen to. Inevitably, harsh things were said, there was never agreement, and one of them would walk away in a snit to end the discussion.

Leroy did manage to do some modest work on my top that was riddled with rips. He bought some naugahyde that was close to the same color, although not an exact match. He cut it into shapes slightly larger than each of the damaged areas and then glued them into place. The result was a unique looking top that resembled a quilt in appearance, but at least I could now repel water on a rainy day. I figured Leroy had resigned himself to opting for function over appearance, which was fine with me as long as there were no more arguments with Diana. They made me very uncomfortable.

I grew increasingly fond of my adoptive owners. My cosmetic needs remained unaddressed but the bond that Leroy and I had developed was much more important to me. We still spent our weekdays at work and on the weekends we still had frequent outings. The children were growing and active. Leroy and Diana had moved into a house in an established, tree-lined neighborhood. I seemed destined to reside outside the garage but every time I felt a little sorry for myself I would reflect back on my life with the twins and it would jar me back to a more healthy perspective.

It was 1971 and I had been part of Leroy's family for four years. It felt like we were on cruise control (I had to imagine it; I didn't have that superfluous feature but I had heard other cars discussing it). When people and cars get settled and comfortable, change always seems to be right around the corner. I don't know why, but it's true.

In this case, the big change was the Rambler. I knew that he wasn't feeling up to par and that little annoyances had started to affect his performance. His miles were piling up, his finish was deteriorating, his tires were worn and he was having trouble starting. He told me one afternoon as we were idly chatting that he didn't know how much longer he could meet Leroy's expectations because he was just plain fatigued and felt he would need some very expensive attention if he were to go on much longer. In particular, his valves were bothering him and he left an embarrassing trail of blue smoke when he was taken out. We both knew that Leroy and Diana had chronic money shortages so he wasn't hopeful about his future with the family.

One Saturday morning shortly after that conversation, the family climbed into him and Leroy backed him out of the driveway. Because Saturdays were normally my time with them, I had a foreboding feeling that something wasn't quite right. As they reached the street, the Rambler and I exchanged knowing glances and the unspoken message that this may be a final goodbye. With a brave wink of his headlight and an ominous cough he drove down the block, smoke trailing behind him. I never saw him again. I will always have fond memories of the Rambler. He wasn't fancy but he had a VW-worthy work ethic. We had become close friends and I was sad that he no longer was of the family.

A few hours later, they returned in a strange car. It was a 1970 Buick and like the Rambler, a station wagon. Compared to the Rambler, though, it was huge. I wondered if I might actually fit into its cargo compartment, not that I had any desire to try it. Although it wasn't legal, Leroy parked him on the street facing me. I had a feeling he was one of those rare humans who knew cars could communicate, and that he was inviting us to get acquainted. Since I was the senior resident, I felt I should initiate the conversation. I introduced myself and noticed that he looked me over with a quizzical expression. I hastened to explain that I had had a rough life before Leroy bought me, and I encouraged him to overlook my odd appearance. He was distant, which was understandable since he had just been purchased and didn't know the family, the neighborhood, his future prospects or me. I said this was his lucky day; that Leroy was a good driver who took good care of his cars.

Neither of us had anyplace to go, so there was plenty of time to warm him up and he gave me a few tidbits. A salesman who did a lot of traveling had owned him, and although he was only a year old he had more than 40,000 miles on his odometer. I was shocked, since I was nine years old and had only 85,000 on mine. He had enjoyed his life on the road. He said his owner drove fast and sometimes scared him as he passed other cars on two-lane roads and set the cruise control at 90 on the Interstate, but overall, it had been a good year. I had to ask what an Interstate was and he looked at me as if I was a rube. He had seen all of Northern California, from Bakersfield to Yreka. I'll confess to some jealousy as he described his nomadic life, as my travels had been limited to the immediate area and I longed to see what else was out there. It sounded very exotic.

We were nothing alike. The Buick was American, big, shiny and almost new. He had a powerful engine, a leather interior, a state of the art stereo system with an eight-track tape player, cruise control, pushbutton windows, power steering and factory air conditioning. I was who I was and knew I would never be anything else. I was willing to extend a wheel of friendship to him but if he lorded himself over me I figured it was his loss and that I'd be just fine. I could tell by the vacant look in his lights that he wasn't really tuning in, but I kept talking just to see how long he could stay awake. It wasn't long before he drifted off, and I shortly followed suit.

I awoke around 6 a.m., my usual time every morning, and saw that the Buick was still sleeping. I looked him over, wondering what it must be like to be so new, outfitted and imposing. I liked myself just fine, but still, a guy can have an occasional fantasy — not that I'd ever admit to dreaming about being anything other than what I am. When the sun shining into his headlights roused him, the Buick gave a couple of grunts and snorts as he slowly awakened. It was apparent he was not a morning car. We didn't have much time to chat, or more accurately, for me to chat and him to listen. Leroy and Diana loaded the kids into the Buick and drove away. I found myself hoping he would adjust quickly to his new life and that we could enjoy friendship like I'd had with the Rambler.

When they returned, Diana was driving and she parked the Buick in the driveway. The Buick asked me if Leroy and Diana were having problems. He had just come from a home where the man and the woman did not get along and he said he felt a similar tension. I thought I might as well be honest with him from the outset. I told him they were, indeed going through a rough spot; that both were trying hard, but weren't making much headway on overcoming their conflicts. I told him Diana always seemed to be unhappy about something and was generally negative, whereas Leroy just wanted peace. I added that in my opinion their relationship was going downhill, and unless they could reach a better understanding of each other's needs it was probably doomed. I hated to lay that on the Buick on his first full day with us, but a Volkswagen is nothing if not honest and straightforward. In my opinion there was little we could do other than be supportive and not add to their difficulties.

The Buick and I settled into a comfortable relationship. I grew to accept our physical differences and accept him as a friend with no strings attached. I felt that he, too, was growing to actually like me. He was awfully stuffy though. I just figured that was the way Buick wagons were. Even so, on occasion he would loosen up and we would tease each other about our appearance. I think I surprised him with my quick wit, but by then I had been subjected to so many insults I had a snappy comeback for any that might come my way.

Our routine was shattered as summer approached in 1973. Leroy and Diana gave up trying to patch up their differences, and they went their separate ways. The Buick stayed with Diana and I went with Leroy. I think he got the better part of that deal. Diana and the Buick stayed in the house while Leroy and I moved to an apartment complex. It wasn't nearly as nice as the house, nor was the neighborhood as peaceful and quiet. I did have a carport, though, so things could have been worse.

To his credit, Leroy adjusted quickly to his new life. He had his moments of feeling blue, which was no surprise, but for the most part he seemed to accept his new circumstances and determined to move on. There were a good number of unmarried people living in our apartment complex and he became acquainted with some of them. I knew their cars more than I knew the people, but I was able to get a good idea of them by those cars. I admired the resident Porsche — what VW cousin doesn't dream of being one? He was white and sleek and he was considerate enough of my humble roots not to lord his Porscheness over me. His owner was a shallow jerk, with ultra-dark sunglasses an expensive razor-cut hairdo and a shirt unbuttoned enough to show off his ostentatious gold chains. His only interest seemed to be seeing how many women he could attract. Leroy was civil enough to him, but I could tell that he didn't think much of him or his lifestyle. There was a dinged up 1968 Lincoln in residence too, and most of us other cars tried to avoid him. He was pompous, he belched noxious smoke and he was usually dirty and filled with food wrappers and empty beverage containers. His only interest seemed to be himself. His owner was a single man who was huge and slovenly. I don't know what kind of a job he had but I heard he was a consultant. Another car told me that "consultant" was just a nice way of saying unemployed. There was one nice little '72 Mercury Capri owned by a quiet woman who befriended Leroy. I thought that was a good thing and I liked her and her car. Leroy got along well with her. Once when they were driving around in me (people seemed to love the unique experience of me) I heard him tell her that he was falling for her. I didn't see him perched on any ledge at the time, though. She said he was too new at the single life to fall for anybody and he said she probably was right. I'm not sure what that was all about, but at least nobody tumbled and hurt themselves.

Although Leroy and Diana were apart, he made it a point to keep in touch with Annie and Johnny. We would stop by the house every other weekend, gather them up and take them to Leroy's apartment. It felt strange to return to that place, as if I was a visitor when I should have been a resident. The Buick was still there. We didn't have much of a chance to talk, as Leroy was always in a rush to get away. He did tell me Diana had been having an occasional male visitor, but he hadn't met any of them personally since they always used the man's car when they went out.

After three months, we stopped going to the house and instead, began taking a much longer drive to a place called Chico, where Diana had moved. It was a three-hour trip for us, each way. That Porsche could have made it in two, but Leroy respected my more limited capabilities. For that reason, I assume, our visits were less frequent and we made the trip about once per month.

Annie, now age nine, and Johnny, age five, seemed happy enough when they came to stay for the weekends. While those two round trips to pick up and deliver them meant twelve hours of driving, Leroy never complained, nor, of course, did I, although I could feel the wear and tear on my engine and tires. The abuse I suffered in my early years was taking its toll. I could still make the trips though, and I determined to continue as long as Leroy remained sensitive to my needs and didn't overtax me. Fortunately, he knew me well by then.

I noticed that the Buick wasn't doing so well. Diana wasn't taking care of it like Leroy had and it was accumulating some unsightly dents and scratches. On one of our visits I asked him how he was doing and he said he did not feel so hot. He was long overdue for a tune-up, and it was easy to see that the once proud wagon had become depressed and self-conscious. Such is the fate of most cars — we inevitably deteriorate. I had my own scars and a patched up top to boot, but I had retained my basic good looks. I am beginning to notice some memory lapses, though. Like right now, for example. I was talking about the Buick and somehow I'm now talking about myself.

Anyhow, it was sad to witness the decline of my old friend. In early 1975 he wasn't there when we picked up the kids, and there was a late model Toyota parked in his place in the driveway. I couldn't tell what year he was, since all those Asian cars look alike to me. We would briefly acknowledge each other, but had little in common and remained strangers. I often wonder what became of the Buick. I hope that whoever owns him appreciates him for the quality car that he used to be and aspired to be again one day.

In 1976 Leroy and I moved again, this time to Santa Cruz where he had bought a condo. I was apprehensive the first time he drove me to our new place, as I had been over that road many times and the memories were not great. I feared Leroy was going to become a surfer and that I would be relegated to my past life of salt in my headlights, beer cans in my back seat and shoddy maintenance. My fears were unjustified, as Leroy showed no interest in surfing. He did enjoy visiting the beach, but he parked me well away from the elements. What did begin to take its toll on me was the trek to his job in San Jose. The road was fast and crowded during the commute times and I was slow. It was pretty stressful for both of us. From time to time he would catch a ride with somebody else and I'd get the day off. I relished them. I loved the weekend jaunts we would take around Santa Cruz, though. It was just that daily commute that was beginning to be a problem for me. My valves kept getting out of adjustment, my fan belt would wear out too fast, my brakes needed relining and I had a wheel bearing issue in my right front.

On one of those days when Leroy had carpooled, he arrived at home in a strange VW, a '72 hard top. He had the same basic lines as mine, but was much newer. As Leroy did when he drove the Buick home for the first time, he parked directly in front of me and we two cars were headlight to headlight. We looked each other over. I was pleased that the VW look had not changed much, despite the years separating us. The first thing we decided was that I would be referred to as "Bug" and he would be "Beetle" to avoid any confusion. I was about to ask him if he was going to be a permanent resident with us when he asked me the same question. The new Beetle said he had just been bought so we guessed, and we turned out to be correct, that this was to be his new home. That made sense to me, since Leroy needed a younger, healthier car for work, but my fear, of course, was that I was about to be replaced.

The new Beetle was nice enough and certainly respectful of my age, so much so that he insisted on calling me "Sir". That was the first time any car had done that and I found it unsettling. I've always been a tough survivor in the trenches, a "car of the people", not some fancy schmancy machine. I asked him why the "Sir" business and he said it was because I was a senior VW, while he was barely at 40,000 miles. I appreciated his deference, but told him to knock it off or he would ruin my reputation.

I figured I'd have to wait and see if I was being replaced or once again becoming a second car. I hoped I wasn't going anywhere because I was very happy with Leroy as my owner and was apprehensive about getting a new one, particularly since the automatic shift was becoming the new standard and fewer drivers knew how to use a stick. I was in no mood to have some clumsy kid learn on me. The new Beetle was equally upset, although for different reasons. He had been uprooted from his original owner and was now in a strange place talking with an ancient Bug. I reassured him he would be fine with Leroy because he knew how to treat cars and in spite of his big feet, he knew how to handle a clutch pedal. We both dropped off, neither knowing our fate.

The next morning and several mornings after that, Leroy drove the new VW to work, leaving me parked at home. I had mixed emotions. On the one hand, I was thankful I didn't have to negotiate Highway 17 anymore and all those rushing cars and slow trucks. But I also didn't yet know what my future with Leroy would be. I was encouraged that he had not brought any prospective buyers around and I figured that the longer he delayed, the better my odds were of staying put. As the weeks passed, I was able to relax a little. Leroy commuted in the young Beetle and used me for weekend pleasure trips. I was happy with the arrangement and he seemed happy as well.

Thanks to that newbie, my life took a turn for the better. He took over the commute duties and I got to rest up for weekend trips to the beach or to escort some woman around to the local sights. I'd seen them all before (the sights, not the women), so I was able to shut down mentally and save my energy. I knew most of the other cars at Leroy's usual stops, although there would be an occasional visitor. One in particular was an uppity dune buggy who sneered as he gave me the once over and made a disparaging remark about my appearance. He said something about slumming with the hippie cars, which was a mistake considering the group he was parked among. I was tempted to just let it go and let the other cars hand him his lunch, but I felt a sense of obligation to protect him against himself, as a dune-buggy is, underneath, a VW like me. So I fired back a response, pointing out that all he was a Beetle with mascara and probably a little light in the shock absorbers as well, judging from his purple metallic paint job. I think he was surprised I was still capable of coherent thought at my age, not to mention razor-sharp barbs. To his credit, his attitude abruptly changed and we all calmed down.

Old people and old cars digress from time to time. The '72 Beetle was just a kid compared to me, but he was respectful and he was a fellow VW, so I cut him some slack. Besides, I was thankful he had assumed the commute duties, or did I already say that? We three — Leroy, the '72 and I — settled into a comfortable relationship. My only regret was Leroy didn't invest much in my upkeep. I was looking fairly rundown, with my faded blue paint and my disintegrating top. And I really was hoping to someday get that driver's side window fixed so I could get rid of the embarrassing stick holding it up. I had overheard Leroy tell a number of lady friends he planned to fix me up when he could afford it, but his child support payments had to come first. I don't know what that means, but I trusted Leroy and I just hoped for some attention at a future date.

Cars come and cars go. In my life with Leroy, I stayed while others went. First it was the old Rambler, then the Buick and then, after a few years of mostly sleeping while the '72 Beetle handled the commute duties, he was gone, too. It was early in 1979 and when Leroy returned home from work, he was driving an ugly little Italian car with a garish yellow paint job and a whiny transmission. He seemed to be brand new and I had to wonder to myself why any human in his right mind would buy such a funny looking thing. Leroy parked him next to me in the '72's slot and when I asked him where he was from he said he didn't know what I meant. All he could tell me was that he was a Fiat, and that Leroy had bought him off a lot that afternoon and had driven him to where we were now parked. In contrast to his paint job, he didn't seem very bright.

The next night the Fiat told me he had met the '72, who had been sold. He passed along the Beetle's regards, which I appreciated, and after that, things began to warm up a little between us, or at least as warm as a German and an Italian can get. I had to confess that I had made a hasty judgment about his intelligence because after he calmed down and adapted to life with Leroy and me he seemed OK. He was a hard worker and never complained about his harrowing commute duties. I was left to continue enjoying my solitude during the week and getting out on the weekends with Leroy and whoever was visiting him, usually a woman. Many of them made disparaging remarks about my appearance and a few told him they thought I was cute. I liked them best. I consider myself more handsome than cute, but certainly not ugly or odd looking as some of them had judged. I think Leroy was using me to screen his lady friends because the ones who didn't care for me tended not to be invited back.

But I digress. Again. In short, Leroy, the Fiat and I all grew comfortable with our three-way relationship and our respective roles. This continued for a little more than three years. I say we were comfortable, but that doesn't necessarily mean friendly. Leroy never seemed to truly bond with the Fiat or give him the respect he so desperately wanted. I had overheard Leroy telling his friends about the Fiat's idiosyncrasies that I must confess would never be found in a German car — his boxy lines, his attention-grabbing paint, his high pitched whine that you could hear from a block away, and the tinny clank he made when his doors closed. He laughingly referred to the Fiat as his "divorce special", but I didn't get the joke.

On an evening in early '82, I celebrated my 20th birthday with a quiet, self-congratulatory flashing of my lights and a discreet humming of "Das Deutschlandlied" ("The Song of Germany"), West Germany's national anthem. Leroy had yet another visitor who was driving a gorgeous Mercedes 450SL that was parked within hearing distance. I must have been humming louder than I thought because I heard him join me in perfect harmony. It was a moving moment. I explained the occasion and he congratulated me on reaching such a ripe old age. I found that thoughtful and generous coming from a car that was so much more expensive, sleek and powerful than I ever hoped to be. I introduced him to the Fiat, and while he was civil, he was not especially warm toward him. We spent the rest of the evening chatting, comparing notes on our backgrounds and talking about cars in general. I avoided making the obvious comparisons between German and Italian cars, but I needn't have worried — the Mercedes seemed to understand common courtesy. It was truly refreshing to me to carry on a conversation with the Mercedes without being made self-conscious about my seasoned appearance. I hoped he would return for a future visit and as it turned out, he did — again and again.

The Mercedes' owner was a nice lady name Liz. She accepted me for what I am and was neither derogatory nor condescending. I guess that helped her pass Leroy's test because she soon became the only lady to visit. Leroy even let her drive me, which came as a shock to me and was an event that gave me considerable anxiety. I have a very sensitive transmission, a moody starter motor, and acceleration issues. Also, most people don't understand that because we are air-cooled, VWs like to be revved up quite a bit before being shifted to a higher gear. When Liz got behind my wheel for the first time I was plenty skittish, but I did my best to start right away. She depressed my clutch, moved my gearshift into reverse, backed me out, and effortlessly put me into low. I belched a grateful sigh of relief. I knew immediately that she was an experienced Bug driver and a good one. Even Leroy, who I could feel twitching in the passenger seat, told her he was impressed.

Once again, I seem to have lost my train of thought. I was talking about the Fiat. I'll try to stay focused as I continue. The Mercedes spent a lot of time with us and after a short while, when Liz moved to Leroy's condo, he was with us full-time. We were one big, mostly happy family except for the fact that both Leroy and the Mercedes were not entirely accepting of the Fiat, for pretty much the same reasons. In early June the problem resolved itself. One morning Leroy drove off in the Fiat, followed by Liz in the Mercedes. When they returned in the late afternoon both of them were in the Mercedes and the Fiat was nowhere to be seen. The Mercedes told me they had driven to Chico and that the Fiat had remained there with somebody named Annie. I had met Annie several times and knew that she was now licensed to drive so I figured Leroy had given the Fiat to her. I thought that was a nice thing to do. I also was hopeful that the Fiat, who always tried so hard to please, would be more accepted in his new environment. He really wasn't a bad guy once you got to know him. Ugly without a doubt, but we can't all be Volkswagens.

Over the summer, the Mercedes performed the commute duties and I assumed weekend beach duties. I think both of us were fine with that arrangement. I didn't have the strain of that daily grind to work, and the Mercedes got to rest up on the weekends. We both were doing what we did best.

This all changed as fall approached. One day a huge, behemoth of a van pulled up and disgorged a couple of bad looking characters who knocked on Leroy's door. I was about to honk my horn in alarm when he invited them inside. Then I overheard the Mercedes talking with the truck and learned that Leroy and Liz were moving to another house. This might have made other cars nervous but I had been with Leroy long enough to know he would look after me. The Mercedes was a little edgy, which surprised me because he had lived in three cities by this time. I advised him to relax; that everything would work out. Later that afternoon, after the truck had departed Liz got behind the wheel of the Mercedes and Leroy behind mine, and we left Santa Cruz behind us.

We ended up in a place called Palo Alto in a parking lot filled with other cars. One in particular had a big grill and was quick to make disparaging remarks about my appearance and flaunt his superiority. I'd heard all these insults before so I shot back with a pointed comment about the bigger the grill, the dumber the talk, and he got the message to calm down. The following morning we were driven to a house in a nice neighborhood that felt a little uptight to me. Most of the other cars I saw were late model, expensive and clean and they acted as if it was their own doing that landed them among each other. I heard the usual ill-mannered comments and I just let them roll off my engine cover. A couple of well-placed glares let them know that I was not going to let them get under my paint. I could tell that they wanted nothing to do with me and when they did speak in our direction it was to the Mercedes, not to me.

This town sure was a contrast to the easy-going culture of Santa Cruz. I'd never seen so many snooty cars in one place and I had to wonder about their value systems. I was confident that none of them knew what synchromesh was, not to mention a carburetor or a wind wing. I was relieved when Leroy moved me into the garage within a couple of days. I was left in peace, out of mirror shot of my gossipy, shallow neighbors.

It was good to be parked out of the elements. I was not in very good shape. My engine was all right for as old as it was, but my body was just a mess. The abuse, age and salty beach air had taken its toll and I felt that had I stayed outside much longer I would have soon dissolved into a rusty puddle on the street. My top had continued to deteriorate and my paint was barely recognizable as the attractive cornflower blue it once was. My fenders, doors and hubcaps were all dented and my bumpers were bent and scratched, sagging as gravity took its inevitable toll. I didn't know what my future had in store, but I had already lived well beyond the life expectancy of most cars and I had no regrets. So I settled into the cool, dark comfort of the garage and waited patiently.

Leroy did not drive me much at all over the next couple of years — at least I think it was that long. I was sleeping a lot and I lost track of time. He started me every week to keep my seals from leaking and my battery charged, and on rare occasions he would take me for short drives. Those were not enjoyable excursions, not only because of the smirks and snorts of the local cars, but more so because my springs, gears, shocks and joints had all stiffened with disuse. Also, since I was isolated most of the time I didn't get to talk much with the Mercedes to hear how he was doing now that he was getting quite a few miles logged onto his odometer. On the few occasions when the garage door was open and we were able to talk, I could tell that he was growing anxious about being traded in.

We didn't even get to say goodbye. On a Saturday morning in the fall of 1986, from the dark interior of the garage I heard the Mercedes being started up and driven away. A few hours later I heard a car pull into the driveway and I could tell from the sound that it was not the Mercedes. Leroy and Liz did not open the garage door so I did not know who was parked in the driveway. In the evening it began to rain and soon it was pouring, and I was glad to be in the garage. I figured I'd get the story soon enough about what had become of the Mercedes.

The next morning Leroy opened the garage to reveal a new BMW convertible parked in the driveway. It was sitting in the Mercedes' spot, covered with water spots. He first stared at me, wide-head-lighted, then the look turned to disgust and then I was completely ignored. It was not difficult to understand that, like the rest of the cars in this status-conscious neighborhood, the BMW found me repulsive without even so much as a token effort to get to know me. So be it. In my long life I had seen cars come and go and it wasn't as if I needed him as my new best friend. It was his loss. Just to yank his timing chain a little, I asked him what the hell he was staring at. He went into a diatribe about the proud history of German auto making and how I was a disgrace to the legacy of all those talented engineers and craftsmen who had worked so hard to earn their sterling reputation. He went on and on, ultimately inviting me to check out his fine lines and flawless construction. I don't think it helped much that I dozed in the middle of his lecture but I figured that was about the most effective feedback I could give him.

Our relationship did not improve. Fortunately, we were usually separated by the garage door. I will confess that I enjoyed knowing the BMW was rankled that I occupied the garage while he was rele-gated to the unsheltered driveway. I had to chuckle when the garage door was open and both of us were in sight of the other cars in the neighborhood. They teased him unmercifully about his taste in ugly roommates. I had come to learn that the fancier the car, the ruder they are. It's as if they actually had something to do with their design and manufacture when we all know that we are the product of ac-tivities well beyond our control. Under normal circumstances I would have come to the defense of the other car in the family, but that BMW was no better than the cars who were verbally harassing him and I felt no compulsion to interfere.

It is my observation that most cars get along, even if they might not feel much mutual respect for each other. We all have our drawbacks but we all have our strengths as well. How else could it be explained that there are so many different makes, models, colors and price ranges? That's not to say that it's a big love fest out there on the roads. But most of us realize that if we don't make an effort to live peacefully with each other it would be a miserable existence at best and pandemonium at worst if we all expressed our feelings by wantonly ramming into each other. Besides, if I did that I would come out the loser. Survivor VWs are more philosophical than physically confrontational.

Over the course of the next year the BMW continued to ignore me as I returned the favor, puffing out my engine cover just a little in exaggerated relaxation whenever the garage door was open and he could see me luxuriating in there, but otherwise paying him no heed. Yes, I was needling him but he certainly deserved it.

————————————

There was a dramatic change in store for me beginning in late spring, 1988. Leroy opened the garage door, got behind my wheel and started my engine like he had done so many times before, but this time he backed me out onto the street. I noticed Liz in the BMW, preparing to follow us. Leroy drove me to a garage and left me there. Naturally, I had no idea what was up, but I figured if it was a garage and not a junkyard that was a positive omen. And it was. Over the course of the next few weeks I underwent a complete restoration. I won't say it was all pleasant, with all that pounding, unbolting and rebolting, sanding, spraying and adjusting. But when it was over I looked very much like the new car I had been some 26 years ago. There wasn't a dent in me, I had new bumpers, my upholstery had been replaced, I had a shiny new paint job and best of all, I was sporting a brand new convertible top. I am not a vain car, but when Leroy took me home I came as close to strutting as a car can. I looked nothing short of fantastic.

I was surprised to see the BMW parked in my spot in the garage. It just didn't seem right to me. It was my space, and now that I was all fancied up, I couldn't imagine Leroy leaving me to the elements. The BMW flashed a condescending look and, I believe, was about to make some sarcastic remark when Liz got in and backed him out. Leroy then parked me in my usual spot and I had to snicker when I saw that resentful look on the ultimate driving machine's grill. Leroy and Liz spent the afternoon rearranging things in the garage, creating enough space to move the BMW in beside me. I wasn't too happy about sharing my space with him but I took solace in the knowledge that he hated it a lot more than I did.

I asked the BMW if he wanted to make peace or continue being a jerk. He denied being a jerk, naturally. It didn't matter to me one way or the other whether he viewed himself as a jerk. It was my perception and that was good enough for me. I figured that if we were going to live side-by-side we might as well make an effort to be civil but if he wanted to continue with the silent treatment, fine. The remainder of the night was spent in an uneasy silence. The next morning the BMW apologized for his behavior the previous evening, and said he hadn't been feeling well because he needed a tune-up. I accepted that modest effort at face value, not pointing out the obvious — that he must have needed that tune-up for a very long time if it explained his attitude. I let it pass, figuring that if he wanted to make peace I would not be the one responsible for our failure to achieve it.

From then on, we were civil to each other, if not friendly. I think we both realized we never would be confidantes, sharing intimate secrets about spark plug gapping, oil circulation issues or the condition of our valve guides. But at least we were talking now. Despite the slight thaw, my opinion of the BMW remained unchanged — he was still a jerk. I don't think he changed his opinion of me, either, but that was fine because I had learned long ago that the important thing is what I think of myself, not what some other car thinks of me.

Especially if it's a jerk.

———————————

The other dramatic change in my life that spring came about in early June when Leroy drove me to Chico with Liz following in the BMW. We stopped at a house and Johnny, whom I had not seen for couple of years, came out to meet us. I'd known him all his life and had watched him grow from a noisy, wet baby into a tall young man who was having trouble growing into his outsized feet. He and Leroy took me for a short drive with Johnny behind my wheel. I had not been driven by anybody other than Leroy for many years so I was nervous at the outset, but although Johnny had his own distinct touch, I could tell that he had potential to be a good driver like Leroy. He had a good sense of when it was time to shift and he did it smoothly, and like Leroy, he was able to negotiate his big feet around my small pedals. We parked at a restaurant and Liz pulled up beside me in the BMW. The three of them went inside, leaving us to bide our time in the parking lot.

When they emerged, Leroy handed Johnny an envelope and my keys. They all said goodbye and Leroy gave my hood a friendly pat before climbing into the BMW with Liz. Johnny drove me to his house for a brief stop, long enough to run inside and bring out a woman with him and excitedly tell her that his dad had given me to him. This was the first I'd heard of it, but now the whole day was beginning to make more sense. I already missed Leroy. The goodbye seemed so abrupt. We had enjoyed such a long relationship together and suddenly it was over. I consoled myself knowing that at least I still had a connection to him through Johnny, and that whenever I found myself missing Leroy I could always pretend Johnny's big feet were his.

Chapter 11

ELEGANT BUT DOOMED

It was the second Saturday of my stay in a used car lot and a man took me out for a test drive. He seemed to know what he was doing as he checked my acceleration, steering, shifting and braking. Cars can immediately sense whether a driver will be easy or difficult to adapt to, and I found myself very comfortable with this driver. He parked me back in the lot and as he walked away I was disappointed, thinking that this might have been a good new beginning for me. When he returned an hour later with the salesman who had been working on finding new owners for all of us, they shook hands and once again he settled behind my wheel and started my engine. I figured I had just been purchased. He drove me away and soon we were parked in front of a small home in a nice neighborhood. I was facing an ugly, odd-looking Volkswagen, which gave me serious second thoughts. I had met many cars in my travels but never had I been parked so close to such a homely, beat up thing as that. I couldn't drive away under my own power, so I held my grill and resigned myself to being there for the moment.

Although he was nothing to look at, I will give the VW credit for attempting to make me comfortable. It was a fruitless effort that first day, but at least he tried. He introduced himself and told me I had replaced an AMC Rambler (not a particularly insurmountable challenge for a Buick), and my new owner's name was Leroy. He added that Leroy also was his owner, and as car owners go, he was a good one — respectful, attentive and a competent driver. I extended minimum courtesy to the VW, as I would to those cars owned by the visitors to my original owner's motel rooms. That is to say, I nodded absently every now and then, and offered an occasional monosyllabic grunt of acknowledgement. This did not discourage him from going on about Leroy and his family and the neighborhood. I had been through a confusing couple of weeks and all I wanted was a little stability and some rest, not incessant conversation with a ridiculous looking Bug. As the day waned and my resistance softened, I did share a few tidbits of my life on the road, hoping that by answering a few of his questions I could satisfy his curiosity enough to quiet him down. The strategy worked, and we both dropped off to sleep as the moon was shining brightly upon us and the cacophonous crickets were serenading at full volume.

I slept well and woke up when the morning sun was shining into my headlights. I regained my focus and noted with irritation that the VW was staring at me. I wondered how long he had been doing that, but I did not deign to ask. However, I did find it unsettling and personally intrusive. He wished me a cheery good morning and once again I responded with a muted grunt, doing my best to ignore him, which was difficult because we were facing each other, about two feet apart. I was grateful when I heard Leroy and a woman approaching. The VW told me her name was Diana, and that she lived with Leroy, along with two children, Annie and Johnny. I was soon introduced to both of these hyperactive little tornados as they rushed out of the house toward me, opened the door and climbed in. The smaller one, who was the one they called Johnny, was out of control as he fiddled with all of my knobs and buttons and climbed all over my seats to the cargo compartment and back again. Annie was a little older and seemed to be more reserved.

Leroy and Diana got in as well, and soon we were driving down the quiet street. Other cars looked as we passed, obviously with envy, as I clearly was the most handsome, stately car on the block. Diana did not appear to be overjoyed to welcome me to the family. She told Leroy they could not afford me and the money could be put to better use for other things, like groceries and bills. Leroy tried to explain to her that the Rambler was in bad shape and would need lots of money for repairs, and that he had negotiated a good deal for me. Diana only expanded her complaints to include Leroy's many other inadequacies. I had just come from a home with a sour relationship and I had a premonition that I was about to become part of another one.

We drove aimlessly for a while until Leroy parked and exchanged places with Diana after encouraging her to give me a try. As she put me into gear I could feel that she was not as comfortable with me as Leroy was, but she was careful. By the time we returned home (it struck me as odd that I already was referring to this new place as "home" but it had become quickly evident that it was). Diana parked me in the driveway and although we were within talking range I was relieved not to have to stare at and be stared at by the VW. She did say that I drove a lot better than the Rambler (of course I did!) but I was way too expensive for their budget. Leroy ended the conversation by telling her he had made the best judgment call he could and didn't want to talk about it anymore. They took the children into the house and I was left to myself for the remainder of the day.

The VW was within hearing distance so I asked him if Leroy and Diana had some ongoing disagreements or if today's argument was an exception. He said he had detected some tension and Leroy seemed to be able to do nothing to please Diana. He felt that both of them were trying to make their relationship work, but that it was continuing to deteriorate. I had to give that ugly little thing some credit for his insightful analysis and I began to develop a modest respect for him. I asked him if he thought we could do anything to patch things up. He replied that the best we could do was to be as reliable and unproblematic as possible and avoid adding to their stress, but it was not within our capabilities to fix whatever was bothering them. I had to admit he made sense and I determined to be as trouble free as possible. To be honest, I felt I had a better chance at that than he did.

Some cars are justifiably humble because they are ugly, poorly built, old or cheap. I am none of those, nor am I the least bit humble. On the contrary, I am a proud, dare I say stately automobile. I am a 1971 Buick Estate Wagon. When I glide quietly over the streets, other lesser cars stare at me with respect and frequently envy in their headlights. I have an exceptionally quiet and smooth V8 engine with a precision four speed automatic transmission. Because my original driver leased me rather than buying me outright, I don't know for sure what my MSRP was, but I'm quite sure it was in excess of $4000.

The year I was born, Richard Nixon was President of the United States and was not very loved. I personally believe this was because he was misunderstood and under-appreciated. He had inherited a nasty, unpopular war in Vietnam and he was the object of the anti-war protesters. About the only good thing that happened in 1971, aside from my debut was the end of cigarette advertising on television. I never smoked, or to be more precise, I never inhaled but I do find the things to be stinky.

My original "owner" was Lewis. Our arrangement was actually a lease, not a purchase. It did not matter one way or the other to me, though, as we cars prefer to let humans quibble about terminology. Lewis was a pharmaceutical salesman. I do not know what a pharmaceutical is. My understanding is that it is a small pill of some sort that humans ingest after asking their doctor if it is right for them. Personally, I never took any pills nor do I approve of them. If something is ailing a car he either goes to a mechanic to get it fixed or he doesn't. If he does, he continues to do his job. If he doesn't he gets progressively worse and soon ends up in a sleazy used car lot, a junkyard or resting on blocks on an unkempt lot. But pills to address our depression, regulate our oil flow, make our tires firm or stop our exhaust from smoking are superfluous and for the weak. I suppose I could understand a Kaiser or a Studebaker taking a pill, but certainly not a Buick.

After spending a few days with him, I learned Lewis' job was to drive from town to town, calling on doctors and trying to convince them they needed to prescribe his pills to people. He also called on drug stores to make sure they were supplied with the pharmaceuticals he had convinced the doctors to prescribe. The whole thing seemed rather pointless to me, but my job was simply to get Lewis to where he wanted to be. He lived in San Jose, which was where he leased me. But he did not spend much time there. He was required to drive as far south as Bakersfield and as far north as Yreka, a distance of 480 miles. Of course, we did not do that every day, as he had to make many stops. On average, we traveled about 175 miles each day, Monday through Friday. Lewis was a good driver but he frequently set my cruise control higher than I felt appropriate or prudent when we were on the Interstate, at 80 MPH or if no police were in sight, at 90.

Lewis returned home to San Jose at the end of most weeks, but sometimes he was so far away that it made more sense to spend the weekend in a motel. When he did, he would often drive me to a restaurant and many times a lady would accompany him on the way back to his motel or she would follow him in her own car. I didn't get much rest on those occasions, as he would end up either driving the lady back to her car in the early morning hours, or I would have to spend endless hours listening to the banal chatter of other ladies' trashy cars until they went away. I didn't mind whiling away time in a motel parking lot, although on balance I preferred my more comfortable garage in San Jose, away from the endless questions about where I am from, where I was going next, where have I visited, in addition to what I consider inappropriately personal questions such as how much do I weigh, what is my MPG, how many miles do I have on my odometer and how much did Lewis pay for me. I have little patience for boorish cars. I developed the skill of pretending to listen while drifting off into my own, more profound, thoughts. The trick was to keep my headlights open and utter an occasional "uh huh" or "I see". Most of the cars I was stuck with were too dense to figure out that I was not engaged at all.

When we spent our weekends in San Jose, Lewis behaved differently. He did not talk much, nor did he seem to be interested in driving me just for the pleasure of the experience. Most of the time he stayed in his house. There was a lady living there as well, who I heard Lewis refer to as Irene. He also called her his wife. Irene never seemed very happy to have us home, nor did Lewis. She would frequently raise her voice and accuse him of something called hanky panky and he would raise his voice back at her, accusing her of not appreciating how hard he works and that it was not his fault if he could not make it home every day. I did not care one way or another. Mostly I was just grateful that I could get a little sleep and recharge my battery in my cool and dark garage. If Lewis and Irene chose to yell at each other that was none of my business. My job is to transport my driver in elegant style and comfort, period.

––––––––––––––

Lewis seemed to be much happier when we were on the road and to be honest, so was I. If there is one thing we cars have in common, no matter what our make or model, it is the unbridled joy we feel as we are driven along a scenic highway at cruising speed. Some, like convertibles and so-called sports cars, probably enjoy it the most. But while I am large, stately and imposing, my size does not detract from my own personal connection with the open road. Traveling is what we are designed to do and traveling is what we do best. To clarify my "so-called" reference to sports cars, I will say I am puzzled by that classification. From what I have seen of them, they are universally noisy and small — frequently seating only two people — and with such tight suspension it is impossible to provide a comfortable ride, which to me is of paramount importance. And to boot, I have never witnessed a single sporting event in one.

My best days with Lewis were the ones when we covered the most miles. A 400-mile straight shot at cruising speed was refreshing and much preferable to those days spent driving around a single town, making countless stops and never exceeding 30 MPH. On our long treks we would zoom along the Interstate, my cruise control set at 80 with frequent accelerations to 90, passing trucks and slower cars, enjoying the sights and smells of the open road. At gas stations I was treated to an oil check and a windshield wash in addition to my fill-up, and was able to meet and compare notes with other interesting cars. I found myself drawn to those most like me, like other large station wagons and Cadillac and Lincoln sedans. I'm quite sure the lesser cars were more comfortable talking among themselves as well, so it wasn't a matter of discrimination by any means. On one memorable occasion I spoke briefly with an actual Bentley. His British accent was difficult to understand, but I found him to be an intelligent, dignified vehicle and unquestionably worthy of my attention. I sensed he had the same reaction to me, despite my being a native of "the Colonies", as he put it.

I enjoyed our summer trips more than the winter trips. In spite of the midsummer heat in the valley, my engine and cooling system worked beautifully. It may have been 110 outside, but my interior remained a comfortable 72. My only problem was the huge numbers of bugs losing their short lives against my headlights and windshield, making it difficult to see. But that was a minor irritant and easily addressed at any filling station.

Winters were more of a challenge. This is not to say that I was not physically up to winter driving, but there were no aromas in the air, the scenery was more stark and depending on our elevation it was often pouring down rain or snow. There were a few days when the roads were covered with snow or ice, and although Lewis had a set of chains for my tires, he did all he could to avoid installing them. That was fine with me. Normally when the roads were approaching the condition that would justify the use of chains, Lewis would find a motel and we would stop there until the weather was more amenable. That was also fine with me. The two times in my life that I had to drive with chains were very unpleasant experiences. With all their clanking, a smooth ride was impossible, my superior suspension notwithstanding. I also drove in constant fear that a chain link would snap and mar my quarter panel although, thankfully, it never occurred.

I always hoped that when we returned home to San Jose, Lewis and Irene would get along but they never did. In fact, each visit — and that was what our stops there were becoming — was more tense than the previous one. Irene would loudly accuse Lewis of hanky panky (to this day I do not know exactly what hanky panky is, but I gather it is not something women like), and Lewis would loudly deny it. Loud arguments would become shouting matches, and ultimately, screaming rants. More than once toward the end of my first year with Lewis I found us driving to a motel in San Jose where he spent the night. It was not a happy time and for that and many other reasons, I was thankful I was a car. We don't get married and we don't know anything about hanky panky. I think we're better off for it.

On Monday morning when we were back on the road, we both felt better. Lewis tuned my FM radio (with custom surround-sound speakers) to country music stations. I would have preferred classical music, but Lewis was in a mood for music about cheatin', drinkin', gettin' a raw deal from a hard-nosed woman, foolin' around and gettin' even. I don't know if classical music has words and if it does, whether the "g" at the end of sentences is dropped like it is in country music. I'm sure that Bentley I met at the service station would know.

Lewis did a lot of talking to himself on that trip, which took us down through the Central Valley and up along the coast. It was clear he was struggling and that something was about to change in our lives. It did, for when we returned to San Jose on Friday, there was a large pile of clothing in the front yard of Lewis' house, along with a bowling ball, a set of golf clubs, books, tools and record albums. Irene was not at home. I knew something was amiss and was tensing up when Lewis let out a loud burst of laughter. "My problem just got solved!" he shouted to nobody in particular. He opened my clamshell tailgate and began stuffing the pile into my cargo compartment. He got most of it in and then strapped the remaining items to my roof rack. Within an hour were we parked at yet another motel.

The next morning we stopped at several apartment complexes. After waiting for him at the fourth one, Lewis came out, parked me in a different spot, and unloaded his possessions. He then drove me back to his and Irene's house. I had a feeling this would not have a positive outcome but I was wrong. Lewis was uncharacteristically cheerful. He went in and returned a short while later with a few more of his things. As we drove away he seemed greatly relieved.

From that day on, Lewis was a changed man. We traveled the same familiar roads but something was different; something I did not feel was altogether positive. We began our workdays later than before, and ended earlier. We spent an increasing number of hours at bars and I could tell that he was not in control of me as we returned to his apartment, or to our motel when we were out of town. He had an unpleasant odor about him when he was in that condition. He also had a lot of lady acquaintances, few of whom I found to my liking because they used incorrect English and smelled of cheap perfume. Irene certainly lacked in many social graces, but compared to these women she was very classy.

I had overheard Lewis laughingly tell one of these ladies that he thought he was going through his midlife crisis. I did not know what he meant but I did know that whatever it was that he was going through, I hoped he would get to the end soon.

Over the next two months Lewis spent more time with various women and less time in his pharmaceutical business. After a full week had passed in which we had not made a single business call, Lewis drove me to an office building in San Jose, parked me and went inside. When he returned a short while later he was accompanied by another man. Lewis had an empty box with him, which he filled with personal items from my passenger compartment, including his collection of eight-track cassettes, an address book, some miscellaneous articles of clothing and a half bottle of something called vodka. The other man watched him carefully and instructed him not to take any company property.

When he finished, Lewis handed my keys to the other man and got into a taxi that had driven up. The taxi asked me what was up with the dude with the box. I did not deign to reply to that lowly classless rattletrap, nor did I know the answer. The taxi sneered at me as his driver eased out of the parking lot with Lewis in the back seat. I did not realize at the time that I had seen Lewis for the last time.

I remained in the parking lot for three days, wondering what had become of Lewis and more important, what would become of me. I had served him faithfully and well, believing that my loyalty would eventually be rewarded so I was not overly concerned and decided to patiently await whatever was ahead.

On the morning of the fourth day a man I'd never met unlocked me, got in and started my engine. He drove me directly to the Buick dealer where I had been leased a year earlier. After a tune-up and a thorough cleaning I was parked in a lot with several other cars. Fortuitously, I was next to another late model Buick so I could engage in an intelligent conversation to find out what was happening to me. He explained that we were in a "pre-owned" lot and that we were for sale.

My head gasket spun at this news. I had met a few used cars in my travels but I had never dreamed I might become one. I had regarded such cars as second class and it was degrading to sit there, day after day, being examined and critiqued by perfect strangers, and for reasons that escaped me entirely, having my tires kicked. I did not know what to expect if somebody new purchased me, as my only experience was with Lewis. Would a new owner be a pharmaceutical salesman? Would he do hanky panky? Would he leave me in a parking lot while he visited bars?

I knew from the first time he settled in behind my wheel that Leroy and I would get along fine. I was greatly relieved when he purchased me. I was beset with unknowns, but I had a sense that things would take a turn for the better, which they did, at least for a while.

───────────────

My new life had some advantages, although I wasn't driven nearly as much and I did miss those heady days with Lewis on the open road. During the week Leroy drove the VW to work so I was used infrequently by Diana for short errands. I quickly adapted to spending most of my days in the garage or the driveway. On weekends Leroy would take me for a spin, either with or without the family, but we never ventured far from home.

I also got better acquainted with the VW. He was disarming and I began to develop a begrudging respect, dare I say fondness for him. We teased each other about our appearance: I accused him of being a random collection of badly fitting recycled beer cans that had been glued together with no plan, with the engine and trunk reversed. He gave it right back to me, pointing out that I was a fat old lady with an imposing clam shell cargo lid that nobody could see around, and with useless fake portholes on my hood, probably to let the excess gas out. Buicks are not known for having a sense of humor but I must confess that I enjoyed the lively repartee with that feisty little Bug.

Regrettably, Leroy and Diana were not getting along as well as the VW and I were. As the months wore on, we could sense increasing tension. Diana's criticisms were more frequent and strident and Leroy's response was more silent. Diana would berate him constantly for not earning as much money as their friends, or not paying enough attention to the children, or not being financially responsible, or not properly taking care of the yard, or simply not communicating. Leroy attempted to tell his side of the story, but when he did, Diana would tell him he was wrong. As a result, they spent as little time together as necessary. I was relieved not to hear their arguments when Leroy was at work. On the weekends, he often escaped by taking either the VW or me for a drive, but they were not happy ventures. We would either wander the area aimlessly or stop at friends' houses where he could relax in a less stressful environment.

I believe that for a car I am unusually insightful, partly because of my experience with Lewis and Irene, but fundamentally because Buicks are uniquely intelligent and sensitive. I felt that Leroy wanted peace in his family more than anything, and he was hugely frustrated at his inability to bring it about. He was doing his very best to make his marriage work and to be a good father, but nothing seemed to work. He was on the verge of giving up. Diana lived in a constant state of anxiety about money and status and was never satisfied. She was afraid that Leroy would leave but that didn't deter her relentless criticism. I had a sense of foreboding that unless there was a dramatic breakthrough they would soon go their separate ways. And so they did.

As summer was approaching in 1973, Leroy came out of the house late at night, carrying a suitcase. He tossed it into the back seat of the VW and they drove away. I did not see him for several days. When he returned, he and Diana had a tense discussion in the back yard that I could not help but hear. They finally agreed on something — that they would divorce. Diana told him that she and the children could not survive if they split things down the middle. All Leroy wanted was to escape, so he told her she could have most of their possessions, most of the proceeds from the sale of the house, and me. I wasn't sure how I felt about that. I had my own anxiety at that point, not knowing where I would be living and coming to terms with not having Leroy drive and maintain me anymore. That evening I told the VW what was going on. Like me, he was not happy but he explained that he was a German, whatever that was, and that Volkswagens do what they have to do. I knew neither of us had a choice about our future, but he clearly was more adaptable than I am.

That weekend, Leroy borrowed a pickup and with a friend, moved his belongings out of their house. He returned and drove away in the VW. We called out goodbye to each other as they left, promising to keep in touch to the extent we could.

I did see Leroy and the VW from time to time, but not very often. And it was even less when Diana sold the house and we all relocated to Chico, which was evidently where she had spent her youth. I had been to Chico with Lewis. It is a friendly, mid-sized university town that in other situations I might have enjoyed settling in, but the lives of Diana, Annie and Johnny were in upheaval and nobody was doing much smiling. All I could do is be a safe, reliable car for them and hope that happiness might return after their wounds began to heal.

Leroy kept in touch with the children and came to Chico every few weeks to take them home with him. The VW and I would visit, but Leroy never stayed longer than it took to gather up Annie and Johnny. As time passed we lost touch. I began to age and as a result of poor maintenance, I was not performing as well as I wanted to. Diana traded me in for a smaller, more economical car in 1975. My life went downhill after that but I am sustained by a few good memories among the unpleasant ones. I believe I deserved a better life, though.

Chapter 12

LIFE IN THE SLOW LANE

My new owner, Leroy, drove me over a mountain road to what would become my new home near Santa Cruz. This kind of highway was a new experience for a sheltered car like me but I found the challenge of the hills and curves to be a fun contrast to my normal staid life. I could tell Leroy had some experience with us Bugs because he knew just when to shift and he did it smoothly. When we stopped, Leroy parked me facing another car, which to my pleasant surprise was also a VW, only older and, well, not that attractive. He was a convertible whose top sported some interesting patches. It was obvious he was quite senior to me, so I respectfully addressed him as "Sir", but he didn't seem to like it. I could tell he was tough and not likely to put up with any nonsense so I abided by his wishes and decided I would just listen, not talk. He asked me if Leroy had bought me and I confirmed he had. He asked if I was going to replace him, and I told him I didn't know because I didn't. That was a little uncomfortable, but I sensed he could handle the truth, and that he would see right through any phony reassurances from me. He said he had been through tough times before, and he was prepared to take whatever was tossed his way. He did reassure me that Leroy was a good owner and a skillful driver, and I had just gotten a lucky break. Based on my first trip with Leroy, I had to agree.

———————

I was born in Mexico but I'm really a German. My concept, design, engineering and parts were all made in Germany, and assembled in a town called Puebla in southeastern Mexico. The year I rolled off the assembly line, 1972, was the beginning of President Nixon's downfall when five White House (or as we called it there, La Casa Blanca — I'm bilingual) operatives were caught breaking into the Democratic National Headquarters in Washington, D.C. This was the beginning of the famous Watergate scandal and it was not a great year for America, with the exception of the return of the last U.S. troops from Vietnam after a long, fruitless war. Personally, I think the most significant event of 1972 was the production of the 15 millionth Volkswagen, which surpassed the Ford Model T and made us the most popular car ever sold. But maybe that's just me.

I look pretty much the same as all the VWs ahead of me, with my plucky, classic lines. There have been improvements over the years, setting us modern Beetles apart from our forebears. For example, we now have an external gas cap so our drivers don't have to raise our hood anymore to fill us up. We also have large windows and the windshield actually curves for better visibility. Our suspension is much more sophisticated, and I boast 54 horsepower — 35% more than the old 40 HP engines of the '60s and an impressive 50% more than the 36 HP of our '50s ancestors. I am proud of my engineering and construction, but I never forget the contribution of my relatives. We Volkswagens stick together.

My first owner was a lady named Doris, an elementary school teacher in San Jose, California. Doris was not an attractive woman but she was refined and she treated me well. She lived alone in a small house and used me primarily for going back and forth to school. Now that I have a broader perspective on life, I realize that my days with Doris were pretty uneventful. Every school day she opened her garage door at 7:45 a.m. and awakened me. She would back me out and struggle with getting me into first gear. Sadly for me, Doris tried, but she never mastered the art of the stick shift. We would lurch and grind along until she was able to maneuver me into third gear. She didn't realize that we Beetles like to have our engines at high RPMs and she always shifted too soon. That would lug me down and I would have to reduce my speed enough to get her to downshift, making for a herky-jerky ride. Once we made it to school I'd be left in the parking lot with the other teachers' cars until 4:00 o'clock, when we returned home.

Aside from that daily commute, my use was limited to errands and a few social activities, normally at a nearby Methodist church. Doris neither smoked cigarettes nor drank alcoholic beverages, and my radio was always tuned to a classical music station. She introduced me to culture and I learned to distinguish between the great composers. My favorite was Mozart because his creations were so complex and lively. I liked Beethoven a lot too, but I didn't care at all for Wagner or Salieri, as I found their works uninteresting and depressing.

The one road trip Doris took me on was to a college reunion in a place called Chico, about three hours away. It was obvious she was uncomfortable away from her routine, with cars passing us, honking loudly if she was not in the slow lane, which she normally was not. She drove in the center lane if there were three, or the left if there were just two. She seemed oblivious to the flashing lights and blaring horns of impatient drivers behind her, as well as the occasional hand gesture which I took to be disapproval when they passed us on the right. Many of those cars sneered at me derisively, but I offered a shrug or ignored them, as my speed was not under my control.

We arrived in Chico late Friday afternoon. Doris parked me in a lot filled with the cars of the other reunion attendees, students and local residents. As other cars came and went, I chatted with any of them who seemed interested in conversation. I learned quite a bit about the town and what it was like to live there, and I found it easy to envision myself being there on a full time basis.

One car in particular struck a chord — it was a vintage Volkswagen. He was much older than I am and it was exciting to see a VW that old still in service. I made it a point to introduce myself. He had a thick German accent I found hard to understand, despite our shared heritage. I was able to discern that he had lived in Chico for many years, and that he had been fully restored. He said he may be old, but he was in better shape than many cars ten years younger than he is. When I asked him when he was built he said something like "Look at der semaphores und you vill know der answer." I didn't know what a semaphore was, so I had to ask. He sighed and rolled his headlights as two lights suddenly flipped out of his doorposts! I'd never seen anything like that. He explained that they were directional signals, but that they didn't work very well on the freeway because of the wind, so his was the last year they were used. That was 1955. I must say I was impressed with that classic. He could have been my great grandfather if cars had such things. As he relaxed he told me some stories from his past, some of which were a bit fuzzy. He had been owned by several drivers, many of whom were young and not particularly easy on him until his current owner bought him two years prior and gave him a complete makeover. He groused that it was his experience that most young people today couldn't properly drive a stick shift with the exception of one guy with huge feet about fifteen years ago, who had traded him for a vain and unreliable MG TD.

That was the extent of my one road trip with Doris. I'm not complaining, but I will admit to being envious when I talk to other cars who have enjoyed more adventures. I found them as fascinating as they probably found me boring. On the bright side, Doris did not put a single dent in me, she kept me in the garage at night and she didn't log many miles on my odometer.

At the conclusion of the school term in the spring of 1976, Doris filled me with several boxes and a balloon with "Happy Retirement!" printed on it. She drove me home, unloaded me and then returned to school for another load of boxes. She seemed both happy and sad, which humans can do but cars can't. We're either one or the other, which makes emotions a lot easier to deal with. We had a quiet couple of months while she kept busy at home doing a lot of cleaning and sprucing up her house and yard. In August I noticed a "For Sale" sign in the front yard. In just a couple of weeks the sign was gone. Then, to my surprise, I found myself parked on the street with my own "For Sale" sign!

With my pristine condition and low mileage I got a lot of attention. A few people stopped by to look me over. A couple of them kicked my tires, which I thought was quite discourteous. I would have returned the favor if it wouldn't have destroyed my wheel alignment. One guy, who turned out to be Leroy, stopped by, checked me out and spoke with Doris about me. He charmed her with his good manners. She let him take me for a spin around the block and I could tell that he had driven a Beetle before. He knew how to shift and when to do it. I did my best to perform for him. When we returned, he talked more with Doris in her back yard and soon they were laughing and she was telling stories about her life in teaching. Eventually, they exchanged some papers, he bid her goodbye, and he drove me away. I saw on the bill of sale he put in my glove compartment that he paid just $900 for me. Doris had advertised me for $1,150 so he got a really good deal. It didn't do much for my self-image though.

The next morning, Leroy drove me over the same road we had traveled the previous evening. It was considerably more congested and other cars were zooming by. We stayed in the slow lane until we would come upon one of several loaded sand trucks crawling up the grade at 10 MPH. We'd dart out and pass them at the first opening and then pull back into the slow lane until we came upon another truck. The trip wasn't nearly as fun as the night before and by the time we ended up at a place called Applied Semiconductor, my nerves were shot. This was nothing like my commutes with Doris. As my engine cooled and my rubber parts reshaped themselves, the cars around me looked me over and asked where the old convertible was. I told them he was still at Leroy's home. They seemed disappointed, so I decided to use the same strategy I'd used the previous night, and listen instead of talk. I gained some valuable insight hearing stories about the other Beetle. It became clear he was a survivor who had no use for pompous or holier-than-thou cars, and that if any of them said anything derogatory or insulting to him, he would give it back in quick order. They all agreed he was a funny looking thing but it was easy to see that he had earned their respect. There was one very old Ford pickup who mentioned he had known the convertible longer than any of the other cars in the lot and that he considered him a true friend. His headlights actually teared up a little when he asked me to pass along his regards in the event the convertible's commuting days had ended. I assured him I would, and I did. I think the Bug sincerely appreciated the gesture.

As the days passed, it was clear I was now the commute car. We didn't know if the old guy would be kept or sold, but the longer nothing happened, the more hopeful he, and by now, I, became. I had grown to like and admire the convertible and he was not selfish about handing out helpful advice and counsel. For example, he pointed out that while Highway 17 can be fun, I have to remember that I'm a VW and that most cars go a lot faster than we are designed for, so I should be happy to stay in the slow lane. He also told me to trust Leroy to keep me tuned up, and not to hold back out of fear of straining anything. The one lecture I didn't need had to do with loyalty to our owner. I was proud of my service to Doris and I fully intended to provide that same level of commitment to Leroy. When I pointed out to him that as a fellow VW he should know loyalty is one of our stronger suits, he acknowledged that as the truth and apologized for belaboring the obvious.

The three of us were fine with each other. I was on Monday through

Friday duty and the convertible was the weekend guy. An occasional exception was when Leroy would drive to Chico and bring two kids back with him. I remembered Chico from my visit with Doris, but the trip with Leroy was much faster and the other cars didn't honk and give us dirty looks. The children's names were Annie and Johnny, and they called Leroy "Daddy" so I figured there must be a relationship of some kind. I didn't know why they weren't living with him if he was indeed their daddy, or why the woman they did live with was so unfriendly. I made a note to myself to ask the convertible his opinion. There was a tired, dirty Buick station wagon in the driveway and he asked me where the other VW was. I had to wonder if there was a single car in the whole state who didn't know him. Anyhow, I told him I was filling in, and that he was fine. I agreed to pass along the Buick's respects. Before we pulled away, he was asleep.

By the time we returned to Leroy's house it had been a full day of driving and both of us were ready for some rest, but Leroy didn't take a break. There were still a few hours of sunlight left — enough time to take the kids to the beach in the convertible. They loved it and came home excited and covered with sand. After they took a bath Leroy fixed a dinner he knew they would like and I could overhear their conversation as they ate on his patio. They talked about their friends in Chico, the men who visited their mother (they didn't like any of them), and asked why Leroy didn't come to live with them like he used to. Leroy tried to explain to them how it wasn't their fault he and Diana didn't live together anymore, and that he didn't think it would be possible for them to get back together. Meanwhile, he said, he wanted be a good dad to them, as he was sure Diana was trying to be a good mom. I could tell all three of them got a little sad for a few minutes, but when Leroy dished the ice cream the mood improved.

The next morning they returned to the beach. He brought them back in the early afternoon, cleaned them up and loaded them into my passenger compartment. I soon figured out that we were on our way back to Chico, and by the time Leroy deposited them and we returned home we were both out of gas, literally and figuratively. We followed this routine every three weeks or so, sometimes making the trip after work on a Friday evening and arriving home long after our normal bedtime. That made for more time on the beach, but those were long, tiring trips for Leroy. I wasn't bothered that much, since moving people from one place to another is my job, and the distance is irrelevant.

On those weekends when he wasn't being daddy, Leroy had a busy life and I met a number of nice (and a few not so nice) ladies. If the weather was warm, they would take the convertible and spend the day on the beach, returning in the late afternoon for a barbecue or socializing with other friends. I liked most of Leroy's friends. There were a few I had doubts about — the ones who were always asking him how he felt about them or the ones who seemed more interested in looking in the mirror than at him or me. The old Bug and I agreed that, even though we had more moving parts, it was a lot less complicated to be a car than it was to be a human male dealing with human females, and we wondered why he put up with them.

Aside from my commute duties and those marathon trips to Chico, my trips were limited. We did visit a town called Chester a few times, where Leroy's parents lived. It was a small town but it smelled good with its clean air and pine trees. Most of our visits were in the summer, but we did go there once in the winter, when it was quite cold and the snow was deep. It was that trip that reinforced to me the superiority of my German engineering. Other cars were complaining of being too cold, some even suffering from frozen radiators and popped freeze plugs. Not me. With no water or antifreeze to worry about, my air-cooled engine worked beautifully. As we drove happily around town I was careful not to gloat. Some of those tired and stalled pickups didn't seem too friendly and I'm sure any smart aleck behavior on my part would come back to haunt me, so I was discreet and avoided headlight contact with the nastier looking ones.

I met some interesting cars in Chester. One was an exceptionally old Ford Model A coupe that was in tip-top shape for a car his age, and refreshingly civil. When I asked him at the gas station how long he had lived in Chester, he told me he had been there for about thirty years. Thirty years! That was six times my age and hard for me to fathom. I told him he must have been well built to last that long, and I could only hope I was as well. He said life had not always been easy, particularly in the early years in a place called Oklahoma, which I gathered, was very dusty.

He didn't go into much detail, possibly because his mind wasn't as acute as it once was. He did recall some of his adventures in Chester and most of the ten or so owners he had put up with. Some he liked and others he was happy to be rid of. He was very satisfied with his current owner, who had disassembled him and put him back together, replacing many of his aged and worn parts, removing his dents, painting him, and housing him in a comfortable garage. I had to agree he looked great. He said his owner liked to take him to rallies and he enjoyed the experience because there were other cars his age with whom he could chat and reflect.

The Model A told me my owner had a familiar look about him and he asked me if he had ever lived in Chester. I replied that I wasn't sure, but his parents did, so he likely had spent some time here as a young man. I added that his name was Leroy and he was a good driver who took care of me. He laughed quietly, saying that wasn't always the case, and that if I ever had a few extra minutes he would tell me some stories about Leroy, who he was pretty sure was the same one who had owned him back in the '50s. He asked me if he had big feet. I told him he did, but that he could still handle a clutch with grace and a delicate touch. When Leroy came out of the gas station office he and the Model A looked each other over and I thought I saw a spark of recognition in their eyes and headlights. When the Ford's owner returned, Leroy asked him about the history of the car. The guy confirmed it had been around town for many years and was somewhat of a legend. Leroy said he might have been one of those owners, although it was hard to tell with all the bodywork that had been done. The current owner said it was entirely possible. The issue unresolved, Leroy thanked him for his time, taking one last fond look at the Model A before he got in and we drove away.

There was a pickup living at Leroy's parents' house, parked in the driveway. But there was just enough room for me to squeeze in next to him. He said he was a '68 Chevy and that he belonged to Leroy's dad. He added that he was one of many pickups in Chester. Most men there needed vehicles like him to haul firewood, take loads to the dump, go hunting and handle other chores beyond the capability of sedans. I was relieved to see no gun rack in his rear window, nor did he have any off-putting bumper stickers. He was a civil, decent truck who didn't seem to have a need to show how tough he was. Like me, he was a manual shift. His was mounted on the steering column, which I found unusual although I didn't mention it. Also, while he had a big V8 engine, he was only a three speed. I asked him what kind of mileage he got, being geared so low, and he said that wasn't his strong suit. He thought it was about 17 MPG. I told him I got upwards of 30 MPG and he chuckled as he said he could see why, with my tiny body and four forward gears. He added that it was doubtful I could carry a half-ton of cargo and I had to agree. I guess if there's one lesson I took away from our Chester visits it is that the car world is made up of many makes, models and styles, and that we all have our own unique place in it. It was a small town but there was a much more diverse collection of cars and trucks there than I had seen in San Jose or Santa Cruz. I enjoyed those trips to Chester and in addition to breathing some wonderful clean mountain air, I learned something with each visit and I met some nice vehicles.

One Saturday morning in the early summer of 1977, Leroy tossed a suitcase into my luggage compartment and pointed me towards Chico. When we arrived, Annie and Johnny were waiting on the front porch as usual, with their bags. Leroy loaded everything and everybody into me and we left. I soon noticed we were heading not back to Santa Cruz, but away. As the day wore on we passed through unfamiliar towns and country. In two hours we were in the midst of the tallest trees I had ever seen! I heard Leroy explain to the children that they were redwoods. He actually drove me through one, which I must say was unsettling. I had seen cars that had run into trees and they usually didn't look very good. But this one offered no resistance at all and when we came out on the other side I, thankfully, had no dents. We continued north, all of us reveling in the new adventure. Nine-year old Johnny was able to appreciate new sights and Anna, at 13 was as well, although her moods tended to swing from glee to darkness for reasons that I couldn't figure out. I just hoped it wasn't my fault.

Our adventure lasted for ten days. I think I enjoyed it as much as they did. We traveled through Oregon and Washington and crossed the border into Canada. I felt quite well traveled at that, since I had now been in Mexico, the U.S. and Canada. I doubted that very many of my peers had achieved such a milestone but I cautioned myself not to brag to the convertible when we returned home. The cars I spoke with in Canada had some strange expressions that took getting used to. When one of them called me "hoser" I first thought it was an insult and was about to return the slam when a nearby VW with British Columbia plates advised me to calm down; it was a friendly term. Most of the cars there also tended to complete their sentence with "eh", which didn't make much sense to me. But then I told myself that maybe some of the things I did as a matter of course didn't make sense to a Canadian car.

In Canada we turned east and enjoyed some stunning vistas of sparsely populated land, dramatic mountains and several noisy, determined trains passing us on the railroad tracks that ran parallel to our route. Because the traffic was light I was able to relax and enjoy the ride on some roads that were a lot smoother than I was used to in California. The only real distraction was a very long song Leroy, Annie and Johnny sang about beer bottles on a wall, which seemed to amuse them a lot more than it did me. We returned to the U.S. in Montana, bearing south. We soon were treated to more impressive sights, including Yellowstone Park and the Grand Tetons. I had seen mountains by this time in my life, but never anything quite so impressive as that range. It was June, but it was cold at night and the mountaintops were covered with snow. It was fortunate that my previous trips with Leroy had exposed me to pickup trucks. Otherwise, I might have been intimidated by the large number of them in Wyoming. A few made snide remarks about my odd shape, but I'd heard it all before and I had learned that the best thing to do when being ribbed by strangers, especially strangers who are larger than I am, is to ignore them.

We returned home after driving through Utah and Nevada, neither of which was the least bit interesting, with mile after of mile of road with no curves, hills or interesting scenery. It was a relief to cross the border into welcoming California, with its green landscape and roads that didn't put a car to sleep.

As our trip wound down I felt it had been a wonderful experience for Leroy and his kids. Nobody complained about being cooped up in my compact passenger compartment for the very long ride though, and as I eavesdropped on their conversations I learned that Leroy was an attentive listener who was able to understand what his kids were going through. He offered some sage fatherly counsel from time to time, probably more than they were eager to listen to. As Annie and Johnny aged and spent less and less time with him as their own lives became filled with activities, I could sense that Leroy felt he was losing them. That may have been his primary motivation for taking the trip with them.

I couldn't help but marvel at the change that had come to my life since Leroy bought me from Doris. I still had a fondness for her and a sincere appreciation for how she had treated me, but I had to conclude that my life with her was somehow a warm-up for my adventures with Leroy. Based on my conversations with other cars who had experienced multiple owners I figured that we all go through radical changes. When the old Bug and I had time to reflect on our lives together, we agreed that despite our very different pasts, we were fortunate to have Leroy as our second owner, even with his size 14 feet on our pedals.

Leroy and I took another trip later that summer, to Santa Barbara. I had never been there and like all cars, I love road trips, so it was an enjoyable few days — at least for me. He did not seem to be in a rush as we enjoyed a leisurely trip down the Coast Highway. I will confess to being uneasy at some of the sheer cliffs leading to the rocky coast of the ocean far below us, but I figured Leroy was no more eager to leap over the edge than I was, so I put my trust in him. We stopped at a little town called Pismo Beach that evening, where Leroy parked in a motel lot. I had enjoyed the day but was more than ready for a break, so that was fine with me. I immediately dropped off and slept uninterrupted until the next morning when Leroy was ready to continue his journey.

We arrived in Santa Barbara a few hours later. I thought it was a pretty place and I felt welcomed when I saw how many other Volkswagens were there. When we drove by a large university the reason became clear: we VWs are reliable, economical transportation and the perfect cars for students. We parked in the driveway of a modest house and when Leroy knocked on the door he was greeted by an enormous woman who put her arms around him and hugged him to her massive torso. I was afraid for a minute that she would suffocate him! When he worked his way out of her embrace she invited him into the house. It struck me while watching that scene unfold that I had ignored the car next to me, an American four-door sedan of a certain age, which is to say, old. (Could that be why it was it was called an Oldsmobile?) I asked him if he knew why Leroy was there and he was just as confused as I was. He said the lady's name was Carol and that she had lived there for a long time, inheriting the home from her parents.

Leroy and the lady named Carol emerged and I braced myself as she worked her imposing rear end into my passenger seat, filling it to capacity and beyond. As we drove away I was able to overhear their conversation. I gathered they had met many years ago when Leroy was a college student. He and two of his friends had visited Carol and some of her friends, and a brief relationship had ensued. Nothing much became of it, though. Carol expressed regret to Leroy that geography had kept them apart. She said that perhaps they could take up where they had left off. I could tell that Leroy was uneasy when he replied. His palms were sweaty on my steering wheel and he almost went through a stop sign, coming to a jarring halt, nearly causing Carol to continue through my windshield. He apologized and explained to Carol that, while he did have fond memories of his time with her, he was only recently divorced. He said he was not yet emotionally stable enough for a new commitment, and it would not be fair to her to, as he put it, "wait until he got his head screwed on right." That struck me as odd, since as far as I knew, people were assembled without screws, nuts, bolts, clamps, wires and all the other things we cars require. When he said that I knew he was not telling the truth.

I was parked at a restaurant and when they returned we drove back to Carol's house. She invited him in but he declined, stammering about having to continue on to Los Angeles for a business appointment the following morning. He tried unsuccessfully to get his arms around her for a hug, told her goodbye and promised to keep in touch. As we drove away he exhaled loudly and uttered a word I had not heard before, but figured was not one he would have used in polite circles. Leroy rarely talked aloud to himself, but on that occasion he did, asking nobody in particular how a woman could pack on 200 pounds in a few short years. I did see a sign for Los Angeles but we sped away in the opposite direction, north on Highway 101, and in my rear view mirror Santa Barbara's lights faded in the distance.

The next couple of years consisted of the by now comfortable routine of commuting during the week and resting up on the weekends. The old Bug continued to chug along, seemingly happy in his life, although it was hard to tell with him because it was rare for him to overtly express his emotions. Leroy continued to make his trips to Chico, although with decreasing frequency. My miles were adding up and my odometer was approaching 100,000. I was still in pretty good shape for a high mileage car but I was beginning to feel my age and I had a sense that I soon was going to need some major work on my valves, carburetor and brakes.

Based on what I have learned from talking with other cars throughout my life, I was aware that one of the most painful events most of us experience is undergoing a change of ownership with no advance preparation. One day you're faithfully doing your job for your owner and the next you belong to somebody else. It's almost as if humans don't even know we have feelings. Sure, we adapt to our new surroundings, but that doesn't make it less emotional for us as we're ripped unceremoniously from our comfort zone and thrust into a new life with no time to prepare for the change. With the exception of abused cars hoping for a better life, we live with a constant nagging anxiety because the only alternative to being sold is probably being totaled in an accident. On balance, being sold is obviously the preferred alternative.

It happened to me that way. I had driven Leroy to work as usual, and that afternoon he came out to see me with another man who looked me over, sat in me, examined my engine and kicked my tires. Again with the kicking! I got an eerie feeling that something was about to happen to me, particularly when Leroy returned a short while later with a small box and removed his personal belongings from me. He gave me a gentle pat on my roof and thanked me for being such a great car, and then walked away. I knew then that I was about to have a change in my life. I regretted that I wasn't able to say goodbye to my old friend the '62 and could only hope that our paths would cross sometime in the future. That evening, the stranger came out, started my engine and drove me away. I hoped he would be as nice to me as Leroy had been.

Chapter 13

NOT EXACTLY A FERRARI

A sad looking vintage VW convertible was parked next to me, eyeing me curiously. I tried to ignore him. I asked if something was bothering him. He asked me where the '72 Beetle was and I told him I didn't know what he was talking about, wondering if perhaps he was having a senior moment. He told me I was parked in the '72's spot. He grilled me, asking who I was, what happened to the Beetle, whether I was a loaner or a replacement car, and other rather personal questions about my heritage. I didn't care for his attitude. I gave him the bare essentials to shut him up, and then shut my headlights and went to sleep.

I may look like a sexy Italian, but I was actually manufactured in a town called Betim, in southeastern Brazil. I'll confess to divided loyalties. My engineering, design and soul are all Italiano, but what kind of heartless car wouldn't feel a loyalty and a pull to the city of his birth? Am I Italian or am I Brazilian? I suppose it's possible to be both but it sure is annoying when cars that were conceived and built in the same country lord their single pedigree over me. Frankly, I think it's rather one-dimensional. I like my mixed heritage.

I'm a Model 128 Fiat. I was built in 1978, the last year we 128s were manufactured. I was designed for export to the USA but I didn't arrive here until early 1979, which meant that I was definitely priced to sell. Aside from the introduction of the cell phone, it was not a particularly good year for my soon-to-be-adopted country, and even that gave me an uneasy feeling about its possible effect on traffic safety. There was a nuclear accident at Three Mile Island, a power plant in Pennsylvania; Russia invaded Afghanistan; and the Shah of Iran was overthrown. Jimmy Carter was President and his economic policies were blamed for the 11% inflation. But the worst thing was the radical Islamists who invaded the US Embassy in Iran and stayed for 444 days. The price of a gallon of gas reached an all-time high of 86¢. Other than my arrival here not much good happened. The best thing we could hope for in 1979 was 1980.

I consider myself to be exceptionally attractive with my four doors and bright yellow paint. I'm a lot roomier than I look and more powerful than my engine specs might indicate, with a 55 HP straight four engine capable of reaching a top speed of 85 MPH, which I think is plenty, if not excessively fast. As far as I'm concerned, anybody who has to drive 85 MPH should have started earlier.

In addition to my 22-MPG capability, one of my most innovative features is my front-wheel drive. I have to wonder why all cars are not similarly designed for better cornering and traction and other Fiats like me agree. We don't have any lobbying power in Detroit, though, so there's nothing we can do about it. Compared to those huge, ugly American cars of my era I was nimble and affordable at a bargain MSRP of $1,971. I'm pretty sure that most of us were sold to either teens or other people who didn't have much money.

That was what happened to me. I was sitting in a new car lot in San Jose, California, among a dozen of my peers. We had recently arrived from Brazil and were still recovering from a little touch of seasickness from being buffeted about on the waves. We landed in Oakland and were soon loaded on a truck to the dealer. We were all hopeful that whoever bought us would appreciate us and treat us with respect. It was a warm June day and when the salesman approached me with a tall man who appeared to show interest in me I did my best to look sharp and eager to please. The guy, who I soon learned was called Leroy, took me for a trial run. I noticed he had really big feet for my small and closely configured pedals, but he was able to manipulate them, easily shifting through all of my four gears and working the gas and brakes smoothly. He seemed familiar with manual shift, which was a huge relief to me because I had heard other cars talking about how automatic transmissions were taking over the world and people who could drive a stick were a dying breed. I was feeling lucky.

We returned to the lot and Leroy went inside with the salesman, emerging a short while later with a handful of papers and my keys. When he got onto my driver's seat and stuffed the papers in my glove compartment, I saw that he had paid $1,850 for me, which was a little lower than my MSRP but certainly not a steal. I bid my fellow Fiats buon giorno as we left the lot and headed for what were then parts unknown.

We drove for about an hour, up a mountain and then down, ending up in a town called Santa Cruz, near the ocean. I had a momentary panic that I was about to loaded onto another ship, but thankfully Leroy parked me, got out, locked me and disappeared into a house, leaving me to endure the stares and personal questions from that vintage bug.

The next morning I was awakened when Leroy got in and started me up. The old VW was still there, staring straight at me. I ignored him as Leroy and I backed out and headed down the road. We traversed the same route we'd come over the previous evening but there were many more cars than before, and not many in the slow lane. I soon found out why as we rounded a corner and passed a big rig full of sand crawling up the grade at about 10 MPH. It was a tense ride and I was relieved when we parked in a lot with hundreds of other cars. Most of us kept to ourselves, dozing or chatting quietly with each other, but one, a VW Beetle, kept staring at me. He asked me if that was Leroy driving me. I confirmed that it was, and that he had bought me the previous evening. When he asked me to convey a message to his old friend, the '62 convertible, it struck me that he must have been the one who that rundown relic had been asking about. As we got better acquainted I learned that he had been owned by Leroy and that I was to be his replacement. I naturally felt a little self-conscious about that, but he assured me it was OK. He said the commute had taken its toll and he was ready for a less stressful existence. He added that although he had fond memories about the bachelor life with Leroy and the convertible, it was time to move on, and that he had no hard feelings. He encouraged me to be nice to the '62, to respect him and give him time to warm up to me. When I described our initial meeting, he said I had rushed to judgment based on appearances, and that once I got to know the '62 and earn his trust, I would have a friend for life. Part of me discounted his advice because he was, after all, another VW and a natural ally. It is a given among cars that those of the same make stick together. I did promise to pass along the '72's greetings and the fact that he had landed on his wheels.

Upon returning to Leroy's house that evening, the '62 looked at me, chuckled smugly, and asked how the commute went. I asked if it was that obvious that it was a harrowing experience. He said he had done the same trip many times and although he ultimately got used to it, it was never easy. He told me I would adjust, but advised me not to get over confident or I'd end up like a lot of other cocky cars he had seen along that route — overturned, smashed up or down an embankment. Heeding the counsel of the '72, I gave him the benefit of the doubt and thanked him for the advice. He seemed genuinely appreciative when I gave him the message from his old buddy, and asked me to wish him well. I agreed, but wondered if I was signing on to be a messenger for those two VWs. I was about to say that we Italians had not experienced very good relations with assisting Germans in the past, but I bit my radiator cap and didn't say anything.

It didn't take long for me to come to terms with my life. I was the commute car and the VW was the weekend car unless Leroy had a date that required a more appropriate vehicle. I worked hard and did everything I could to please Leroy, but I never felt that we had bonded. My feelings were hurt more than once when I overheard him tell a passenger that I was his "divorce special." I don't know exactly what he meant and I don't even know what a divorce is, but I got the feeling that he wasn't complimenting me. He would laugh as he pointed out that my sleek lines were boxy, that my yellow paint caused people to mistake me for a taxi, that my engine would whine when the RPMs were high, and that my pedals were too close together for his big feet. I had to agree with the last one, as more than once he had aimed for the brake and hit the clutch, resulting in some piston-wrenching moments. As for my appearance and color, well, those were a matter of taste and mine is obviously more refined than Leroy's. And I, like all cars, will protest as RPMs increase to the breaking point. I would have advised him to slow down or shift, either of which would make my whine magically disappear. Regardless of his feelings toward me, I was built to do a job and I was determined to do it well. I have to confess I would have enjoyed it a lot more had I felt appreciated.

We had a few trips together that were not simply commutes.

Every few weeks we drove to a town called Chico where he picked up Annie and Johnny, who turned out to be his children. We would drive back to Santa Cruz and two days later we would repeat the round trip, depositing them in Chico. I liked to get out on the open road but I had to wonder why Leroy didn't have Annie and Johnny live with him. That would have saved a lot of gas and time. But that decision wasn't mine to make.

———————

On one memorable occasion — I think maybe it was the highlight of my time with Leroy — we traveled to a town by the name of Chester. I really enjoyed that trip because it was a place I had not seen before and also because there wasn't much traffic and we had a mountain road practically to ourselves. It took us more than four hours to get there, four hours of pure joy. Leroy didn't have to do a lot of shifting, so we just cruised along with my cassette player blasting some classic Willie Nelson and Jerry Jeff Walker until we reached the city limits and he turned down the volume. He pulled up and parked in the driveway of a house, and went inside. I noticed a '68 Chevrolet pickup parked nearby, so I asked him if he knew where I was and what Leroy was doing. That's when I learned we were in Chester. Leroy had lived here at some point, in the very house where we were parked. The pickup guessed he had come home to visit his parents, which made good sense to me even though I don't have any. Parents, that is. I have plenty of sense. The pickup was nice, which I appreciated. Sometimes trucks scoff at my size and limited cargo space but he didn't even seem to take note of our differences.

He told me there weren't many cars like me in Chester; that most people drove pickups like him or big American cars. He said one of the main reasons might be the difficulty of finding spare parts for foreign cars in that part of the country. I thought better of pointing out to him that even if I was manufactured in Brazil, I am just as much American as he is and have never spoken any language but English. Foreign indeed. But the pickup was nice enough and I was in an excellent mood after my trip, so I let it pass. Cars like me might be rare now, I thought, but within a few years we will be the trend-setters with our revolutionary front wheel drive, economy of space and better than average gas mileage.

I didn't see Leroy again that day. As we became acquainted, I learned the pickup had originally been purchased by Leroy's parents in 1968. He had enjoyed a relatively stress-free life, although he confessed it could be boring at times. He longed to test his hauling strength but had accepted the reality that he was going to lead a pampered life compared to the other pickups in Chester. One feature of living in a small town like Chester is the limited number of places to go and essentially no commute. He was eleven years old and had only 20,000 miles on his odometer! I wasn't even a year old yet and I had already clocked almost 13,000. He said he had a big V8 engine and a three-speed manual transmission so there was power to spare, but in the winter, when the roads were covered with snow it could be slippery. I was embarrassed, but I asked him what snow was. He looked at me funny, as if everybody except abject fools knows what snow is, but he patiently explained it was white stuff that falls from the sky when the weather turns cold, and accumulates into large piles and gets packed onto the roads. This makes the roads slick and sometimes the cars and trucks have to have chains installed. Again, I had no idea what he meant, but this time I just played dumb. Chains? Why? In case you get stuck and need something to hook to in order to be pulled out of your jam? Why not a rope, which is much lighter and easier to manipulate? When I happened to mention later in the evening that I have front wheel drive, he said it would be very handy in the snow. I took his word for it.

I slept soundly, probably because of the high altitude. I woke up refreshed, filling my intake valves with clean, pine-scented air. Leroy emerged in the early afternoon and took me for a cruise around Chester, which didn't take very long. We drove to one end of town, did a U-turn, drove to the other end and repeated. Then we drove around town, briefly stopping in front of the high school. We finally parked at a place called the Frosty Freeze.

When Leroy went in, I found myself next to a very old but nicely reconditioned car. He told me he was a 1937 Plymouth. I couldn't believe a car so old could still operate but I didn't want to insult him. As if reading my mind (maybe old cars can do that, which gives me something to aspire to), he told me that fifteen years ago, after a hard life, he was about to be consigned to the junkyard when a guy named Larry bought him for $50, towed him to his home, and parked him in a big garage. It was there he was restored from bumper to bumper, and for two years was not driven at all. He said by the time he emerged from that garage into bright sunlight he had not seen for so long, he had no dents, a rebuilt engine, new upholstery and a fresh coat of paint. He was enormously grateful for Larry's skill and com-mitment, as it meant he was still alive.

The Plymouth had lived in Chester for more than 20 years, and said at one point he was owned by a guy who looked a lot like my owner, except he was thinner and had more hair. When I told him his name was Leroy he asked me if he had big feet. I confirmed that he did and it erased all doubt. Leroy came out of the Frosty Freeze talking with a guy who seemed to be an old acquaintance. The guy looked at me and laughed, asking Leroy if that bright yellow paint made me go fast, or did it just attract bees? I was disappointed when Leroy joined in on the joke and even remarked about how difficult it was to pick up women in a car like me. Well, I might not be one of those smug, obnoxious Corvettes, but I have my definite advantages, even if he doesn't recognize them. While I was considering how to get even, Leroy mentioned when he was a kid he owned a Plymouth just like the one beside me. He said it was pretty thrashed, and some of its parts might well have ended up in this one. Had he bothered to research it, he would have been surprised to know what I already learned in ten minutes of listening — not one of his strengths — that this Plymouth was the very one he had owned. But the conversation ended there and Leroy got in and we drove back to his parents' home.

That night I asked the pickup if he knew the Plymouth. He said he was familiar with him, and that he had lived in Chester for many years. He was surprised when I told him that the Plymouth had lived at the very house where we were currently parked, back in the late 1950s. He said he was acquainted with a vintage Model A Ford who had been in Chester for a long time and also claimed to have lived at Leroy's parents' house for a short time. I asked him what a Model A Ford was and he said he didn't know a lot about them other than they once dominated the U.S. auto market way back in the 1920s and '30s. He said there weren't many left now, but that the one in Chester had, like that Plymouth, been restored to its past glory. He encouraged me to introduce myself if we had the opportunity to meet, cautioning me that he may be hard to understand at first because of his Okie accent. I already felt stupid for not knowing what snow or a Model A Ford were, and I was too embarrassed to ask him what an Okie was. I figured I'd find out if I ever met the Model A Ford.

We left Chester the next morning. Once again, Leroy inserted a cassette and turned up the volume as we sped along the highway toward home, with me brilliantly negotiating the curves of the mountain road. We stopped in Chico to take Annie and Johnny to lunch. Annie had recently passed her driving test and asked Leroy if she could drive me. She assured him she had driven a stick shift, so he gave her my keys.

As we started out it was obvious to me that Annie, if she had ever driven a stick at all, either hadn't done it often or was a slow learner. She rammed my clutch to the floor, ground me into low, mashed my accelerator down and suddenly released the clutch. I had no choice but to lurch dramatically and kill my engine, lest we go careening down the road at top speed. Leroy told her to try it again, with less gas and more gentle shifting. I could have kissed him for that if I had lips. Annie once again depressed my clutch, this time slipping me into gear without grinding, and when she stomped on my accelerator Leroy told her to ease up and try to be one with the machine. That made good sense to me. So Annie gave me less gas and let the clutch out slowly, allowing me to move forward more gently. When it was time to shift into second gear she once again ground my gear but she eventually found the right spot and we proceeded jerkily toward third. She was better at this one, although she was going way too fast for the neighborhood, so Leroy, who had visible sweat beads on his forehead, advised her to slow down. She did so by stomping on my brake which worked, but it was anything but smooth, partly because of her heavy foot and partly because I was so nervous. I suddenly slowed to a crawl, nearly throwing Leroy through my windshield and Johnny up to my front seat. And making the situation worse, when she applied my brakes she failed to depress my clutch, so once again I lugged to a stall and my engine died. Had I been manufactured with sweat glands they would have been operating at full tilt by now.

Leroy suggested that we should all go for a drive before lunch, and guided her out of town onto a more deserted road. He had her practice her starts and stops. He assured her she was doing fine. I wasn't so sure. Even so, after twenty minutes, she did seem to grasp the concept of coordinating the gas, the clutch and the gearshift. Leroy let Annie drive back to town, and we found a spot in a parking lot so she didn't have to demonstrate her parallel parking skills on me. I think she was as relieved as I was.

After lunch, Leroy took over the driving duties again and we deposited Annie and Johnny at their house before continuing our journey home. I don't know how humans feel about this, but we cars think it's always nice to get home to familiar surround-ings, where we recognize the oil spots and potholes and the other cars we have come to know. The '62 Bug had been sleep-ing (probably all weekend) but awoke to ask me about our trip. I told him about Chester and the other cars I'd met. He said he wished he could have talked with them as well, as he considered himself a member in good standing of the codger club. He said hearing about the Model A and Plymouth still operating at their ages gave him hope that his days might be extended too. Then he went back to sleep.

————————————

My life with Leroy and the '62 didn't take any serious turns dur-ing the next year. I continued my commute duties as my odometer reached nearly 50,000 and was climbing every day. My front end had a few small dings here and there from little rocks being tossed up by cars in front of me, and my doors had some pockmarks I got from careless people in parking lots. But overall, I was in pretty good shape. Leroy, to his credit, did keep me tuned up, clean and in good tires. My only regret was that despite my unwavering loyalty and dependability, I never was able to totally win his affection. I worked hard to prove my worth by being reliable, quick to respond, and easy to maneuver. I had come to terms with the reality that my design was what it was, and that I was not a Porsche or a Ferrari. I knew, though, that Leroy's deep down wish was that I was one. I eventually resolved to live with my disappointment and simply to do my job, the alternative being to live in a constant state of anxiety like the ugly but well-meaning AMC Pacer I was acquainted with from the Applied Semiconductor parking lot. That guy looked like he'd been designed by a practical joker. The other cars ignored him and even his owner ridiculed him openly, making fun of his boxy rear end and the way he rode so high off the ground. I wanted to counsel him to relax and accept who he was but I never got the feeling he was open to sug-gestions. We cars of the 1970s are not known for our beauty. So be it. Neither were men's fashions, with those ugly polyester pants, open shirts, gold chains and boots with zippers on the sides. Men, though, can change themselves. Cars can't.

Speaking of change, I noted that Leroy's lady guest list had begun to thin out and that he seemed to be spending more and more time with one particular woman he called Liz. Compared to the many visitors he had entertained over the years, I thought Liz was one of the better ones. She smelled good, was able to carry on an intelligent conversation and she made Leroy laugh. They spent a lot of time together on the weekends and I grew to like her quite a bit, perhaps because she never once made fun of me and actually chided Leroy at one point when he was ridiculing my appearance yet again. She told him he should be more sensitive because for all they knew cars had feelings too, and how would he feel if his car made fun of him? I couldn't believe what I was hearing in my side mirrors! That was the first time I'd ever heard a human acknowledge what all cars already know and while I was really pleased to hear the words, it was a little eerie, as if she had been listening in on my conversations. It made me wonder what else she knew about my private thoughts.

———————

It was autumn, 1981 when our comfortable routine came to an end and my life began to change. Liz moved in with Leroy, which met with my enthusiastic approval. The '62 Bug didn't care one way or the other so long as his basic needs were met, and Leroy did attend to them. Liz owned a car that had no doubt cost a lot more than I did. It was a 1974 Mercedes-Benz 450SL. He was a few years older, but I have to confess that he was a sleek looking two-seater with his pale blue paint and removable hardtop. We never did really warm up to each other. I was self-conscious about my boxy appearance and bright yellow paint. Most of the time it had not bothered me, but now I was comparing myself to the Mercedes, which made me feel clunky, if there's such a word. I was in awe of him. He was aloof, although the VW was also sort of blue and clearly was a convertible. And both were Germans, which I thought would help them bond. But the Mercedes essentially ignored the VW, who wasn't bothered in the least. Both were polite enough to acknowledge each other with a distant nod but that was as far as it went.

I went out of my way to be welcoming. The Mercedes wasn't very forthcoming, however, and while he responded to my questions his responses were perfunctory and he offered neither additional information nor questions of his own. I thought it curious and disappointing that a person as nice as Liz could have such a snob for a car. Because we all had to park together, I thought it would be a more pleasant experience if we three all got along, and I was hoping that the Mercedes would warm up after he got to know us. But he didn't. For reasons known only to him, he remained essentially a stranger.

I had met other cars with a similar attitude and I always wondered why they weren't more social. Although we're all different makes and models, we're all cars, sharing the fundamental purpose of getting people from one place to another. Just because one is expensive, fast, shiny, customized, dinged up, old or new doesn't, at least in my headlights, make one better or worse than another. But I had not driven a mile in that Mercedes' tires and was in no position to judge him. As mature cars do, I accepted the situation and figured I had given the Mercedes the opportunity to be friends if he chose to.

The one advantage I realized was that my commute duties were eased, as Leroy and Liz took turns with us. That was fine by me. The days I remained home were quiet because the VW spent most of his time sleeping. I took the opportunity to get some rest myself, and during the hours when I was awake I'd think about random things, such as how Annie was doing with her driving, whether that pickup in Chester ever got to go on a road trip, how I might win the affection of the Mercedes, whether the '62 would ever get a paint job or if he even cared, and what my future might hold. I don't really think I'm neurotic so much as introspective.

By the time spring arrived the next year, 1982, I was ready for it. We had gone through an unusually wet season. There were an alarming number of accidents during our commute caused by impatient drivers who were in a rush to get to either work or home, but lacked the skills to do it safely. It seemed like at least once each week traffic would slow to a crawl because one car had run into another or had careened off the road. As we crept by one of these scenes in late January we were parked for a few minutes beside a Highway Patrol Ford with his red lights flashing. I had always envied those guys with their powerful engines, their skilled drivers and all the goodies in their passenger compartments like radios, radar guns, and weapons. But when I glanced at this particular Ford's headlights all I saw was exhaustion. I asked him if he was OK. He said he was, but just barely because this was the fifth accident he had worked that day and he was tired. He said it was days like this that made him want to retire from the Highway Patrol and just be a regular car like me. I would have been delighted to trade places with him and experience some of the excitement he got to see every day, but I would have made a pretty funny looking police car. That short conversation made me realize the importance of accepting our lives as they are played out and not always longing to be some car we are not, because it may be the car we want to be doesn't want to be what he is either.

As the weather gradually improved, so did my morale. All three of us cars at Leroy's relished the warm days, basking in the bright Santa Cruz sun. The Mercedes remained distant and I had resigned myself to the reality that we would never be close. At least he wasn't hostile. The '62 was beginning to complain from time to time about his condition, but not excessively, for that was not his nature. And he certainly had just cause. He was developing a serious rust condition exacerbated by the salt air, and his top was beginning to disintegrate. His engine had nothing serious the matter with it, though, other than being unable to stay properly tuned. He did complain that his valves needed constant adjusting. His headlights were loose and out of focus, making it difficult to carry on a conversation because it always seemed like he was looking elsewhere. Overall, he was not in bad shape. His ailments would not be that difficult to address. I think he was just enjoying being a crabby old curmudgeon.

———————

A Saturday in early June 1982 turned out to be a significant day for me. It began around 7 a.m. when Leroy opened my glove compartment and removed his personal items that had been there for so long, things like old receipts, a wine opener, a few maps and a roll of film he had long forgotten about. He also took all of his cassette tapes, which I found curious. After cleaning me out, he started me up and we drove off. I was surprised to spot Liz and the Mercedes behind us but I figured our humans knew what they were doing. Before too long I recognized the now familiar route to Chico so I settled in for the drive to fetch Leroy's kids. The Mercedes was still behind us and I wondered why Leroy and Liz didn't just travel together. It made no sense to me, but then many things humans do don't make sense to me.

When we arrived at their home, Annie and Johnny were sitting on their front porch. They met Leroy half way and did those human hugs. Liz, who had parked behind us, got out of the Mercedes and greeted the kids, and then got back into her car, telling Leroy she would wait for him there. Hmm. It soon came to me that we were not going to carry Annie and Johnny back to Santa Cruz, and I wondered what going on. It seemed like we had traveled a long distance just to say hello. I soon found out.

Annie was graduating from high school that evening. Leroy told her how proud he was, so I suppose that must have been some sort of accomplishment. After he praised her, he handed her the keys to my ignition. That's when things started to fall into place. I was being given away. Or maybe not, because Leroy told Annie to drive me to the restaurant they occasionally frequented together, adding that he would follow in Liz's car.

When we arrived at the restaurant, the Mercedes and I were parked along side each other. This turned out to be one of the few times the Mercedes ever initiated a conversation with me, as he asked me where we were. When I told him we were in Chico, I asked if he'd ever been driven up this way and he said he didn't believe so. He made a derisive comment about country hicks and for the first time since our acquaintance I snapped at him, and told him that it is a mistake and an unfair judgment to make hasty assumptions based on such limited data. That response caught him off guard and he actually apologized. I felt as if maybe we had reached a breakthrough in our icy relationship now that I had called him on his snooty attitude.

When the four of them came out of the restaurant a short while later there were hugs all around, and I heard Leroy tell Annie that I might be homely, but I was reliable. This was turning into a really weird day. First, the Mercedes and now Leroy was showing a little respect. I had become so inured to being a humble little workhorse that it was almost uncomfortable. The humans couldn't see it, but I was blushing under my yellow exterior. As Annie and Johnny climbed into my passenger compartment, Leroy told her he would mail the pink slip. She told him she loved him and she loved me and that she'd take good care of me and avoid the drag races, which made him laugh. I didn't get the joke if there was one. After assuring her that they would attend the evening ceremony, Leroy and Liz got into the Mercedes and drove away, leaving me with Annie behind the wheel. It began to dawn on me that I might be remaining in

Chico.

And I did. It took a few days for me to understand that Annie was now my owner. I was OK with that because she seemed to really care for me and was actually proud of me. Her driving skills had improved, thankfully, and she was an adequate stick shift driver now. I did regret not having said goodbye to my old friend the '62 Bug and I could only hope that one day we might see each other again. Meanwhile, I resolved to settle in with Annie and continue doing what I do best, which is get my passengers from point A to point B with reliability and consistency. I found myself looking forward to a new phase in my life, living in a college town and being close to the open road.

Chapter 14
NEW BEGINNINGS

The first time I was parked at Leroy's house I was next to a garish yellow, boxy little Fiat and an exceptionally ugly vintage Volkswagen convertible. I looked around for other cars that might have been worthy of my attention and saw none, so I chose to ignore those two. The VW clearly was fine with that arrangement. After a brief hello and a quick once-over, he just went to sleep. As for the Fiat, I found him to be as needy as he was uninteresting. He asked way too many questions, some of which I answered out of common courtesy. I hoped this would satisfy him but he continued to pester me until he eventually came to understand that I had no interest in him. This is not to say that he was bad or that I was casting judgment; I simply preferred to associate with cars of my stature. Clearly, he would never achieve that. He was cheap, tinny and undignified and I am sure would have been more at ease among cars of his station. I remained as aloof as I could without being unpolished, hoping he would get the message. He eventually did and gradually we developed a civil, if not friendly, relationship.

The VW was, like me, of German heritage. I felt this common bond, however vague, was worthy of granting him special treatment so I made a point to be as nice to him as I could without indicating to him how repulsive I found him to be. I must say, however, the more I got to know him, the more impressed I was. He had been abused as a young car and while many would have given up and settled for a trip to the crusher, he was determined to live as long as he could, serving Leroy and quietly observing life around him. He was wiser than he looked. I figured that was because he was of German design and construction. To be sure, his appearance left much to be desired. He compensated by displaying a quick, acerbic mind and I grew to respect him.

Although I think boasting is inappropriate, I do believe I am one fine looking piece of automotive genius. I'm a Mercedes Benz 450SL roadster and if I am not king of the road, I am unquestionably the first runner-up. I was built in West Germany in 1974, thankful to be a German because America was in an awful mess. President Nixon resigned in disgrace after the Watergate scandal and the economy was out of control with inflation reaching 14%. Gas, which I find quite tasty and tend to use quite a bit of, was selling for an all-time high of 53¢ a gallon. To help drivers use less gas, the national speed limit was reduced to 55 MPH, which was nothing short of an insult to a precision machine like me, comfortable when cruising at 80. As far as I'm concerned, if my driver has to worry about gasoline consumption, perhaps he has the wrong car and should consider one of my more humble cousins, like the Volkswagen. I find it tacky to even discuss the price of fuel. It is what it is.

I'm a stunning two-seat roadster. I believe my MSRP of $36,500 was an excellent value, as my owner was able to enjoy not only my exquisite good looks and comfort, but also a smooth four-speed automatic transmission and a big V8 engine that could generate up to 222 horsepower. I am a convertible with a top made of solid metal that is easily removable. We can't all be sleek, elegant and fast. I'm just happy that I am.

_____

My original owner was a well-to-do lady named Edith who lived in a very nice neighborhood in San Francisco. In my parking garage I was amidst a comfortable peer group of other Mercedes along with BMWs, Audis, Cadillacs and Porsches. It did not escape me that most of the truly fine automobiles were of German design and manufacture. For American mass produced cars, the Cadillacs were certainly top tier. Personally, I found them to be excessively large and, well, obese. At least there were none of those offensive Asian cars in our garage with their whiny engines, rattles and ill-fitting doors that required what I judged to be undue slamming. I thought they were just tacky and I was happy to be parked amongst other fine cars of my stature, as I am sure they were, in their own crowded, noisy, unheated, oily garages.

Life with Edith was safe and uneventful. Our trips were mostly shopping excursions and I became very familiar with public parking facilities. A seasoned consumer, Edith knew where the upscale garages were located so I was rarely subjected to being parked near cars that were not of my station. One store Edith frequented offered valet parking. This sounds like a creative idea and an excellent customer service gesture, and I'm quite sure Edith found it to be a major convenience. What she did not know, however, was that valets can tend to be less than gentle once out of sight of the owners. I was subjected to some harrowing rides and near misses with valets, and when I was parked it was always outside, surrounded by cars of all makes and models, frequently making it an uneasy experience for me. I do respect the lower class cars, but I would prefer not to associate with them. I'm sure they, in turn, are most probably more comfortable among their own kind. Some of them, particularly the scratched and dented vintage Chevrolets, Fords and Dodges, would eye me with open hostility. I avoided headlight contact with them, not wishing to give them any reason to nudge me or push me down a hill, which is an ever-present danger in San Francisco.

Edith was a nice enough lady and she seemed to respect me, but she knew nothing about cars aside from how to start, drive and park us. Her daughter, Liz, lived in Palo Alto during my early years and we would make frequent trips to visit her. I enjoyed those invigorating jaunts down Highway 101 and particularly the more scenic and faster Highway 280. Edith did not come close to testing my limits on the open road, but at least we would get my RPMs up enough to blow out some of the carbon that had accumulated on my pistons. Those trips were less frequent than I needed, unfortunately. That, plus the fact she could not seem to remember to take me in for my scheduled maintenance, meant my engine was aging prematurely. I still looked good because I was used so little, but by 1978 I began to emit embarrassing clouds of blue smoke from my exhaust. Like people, cars need exercise and I was not getting what I required. Edith did not notice that we were trailing visible exhaust, as she rarely looked in my rear view mirror except to adjust her hair and makeup. I kept hoping Edith would eventually notice my blue smoke and have my engine repaired. She never did.

In 1979 my heater relay stopped working. As a result, my heater was on full blast all the time my engine was operating. Because Edith never ventured far, she did not bother to have me repaired, so now I was overheating my passenger compartment as well as belching exhaust. She was making fewer trips to Palo Alto by then, and when she did and I became too warm, she would simply open a window. If it was raining she would open only the one on the passenger side. That cooled things off, but my upholstery got soaked. I was as powerless to do anything about either of my problems and I eventually resigned myself to living with my flaws and hoping nothing more serious would beset me.

The following year I spent considerably more time in her garage, with rare shopping trips and no trips at all to Palo Alto. When Edith did take me out I could not help but observe that she had lost considerable weight and that she did not look well. My concern for her grew through the year and it peaked when eventually she stopped driving me altogether. From that August to February 1981, I was parked in the garage, unused. My battery slowly drained and I drifted into a dreamless sleep. I was awakened when a new battery was installed and found to my surprise that Liz, not Edith, was starting my engine and pulling out of the garage. I was groggy. My exhaust pipe was smoking more than ever, and my heater still was not operating properly. Liz started down toward Palo Alto, but before we reached the freeway she pulled into a gas station where an employee showed her how to remove my heater fuse. That made things cooler, but after ten miles she stopped and reinserted the fuse. It wasn't long before it was again too warm, so she stopped and removed it once again. This continued all the way to Palo Alto. I believe we stopped five times in total as my passenger compartment ranged from uncomfortably warm to uncomfortably cold.

Liz parked me in her garage. It was smaller than the one in San Francisco and I was the only car in it. I actually enjoyed spending that night alone with no other cars keeping me awake with their conversations, their smells and the creaks, pops and hisses of their engines as they cooled. I assumed we would be returning to Edith's home the following day so I decided to enjoy my sleepover with Liz. As it turned out, we did not return to San Francisco the following day. Instead, she drove me to a Mercedes dealer and left me there. I felt some anxiety, but that was soon put to rest when I was driven into a service bay and put under the care of a mechanic who I could sense was exceedingly competent by the way he handled his tools. The last thing I remember was the removal of my battery cables, at which time I went into a deep sleep.

I was awakened when they were reconnected and I immediately discerned that something felt different. The mechanic started my engine and I was astonished to feel my pistons and valves working much more smoothly, and most important, there was no longer any of that unsightly smoke coming from my rear end. My engine had been repaired! If I'd had arms I would have given Liz a big hug. As an added bonus, I noted with considerable relief that my heater had been repaired. I felt like a brand new car and I was ready for any adventure the roads might toss my direction. My life was getting so much better!

Sadly, I never saw Edith again. My worst fears were confirmed when I heard Liz explain to a passenger a few days after my repairs, that I had been inherited. I wanted to go to Edith and pay my final respects, but I did not know where she was. I did know she was no longer in her San Francisco flat and I likely had seen the last of my old garage mates. Such is the life of the car. Acquaintances pass through our lives and we have no control over where we will be parked or who might be next to us. I accepted my new life and was optimistic that Liz and I had begun our relationship on a most positive note with my much-needed repairs.

———————

Liz and I quickly grew comfortable. I liked the way she drove me, with confidence and on occasion, unbounded speed. One time we were pulled over by a Highway Patrolman who told her his radar had shown us going 90 MPH. To my amazement, Liz flirted her way out of a citation by explaining to the patrolman that she had just inherited me, and was not yet familiar with me. She said she did not realize how fast we were going, and that she was preoccupied with memories of her dearly departed mother. I had never heard her speak so softly, so sincerely and so convincingly. It worked, because the patrolman very politely cautioned her to use more restraint in the future, and then he wished her well. I was impressed with Liz, who held me to 75 for the rest of our journey.

My life with her was a lot busier and interesting than it had been with Edith. For one thing, she had many friends. Many of them were men, most of whom I did not like. The ones I approved of were polite to her, drove me with respect and skill, and did not smoke. They were in the minority. I wondered why Liz put up with the others. Thankfully, most of them soon disappeared so I gave her credit for her discriminating taste. After a few months I became acquainted with Leroy, who I thought was worthwhile and apparently so did Liz, for his visits became more frequent and her visits to him in Santa Cruz did as well. I loved those trips with the sharp curves and hills to his house. And when Leroy drove me I could tell he understood cars, our needs and how to coax the best from us. He had unusually large feet but they did not affect his driving. That impressed me.

In the fall of 1981 I became a permanent resident at Leroy's, after Liz moved her belongings there. Aside from having to spend my parking time next to the boring Fiat and the seedy VW, I began to enjoy myself. Leroy and Liz commuted to work in me and I reveled in being out on the road among all those other cars, showing my stuff and being admired. Lesser cars would move aside when I approached them and they saw my distinctive three-pointed Mercedes Benz star in my grillwork. This has been our proud emblem since 1910, the three points of the star signifying our superiority "on land, on water and in the air". I don't know much about our history in the water or the air, but I do know that no car is better on land.

My weekends were quiet. If the weather was nice, Leroy and Liz would often take the old VW to the beach. He didn't say one way or the other, but I sensed that he enjoyed being put to use after resting all week. The Fiat was used less and less, and I could tell that he was bothered. He mostly just sat, fretting about being idle. I did feel sympathy for him, but it was patently obvious that I was much better qualified for commute duties and that the VW was more fun on the weekends. So I wished he would stop complaining and accept his situation in life. After all, we can't all be Mercedes Benzes.

On a fine spring day in 1982 Liz settled into my driver's seat and started my engine. We followed Leroy in the Fiat to the highway and drove for three hours, ending up in a town I'd never heard of called Chico. We stopped in front of a house. Liz got out long enough to greet Annie and Johnny, Leroy's children, who then climbed into the Fiat with Leroy. I had met Annie and Johnny on previous occasions when they spent weekends with Leroy, and had always wondered where they resided when not in Santa Cruz. We followed Leroy to a restaurant where Liz parked me next to the Fiat. The Fiat told me he had been to Chico on several occasions and proceeded to give me volumes of useless information, none of which held the least interest for me, and even snapped at me when I offered my impression of the town. Everybody returned to us and Leroy handed Annie the keys to the Fiat. She and Johnny climbed in and left. I correctly assumed that the Fiat would now be living in Chico. I thought that would be best for everybody, actually. Especially the Fiat, who would be a lot busier with Annie at the controls.

We stayed in Chico for the remainder of the day. I was parked at a motel until the early evening when Leroy drove me to a large high school parking lot and left me parked among hundreds of other cars. I saw many people Annie's age who were wearing robes and flat hats with little tassels on them. Since teenagers normally do not dress alike, I gathered this was a special event of some sort. Leroy and Liz were there for a couple of hours, after which Leroy drove to a different restaurant than we had visited with Annie and Johnny. When we returned to the motel I had trouble sleeping because young people were driving around in their cars, singing and yelling and honking horns.

When we left Chico the following morning I mistakenly believed we were returning to Santa Cruz. Instead, Leroy pointed me the opposite direction. It was unfamiliar territory but it was a pleasant drive as we began to climb in elevation, where the weather cooled and the sights and smells were new and enticing. It was a curvy road and I was proud to show off my remarkable ability to corner and accelerate, smoothing out the roads twists, turns and hills. It was easy to sense that Leroy enjoyed that drive as much as I did. I was a finely tuned machine and he was one with me, driving me precisely as I would have driven myself. It was a memorable afternoon indeed.

However, I must confess to some uneasiness as we entered the small town of Chester. I could see the other cars looking at me curiously, with something less than welcoming, admiring warmth. Most of them were pickups and older, functional American cars. Not that there is anything wrong with such vehicles, for there certainly is a place for them. They simply were not of my elite status and we had little in common. I was filled with anxiety when Leroy parked me in the driveway of a home, next to one of those unsightly pickups. After he and Liz went into the house I ignored him, concluding that he was likely too ignorant and parochial to have anything of interest to say to me, or to understand anything I might say to him. I recalled those occasions in San Francisco when I was unfortunate enough to be parked by valets in disgusting public garages. I used the same technique that day in Chester as I did then — not acknowledging those around me and feigning sleep.

That pickup, though, did not pick up on my hint, if you will pardon the pun. He continued to stare at me unabashedly until I acknowledged him with a curt hello. He responded with his own howdy and just kept staring at me. When I asked him if something was wrong, he replied that he knew of nothing that was wrong, again adding no comment beyond that curt response. When I could stand it no more I asked him why he was staring at me, and he replied that he had never seen a car like me and he was trying to figure out what kind I was. He sounded more naive and unseasoned than hostile so I explained what I was and gave him with a short history of my lineage. He listened courteously, but did not ask me to expand on any details. I thought this was unusual, as most cars would belabor me with additional queries, so I asked him if he had any further questions. To my surprise, he said he did not. I was compelled to ask why. The pickup simply replied it was none of his business. I was taken aback and felt a grain of respect for him, thinking that perhaps he was more discerning than I had initially concluded, and that I had allowed myself to be deceived by his clumsy appearance with his high cab, long open bed and unimaginative brown paint.

He taught me a valuable lesson in that brief meeting about making hasty assumptions based on outward appearances. It was both an enlightening and a humbling experience. We spent the night beside each other, talking little but at least in my case, growing more comfortable. By morning I was even more intrigued that the pickup had so little curiosity about me. This was a new experience, and his lack of prying or asking inane questions earned him my begrudging respect.

In the morning, Liz and Leroy climbed into my passenger compartment and we explored Chester, which did not take very long because it is such a tiny town. Once again, the local vehicles were staring at us so I endeavored to put my best wheel forward and render us worthy of the attention. We went from one end to the other and then back again, with Leroy providing a narrative description of the geography, businesses that had come and gone, reminiscences, and homes he had visited as a child and young man. I gleaned from this dialog, which was probably much more interesting to him than to Liz and me, that Leroy had spent his childhood in this unsophisticated place. As we drove past a real estate office he told Liz the building formerly housed something called a Frosty Freeze and that he had whiled away many hours there. He also pointed out a run-down grocery store where, as a teen he had worked for a meat cutter, and the gas station across the street where he had learned to service cars.

The only things of interest I saw during that brief tour were two cars, the likes of which I had never before witnessed. Both were parked on side streets that we did not enter, but they were so unusual that they diverted my attention, if not Leroy's. One was a small boxy thing that looked well cared for but was astonishingly old. The other was also vintage, but newer and a bit more rounded, also well cared for. Leroy pulled into the gas station to fill my tank and with considerable relief I noticed that we were adjacent to a late model BMW 740i rather than one of those ignorant pickups. I spoke briefly to the BMW. He seemed friendly enough, so I asked him about those two odd cars I had just seen. He explained that one was something called a 1931 Ford Model A coupe, and the other a 1937 Plymouth four-door sedan. Both had resided in Chester for many years and were not driven much except in parades and other special events. He opined that we should both hope to live as long as those classics, and I must say I agreed with him, so long as other cars would not think I was as strange looking as I thought those two were.

I spent that evening once again adjacent to the pickup. I thought I had been less than polite at our initial meeting, as I had asked him nothing about himself. So I attempted to strike up a conversation, which turned out to be a challenge. Once again, he was civil enough, but taciturn, responding to my queries but offering little elucidation. I managed to glean that he was a 1968 model who had lived his entire life — fourteen years to date — in Chester. He expressed no curiosity about life beyond it. He said he was purchased to be a reliable vehicle and to haul things when necessary. Beyond that, he had no aspirations other than to do his job well. That sounded to me like an awfully mundane life, yet I couldn't help but admire his strength of character. By morning he had reinforced to me with his dignified and straightforward mien that I should refrain from jumping to hasty conclusions based on initial impressions.

We left Chester the next morning but to my puzzlement, we continued east rather than returning to Santa Cruz. I was treated to more new sights and smells as Leroy skillfully guided us over the highway. When our driving day ended, four hours later, we parked at an imposing hotel at a place called South Shore at Lake Tahoe. Leroy and Liz took their luggage and left me in a large parking lot filled with cars of every imaginable make, from lowly Chevrolets and VW Bugs to high end Porsches and Mercedes such as myself, with everything in between, and even an egomaniacal Ferrari parked at an angle, selfishly occupying two spaces. On the bright side, there were very few pickups and those I did see were clean and looked as if they had never been used for hauling anything other than groceries.

It was just after dusk when Leroy and Liz returned and we drove a short distance, pulling up at a place with a sign that said it was a chapel. I do not know what a chapel is but they acted like they did. They went in, and a half hour later they returned, giggling and joking about what must have a hilarious experience there. They were more lighthearted than I had ever seen them as we returned to the hotel. As they walked away Liz remarked that she could not believe they were married. I guess that was important but I don't know why. Cars do not get married. Not wishing to try to solve things I do not comprehend or are of no importance to me, I went to sleep.

We departed South Shore early the following morning and took a different route, climbing up and over a mountain on a wide road. When we had been driving in the flat valley for a while and I began to recognize some of the landmarks, I concluded we were on our way home to Santa Cruz. We arrived in the early afternoon and after I was unloaded I was left alone to relax and reflect on my most eventful trip. The old Bug convertible asked me where the Fiat was and when I told him he now belonged to Annie in Chico, he just shrugged. I surmised that by this stage in his life he had seen so many other cars come and go that he had learned to accept the inevitability of change.

———————

I was now the sole commute car for Liz and Leroy. I must confess that the challenge of the drive between Santa Cruz and San Jose notwithstanding, I eventually tired of the routine and found myself longing for a more exciting road trip where I did not know to anticipate every bump and idiosyncrasy of the route, and did not have every iota of landscape memorized. This is not to say that I shirked my duties in any way, for I most certainly would never do such a thing. It was simply a case of becoming bored with the same drive, five days per week. The thrill was gone.

My hope for change was realized on the day when a large truck pulled up in front of the house. He informed me in rather crude English that he was a moving van, and that he was going to haul the furnishings from, in his words, "dis dump" to "anudder joint." Three large, unpleasant, smelly men spent the day loading the truck and in the late afternoon they drove away. Shortly thereafter, Leroy emerged from the house and got into the VW, Liz settled in my driver's seat and we all pulled onto the road, bound once again for the road to San Jose.

This time we did not stop in San Jose but continued north and stopped in Palo Alto. Leroy and Liz parked us in a motel lot. I asked the old Bug how his trip was and he snapped at me and said that everything was just fine, and why shouldn't it be and what was it to me, anyway. I bit my fan belt, refraining from a snappy riposte. It was obvious that he was exhausted but his pride would not let him admit it, so I ignored his curtness. Actually, I was impressed that he made it all that distance but I feared that if I complimented him he would misconstrue my remarks as patronizing, so I kept silent. We spent a quiet evening with the exception of a minor confrontation with a BMW who took exception to being parked next to the VW, who he evidently considered to be of a lower class.

When he made a disparaging remark about how Palo Alto seems to be letting just about any car into its city limits these days, the VW squinted at him through his headlights and asked him if he had a problem. He added a snappy comeback about how BMW must stand for "Bothersome Mediocre Whiner", and that if he wanted to mix it up a little he was game. Given the relative condition of their paint jobs, the Bug had a lot less to lose if it came to that. The BMW was taken aback by the aggressiveness of the Bug's response and he wisely chose to shift his attention elsewhere. The other cars within hearing distance guffawed, enjoying the scene of a smug BMW being put in his place by a vintage VW.

The remainder of the night was incident-free. I must say I admired that old VW for his unwillingness to let personal insults go unanswered. Most of us concurred that BMWs were generally overrated, snooty cars with overly aggressive, obnoxious drivers that matched their personalities. As a group they were disliked, their impressive engines and construction notwithstanding. We Mercedes Benzes are as well designed and built if not better, and even more expensive. We are recognized for our reliability, comfort and performance, yet we never flaunt it, not even my 1955 cousin, the 300 SL Gull-Wing coupe. We were in universal agreement that if any Mercedes had earned the right to strut amongst his peers, this one was the worthy candidate. Yet, he never did because above all, we Mercedes automobiles are dignified and self-restrained, and unlike BMWs of every ilk we prefer to let our many assets speak for themselves.

The following morning the Bug and I were driven to a house in a quiet Palo Alto neighborhood where I saw the van parked in the driveway. The same large, off-putting men were waiting for us. As we approached they emerged from the van's cab and opened his rear-loading door. Leroy greeted them, unlocked the house and they all went inside except, of course, the van, the Bug and me. Soon the men began to unload the van, carrying things into the house. I had never seen the things humans keep in their houses so this was a real headlight opener for me. Most of the things were a mystery, like the big box with the glass window in the front; the tall, heavy metal box with big doors on the front but with no wheels; the large, floppy square thing with the tag that read "Do not remove under penalty of law" on it; and boxes upon boxes of who knows what? Cars have no need for such things. We're perfectly happy as long as we are not abused and we are well maintained. I believe our lack of material possessions lets us be happier and less stressed, and that if humans would take a lesson from us they might live longer.

By early afternoon the van was empty and driven away. The Bug and I remained parked on the street while Leroy and Liz presumably organized their belongings in the new house. We had come to realize that we were most likely going to live in Palo Alto now. The VW had never been there. I had, but I lived in a different neighborhood at an apartment complex. This location was much more calm. A few people walked by, looking at the house with curiosity and at us as well. I received the usual admiring glances. The old Bug, though, did not. We heard a few disparaging remarks like "What in the world is that thing?" and "There goes the neighborhood." It is good that humans cannot understand cars when they speak or they might have been shocked at the Bug's attitude. I confess to never having heard some of those words before and I suspect they were not in our owners' manuals.

Over the next week we familiarized ourselves with our new surroundings. Most of the other cars in the area were friendly enough. A few were distant and self-absorbed which was quite a contrast to those friendly, outgoing cars in our old Santa Cruz neighborhood. I did feel some sympathy for the Bug. When other cars spoke it was always to me and he was either ignored or sneered at, but never engaged. That was too bad. I had come to know how wise and decent he really was. They were missing out on getting to know a unique individual by making the faulty assumption that his ragged appearance reflected his inner soul. The Bug appeared relieved when Leroy cleared a space in the garage and moved him there. To be honest, I think we all were. I liked and admired that pugnacious little guy, but his presence and his take-no-prisoners attitude were stressful.

When Leroy returned to work it was to a different place. The parking lot was smaller, as was the building where he spent his days. The sign on the exterior read "Silicon Valley Consulting, Inc.". As we returned home that evening Leroy was in high spirits, carrying on about what a great opportunity his new job was. He said he had stayed too long at Applied Semiconductor and that this new job was reenergizing. I knew just what he was talking about. With each of my relocations, first to San Francisco, then Palo Alto, then Santa Cruz and now back to Palo Alto, I felt new excitement as I anticipated the new scenery and other cars I might meet. We cars may not grasp the details of what people do when they are at work but we do understand their conversations and we are able to sense their moods. When our drivers are happy, we are happy and I was very pleased with this change in Leroy.

As I reflected on the past few months it made me realize that there had been some radical changes taking place. First, that odd-looking Fiat was given to Annie. Leroy and Liz got married and moved from Santa Cruz to Palo Alto. Then Leroy had a new job. I felt the beginning of a gnawing concern that perhaps a change was in store for me as well, although there was no logical reason. It was just a nagging, nonspecific anxiety.

As it turned out, there was no basis for my fears, at least not yet. I was much relieved as we adapted to another routine of commuting to work and occasional weekend forays. Leroy, Liz and I were a tightly knit team and I lived in dread of that that one day we would be broken up. I resolved to give them as little justification for change by concentrating on smooth performance, avoiding accidents, treading lightly and evenly on my tires, and making all my fuses, wires, hoses and belts last as long as possible. In short, I vowed to live up to the high Mercedes Benz standard. I must say I believe I did quite well at it too, giving Leroy and Liz no cause to take me to a shop other than for routine maintenance.

The next few years were comfortable, but I was beginning to feel my age. Sometimes I was slow to start and was having trouble waking up as quickly as I had when I was new and frisky. Also, I developed a "thunk" in my right front shock absorber and a few other minor squeaks and rattles that were audible but not serious. Most of the time they were not an issue, but when we encountered a pothole or a rough stretch of road, it was embarrassing. Overall

I continued to provide reliable, comfortable transportation. And I still looked good.

The undeniable fact, however, was that I was nearing 200,000 miles on my odometer. Had I been an American car I'm sure I would have been recycled by then. But even a Mercedes has a finite life span. Rather than allow myself to obsess about my aging, I tried to live in the moment, squeezing every bit of adventure I could out of life before my ultimate fate, whatever that might be. I relished those trips to Chico when Leroy would visit Annie and Johnny, although they usually entailed just a drive up, a wait in a restaurant parking lot and a return trip. There were some occasions when Annie would drive to Palo Alto in that odd little Fiat for the weekend. We still did not have much to say to each other, but at least we were civil. I will confess to thinking that his presence detracted from the beauty of our upscale neighborhood, but I remained silent.

My favorite excursions were the ones to Chester. After that disconcerting first visit, we returned four or five times. I adjusted to being stared at and actually got to the point where I welcomed it and I would even preen a little when I found one of those rusty, banged up pickups with gun racks and bumper stickers staring at me.

The principal reason I had come to relish the Chester trips, though, was the quality time I got to spend with the '68 Chevy pickup. Paradoxically, I now had almost twice as many miles on me as he did, yet I thought of him as so much more worldly. He just had a quiet aura about him and a clearheaded philosophy about vehicles and our roles. With each visit my respect for his wisdom grew. I also felt that he was warming to me a little. And I found myself wondering why it should matter if a simple, unsophisticated American half-ton pickup likes me or not. This was a new experience for me and it was both humbling and broadening. I felt imbued with his Zen-like acceptance of life's exigencies and where we properly fit in the universe. This was truly headlight-opening for me. It slowly dawned on me that my attitude had been shallow indeed as I shunned lower vehicles and looked down my hood at them for no reason other than my own perceived status and self-image. That noble truck, while saying so little, made me realize that I needed to reexamine my value system if I hoped to become as elegant on the inside as I am on the outside. I shall be forever grateful for the influence he had on my life.

––––––––––

The inevitable separation from Leroy and Liz came to pass on a Saturday morning in early autumn of 1986, when they drove me to San Jose and parked me on the street in front of a car lot full of BMWs. I don't think it's any secret that this is the last place I wanted to spend any time. I had never been so uncomfortable in my life, sitting there on the street with twenty BMWs leering at me and making disrespectful comments. There was a time in my earlier life when, put into that situation, I would not have deigned to speak to them or even acknowledge their existence but would have stared straight ahead and reflected on what a fruitless waste of mental energy it was for one model of expensive German cars to ridicule one another. By this point, though, I had mellowed. I responded courteously to queries about my background. I did sense, though, that I was a minority in a less than friendly environment. My life's lessons from the old Chevy were put to good use that day, inspiring me to be polite yet distant and avoid the temptation to make snide comments.

My fate was sealed an hour later. Leroy and Liz returned and gave my keys to a man whom I had never met. He got behind my wheel, started my engine and drove me away. I was thoroughly confused. He accelerated me, slipped me into neutral and raced my engine, slammed on my brakes, sped up and took a corner faster than I was accustomed to, and then worked his way back to where we had started. I had the sense that I had just been through some kind of a test. I was grateful for one thing which was that he parked me out of view of that smug line of BMWs. Leroy emerged, removed his personal effects and gave me a pat on my roof as he returned to the building. A few minutes later he and

Liz walked past me and climbed into (and it pains me to say this) a new BMW 325i convertible. They drove away and I was overcome with sadness and anxiety.

The next couple days were like a bad dream, only when I awoke I was still in it. First I was taken into a garage where fifteen other cars were in various states of maintenance. I was examined from bumper to bumper and my engine was tested with strange electronic equipment that tickled uncomfortably. After I was tuned up I actually felt pretty good physically, but I was still disoriented. Next I found myself in a body shop where a man removed and smoothed my dented areas, painted me and replaced my lenses. When he was through I felt and looked much younger than my twelve years. I retained a dimming hope that I had just been left there for a makeover but that hope was dashed when I was parked on the lot surrounded by cars of various makes and models. I had seen used car lots before, but I had never been a used car, nor been sold except when I was new. When I expressed my displeasure at this experience to another Mercedes parked next to me, he advised me to get over myself. This was his third experience in a used car lot and he had no sympathy. He was an aging (1968) 250 sedan who, with 247,000 miles on his odometer, had clocked more than I thought possible. He told me he was exhausted and ready to call it a life, but that for some reason people like the looks of him and were determined to prolong his misery. I suppose that by comparison I had less to be unhappy about. That did not significantly reduce my discomfort about my unknown future, however.

My tenure at the used car lot was mercifully short. In just three days I was purchased and driven home by a young professional woman who actually reminded me somewhat of Liz, although she needed more experience behind the wheel before I would be truly comfortable with her. I determined to take on that project with pride and to continue doing what we Mercedes Benzes do well — serving our owners to the best of our ability. Meanwhile, I relished my fond memories of Liz and Leroy and hoped that one day our paths would cross again.

Chapter 15

PURSUING THE ULTIMATE IMAGE

L
eroy and Liz bought me in San Jose. They offset some of my cost by trading in a 13-year old Mercedes Benz. He still looked OK but there was no way he could keep up with us newer cars, even if he was a German. We BMWs do respect our Mercedes cousins, although we consider them to be a bit stuffy and staid. I have heard unconfirmed reports that they consider BMWs to be upstarts who are overly focused on speed and preening, rather than upholding the dignified German image. They're entitled to their opinions even if they're stuck in the past. There's plenty of room on the roads for both of us — as long as they stay out of the way.

If I do say so myself, I am one fine-looking creation. My looks are exceeded only by my astonishing performance. They just don't make many like me anymore with my advanced engineering, creative design and tight construction. There are more expensive cars out there and even a few that can go faster. But the expensive ones don't perform like we do and the faster ones cost more and are not nearly so attractive.

I was manufactured in Germany by Bayerische Motoren Werke AG. In English we just call it Bavarian Motor Works because not everyone is blessed with the ability to speak our mother tongue. I am a model 325i cabriolet with a four speed manual transmission. I was built in 1986. My straight six fuel-injected engine is as powerful as 168 straining horses, which is more than most herds, and I can leap from 0 to 60 MPH in a mere seven seconds. My top speed is supposed to be 138 MPH but I've never tried it. And if required, which it usually is not, I can generate 6,500 RPM. We BMWs boast a rich heritage, from our old Radio Flyer aircraft engine days serving our country in the First World War, to motorcycles in 1923, and since 1929, automobiles. There is a well-founded reason that we are billed as "the Ultimate Driving Machine" because we simply are. I am proud to sport the impressive BMW logo on my hood and my trunk.

People who drive us are generally high achievers in their careers and have demonstrated abilities above the crowd. Sometimes they are referred to as yuppies (young urban professionals), self-absorbed jerks, or just plain inconsiderate drivers, and are often described with more colorful language. Many of them are attorneys and financial managers. I believe the stereotypes are all unfairly negative because those who do not drive us are jealously inferior. We're not for everybody, particularly those who go too slow in the fast lane.

Leroy and Liz paid $24,800 for me in the autumn of 1986. Politically, it was a year of upheaval, making me very happy I am a car instead of a human. President Ronald Reagan called the leader of Libya nasty names; the president of Haiti fled to France; the Philippine president slipped out of his country to avoid prosecution for corruption; and the Panamanian president was arrested for selling illegal drugs. All in all, it made us all wonder why people can't just mind their business and do their jobs like we cars do. To top all this off, the Challenger rocket ship exploded just after launching, tragically taking the lives of the crew of seven; and in Russia the Chernobyl nuclear power plant was incinerated in a disastrous explosion. I believe we BMWs were about the only saving grace in an otherwise bleak year.

When Leroy first settled in behind my wheel I will confess to a momentary panic regarding the size of his feet, which are enormous. I envisioned a disastrous first day with my new owner's shoes covering my clutch, brake and gas all at the same time. It was a major relief when I felt him working my pedals as we drove from the dealership. In spite of their size, Leroy's feet managed to press only one pedal at a time and not only that, he did it with surprising finesse. I could tell that he was not a novice with a stick shift. Liz asked him why he was so insistent on a manual shift and his response was perfectly cogent: he told her that if they were going to drive a hot sports car they should go all the way and make it a true ultimate driving experience. He added that automatic transmissions were fine for Buicks, but not for zippy BMWs. How right he was! It's an option for us and I'm thankful I was built with a stick shift as was right and proper. I feel sorry for any 325i with an automatic transmission because there is no way they can enjoy the life we deserve.

We drove to Palo Alto. Because the day was cool and it was about to rain, Leroy had not retracted my convertible top but I figured there would be plenty of opportunities for that. He was cautious to a fault, maintaining the speed limit and keeping the official DMV recommended distance between us and the cars in front of us. In other words, I was disappointed. BMWs do not enjoy following rules, and our owners typically are skilled to the extent that they should be exempt from rules, aside from the ones they make up. We're quite good at darting in and out, changing lanes, tailgating and exceeding the speed limit. We were designed with these abilities and we love to exploit them. When we're stuck with a driver who does follow rules we are frustrated, as I most decidedly was on that first trip with Leroy. I could only hope that he was exercising undue caution because it was his first time behind my wheel and that, with time, he would learn to enjoy my very special capabilities to their maximum.

He parked me in a driveway of a nice enough-looking house but he did not open the garage door to move me under cover. That was puzzling. I was brand new, yet he was leaving me out in the rain. This is not to say, of course, that rain affects me one way or the other. It just seemed rather disrespectful. I sat there all night and when the rain did begin it was intense, but it let up fairly quickly just before midnight. When Leroy emerged in the morning he did so through the garage door, which he raised from the inside. The sight before me caused me to gasp. Occupying my rightful space out of the elements was the most hideous, ugly, unkempt disgrace to the German nation that one could imagine. It was an unspeakably old Volkswagen convertible, dented and rusty, with a torn and patched roof. I had to avert my headlights because I could not bear to look at such a disheveled insult to German engineering. I assumed that Leroy would move that horrible thing out of the garage to make room for me.

That was not to be. He lowered the garage door and climbed into my passenger compartment, started me up and backed me out to the street. We headed for the freeway, but instead of entering it Leroy crossed over and turned onto a frontage road. Because it was so early and a weekend morning, there was no traffic. He looked into my mirrors, then at the road in front of us, and suddenly mashed his foot down on my accelerator. That was more like it! I leapt into action, leaning forward, squeezing every ounce of energy I could muster as Leroy shifted smoothly through my four gears, and quickly climbed to 60, then 70, and before I was even trying, 90! The road was still damp, but I was gripping as if I had glue on my tires. I was preparing to hit my maximum speed when suddenly Leroy's formidable shoe was pressing on my brake pedal, hard. I instantly reduced my speed and then stopped. I was proud of my performance on this first test, yet troubled that

Leroy ended it before I could truly demonstrate my skills. He turned me around, and once again we were off like a shot, quickly reaching 90 and even a bit more. Our intersection was rapidly approaching so he again slammed on my brakes and slowed to the crawl it would take to turn back onto the main road and find our way home. I allowed myself a glimmer of optimism that my life was about to improve.

We parked once again in the driveway. Leroy opened the garage door, leaving it up as he went into the house, and I found myself staring at that unkempt Bug. I was startled when he suddenly asked me what the hell I was staring at. So I told him he was a disgrace to the German legacy and that it would be best if he remained out of sight, and that I was willing to sacrifice my rightful place in the garage to accomplish that. I thought I had communicated my feelings quite clearly and I was taken aback by his reaction. He muttered a couple of barely intelligible obscenities and remarked that I had not yet earned enough credibility to pass judgment on him or any other car, and although I might be new and shiny, I was nothing more than a chick car. Well! We obviously had not gotten off to a good start. That was fine with me — I had no desire to form any kind of relationship with him and I sensed that his feelings were mutual.

Later that day it was Liz's turn to drive me. I noted with relief that her feet were not as large as Leroy's. She also felt much lighter in my driver's seat. We were a good fit. When we started down the road it was apparent that Liz was familiar with manual transmissions, for there was no grinding or lurching. She didn't kill my engine once as she moved through the gears. She was more conservative than Leroy, but I reminded myself that this was our first drive together. I was optimistic that with time and familiarity, Liz had the potential to develop into a credible BMW driver. Sitting beside her, Leroy gave her tips such as encouraging cars in front of us to move aside or speed up by tailgating and flashing my lights, or having me dart in and out of traffic to gain the advantage. At first, Liz just laughed at him but when she realized he was serious she became annoyed and advised him to stop offering stupid unsolicited advice that could result in a ticket at best and a totaled car at worst. I absolutely agreed with Leroy. Liz clearly did not, and things got a little tense between them. By the time we returned to their house they were not speaking to each other. So there I was, parked in the driveway, staring at that disgusting Bug and feeling as if I was somehow the cause of some marital stress. I had done nothing wrong but I didn't like the way things were starting out with my new owners.

———————

It was with considerable relief on Monday morning, when Liz again was driving, to find that she and Leroy had apparently worked through their differences. They chatted amiably and Leroy tuned the radio while Liz focused on the driving. This was my first experience with a rush hour and I was stunned at the traffic, which was progressing at a crawl. Liz, though, carefully maneuvered me into the carpool lane. We were able to pick up some speed there but not nearly enough to please me. And as I could have predicted, there was a lumbering old Chrysler in front of us, oblivious to the fact that we wanted to get around him. We had no choice but to follow his outsized rear end until he moved over in preparation for his exit from the freeway. As we shot by I yelled out "Thanks for nothing!" and in return was given an icy stare. It was almost as if that sluggish Chrysler felt he was entitled to hog the carpool lane with no consideration for those of us who need to demonstrate our full potential at every opportunity.

We arrived at an office building and stopped long enough for Leroy to get out. Liz and I continued to another office where she locked my doors and went inside. A short while later she returned in the company of two other women and a man, all of whom looked me over with care and said nice things to Liz about my design. The women seemed particularly impressed that I was a convertible, while the man, for some odd reason, kicked my left front tire. I immediately disliked him. They all returned to their office and I was left in the parking lot until later in the day when Liz returned and we left to go pick up Leroy and drive back to Palo Alto.

This, as it turned out, was to be my routine during the week. It wasn't very exciting and I soon found myself dreading Monday mornings and looking forward to Friday evenings. Odd as it may sound, I could sense from their bantering that Liz and Leroy felt the same.

I loved the weekends. It seemed like we went someplace new with each of them, and I had soon been exposed to San Francisco, the Wine Country, Lake Tahoe, Santa Cruz, the north coast and a place called Chico. Traffic was heavy at times but at least we were not stuck in a commute routine. There was always something new to see. Most of the time we were able to speed along as fast as we wanted, or at least a fast as we could get away with. Liz was beginning to drive me like a proper sports car with occasional glimmers of aggression and gradually increasing speed. Leroy was the one who brought out the best in me. He drove me as a BMW ought to be driven, with quick getaways, smooth shifting and excessive speed. I came to an early conclusion that speed limits were created by stodgy people for marginal drivers in low-performance cars. I just did my best to help Leroy free us from those arbitrarily and unrealistic bonds. We became adept at weaving through traffic and letting slow cars in front of us know we needed to get around them. We were often the target of glares and, as Leroy called them, one-finger salutes. I didn't care. Slower cars with slower drivers simply did not understand the concept of a BMW. If all cars were BMWs the world would be a much happier place and we would all be able to get from point A to point B a whole lot faster.

I was both pleased and mystified the first time we went to Chico. I was pleased because Leroy and I were going somewhere new with no commute traffic. I was mystified because I did not know our destination. It was a long drive through uninteresting countryside but the road was fast. He had put my top down and I could tell that he was enjoying the ride as much as I was, with the wind blowing through his hair and my radio cranked up high enough to hear it above the din. Liz was not with us that day. I know Leroy was fond of Liz but he was enjoying a day to himself on the open road, as was I. As we zoomed along in the fast lane at 80, occasionally creeping up to 90, he sang along with the radio as he kept a constant watch in my mirror for those cars with the red lights and sirens. Inevitably, there were a few underperforming cars who slowed us down from time to time. Leroy would gracefully scoot me around them at the first opportunity, either on the right or the left, and resume our more natural speed.

We arrived in Chico in a couple of hours and Leroy stopped in front of a house, rather than the usual hotel or restaurant. There was a boxy, yellow Fiat parked in the driveway who looked at us with curiosity. His rear was covered with decals and bumper stickers, informing me (and anybody else who happened to look at them) that his driver was attending Chico State and a member of Theta Sigma Upsilon; children should be fed; Republicans are evil and greedy; and war is stupid. I was neither informed nor interested in any of this and found the decor to be distasteful. It was not my place to give the Fiat my opinion, though, so I refrained. I figured he had enough of a burden simply being ugly, old and bright yellow and did not need any feedback from me to reinforce how vastly different we were.

A rather stern looking woman answered the door when Leroy rang. She did not invite him in. He stood there for a few minutes until an attractive young lady came out to greet him with a hug. The stood on the porch chatting until another person appeared, a tall, gangly teenager who looked quite a bit like Leroy. I noted that his feet were similarly outsized. The three of them climbed in and we drove away. I heard the lady call Leroy "Dad" so it began to dawn on me that they must be his children. He called them Annie and Johnny. I was puzzled that they seemed to be living with another woman who did not care much for Leroy, and that Liz was excluded from all of this. I assumed it would make sense at some point. We parked at a restaurant where Leroy found a spot on the end like he usually did, which minimized my chances of having my flawless doors dented by careless neighbors.

After my three passengers went inside I heard a voice with a distinctive German accent asking "Vas dat Leroy?" I looked around and discovered that the question had come from an extremely old but beautifully reconditioned Volkswagen. It was clear that I was technologically superior and more roadworthy, yet I figured I should treat him with deference, given his age, his German roots, and the fact that he exuded about as much class as a Bug could possibly muster. I replied that yes, that was Leroy. The Bug told me I might not believe it, but Leroy had been his owner some 25 years ago. I naturally harbored some doubt that his memory could be that sharp but when he described Leroy's driving skills and big feet, I was persuaded that he was telling the truth.

The Bug told me he had been driven by Leroy when he was a college student in Chico. He regaled me with stories about their time together, his most memorable among many being a trip to Mexico during spring break. He spoke of his youth with fondness. And while he now looked and felt better than he could ever recall, he missed those carefree and adventurous days with Leroy the college student and frat boy. Now that he had been carefully restored he led a pampered existence. He was not complaining, he said, he was just nostalgic. When I asked him why Leroy had sold him he told me he had not been sold, but rather traded for a cute but totally unreliable MG.

Leroy, Annie and Johnny returned and as we drove away I told the VW, who Leroy had not even seen, that it had been a pleasure meeting him. We meandered around Chico as Leroy and the kids chatted. I gathered that Annie was in her final year of college and Johnny had just enrolled. Johnny asked Leroy if he could take a turn behind my wheel. Leroy agreed, much to my trepidation.

As Johnny pulled into the traffic I could sense that he had some experience with manual transmissions but he wasn't nearly as adept as Leroy. He raced my engine before engaging me in low, and jerked his way through my gears. Like Leroy, though, he seemed to have adapted to his big feet, and he managed to avoid stepping on two pedals at once. I felt he had some potential but that he was not yet seasoned. Annie didn't seem to notice or care one way or the other.

Leroy asked Annie if something was bothering her so I guess she was not always as quiet as she was on that day. She replied that her mother was driving her crazy and that she could hardly wait to move out. Leroy told her all mothers and daughters have occasional stressful moments, and pointed out that she had just a few more months more of school, after which she would be able get a job and gain some independence. He asked her to be patient because paying college expenses for both her and Johnny was a strain and he couldn't afford to pay for her to live somewhere else. She told him she knew that, but just needed to vent. I know cars have vents, but I wasn't aware people did. Anyway, she calmed down and the three of them continued chatting as Johnny drove us aimlessly around Chico.

We returned to Annie and Johnny's house and while they continued their conversation for a few more minutes, the Fiat and I had one of our own. He asked me where the Mercedes was and I told him that he had been traded in as part of the deal to acquire me. I added that I had never actually met the Mercedes just in case I was about to get some questions I could not answer. I was surprised to learn that Leroy was the Fiat's original owner. I couldn't imagine somebody with the discerning taste to buy me would deign to be seen in such a funny looking thing, although I kept that thought to myself. Just because he was ugly was no reason to insult him. He said he had been living in Chico for four years and while he missed Leroy, he had a pretty good life with Annie and hauling her sorority sisters around, although they could be noisy and screechy. He asked if the '62 Bug was still living with us. I said regrettably he was, and not only was he in residence, he also was occupying my rightful place in the garage. The Fiat advised me not to pass hasty judgment on the VW. He had experienced a hard early life, had been with Leroy for many years, and had earned his right to covered parking. He told me more about the Bug's past and although I still felt some resentment, I began to get a glimmer of understanding.

I enjoyed my trip home from Chico. Leroy was in a hurry and I was up to the challenge, weaving deftly in and out of traffic and urging cars who clearly felt entitled to a slow trip in the fast lane to move over. With those who held their ground, Leroy and I simply eased around them on the right. A few of them gave us some rather descriptive feedback, of course, which I ignored. The last thing I wanted was a confrontation at 80 miles per hour so I just pressed on. It was a fun three hours, since I was finally doing what I was designed to do — exceed the speed limit and treat the freeway as a slalom course.

Another memorable road trip was to a place called Chester. Leroy, Liz and I left Palo Alto on a crisp autumn Saturday morning, heading for Chico. I assumed we would be stopping there for another visit with Annie and Johnny, as was Leroy's almost monthly routine. But we continued on, and I soon found myself on my first mountain road. What a thrill! I was born for this! There wasn't much traffic to impede us, and Leroy clearly was familiar with the road so I let myself go all out, zipping through the curves as we climbed into the mountains, with Leroy allowing me to speed up on the straight stretches, break slightly before the curves and then accelerate through them. I could sense Liz was uncomfortable with our performance and decided to let Leroy deal with that. My job was to get us to wherever it was we were going and to have a load of fun doing it. I had never dreamed that driving could be so exciting. When we approached Chester after almost an hour and a half of sheer joy, I reluctantly slowed down.

I was not prepared for what confronted my senses in Chester. I had seen a few pickup trucks but never so many in a single setting. With the exception of the old Bug, my peers in Palo Alto were pretty much like me, that is to say, expensive, clean, late model and more often than not, German made. There were a few upscale Japanese cars and even fewer American cars. We BMWs, Mercedes Benzes, Porsches and Audis were comfortable with each other. We had little respect for the big boxy American cars that looked like they had been designed by a committee, leaked fluids and accelerated slowly. The Japanese cars were a cut above, but not at our level. In addition, they spoke with an accent that was hard to decipher so the upshot was that they stayed among themselves, as did we Germans. We all understood the unwritten rules and it made for peaceful coexistence. In Chester, though, I felt self-conscious flaunting my good looks around those pickups — hulking dullards with dents, mud-splashed fenders and bumper stickers encouraging people to eat spotted owls.

Leroy pulled up to a house and parked me adjacent to one of those awful things. This one was and old, brown dirty Chevrolet truck who did not look approachable, which was fine by me. Leroy and Liz unpacked my trunk and went into the house. I noticed the pickup staring at me but I did not sense much interest on his part, which told me he was not that intelligent. I opted to ignore him. He did not ask a single question about me, nor did he show the least bit of respect for my advanced engineering and sleek design. I figured he was either intimidated or just slow. We spent the entire afternoon and all night side by side, with not a single word passing between us.

Late the following morning Leroy and Liz took me on a tour of Chester. I was not impressed. Clearly, there were no zoning laws, as the streets seemed to wander randomly and the houses were radically inconsistent. Some were nice, tidy and inviting and others were patched up ramshackle places with dead rusty cars and live hostile dogs in their yards. This was definitely not Palo Alto. As we drove up Main Street to the end of town, then turned around and reversed our course, it struck me that other than me, there wasn't a single BMW in sight. Many vehicles were of the same ilk as that odd truck I had spent the evening with so I had little to say to them. They eyed me as we drove by. I believe I detected envy but it may have been suspicion — some of those less advanced headlights are difficult to read. And I have to say that a few of the comments I overheard were not what I would call flattering. There was no question that I was superior in every way, yet I was beginning to feel a twinge of discomfort. I was well and truly out of my element and I began to long for the familiar environs of Palo Alto.

I met one car who, like me, was different from the crowd but in an entirely different way. Leroy had pulled into a gas station next to him and I overheard him talking with the owner. I learned he was a 1937 Plymouth who had lived in Chester for many years, and that Leroy had actually owned him in the late 1950s! I asked the Plymouth if that was true and he said he did recall a guy named Leroy with big feet who had owned him for a short time. The Plymouth said it had been fun, but a bit rough on him — he'd almost had his fender ripped off, had a bullet shot through his door and had been treated with something less than respect. He was on the verge of going to the crusher when a highly skilled local guy bought him for almost nothing and spent four years reconditioning him. I had to admit that he looked as if he had just been driven off the showroom floor. He said he was quite proud of his looks now and grateful to have been saved from the scrap heap. But the tradeoff was that he spent most of his time under a dust cover in his owner's garage, started up perhaps once a month to keep his seals tight and his battery charged, and driven very rarely, mostly for special occasions. He hastened to add that he was not complaining because his life was surely easier than most of the cars in the area. Based on my brief tour, I had to concur.

We returned to the house where we had spent the previous night. Once again I was parked next to that dullard of a truck. We spent the entire afternoon and night in silence. Rather than attempting to enter into a lucid dialog with an inferior car who would add so little, I pointedly ignored him once again and spent the night sleeping fitfully with nightmares of being pursued by an angry mob of filthy, mechanically unsound pickups.

It was with a huge sense of relief, at least for me, that we left Chester the next morning. Not only was I leaving this unwelcoming place, but also I was eagerly anticipating another thrilling challenge on the mountain road. As the town faded into the distance of my rear view mirror, I felt as if a burden had been lifted from my springs. I was back in my element as I once again gripped the road with Leroy skillfully guiding me through those magnificent curves. I knew that there was no way any of those clunky pickups could perform likewise. I wondered why anybody would buy such a vehicle. Humans can be difficult to understand.

We continued commuting during the week and taking occasional trips to Chico and other destinations on the weekends, but not to Chester. I heard Leroy explaining to Liz he did not want to go while it was snowing because he did not want to risk a dangerous ride. I don't know what snowing is but I was hurt that Leroy did not believe I could handle whatever came my way. Nevertheless, we did not return to Chester until the weather was warmer and I was never allowed to demonstrate that I could do just fine in snowing. And when we did visit Chester, that off-putting pickup was always parked in the same spot in the driveway. I think we returned four or five times over the ensuing years. I was parked next to him but we never exchanged a single word. I think he was missing out.

I felt I had established myself in our Palo Alto neighborhood by now and that the other cars were affording me the respect I deserved. This is not to say that they were friends. No, I believe the price of deference often can mean a life of solitude. I will confess that I sometimes came close to a feeling of envy when I saw them talking among themselves and sharing their stories about mechanical aches and pains, their exploits and the habits of their drivers. They did not include me in these conversations. I assume this was because they were intimidated and aware that they would never rise to the stature of the Ultimate Driving Machine. I accepted this with dignity, although I would have welcomed the chance to be included and to let them see that deep down I was just like them. Not that I was, of course, but I was confident I could fake it.

One Saturday morning Leroy opened the garage door, climbed into that odious Bug and started it up. He did this almost weekly, presumably to keep the battery from dying. In my opinion we all would have been better off if the battery and the VW had both died. On this day, though, Leroy backed the VW out of the garage. Then Liz got behind my wheel, started my engine and backed me into the street. Leroy and the Bug drove away with Liz following. I was mortified that other cars might think we were together so I pretended that it was merely coincidental that Liz and I happened to be traveling along the same road.

We followed them to an industrial area filled with warehouses, a beer distributor, a landscape supply store and a few auto repair shops. Leroy parked in front of one of these and went inside while Liz and I waited on the street. He returned in a few minutes with another man and together they walked around the VW, inspecting it closely while the man made notes on a clipboard. When Leroy rejoined Liz and me I was delighted that the Bug was not returning home with us. This was a good day indeed.

At long last, I was parked in my rightful place in the garage. It smelled a little like an old, stinky car but that was a minor annoyance, as I luxuriated in my new surroundings. I could relax in the privacy of my own space, out of the view and mirror-shot of the neighborhood cars. After the door was closed and the light extinguished I experienced a newfound inner peace that I had never felt before. There was nobody to impress, nobody to frown at, nobody to compare myself (favorably, naturally) to. It was just me and that was fine. I allowed myself sag a little. I slept a dreamless and restful sleep for the entire remainder of the weekend.

I was awakened with a start on Monday when Leroy and Liz opened the garage door and got into my passenger compartment for their commute to work. I was unusually mellow as we left the house, thinking all is good with the world. But shortly after getting onto the freeway I was once again back into my normal mode, impatiently glaring at other cars impeding me, disgusted by the appearance of most of them, and preening as they stared enviously at me while we zoomed by. I was behaving as I was intended to and as others expected. One difference was that I found myself reflecting on what a peaceful weekend I had enjoyed in the garage. I decided to categorize that as a guilty pleasure. If it was a one-time experience, I would tuck it away as a fond memory. But if it was a preview of a new living arrangement I would welcome it with considerable enthusiasm. So I was encouraged when I once again found myself in the peaceful sanctity of the garage that evening.

One might understandably conclude that it would be difficult to shift from my usual Ultimate Driving Machine persona to quiet garage time on a daily basis, but I was able to compartmentalize my life and do very well in both situations. I was my old self out in public, but once that door closed on my rear bumper my life was mine alone and nobody's business. I relished those private moments, but I was unaccustomed to the introspection that my time in the garage invited. If I found myself thinking too deeply about anything, such as how I might feel if I were treated as I treated other cars, or how I might compare to cars ten years in the future, or whether Leroy and Liz were thinking of trading me in, I would force myself to snap out of it and go on to another subject. Probably the only thing I do not excel at is self-criticism, not that I deserve very much of it.

Three weeks passed. By now, I had become accustomed to my new routine and was thoroughly enjoying my life with Leroy and Liz. It all came crashing down when we once again drove to the place where we had left the Bug. We parked and Leroy went inside. Shortly the big sliding door to the building opened and Leroy was backing out a strange, yet oddly familiar car. I looked closely at it, and he at me. No, it couldn't be! It was the VW. His dents were gone and he had a shiny new paint job, new bumpers and a brand new convertible top. I had to grudgingly admit that he looked pretty impressive — for a Bug. Liz and I followed Leroy home and I watched with regret when he opened the garage door and drove the newly restored VW in and parked. Once again, I was relegated to parking on the driveway. I was resentful.

It was a two-car garage, but like most of them, half of it was used to store things, leaving room for just a single car. That afternoon, Leroy and Liz rearranged things to create enough room for a small car. Leroy moved the Bug into the new space and then parked me beside him. To be sure, I had mixed emotions. On the one hand, I was not being forced to relinquish my space. On the other hand, I now had a roommate whom I neither respected nor liked. After Leroy closed the garage door, the VW and I were left alone, in the dark, side by side. It was uncomfortable. Aside from our initial unfriendly introduction, I had never spoken to him, nor he to me. I quickly resolved to continue with that arrangement. Our mere proximity in tight quarters did not bring with it an obligation to befriend him. I was taken aback, therefore, when he spoke to me and asked if I was going to continue being a stuck up jerk. This was not a good start. I replied that if I had given him that impression it was his problem, and that I may be aloof for good reasons, but certainly not stuck up. He replied that as far as he was concerned, the two are the same, and that if I wanted to be civil that would be fine, or if I wanted to continue being a stuck up jerk that would be just as fine. I resisted another snappy comeback and chose to remain silent for the remainder of the day and night.

When the garage door opened the next morning I was surprised to see Leroy and Liz get into the VW instead of me. They drove away and I was left to ponder the new situation. I concluded this whole thing was beyond my control and the smart thing would be to make peace with it. This meant despite my negative feelings toward the Bug, I should lower my standards and be more approachable. When they returned that evening I did just that. I apologized to the Bug for my reticence, explaining I was due for a service and was not feeling 100%. He said it was no problem, and if I wanted to be a friend it would be fine, but if not, he had been around for almost 27 years, long enough to realize that not every car can get along with all others, and he had no interest in forcing a relationship that was not meant to be. In other words, it was my call. I thought it was pretty clever of him, actually — a strategy I would expect a BMW to come up with, but not a lowly VW. The conversation established the ground rules for our relationship and things went more smoothly between us after that. We both accepted the reality of sharing the garage and resolved to make it as pleasant as we could.

––––––––––––

It was a sunny Saturday morning in June of 1988. Leroy got behind the wheel of the VW and Liz behind mine. We drove out of Palo Alto and headed toward the by now familiar route to Chico. I still enjoyed those trips although on this one we were going much more slowly because we were following the Bug. We arrived in Chico and pulled up at the house where Johnny lived with his mother. Annie had sold the ugly yellow Fiat and was now living in San Francisco. Johnny came out to meet us and immediately went to the VW and looked it over, gushing about how fine he now looked and paying absolutely no attention to me. Leroy invited him to drive to the usual restaurant for lunch. Liz and I followed. We were parked next to each other and I asked the Bug if he had ever been to Chico before. He replied that he had, although not for about 15 years but it looked pretty much the same except for the cars. We both noticed one drive by on the street that was not at all new. It was a nicely restored MG, one of those classic TD models from the early 1950s. It didn't look nearly as sleek as I do, of course, but its classic lines were impressive. We made brief headlight contact as he went by but there was no conversation, which was too bad, as I was curious to learn if he spoke with a British accent.

When Leroy, Liz and Johnny emerged from the restaurant they stood by us and carried on with their conversation. Leroy handed Johnny an envelope, telling him to get to DMV right away, and then he handed him the keys to the Bug. There were people hugs all around, after which Leroy and Liz climbed into my passenger compartment and Johnny got behind the wheel of the VW. When he started up and drove out of the parking lot it dawned on me, and probably the Bug, that Johnny was now his new owner. The lives of automobiles can take sudden twists and turns, even when not on the road. Without any warning, the VW was out of my life. Just when I was beginning to accept him. Not like him, necessarily, but accept him.

I was now an only car. It was a good life. I no longer had to share the garage or suffer the embarrassment of being identified with a humble Bug. I now was on a par with my neighbors. We had similar values so there was none of that annoying soul searching the VW loved to pester me with. We could now talk among ourselves about things we considered important, like being clean, being looked at with admiration by lesser cars, the joys of tailgating and living on a tidy street with no ugly cars around to detract from the beauty.

Leroy and Liz continued to use me for their commute. Both were happy in their jobs and were doing well because they were able to take me on several trips to upscale places like San Francisco, Lake Tahoe and Los Angeles where I would always be parked by a uniformed valet who treated me with care. On a number of occasions I was parked at the airport for two or three weeks at a time while Leroy and Liz took vacations to Europe and Hawaii. I cared nothing about Hawaii, but I was envious of their trips to Europe, my homeland. Nothing would have pleased me more than being taken along with them on the Autobahn where cars like me are allowed to be driven as we were intended. But that was not to be, so I made peace with my life in Palo Alto, which on balance was just fine.

I had observed on our street that older cars often disappeared, being replaced by new models. Most of them were top of the line German cars like myself, but many of them did not stay longer than two or three years. As an '86 model, I soon found myself the senior citizen of the block. The new cars talked with each other, paying less attention to me. They were courteous enough, but we had little in common. It was all about the latest innovations of fuel injection, airbags and electronic technology and I found myself feeling left behind. I still considered myself to be a beautiful machine and certainly worthy of more respect than I was being afforded but it would have been beneath my dignity to grovel. So I kept to myself when in the driveway, and was always relieved when I was alone in the garage, out of sight and mirror-shot.

On a nippy day in January of 1991, I was driven to a local Porsche dealer where I had a foreboding feeling that I was about to be traded in. I suppose I was somewhat consoled that at least my replacement was a fellow German, even if from another family entirely. But like all cars who find themselves for sale on a lot with others in the same situation, I was anxious about my future. And I was frankly resentful of the ignominious end of my relationship with Leroy and Liz. I knew that only very rarely does a car remain with a single owner for his entire life. But I was still hurt. I had tried so hard to be their Ultimate Driving Machine, only to be shunted aside and forgotten. To my considerable relief, though, Liz drove me home a short while later with Leroy following us in a brand new Porsche. She parked me in the garage and the two of them left in the new car while I pondered my future and the pending relationship with a new garage mate.

A short while later the garage door opened and the Porsche was parked next to me. We were distant at first and simply eyed one another. As the older resident, I felt I should make the first move, so I introduced myself to him. He did likewise. I told him my previous garage mate was a lowly Volkswagen and that I was pleased to now be in the company of a much classier car like him. That evidently was a mistake, as he quickly pointed out that the Volkswagen had been invented by the founder of Porsche and they were close cousins. He said there was much mutual respect between VWs and Porsches. They are vastly different cars filling vastly different roles but they share the common values of solid performance and reliability, and loyalty to their owners and to each other. I was about to point out the many flaws I had observed in that VW and how, by comparison, I was an Ultimate Driving Machine. But I restrained myself.

He told me that he was Leroy's car and that I now belonged to Liz exclusively. I liked Liz well enough but I had concerns about becoming the "chick car" that awful VW had called me. It quickly became apparent that Liz was my sole driver now, and the Porsche was Leroy's domain. I had no say in the matter, naturally, so my feelings were irrelevant. I had to adapt to the new arrangement. I did miss being driven by Leroy. Liz was good but it was not nearly as thrilling with her at my controls. I consoled myself with the fact that I at least had not been traded in or sold, and that on balance I was much better off with Liz. The Porsche never acknowledged it, but I knew I still was the Ultimate Driving Machine.

Chapter 16
PESKY AMERICAN SPEED LIMITS

As we approached the dealership at the end of the test run, the sales guy asked Leroy what he did for a living. Leroy said he was a management consultant. I did not know what that was, and I guessed the sales guy did not either, as he asked Leroy if he thought he could secure a loan to buy me. Leroy shrugged and said it didn't matter; that he'd pay cash if they would come down on the price a little. I could feel the sales guy squirming in the passenger seat as Leroy told him he was prepared to write a check for $66,000 and drive me home. They pulled into the lot and the sales guy asked Leroy to wait a minute while he discussed me with his boss. He came back five minutes later and told Leroy he could have me for $68,000. I thought that was a reasonable compromise, but Leroy said no thanks and started to walk away. The sales guy gave in at that point and said he would accept the $66,000, even if it meant no anniversary present for his wife. I knew right then that Leroy was not a man to be trifled with — the ideal Porsche owner.

Not every car can be a Porsche and not everyone can be a Porsche owner. We are designed to be operated by only the most discriminating of drivers — those who can appreciate truly advanced engineering, smooth handling, exceptionally responsive performance, and sleek yet subtly understated lines. I am a proud Carrera 2 Cabriolet. I come from a long line of distinguished 911s, which boasts the longest production record of any sports car in the world, dating back to 1963. We all were built in Stuttgart, of course, by highly skilled and dedicated German craftsmen. My efficient flat six engine needs only 130 horsepower to reach 130 MPH, and it will do it in a hurry. As I progress smoothly through the five speeds of my manual transmission, my rear spoiler self-adjusts to make certain I don't become airborne. Not everybody can afford me. My MSRP was $70,690, which was more than double the average annual household income in the USA the year I was built, 1991.

Germany had been reunified the preceding year. We Germans were very proud of that accomplishment and were confident that we were up to the challenges of merging the Eastern and Western sectors of our country after 46 years of separation. 1991 also was the year Boris Yeltsin became the president of Russia; and the year that the United Nations, at the urging of U.S. president George H.W. Bush, invaded Iraq to persuade them to stop their invasion of Kuwait. It worked.

Before Leroy purchased me, I had been test driven by three other guys and I didn't like any of them. One obviously had learned to drive with an automatic transmission. He ground and jerked his way through my gears as he lurched down the street, causing both the sales guy and me to wince. The other two knew how to drive me, but lacked the innate feel that truly skilled drivers have with their machine. Oddly, both of them were lawyers who refused to listen to the coaching of the sales guy on how to get the most out of me. I will confess to being wary when Leroy took me out for my test drive with him because I did not think his substantial feet would be able to negotiate my small pedals. But the moment he eased me onto the road I could sense that this was a guy who knew his way around a stick shift. We had an immediate bond.

We left the dealership, following a lady in a BMW, and ended up at the same house. She parked the BMW in the garage and then joined Leroy for our first real drive together. Her name was Liz and she seemed pleased that the BMW was now going to be her car. That made sense to me, since it looked like a car more suited to women than to men and there was no question that I am a man's car. Leroy was tentative with me at first, but it wasn't long before he relaxed and so did I as he became familiar with my acceleration, turning and braking.

I was parked in the garage next to the BMW. I was familiarizing myself with my new surroundings when he introduced himself. I did likewise. For some reason, he felt compelled to point out that I was a much more worthy garage mate than the previous occupant, a lowly Volkswagen. I took umbrage at that and I told him so. He clearly was not aware of the long-standing close connection between Porsches and Volkswagens, both of which are exceptionally reputable and committed to superior service. He quickly backtracked, apologizing for offending me. That made me respect him even less: if he had an opinion about something he should have been honest about it, rather than change it to appease me simply because I'm more expensive than my VW cousins.

As it turned out, my first impression of the BMW — that he was shallow, insecure and opportunistic — was accurate. When he said that he was an ultimate driving machine I asked him to give me some specific justification for that opinion. I don't think he had ever been called on it before because he stammered and stuttered, and mumbled something about acceleration and handling. I just looked at him. There is no question that I was vastly superior in those two qualities. Ultimate driving machine indeed. I allowed him to prattle on while letting my mind drift. I would have enjoyed comparing performance capabilities with another Porsche, but I had no desire to discuss them with that BMW, who so clearly was not in my league. I thought it best to be polite but distant. I had to live next to him, but I had no need to be his best friend.

Leroy and I quickly became a team, anticipating each other's moves and operating as a cohesive unit on the road. He did not succumb to the temptation of so many new Porsche owners to show off by driving too fast, tailgating, peeling out or other rookie behavior. We both knew my capabilities and there was no need to impress anybody. Therefore, when we were commuting I rarely was shifted higher than fourth gear. When we were on the open road on weekends, however, it was a different story. He let me go as fast as he could without getting a citation, shifting me with smoothness and confidence at just the right RPMs, deftly darting around traffic and accelerating through the turns without being obnoxious. I could be much more aggressive, of course, but we both were well aware that California roads were not the Autobahn and we behaved accordingly. Leroy drove me very well and he kept me clean and tuned up. Life with him was excellent from the very first day.

I am a sports car. I hug the road and my suspension is tight, allowing my driver to feel every irregularity and pebble on the road. This almost intimate connection to the highway is one of a number of advantages that make driving cars like me such a thrill. I will confess to having one drawback, which is my compact interior. The driver can enjoy my ergonomic design, but the passenger can suffer some discomfort with the narrow bucket seat and limited legroom. I believe the original concept was that we would be operated with the driver as the sole occupant. The second seat might well be viewed as an afterthought. It's fine for a smallish, thin person but not a chubby or leggy one. Willowy Liz was fine on short excursions, but long road trips were uncomfortable so when Leroy felt the need to take one, he went solo.

Our first significant excursion was to Oregon after the weather had warmed up enough for Leroy to put my top down. I didn't know our destination, or even what or where an Oregon was. That was not important. Like Leroy, I looked forward to a road trip, but from a different perspective. I longed to get out on the highway and just go, exercising my engine and wheels as we cruised along. I was delighted to find us on an Interstate highway, pointing north. Leroy put me in cruise control, holding me down to 80 MPH that put no strain on me whatsoever. I didn't exceed 3,000 RPMs as long as I was in fifth gear, where I was for most of the day. My radio was on, the sun was shining, I had a full tank of gas and my engine had recently been serviced. Life was good. I could tell Leroy was reveling in the experience as much as I was. We covered 400 miles that first day, stopping in a town called Roseburg. I was disappointed that we had to stop. I could sense that Leroy was getting tired, though, and it was probably best. Cars can go a lot longer than people do without rest, but then people seem to live longer. I wonder if people know something we don't. I shut down for the night, listening to my engine and parts creak and crackle as they cooled and settled into place.

Early the next morning Leroy was refreshed and ready to hit the road. We once again headed north, stopping for a break in Portland so Leroy could fill my tank with gas and his own with whatever it is that people fill theirs with. Then we turned east, traveling parallel to a wide river, ending up after 300 miles in another town called La Grande. We stopped for the night. We spent the next couple of days there, making short trips so Leroy could visit people he evidently knew. Some of them bore a resemblance to him so I figured there might be some sort of family relationship, like the one we Porsches have with VWs and Karmann Ghias.

When we left La Grande I was ready, not because I disliked the town, but because I had a need to get back on the road. That was the life for me, out there with the wind, the exhaust from other cars and navigating the bumps and ruts as we sped our way south. This is what I was designed to do and I reveled in it. The road was mostly two-lane so I couldn't go as fast as I had on the wider roads. When we found a long stretch with no traffic, Leroy mashed on my accelerator and I took off instantly, climbing quickly to 105 and ready for more until he let up and slowed back down to 80. I was reluctant to give up that burst of freedom and would have preferred to see how fast I actually could go but Leroy, wisely, knew that those roads were not built to accommodate a Porsche's full capabilities. I spent more time that day holding back than testing my speed. We passed many big American cars who seemed perfectly happy to lumber along at 60 or 70, barring our way until Leroy could find a way to scoot around them. As we passed I could see how complacent and bored they were, with their droopy headlights and the unexciting, unchanging hum of their inefficient engines. Watching them reinforced in me that I was fortunate to have been created as a Porsche. Regrettably, the roads in this country are far beneath my potential. Leroy stopped in Winnemucca, Nevada for the night, needing a rest as usual, while I as usual, didn't.

Another 300 miles the next day got us home. The highlight was the stretch from Tahoe down to Sacramento. It was no challenge at all, but the scenery was nice and the road was wide enough to let us go as fast as Leroy would allow, which wasn't enough to suit me. We did get up to 90 a couple of times, which was fun but short lived. After that outing I found the city streets and the garage with that insecure BMW stifling, but I consoled myself with the thought that there would be other trips in my future because I knew Leroy enjoyed them as much as I did.

We did go on another road trip before long, and this time Liz came with us. When they tossed their bags in my back seat and climbed in I did not know our destination but it didn't matter. We were going someplace and that was enough for me. I was hoping, naturally, for an opportunity to have my capabilities tested, although I had learned that California roads, not to mention the traffic laws, were not designed with us Porsches in mind.

Our first stop was a town called Chico. We stopped at a restaurant. Leroy parked me next to a vintage VW Bug convertible who, considering his age, appeared to be very well maintained. I found it puzzling that Leroy and Liz recognized him. They walked around him, commenting about how Johnny was taking such good care of him. I didn't know who Johnny was but I figured he, like Leroy, had a certain respect for us cars.

When they went into the restaurant I struck up a conversation with the Bug. Despite my being a newer, faster and more expensive car, I was respectful, as the VW and I had a shared ancestry. When I introduced myself as Leroy's car and noted that they seemed to know each other, he confirmed that they did. He was taciturn at first — I had the feeling he might be a little defensive. But he seemed more at ease as we got acquainted and he realized I was not going to lord our differences over him. On the contrary, I offered my sincere compliments about his pristine appearance and condition. He looked at me guardedly at first, as if awaiting an insulting punch line, but it never came, at least from me. There was a brief, uncomfortable silence before he confirmed that he had, in fact, been owned by Leroy for many years and that Johnny, Leroy's son, was now his owner.

As the Bug gradually opened up, I found myself intrigued by his life history. He was almost 30 years my senior! I was in awe that a car that old could look so good, have such a keen memory and had lived through so many adventures. His early memories were of being owned by some obnoxious, uncaring, spoiled twin boys who, if they were still alive, would have been almost 50 years old by now. Based on his description of their out-of-control life styles, it was doubtful either was still around. The Bug did not think he would survive the abuse they heaped upon him and he had resolved to put himself into a permanent sleep when, at the last minute, Leroy bought him and gave him a new life. He talked about his happy days in Santa Cruz, where he didn't mind that the sun and salt air took their toll on his body. When he reflected on his life in Palo Alto it was much less positive, as he and the BMW never did bond. He said the BMW was just a plain old jerk, and so were most of the other self-centered hoity toity cars in that snooty neighborhood. Even after Leroy had invested in his restoration he felt like an outsider there so he was relieved when Johnny took him to Chico. He considered a college town to be just the right place for him. I couldn't help but notice that when other cars passed by on the street they would often acknowledge him. At first I thought they were greeting me. As a Porsche I was accustomed to that. When I realized they were greeting the VW I was both impressed and happy for him. He had certainly paid his dues for the right to the life he was leading.

The Bug asked me if the BMW was still a stuck up jerk who fancied himself as the ultimate driving machine. I was amused to hear that accurate description — not that the BMW was an ultimate anything, but that he did indeed present himself as an unquestionably superior piece of automotive engineering and construction. However, it is not my nature to gossip or say negative things about other cars so I deflected the question by asking the Bug why he felt the way he did about the BMW. He replied that he had been subjected to abuse for most of his life by other cars who somehow considered themselves to be better than he was. He believed all cars are special in their own way, possessing both strengths and weaknesses. By the time he met the BMW he was fed up to his wiper blades with egocentric, insecure cars who had to affirm their worth by putting others down. I thought this was certainly insightful, and that the BMW could learn some things if he would allow himself to listen.

Leroy and Liz emerged from the restaurant with a tall young man who resembled Leroy (especially with respect to his substantial feet), so I assumed he was his son Johnny and the owner of the Bug. While Leroy and Liz again walked around the VW, reflecting on their time together, Johnny carefully examined me. It was obvious he would have loved to own me or a car like me. His dad noticed as well, and advised Johnny if he continued to do well in school and found a decent job, a Porsche was not beyond his reach. I was thinking this would take Johnny a long time but I certainly couldn't fault Leroy for encouraging him. As we drove out of the parking lot, I told the Bug how much I had enjoyed talking with him. He seemed to appreciate the gesture.

We left Chico and before long we were climbing into some mountains and the road became curvy. We sped along with Leroy shifting, steering, braking and accelerating smoothly. It was over all too soon as we drove into a small town called Chester. It seemed nice enough, although the cars were not like the ones I was accustomed to in Palo Alto. I did not see another Porsche at all, and few Mercedes or BMWs for that matter. There were plenty of American and Japanese cars, and many pickups as well. In fact, when we parked at a house, I found myself beside an old Chevrolet half-ton. After Leroy and Liz had gone into the house I introduced myself. He was civil enough, but not very forthcoming and I told myself that he was probably just old and tired. That was fine with me, and I respected his privacy.

I was curious about the place called Chester, though. I asked the Chevy if he had been there for a long time and he replied that he had spent his entire life there. He was manufactured in 1968 so this made him a respectable 23 years old. I had not met many vehicles of that age. As I had with the elderly VW earlier that day, I admired him. I did not detect any hostility or rudeness, just a quiet confidence and no particular need to impress. I felt I could learn a thing or two from a vehicle that had been around for so many years but I also was sensitive about appearing nosy or brash, so I approached him gingerly. Asking questions and listening carefully, I showed him I was sincerely interested in his history and views. He slowly opened up. I learned he was not driven very much, and was used mostly for short hauls with loads too big for a car trunk. I was amazed to learn he had only 40,000 miles on his odometer! Although his paint was faded in spots, he had no dents at all, and he still had his original upholstery.

The Chevy told me that in his youth he had longed for a life like mine, exploring new places and experiencing sights and sounds he was missing out on in Chester, as well as the chance to get acquainted with other cars and trucks. He eventually made peace with the fact that his was to be a different kind of life, designed as he was more for utility than comfort. His big V8 engine did not get very high mileage per gallon, and despite his large bed, there was no place to store luggage away from the elements. He said he had learned through the years that every vehicle has a distinct purpose and the well adjusted and happiest ones were those who accepted their roles without bitterness or resentment, as he had. Although he had little to compare it to, he thought Chester was a good place to live, with nice people and cars. By comparison, he mentioned the BMW that Leroy and Liz had once brought to town. He felt that car was overly anxious about his station in life and until he was able to come to terms with his preordained role, he would never be at peace. I heartily agreed, although neither of us felt the need to discuss the BMW.

As the afternoon waned into evening, and then night, we continued chatting. The Chevy had loosened up by now and we had reached a comfort level. He revealed that his first impression of me was not very positive, a hasty conclusion he was not proud of because it was based solely on my appearance. He had never seen a car with sleek lines such as mine and had assumed I would have a superior, boastful attitude. He was pleasantly surprised that I was nice and I had to chuckle as I told him I had made my own hasty assumptions about him, thinking that he was probably an old grandpa of a car who would have little of interest to say. We agreed that it was a positive learning experience.

The night wore on and I felt an almost luxurious fatigue from the day's adventures. I'd made two very interesting acquaintances and I had traveled an unfamiliar and fun road. Now I was in a higher altitude than I was accustomed to. As this combination took its effect on me, I found myself drifting into an enveloping sleep and I peacefully let it overtake me as my squeaking and mildly popping springs and joints slowly relaxed.

I saw more of Chester the next morning when Leroy and Liz took me for a spin. It was surprising to see what a small place it was and I found myself wondering if people got claustrophobic living there. Leroy drove from one end of town to the other, which took not more than five minutes, and then we diverted onto some side streets. As we drove by one house I noticed an extremely old car looking at us. I had never seen anything like it. Leroy exclaimed to Liz that he had formerly owned that car, a 1931 Model A. I had never heard of a Model A, but I did know that 1931 was more than sixty years ago. I was awestruck. Not only did the Model A seem alert, he looked to be exceptionally clean and well maintained.

A few houses away we came upon another odd-looking car, and like the Model A, it seemed to be in unusually good shape. I heard Leroy tell Liz it was a 1937 Plymouth, and like the Model A, he was a previous owner. Liz asked him if he had owned every car in town. He chuckled as he told her not all of them, just the best ones. I had never heard of a Plymouth. I'd never given it any thought, but it occurred to me that car brands come and go. I wondered — and I still do — if, like the Model A and the Plymouth, the Porsche name will fade into obscurity and be forgotten.

I spent the rest of the afternoon parked next to the pickup, napping and idly chatting. I learned that most of Chester's employment was at a lumber mill. The Chevy explained to me what lumber is, what it is used for, and how it starts out as trees. I was fascinated that people are able to change a tree into a stack of lumber. Humans are a source of never-ending surprises.

Leroy and Liz emerged from the house at dusk. They had changed their clothes. We drove back into Chester and parked in a lot with several other cars. On the way there, they discussed how high school reunions can be fun but intimidating. Not knowing what a high school reunion was, I listened carefully to understand in the event I would somehow be affected. It turned out there was nothing to worry about. Leroy locked my doors before he and Liz went inside a large building that was already full of people in noisy conversation and we cars were left in the lot to either get acquainted or ignore each other. I acknowledged the late model Thunderbird next to me and he returned the favor, so we compared notes. He was from another town up north and like Leroy and Liz, his owner was here for a high school reunion. A few other cars chimed in and said their owners were attending as well, and it turned out that while none of us was actually from Chester, all of our owners had spent their youth here. I gradually learned what a reunion was, and realized I had no interest in such things. We cars live in the moment and do not revel in history. We have little desire to reacquaint ourselves with cars from our past. There's no point. Cars move better forward than in reverse.

After a couple of hours, Leroy appeared in the company of two other men he called James and J.C. They teased Leroy about having a car that was beyond his capability but I could tell they were impressed with me. James was complimentary, admiring my classic lines and asking appropriate questions about my handling, speed, comfort and mileage. I could tell that J.C. was impressed as well, but he hid it behind bravado, telling Leroy he was too tall for me and that his feet were too big for my pedals. J.C. was very nearly right on both counts. For some reason, J.C. kicked my tire before the three of them went back inside. I'd have kicked him back if I could.

The Chevy and I were in for a big surprise the next morning. Leroy and Liz loaded their bags into my luggage compartment but instead of getting behind my wheel, Leroy got into the Chevy and

Liz prepared to drive me. The pickup asked me if I knew what was going on. I didn't, but I did offer him reassurance that Leroy was a safe driver and that regardless of what was happening, he should trust him. Before long we were both on our way back toward Chico. The trip back wasn't nearly as much fun because Leroy was cautious with the pickup, easing him around the corners and taking it slow, presumably because he had neither power steering nor power brakes. I could tell the truck was working hard and I was impressed at the competent job he was doing. Naturally, I would have preferred to challenge that road but I knew there would be other opportunities. The main concern was getting safely to Chico. We arrived after almost two hours and paused at a gas station to fill our tanks. The Chevy said he was fine, and had enjoyed the drive. This was his first trip over that road and to Chico, and he felt invigorated. He thought Leroy had done a credible job with his driving which was quite a relief because he had a three-speed column mounted stick shift and not everybody was comfortable with them. Leroy seemed to be.

We arrived in Palo Alto late in the afternoon. Liz parked me in the garage and the Chevy was left on the driveway. When the garage door opened and the BMW, who had been left behind, spotted the old pickup, he asked me what he was doing there. I suggested he ask the pickup himself, rather than use me as an agent. He said he'd rather not speak to him and I told him it made no difference to me. I thought to myself it probably didn't matter to the Chevy either. He had glanced at the BMW and said nothing. If the BMW wanted to act icily that was his choice. The pickup exhibited no indication of caring one way or the other. I opted to mind my own business. I had come to strongly admire the wise old truck and I wasn't going to let the opinion of an insecure BMW influence my feelings toward him.

Within a couple of days we all knew the Chevy now belonged to Leroy and would be staying with us. I thought this was great, as our bond had continued to strengthen. The BMW made no secret that the pickup was out of his element in Palo Alto, and the way he denigrated him to the neighboring cars was downright embarrassing and less than classy. Some cars on the block were amused by his behavior and egged him on, others ignored him, and a few enthusiastically agreed that this block was no place for such an unsightly utility vehicle. To his great credit, if the Chevy was concerned about what others thought of him, he didn't show it at all.

Sometimes bad things happen to those who least deserve them. Such was the case one night when Leroy had left the pickup parked on the street. It was about 2 a.m. when I heard a loud screech directly in front of the house, followed by a mirror-splitting crash of metal crunching against metal, and then a sudden, eerie silence. The BMW and I were, as usual, parked in the garage. We looked at each other, knowing that those noises were not good omens. We heard stirring in the house and before long, sirens. The garage door was raised and Leroy rushed in to retrieve a fire extinguisher. It was then that we could see an older Volvo with his front end completely crumpled beyond recognition, jammed against the bed of the old Chevy. It, too, was severely damaged. A couple of teenage boys were milling about and another was lying on his back on the lawn with his arm across his forehead. Beyond that, the two vehicles appeared to be in much worse shape than the boys.

Unlike humans, we cars do not experience physical pain. That is truly fortunate, for if we did, both the Volvo and the Chevy would have been in agony. They were unconscious, though, and I was unable to ask my old friend how he was doing. An ambulance came and carried the injured boy away and the police, after making a report, took the other two boys. I was able to discern that all had been drinking beer, which led to the accident. The two who went with the police pleaded to be released, but to no avail, and the policeman told them they would be spending the night in a place called Jail. I had never been to Jail and didn't know where it was. The boys obviously did not want to visit that town.

The activity continued as neighbors came to view the accident and offer their opinions, questions and assistance. Tow trucks arrived and hauled the damaged vehicles away. Neither had awakened yet, which perhaps was just as well. About the only positive thing was that Leroy did not have to use that fire extinguisher. By 4 a.m. the excitement had waned. People returned to their homes and Leroy shut the garage door. I was unable to get any rest for the remainder of the night, worrying if I would ever see the Chevy again, and what his future, if any, held in store. I'm a patient car, but when the BMW muttered something about the neighborhood being a nicer place now that the pickup was gone I very nearly opened my passenger door to smack him a good one. Of all the insensitive things I had heard him utter, that was the worst. It pretty much confirmed to me that although we may be destined to reside next to each other in that garage, I was not required to converse with him. I spoke to him only one time after that.

Our lives slowly returned to normal. I missed the truck and I knew Leroy did as well, but I figured such is the way of life. He had lived far longer than most vehicles. Nevertheless, I continued to mourn. My terse relationship with the BMW did not warm. On several occasions when he attempted to start a conversation with me, I refused to acknowledge him. He seemed eventually to get the message and we lived next to each other in a heavy silence.

It had been nearly a month since the accident when, one afternoon, Leroy and Liz got into the BMW and drove away. Liz returned a short while later, but Leroy was not with her. She left the garage door open. Then I saw Leroy pull up and park in the driveway in a new truck. But wait! It wasn't new at all. It was the same model as the old Chevy. Leroy was driving a sparkling replacement with no dents or scratches. As I looked him over, though, I noticed he had the same license plate number as the original pickup, which was odd. Then he spoke to me and I knew this was the same Chevy and that he had been restored. He looked far better now than he did after and even prior to that tragic accident. I told him it how great to see him again and I asked him what had happened. He said he wasn't sure and he was hoping I could enlighten him. He had just dropped off to sleep when he felt a violent push from the back of his bed and woke up in the yard of a body shop, next to an old Volvo who appeared to be totaled. I explained he had been rear-ended by that Volvo, after which both were towed away. I told him he looked like new and he modestly lowered his headlights as he thanked me, joking that he picked a radical way to achieve his new look and would not recommend it. I asked if there were any residual effects from the accident. He said on close inspection one could see the new bed did not line up perfectly, but otherwise he was just fine. His engine had not been damaged, nor had the front end. He claimed that on balance he had come out of the event quite nicely. I agreed, telling him I had given him up for gone and was relieved to see him back in action. He mentioned that the Volvo had not been so fortunate — he had never awakened and was now a cube of freshly crushed scrap metal.

As might be expected, Liz's BMW was not as pleased about the Chevy's return as I was. I heard him mumble something that sounded like "Must he be parked at our house?" as he eyed the pickup. I thought it was highly insensitive, but then I had come to expect that from the BMW. I doubt very much if the pickup gave it a second thought. I am certain Leroy, the Chevy and I were all pleased to see his return, each for our own reasons: Leroy because he got his pickup back; the Chevy because he was still alive and among friends; and me because a respected old friend who I thought was gone forever had miraculously returned. Some cars go too quickly and others after a very long life. That's just the way things are.

On a sunny Saturday afternoon in July 1996, Leroy and Liz lowered my top and we struck out for parts unknown. Leroy pointed me west and we soon found ourselves cruising down the Coast

Highway toward Santa Cruz. I had been on the road before and it was one of my favorites with a few hills and corners that, while far from challenging, were fun. I heard Leroy explaining to Liz he felt it was time to sell his business. He said he had started it from scratch and grown it into a thriving enterprise that was highly respected, but that he no longer was enjoying it. Liz was, as always, supportive. She told Leroy she also was getting restless with her job and finding it less satisfying each day. Liz suggested perhaps they should make a clean break and leave the area completely. She said she was drawn to a place called "the wine country" which I had never heard of. Leroy said he had not spent much time there, but he certainly was open to leaving Palo Alto. I couldn't tell them, but so was I. It was safe, pretty and peaceful, but came with an attitude I did not share. Too many of the cars I had met were expensive, shallow and vain. I believe the BMW was more connected to our neighborhood than I was, and unquestionably more than the Chevy.

It was late in August and neither Leroy nor Liz went to work for the entire week. Instead, they put the Chevy to use, loading him up for trips to what he told me were the dump and the thrift store. I could tell by his elevated mood that he was happy to be of service, doing what a pickup was designed to do. Late that week a moving van parked by the house. By the end of the day, it had been filled and driven away. Leroy and Liz left with the BMW, and the Chevy and I were left alone at the now empty house.

Early the following morning, Leroy and Liz returned. After a quick walk through the house, they left again. This time Liz was in the BMW and Leroy was driving the Chevy. They closed the door and I was once more left alone in the otherwise empty garage with a growing concern that I would never see them again. My fears were unfounded, as they usually always were, when in the late afternoon the garage door opened. The BMW was in the driveway with Liz behind the wheel. She backed out and drove away and Leroy settled into my driver's seat to follow. We stopped at a nearby motel where the BMW and I were parked adjacent to each other. It was contrary to my vow of silence toward him, but I was compelled to ask him where they had been and what had become of the pickup. He said he and Liz had followed it to a place called the Napa Valley, where it had been left behind at a house with a dusty driveway. He added that it seemed a fitting place for the Chevy and good riddance. His sarcasm made me regret I had asked the question.

We spent the rest of the night in silence. The following morning Liz and Leroy returned and we headed out of town. Two hours later we turned off the highway onto a dusty road and parked at a house surrounded by what I later learned were called vines. To my relief, I saw the pickup parked there. I could tell he felt the same about seeing all of us, with the possible exception of the BMW, of course. Before we had a chance to talk much, the van from the previous day approached. The space was limited by vines, trees and a narrow road, but his driver was skilled and managed to maneuver him into a position that allowed him to be unloaded efficiently. By mid-afternoon Liz and Leroy's belongings were in the new house and the van had been driven away. All three of us vehicles probably knew by then that this was to be our new home.

Our lives took on an entirely new routine. No longer were the BMW and I driven to work and left in a parking lot all day. Leroy and Liz did not have jobs any longer. It seemed to make them a lot happier. I was relieved to be out of Palo Alto and except for the chronic dust on my body and in my filters, I was at peace. Leroy would take me on drives, where there was nothing but acres and acres of vineyards. There were some luxury cars, along with a good number of pickups and utility vehicles. I was pleased that they all seemed to get along with each other. That was a refreshing contrast to Palo Alto where so many of the cars spent their days comparing themselves with each other. The pickup was very happy as well, seeming to have found his element. He didn't mind the dust at all and he clearly enjoyed being used to haul things such as trimmings, supplies, plants, equipment and the countless other things on a ranch which required his capabilities.

To the surprise of neither the Chevy nor me, the BMW had trouble adapting to our new country lifestyle. He grumbled constantly about needing a wash and looking like a common low class car. Naturally, we ignored his meaningless carping. As it turned out, his life at the vineyard did not last very long. In October, he was driven away with Liz and Leroy. We expected them to return in the afternoon and were somewhat taken aback when they returned in a brand new odd-looking little car. After Liz parked it, I introduced the Chevy and myself. He had a British accent and was difficult to understand at first, but I gleaned that he was called a Mini. He was feisty little thing, as small cars are wont to be, but friendly enough. He told us he had been purchased by Liz in San Francisco, and that the BMW had been part of the deal as a trade. I breathed a sigh of relief that the BMW was out of my life, German or not.

My own life was about to take a dramatic turn as well. Leroy had taken me to a place for servicing and the mechanic had advised him that we Porsches are not designed to be driven in chronically dusty conditions like utility vehicles, and that I was too handsome to be abused like that. I agreed that the dust was affecting my performance but I didn't particularly care whether it covered my body. But Leroy heeded the mechanic's counsel. He sighed heavily as he arranged to leave me there with a sign in my window advertising me for sale. It didn't take long. By the first of November I was the property of a new owner and I never saw Leroy, Liz or my old friend the Chevy again.

I am treated well, but I do miss Leroy. He was a considerate, skillful owner and I am fortunate to have been driven by him. But it was time for me to go, so I went. That's what we cars do.

Chapter 17
WISDOM

After 24 years of a sedentary Chester existence, my life took a dramatic twist in 1992. I suppose my new adventure began when Leroy and Liz visited, this time in a sleek, fast looking car with an impressive deep throated rumble in his engine. Leroy had difficulty getting out when they parked beside me. He was tall and the car was low, so he had to so some uncomfortable twisting and grunting when he got out and stood up. He grinned as he told Liz that was the price he had to pay for driving a Porsche, which I gathered was the brand of this strange looking beast next to me.

At first I said nothing, not knowing if the Porsche, like the BMW before it, would give me the silent treatment. He turned out to be a little more forthcoming. He introduced himself and began peppering me with questions about Chester. Before long I concluded that he had no hidden agenda and was sincerely interested, so I loosened up and responded to his inquiries. I also learned that he had a five-speed floor mounted manual shift and a huge engine that was more powerful than mine, despite his being about as tall as my door handle. He said he was built for speed and high performance, not necessarily for comfort and definitely not for hauling things. We both chuckled as we pictured ourselves in switched roles with me screaming through the curves of a mountain road and him with a load of hardware supplies behind his driver's seat.

It was fortunate that we enjoyed each other's company because the following morning Liz climbed into the Porsche and Leroy into me, and we headed out of town with Leroy and me in the lead. I was relieved he had a good understanding of my manual shift and how to baby me around the corners when we started down a mountain road that I had never traveled before. Although the road had many curves and required a lot of braking, I was giddy with the new sights and being on my first real road trip. We ended up at a Chico restaurant. My senses were overwhelmed! Not only had I just been driven on the longest journey of my life, but we were now in a town that had more traffic than I had ever imagined possible, with cars going every which way and some strange light mechanisms at many of the intersections that somehow coordinated the starting and stopping of the cars trying to get through. This was a marvel to me, as I thought it perfectly normal to coast through stop signs. I could see that wouldn't work here. I had heard of Chico before from visiting cars, and I had been told that it was much busier than Chester. Even so, I was not prepared for this level of activity. After all this excitement I was grateful for the opportunity to take a nap.

As we continued our journey we emerged from the mountains so the roads were straighter and a lot faster. Soon we were on one that had two lanes in each direction, which was yet another brand new experience. We cruised along at 60 MPH in the right lane while cars zoomed by us on the left as if we were standing still. It was disconcerting at first, but before long I gained some confidence and grew accustomed to the pace. At the end of a tiring day, we arrived at a house on a tree-lined street. Liz pulled into the driveway in the Porsche and when she opened the garage door I caught a glimpse of that unfriendly BMW. I could tell he was not happy to see me but I didn't dwell on it.

Leroy was now my owner. I had mixed emotions about that. For one thing, I had a built a strong bond with Leonard, my original owner — what car wouldn't over such a long period?! I also had a deep affection for Chester and the rich life it had afforded me. Now I was with a new owner in an environment that represented a dramatic contrast with the comfortable surroundings of Chester. As I looked around me I did not see a single pickup. Most of the cars were late model, some with names I recognized, like BMW, Mercedes, Cadillac and Porsche, and others I had never heard of, such as Saab, Volvo and Maserati. I will confess to feeling out of place in that upscale crowd.

I was built in 1967, although I am officially a 1968 model so that's the year I relate to. It was a year of dramatic social and political upheaval. Humans have a real knack for getting themselves into jams and harming each other. They should take a lesson from cars and just get along, accepting each other's differences and yielding the right-of-way from time to time. It was in 1968 that two highly influential Americans, the Reverend Dr. Martin Luther King and Presidential candidate Robert Kennedy were both brutally assassinated. Some referred to it as the worst year of the century, with a raging war in Vietnam, racial strife at home and that political violence. Others, though, viewed it as the dawn of a new era of retiring the old evils and ushering in a new, progressive social consciousness. I'm only a vehicle so changing society is not my job. For that I am most thankful.

I'm a 100% American half-ton Series 10 Chevrolet pickup. I'm considered a "light duty" truck but I have to say that I have always been up to any challenge put to me. Although General Motors is headquartered in Detroit, I was actually built in Fremont, California and I have never left the state. I'm equipped with a V8 engine that can generate up to 287 horsepower – maximum power that

I've never required. My gearshift for my manual three-speed transmission is on the steering column. The old timers refer to that as "three on a tree." At about 17 MPG I don't get very good mileage but in 1968 leaded regular gas cost only 34¢ a gallon.

Leonard had purchased me in Susanville for $2,486, which was a very good price then and would be even better now. He took me to Chester where I spent the first two dozen years of my life in relative comfort. Leonard respected machines and he paid a great deal of attention to my needs. He had me serviced regularly, he replaced my tires when they aged, and he was always a careful driver with the possible exception of running through an occasional stop sign. Stop signs didn't matter that much in Chester. I was used mostly for commuting to work, just a mile from Leonard's house, so I didn't run up many miles on my odometer. In fact, I averaged just under 2,500 per year during the entire time he owned me. I was used on occasion to haul trash to the dump or equipment and supplies from the hardware store that would not fit into a sedan, but all things considered I had a very easy life. I thought I was underutilized but I did not make an issue of it. My job is to be a solid, reliable vehicle. That was my commitment to Leonard as it continues to be to Leroy.

There were many pickups in Chester. Some, like me, were treated as commute cars, while others were worked harder, some to the point of abuse when they were taken onto unpaved, rutted and often muddy roads for deer hunting or firewood gathering. Most of them were quickly pocked with dents and dings and their beds seemed always to have traces of wood, animal pelts, old tires, rusted tools and beer cans. For some reason, perhaps an unspoken code, most of them also had bumper stickers that expressed the attitudes of their drivers, such as "Lumberjacks need love too", or "I have guns and I vote". When I would have occasion to speak with one of these trucks that always seemed to be old before their time, I got a sense that they considered me to be pampered and somehow less "pickuply" than they were. I learned early on not to let the comments and observations of others affect my own conclusions or my self-image. That attitude has served me well through the years.

_____

The onset of my first winter in Chester came as a shock. I had never seen snow or ice before, nor had I ever been subjected to such cold weather. I was too long to fit into Leonard's garage so my parking spot was on the driveway, exposed to the elements. When I awoke on that November morning in 1968 and found myself covered with snow I felt a momentary panic. I had no idea what that stuff was. It was cold, white, and continued to pile up on my hood, cab and bed throughout the day until it was more than a foot thick. I felt my radiator water begin to gel and my oil thicken in my crankcase. I was in fear that I would end up buried in the whiteness, never to be heard from again.

To my considerable relief, Leonard emerged from the house in the afternoon with an implement in his hand that I learned was called a shovel. He cleared the driveway in back of me, all the way to the street. He then used his arm to sweep the accumulated snow from my cab and hood. When he got in and tried to start me, I was reluctant at first because I was so cold and my carburetor was getting too much air and not enough gas. By using my hand choke, Leonard compensated and I was able to start. He eased me out of the driveway onto the street and we headed toward town. I was relieved to be going so slowly, as the road was slippery. On our brief journey I saw three other pickups that were not on the road where they should have been. They were clumsily parked, if that's the proper term, askew in various positions off to the side. One was turned completely around and another was nosed into a pile of snow that somehow had been removed from the street. When Leonard applied my brakes I knew this was what had caused those other pickups to leave the road. I could feel how slick it was and I realized that Leonard's gentle pumping of my brakes (instead of slamming them toward the floor as those other pickup drivers no doubt had) prevented us from plowing into the snow bank to join them.

Although our trip that afternoon was just a brief errand to the post office — a routine I had experienced many times before — it felt like it was taking hours. We made it home and when I was safely in the driveway I was no longer concerned about the snow once again piling up on my body. I was not at all eager to get back out on the road but I knew that I'd better reconcile myself to that inevitability.

Later that same afternoon Leonard installed some uncomfortable chains around my rear tires. They were made snug as he cinched and tightened them with a rubber connector. I figured he knew what he was doing, so I accepted it. He then put six heavy sandbags in my bed. I figured we were going to haul them somewhere, but it turned out they stayed there for the entire winter. Between the chains and the added weight of the sandbags, our next trip on the snow-covered road felt much more safe and in control. I didn't realize it at the time, but I was learning about winter in this first of many to follow.

Everybody, cars and people alike, seemed to be in a good mood at the onset of winter, but as the days become weeks and the weeks became months, what was new and fresh in November became tiresome and ugly by March. Toward the end of that month, though, the sour moods melted away with the snow and there was a palpable feeling of newfound optimism. We vehicles were all filthy by then from not bathing for the entire season and we were covered with mud and splattered slush. When Leonard washed me I knew spring had officially begun. That routine repeated itself each year that I lived in Chester.

My life took on a comfortable predictability during the next years. I saw many cars come into Chester and eventually leave. Some were traded in for new models, some were abused to the point of being worthless, and some were wrecked. Leonard, meanwhile, continued to treat me well and not add many numbers to my odometer. I had learned early in my life, or perhaps it had been designed into me, that my job is not to change the world, but to live in it; that I could learn a lot more by listening than by talking; that if owners are good to their vehicles, the vehicles return the favor; that life has a beginning and an inevitable end and nobody or nothing lasts forever. These sound philosophical tenets are what I have used to steer myself through life. I am acquainted with many other cars and trucks. Some accept things as they were and those are the ones at peace. Others seem intent on changing their environment or fighting against things that are out of their control to change, and they always seem to be in a state of unhappy anxiety.

As cars came and went throughout Chester, so did they at Leonard's house. It made perfect sense to me that a man should own both a car and a pickup, as our roles are entirely different. My job is to haul things; the job of a car is to haul people. When I first arrived a '68 Chevrolet Impala was in residence. He was still new and shiny, and was kept in the garage so we didn't get to speak all that much. He was nice enough, and as a fellow Chevy, we had an unspoken bond. Although they shared him, Leonard's wife Dolly was the principal driver of the Impala. It became clear almost immediately that the Impala was the family car and I was the utility vehicle. Those roles suited both of us. Every four years, Leonard and Dolly would replace their sedan, always a Chevy, with a new one. The '72 was a Malibu model in a sporty black color. I must admit that I was impressed with his sleek body style and his spunk. In 1978 he was replaced with a new, smaller Malibu who was, in turn, replaced in 1982 with a Caprice Classic, and in 1986 a Cavalier replaced the Caprice. In 1990, Leonard surprised me when, after driving the Cavalier away, he returned before long in a brand new Cadillac DeVille. During my long tenure with them, this was the first car Leonard and Dolly had purchased that was not a Chevrolet. I must say, he was a handsome car and Leonard was terribly proud of him.

At first the Cadillac was aloof, exuding a rather superior air. I had seen attitudes like that in other cars and figured that if they wanted to act like that they must have their reasons and that it was none of my business. Nevertheless, I thought it best to be courteous. He had been with us for a few weeks before we first spoke in the driveway. I introduced myself, telling him that I had lived in Chester for several years, all with Leonard and Dolly, and that if he had any questions he should feel free to ask. He thanked me for my interest, but beyond that said nothing. I had the sense that he was uncomfortable in my presence, not realizing that I am neither a competitive nor a judgmental vehicle. Or it could have been that he felt I was beneath his station in life and that he had decided not to associate with me. That had been my experience with some of the more expensive cars. I let it ride, figuring that when and if he chose to open a dialog with me, I would reciprocate.

A few weeks passed and we found ourselves once again parked adjacent in the driveway. He acknowledged me for a change, and asked if I could give him my opinion on something that had been puzzling him. I told him I would try. He told me he had been uneasy from the first day in Chester with the looks and comments from other pickups like me, and that he did not know why they disapproved of him. He said it was obvious to him that he was an exceptional vehicle, and the reaction from others should be respect, not derision, and did I not agree? I didn't want to hurt his feelings, so I chose to be candid and straightforward, figuring that it would be up to him how to handle it.

I told the Cadillac that in my opinion there is a role for every vehicle and that just because one is big and expensive and another is small and dented and others might be ugly, huge, old, new, smart, stupid or whatever, we were all cars sharing the same roads of life. What we are is not a reflection of anything other than our design and construction. It has nothing to do with us intrinsically. He was created to move people with grace, style and comfort. I was created to haul things. Our differences have nothing to do with our relative worth; that should be determined by how well we do whatever is expected of us. Some cars and trucks seem to believe that they are more important or worthwhile because of what they do, but that's shallow thinking. Those pickups who sneer at expensive cars are most likely compensating for their own perceived inadequacies and pushing up their own self-images by pushing down on others. I told the Cadillac that there were many cars and trucks in Chester that I admired and others that I did not care for. I, too, had heard an occasional insult uttered in my direction but I chose to ignore them because the opinion of the one uttering the remark meant nothing to me. Indeed, the most important judge of my character is me, not some other vehicle with a personal issue.

I apologized to the Cadillac for my diatribe. He was staring at me wide-headlighted, and almost speechless. He told me that on the contrary, he found what I was telling him to be of great value and most reassuring, and that he had seriously misjudged me. That was sort of embarrassing, but appreciated. He thanked me for my insight and told me that he would try to adopt my attitude. And he did. From that day forward, we were friends and confidants. An unlikely couple to be sure, but with the common denominator of self respect and recognition that differences don't necessarily have to contain negative connotations but in fact add to the richness of the vehicular world.

———————————

The heady summer days in Chester more than compensate for the tiresome winters, helping us to forget about all the snow, slush, mud and slippery roads. During the day the sun is warm but not too hot. And the nights are cool and pleasant. On one such day in 1976 I was quietly dozing in the afternoon when an odd little car was driven up and parked next to me in the driveway. I had seen similar cars before, but never up close and I thought he was about the strangest thing I'd ever seen. He was tiny, at least compared to me, and to describe him as aerodynamic would have been about the farthest thing from the truth I could imagine. His lines sloped down in the back as well as the front and it was difficult to discern which was which. His interior was spartan at best, with two far from luxurious bucket seats and a rear seat which looked fine for hauling small children, dogs or groceries, but certainly not fully grown humans.

I recognized the driver as Leroy. He had been to Chester before to visit Leonard and Dolly. When he went into the house I paid my respects to the odd little car. He said that Chester seemed like a very nice place that smelled good, but that some of the other pick-ups like me intimidated him with their hostile looks and demeaning snorts. I advised him to ignore them, especially the ones who made the most noise, who were probably the ones least worthy of any attention. He seemed relieved at that. I asked him what kind of a car he was and he told me he was a Volkswagen, which is a German car. I learned that he had a four-speed floor shift and that he averaged 30 MPG, which was almost double mine. He said one drawback was his limited horsepower, making it a challenge to drive on hills, but for the most part he was a reliable, functional trouble-free car. He said Leroy had purchased him from an elderly lady and that he now lived in a place called Santa Cruz with him and another, much older Volkswagen. He seemed like a decent car and although we were dramatically different, we got along fine. I saw him a few times after that and he always seemed happy to be on a road trip. I couldn't really relate to that, never having been on one myself, but I could imagine how it must feel to be out on the open road with the wind blowing against my cab, seeing and smelling new and different things.

Leroy and the Volkswagen visited one time in the winter and I was concerned that the cold and the slick roads would be too much of a challenge for him because he did seem rather fragile compared to most local cars and trucks. He surprised me by pointing out that his engine was in his rear, which provided additional weight to help with his traction. I was taken aback, having assumed all engines were in the front. I tried to visualize what kind of a pickup I would be with a rear engine and I found it amusing to picture my bed in the front. That would have been odd looking indeed.

The Volkswagen also told me his engine is air cooled, thus taking away any worries about freezing radiators. This made absolute sense to me and I wondered why I wasn't air cooled as well. The new information assured me that the little Volkswagen was perfectly equipped to get through a Chester winter, and I had worried needlessly. He may have been funny looking, but the little Volkswagen was a well-designed and manufactured car.

I saw the Volkswagen a couple of times each year, usually for a day or two. I did enjoy those brief times, hearing about life outside Chester. I knew it was not the center of the cosmos, and I always have felt that the more we can learn about other places and other ways of life, the wiser we become. I was acquainted with almost every other pickup in town. Some of them felt as I did. Others did not, and were of the opinion that Chester was the most important place ever, and that there was no need to look beyond the town as long as their engines were tuned and they had a comfortable place to park. To be honest, I found conversation with these narrowly focused acquaintances to be uninspiring. I was no one to talk though, since like most of them, I had rarely been away from my only home.

In the spring of 1979, after once again successfully negotiating myself through winter and its harsh elements, I saw Leroy drive up and park beside me. This time, though, he was not in the Volkswagen, but rather in a bright yellow, boxy subcompact car. I had never seen anything like him before. He was a bizarre looking thing and I had to keep reminding myself that appearances can be deceiving. I greeted him and at first he seemed a little intimidated, probably at my size. But I made it a point to speak calmly and politely and he soon relaxed. I told him I did not mean to pry, but was curious as to what kind of a car he was. He told me he was a Fiat, from Italy. I had never heard of either but I assumed it meant he was not made in the U.S.A. I mentioned he wouldn't see many, if any, cars in Chester like himself but not to be discouraged; that locals preferred larger, utilitarian vehicles and further, that parts for foreign cars were hard to find in this part of the country. As he became more comfortable and our conversation went on I learned he had never seen snow before and did not know what it was. I explained as best I could, and added that driving could be a challenge when the roads get slick. That's when he told me he had front wheel drive. I thought it was a real revelation and one that made a lot of sense. If I had front wheel drive I believe I would have been able to negotiate the snow and ice a lot better. I also learned that he had replaced the Volkswagen, although he did not know what had become of him.

Leroy and the Fiat explored Chester in the morning. When they returned, the Fiat said he had seen a lot of trucks like me and was thankful he had gotten to know me beforehand, so he wasn't intimidated by their size. He did not understand why a few of them had made unfriendly remarks and I assured him the problem was the uncouth pickups, not him, and to not let it get under his paint. Interestingly, he mentioned that he had met the restored '37 Plymouth that had lived in Chester for so many years, and that the Plymouth told him he had once been owned by Leroy. I had not been aware of that. I was probably in the very parking place he had occupied some twenty years prior! I never cease to be amazed at how much we can learn if we listen more than we talk, and the more we learn, the more we realize we don't know.

As with his Volkswagen predecessor, I did not see the Fiat that often. Over the next three years he and Leroy made those quick visits, and then he was gone, replaced by yet another car that also was quite unusual, although in a far different way. It was a warm, sunny late spring day and I was enjoying the quiet solitude of my driveway when my reverie was interrupted by the presence of another car beside me. I had never seen him before, nor had I ever seen another like him. Leroy emerged, along with a woman I had not met. After they went into the house I couldn't avoid staring at the new, strange car beside me. I know it was not very polite but I was intrigued.

He was a sleek, two-seater convertible set close to the ground. I could immediately sense from his lines and solidity that he was a car of some note. After a quick once-over and a curt hello, he ignored me. I bade him welcome and introduced myself. He said nothing. I must have made him uneasy with my continued focus, because he eventually asked if something was bothering me. I apologized and explained why I was so fascinated. I asked him what he was. He said he was a Mercedes Benz, which is a strange sounding name, but probably no more so than Chevrolet. He asked if there was anything further I wanted to know about him and I replied that I am always eager to learn new things but didn't want to pry. I could sense that he was loosening up a little then, and he explained that he was of German manufacture. I told him I was acquainted with another German car, a Volkswagen, whom I had become friendly with. He rolled his lights at that and pointed out that just like not all American cars are alike, neither are German cars. Point taken.

As the afternoon waned and sunset approached, the Mercedes asked me about Chester and why he got so many stares as he drove into town. I explained that they were probably the result of curiosity. I tried to help him understand the culture of the town and why people there drove pickups instead of sports cars. At the risk of overstepping my bounds, I encouraged him not to make any snap judgments; that we all have a role and looks can be deceiving. I explained to him that my personal belief is that a high priced Cadillac is no better than an economy priced Ford. If the Ford does his job better than the Cadillac does his, the Ford is the better car. He seemed to accept the advice in the way I had intended it.

The Mercedes was taken out for a drive the following day, after which he was again parked beside me. We chatted amiably off and on during the night and I had the sense he had relaxed and was able to open up a little bit. He said he was first owed by a lady in San Francisco, which evidently is a large town with many cars of all stripes. He then was owned by the lady's daughter, Liz, who was the one with Leroy. He and Liz had lived for a while in Palo

Alto but now were living in Santa Cruz. I asked him in passing if he was acquainted with a yellow Fiat Leroy used to drive, who also had lived in Santa Cruz. He acknowledged that he knew the Fiat, although they had little in common. I learned he was now living in Chico and being driven by Leroy's daughter, Annie. I told the Mercedes that after I got to know the Fiat I was able to see his value and had grown to respect him. I don't think the Mercedes shared my opinion.

Leroy and Liz loaded their things into the Mercedes the next morning and left Chester. Like my experience with the Fiat and that Volkswagen, I saw him a few times after that and we developed a mutual trust and respect. I had the sense he was actually seeking my counsel on how to better get along with other cars and be more accepting of their differences. It was in his DNA to feel superior and I could tell while he knew the right thing to do, it was difficult for him to follow through. I told him I could not live his life for him or presume to tell him how he should live it, preferring to mind my own affairs instead of telling others how to behave. I emphasized that all I can do is act as my conscience dictates, not how some preconceived notion tells me to, and that there is nothing of value in degrading or looking down on others. I believe he was listening, but if he wasn't, that was his problem, not mine.

———————

My life continued in its uneventful fashion over the subsequent years. I would be taken on brief errands but no long trips and had actually resigned myself to the probability that I would most likely never leave the Chester area. That was fine, although I certainly would have enjoyed seeing some of those other places I head heard about from Leroy's cars. This is not to say I would have liked to relocate. I thought Chester was a pretty nice place despite having nothing to compare it with. But it would have been broadening to travel to other places. I had resigned myself to doing so vicariously, mostly through the headlights of Leroy's cars.

In the autumn of 1986, Leroy and Liz once again surfaced in

Chester. I was surprised, but not shocked, to see them in yet another car and yet another exotic one at that. This one was a white convertible, although more of a sedan than his Mercedes predecessor was. I could see that he was almost new and also that he was preening while parked beside me. He refused even to look at me, which I found a little disconcerting. He said nothing in response to my greeting and I got the message. I figured if he wanted to converse, I would engage him. He didn't say a word the entire afternoon or through the night.

The following morning, Leroy and Liz drove off in that strange car. I noted the initials "BMW" on his logo. I do not know if this was what he was called or if the letters stood for something. I was fairly certain they did not stand for "Big Mouth Wheels", as he still had not uttered a word. When they returned the silent treatment continued. I thought the BMW might have had other things on his mind, was exceedingly shy, incapable of talking or was simply a jerk. We spent another silent night and the next morning he, Leroy and Liz were gone. In the five years of his sporadic visits we did not exchange a single word! I found this to be pretty unusual, although I figured he must have had his reasons for acting like he did, and if that was the way he needed to be, it was up to me to accept it.

After Leroy bought me from Leonard and I had been relocated to Palo Alto, the Porsche did his best to help me make the transition while the BMW ignored me. The Porsche took the time to explain to me what kinds of trees were dripping their sap on me, how the lawn sprinklers knew to go on at 3 a.m. by themselves, what the purpose of a street sweeper was, and why there were so few pickups like me in Palo Alto. The BMW, though, said nothing and even seemed to be embarrassed that I was parked in front of Leroy's house. I tried, but was unable to understand why outward appearances were so important to him because I had always felt that substance was much more important than image. Perhaps this was the influence Chester, with its collection of hard working, unpretentious, dented vehicles, imbued in me.

Leroy was considerate of me. He always remembered to use the hand choke when my engine was cold, and he saw to it that my oil was maintained at the proper level and that I was tuned. But I continued to feel out of place and underutilized. I was not used to haul anything and because I was parked on the street for extended periods of time I couldn't help but overhear judgmental comments from some of the neighborhood upscale cars. I began to wonder if these were, like the BMW, typical of Palo Alto.

———————

One spring night as I was in a deep slumber I felt a fairly sizable bump to my rear end. I recall nothing after that until I awoke later in a body shop, confused and disoriented. My entire bed and rear bumper had been removed and I couldn't help but feel self conscious in my nakedness. I knew that my frame was bent somewhat, which puzzled me. I was parked next to a badly damaged Volvo. As I took a closer look at him I could see he had been totaled and would likely be destined for the crusher. It took a full month, but eventually I had a replacement bed and rear bumper mounted, and I was encouraged when I received a paint job. I think I looked much improved. I was still at a loss to explain what had happened to me, though, and where I was and where Leroy was.

A couple of days later, after my new paint was dry, I looked up to see Leroy approaching. We were both pleased. I was relieved to see a familiar face and I could tell he liked the looks of my makeover. He got in, started me up, and we drove away, arriving in short order at his house. Despite my never having felt truly welcome in the neighborhood, I was happy to be back in familiar territory. The Porsche let me know I had been rear ended the previous month by the Volvo I had seen in the body shop. He said the driver had been a teenager who was apparently showing off, drinking, stupid, or all three. Police cars, an ambulance, rubberneckers and tow trucks had all been on the scene and the way he described it I was sorry I had missed all the excitement. I guess I was the star of the show, playing my part when I was unconscious. I tried to look at the upside of the whole event. Rather than being sent to the crusher like that Volvo, I was now sporting a brand new paint job on a dent-free chassis so I had nothing to complain about.

The next few years were uneventful. I mostly sat in front of the house. This was very similar to my life in Chester so I had no trouble adapting. I continued to wonder why the BMW was so unfriendly. The Porsche made up for it and I believe that despite our radically divergent appearances, construction and purpose, we became good friends. I was used on occasion for trips to the hardware store or just to go on a drive to keep my battery charged and my seals tight. To be sure, I would have welcomed the opportunity to make more of a contribution but for in general my life was sedentary.

A big change took place in 1996, just after my 28th birthday. That was when we left Palo Alto for good and moved to the Napa Valley. Leroy and Liz had sold their home and bought a place in the country. It took some doing to move their belongings (people definitely require more creature comforts than we vehicles do) — they actually had to hire a van with some strange looking characters doing the loading and unloading. I was pleased because I was packed with some of the more fragile items that Liz did not want in the van. I was extra careful on the drive and in a jubilant mood now that I was being used for something important.

After Leroy and Liz saw to the unloading of the van and all three of us cars were at the new location, we all heaved a sigh of relief and set about making the adjustment to our new lives. Leroy and Liz seemed very satisfied, the Porsche was optimistic and I was euphoric. The BMW was the only one of us who was not comfortable in the new surroundings. He complained incessantly about the dust, the isolation and the absence of his Palo Alto friends.

That puzzled me, as it was clear to me that most of those cars he considered to be his friends were far from it. Some were like him in that the most important thing to them seemed to be what others thought of them. Others were laughing behind their radiators at him while they pretended to be friends. And I heard one car utter "good riddance" as the BMW was driven away for the last time. The BMW didn't seem to notice and it dawned on me that his entire life had been devoted to impressing others rather than living up to a higher, more meaningful personal standard. That made me sad for him.

We lived down an unpaved gravel road. I had no trouble adjusting and being covered in a film of dust was actually refreshing, particularly now that I was getting used almost daily as a pickup should be used. I quickly memorized my way to the hardware stores, the recycle center and the dump, and before the year was out I found myself being used to haul grapes, barrels and winemaking equipment. And on almost every trip I received friendly nods from other pickups and admiring looks from envious humans, many of who asked Leroy if I was for sale. Fortunately, he turned them down. For the first time in my long life I felt as if I was being fully utilized and appreciated, and I was relishing the experience.

The Porsche was doing his best to accommodate himself to his new environment but I soon began to see signs that he was having some difficulties. He developed a chronic cough and a few other ailments that were most likely the effect of dust particulates on his engine and joints, which were not designed for vineyard living. He spent an inordinate amount of time in the repair shop having things addressed, such as his oil cooler, fuel injectors, filters and brakes. And while I looked natural in my unwashed condition, he looked out of place. As I would have expected, he never uttered a single complaint. But I could tell he was suffering.

The BMW, predictably, continued to complain. The Porsche and I ignored him to the extent possible. It was easier for me, since he never addressed me anyway, but I'm sure the Porsche tired of listening to him. I would think it would have been particularly difficult to tolerate from a fellow German. He likely would have been more philosophical about it if the BMW were Japanese or better yet, French. But living with a fellow German with such a negative attitude was exceptionally difficult for him to accept. On one occasion after listening to a string of complaints about the dust, the coyote noise, the hard water, the absence of other cars that could meet his high standards and having to sleep in an open carport, the Porsche had heard enough. He let loose with a string of invectives that shocked both the BMW and me, although for different reasons: the BMW because no car had ever addressed him with such outrage and me because it was all done in German, yet I could not fail to pick up on the meaning, even if the words escaped me. The Porsche's feedback did not influence the BMW's attitude, but mercifully it did quiet him down for a couple of days.

I guess Leroy and Liz sensed that the BMW was a poor fit for country living because it wasn't too very long before they drove away in it and returned later in a funny looking little car with a distinct British accent. He told us he was a Mini. The Porsche asked him what he was a mini of and he replied that no, that was his actual make, not an adjective. We bantered good-naturedly over that one and wondered if the Porsche should hereafter be known as a Fastie and me as a Maxi. We were relieved to learn that the Mini had a sense of humor and was able to go along with the teasing. We were pretty certain the BMW would not have found us at all amusing.

It wasn't very long after that when the Porsche, like the BMW, disappeared from my life. He had been suffering from his chronic dust-related ailments for some time. He was doing his best to deal with them but it was a losing battle. He was just too finely tuned and precise to spend so much time where we were and he was getting progressively worse. That final day when Leroy emptied his passenger compartment of his personal belongings and started him up, the Porsche and I looked at each other, knowing that this would likely be the last time we saw each other. I wished him all the best and told him how much I had enjoyed our relationship, and he told me he felt the same, but he knew it was time for him to move on.

———————————

I was happy on the ranch from my first day there. I felt useful, appreciated and comfortable. Leroy drove me more than I had ever been driven before and we developed a strong bond as the years passed. He kept me tuned and lubed and was able to repair the minor things that occasionally afflicted me, such as burned out lights, leaking hoses, mice nibbling on my wires and at one point, a loose engine mount. It's now been 15 years since we moved here — 15 great years. Other cars have come and gone, mostly being driven by Liz. I got along well with all of them and I will confess that I was relieved that none of them was another BMW. I suppose most cars my age would be in their final years if they were still around at all, but I don't feel old. Sure, I look dated compared to the fancy pickups on the road today with their air conditioning, bucket seats, cup holders and sound systems. I have none of those amenities and that's just fine with both Leroy and me. And I just love it when he brags, which he does with embarrassing frequency, that I still have less than a hundred thousand miles on my odometer. I think I just might last as long as Leroy does.

Through The Headlights

EPILOGUE

"Leroy? Is that you?"

"Huh? Who's that?"

"It is I, your pickup. You'll be able to concentrate when you stop spinning around and get your bearings. It's going to be OK. Take a deep breath and reeeelaaaaax."

"What the... Where am I and why am I talking with a pickup? This is beyond weird."

"C'mon, trust me. You've trusted me for a lot of years and I've never let you down. Well, except for that time we got stuck in the mud at the vineyard, but we both know that wasn't my fault. It'll be better if you calm down and let me explain."

"Let a pickup explain something? Now *that* makes a lot of sense."

"I'm telling you, it *will* make sense if you will act like the Leroy we all know and open yourself up to some possibilities that might seem odd at first. Really. Trust me. If you can't trust a '68 Chevy, whom can you trust?"

"I must be dreaming. Tell me I'm dreaming."

"Well, you *are* asleep. But believe me, this is no dream. I'm real and so are you, and this is a real experience we're having."

"How can I be asleep, not dreaming, but having a real experience talking with a pickup? Last time I checked, vehicles were inanimate."

"Y'know, I've pretty much liked all the humans I've met but I have to tell you that the one thing you all seem to have in common that both mystifies and irks me is a closed mind. Why do people all assume that they are the only things in the universe who talk and that all the rest of just sit around, dumb as posts, waiting for you to use us? People talk with each other, animals talk to each other, and for all we know, bugs, flowers and trees talk to each other. Where is it etched that humans, just because they happen to have tongues, thumbs and prehensile capabilities, are the only species that talk? Don't you think that's a tad presumptuous?"

"OK, you've made your point, but you must admit that our having this conversation is pretty much outside the lines of rational thought. In defense of us humans, the fact is that nobody, or at least nobody in my realm of experience, has heard any species talk except humans. Other animals do make noises that we presume to be communication, but they don't carry on conversations that make sense to the human ear. And as for inanimate objects like you, we never hear dialog. You might emit occasional belches, coughs, pings and roars, but certainly nothing resembling words as we know them."

"What's weird to you may be perfectly normal to a vehicle, Leroy. All you have to do is open your mind. I understand how difficult it must be to overcome a lifetime of assumptions, regardless of their accuracy. I, like all vehicles, do in fact communicate. Humans don't normally hear us, but cars talk to each other all the time. You can hear me now because this conversation is taking place between our spirits, not our physical beings. I urge you to accept and enjoy the experience. I'm here at the request of some of the other cars you've owned in your lifetime. They appointed me to get in touch with you. They did this because you treated them well, and they would like to express their appreciation. Then you have a decision to make."

"OK, I'll tentatively acknowledge carrying on a conversation with a pickup truck and hope it's not one of those mindless television shows in which people are entertained because I'm doing embarrassing things. Now if you can tell me what's going on I would be very grateful, although I won't agree yet to buy your explanation. I'm pretty new at talking to cars and this might take some time."

"That's fine, Leroy. I can assure you that this is no television show. I'll try to explain what's going on and maybe you'll understand and perhaps even appreciate your situation."

"Nothing personal, or should I say vehicular, but I rather doubt that. But give it a shot and I'll try to be open minded."

"Fine. To begin with, you are on an operating table undergoing major surgery. You had a heart attack, which I gather is even more serious than a blown head gasket would be to me. You are heavily sedated and traveling in that iffy zone between life and death. You might pull out of this and you might not. Your fate is partially determined by the skill of your surgeon, by what he finds during the procedure and whether it's repairable, and to a very large extent, by your own motivation. To put it simply, you need decide if you want to live or die."

"Well, now that you mention it, I do recall having some pain in my chest and blacking out, so that might help explain the part about the O.R. Oddly enough, that doesn't seem nearly as unsettling as finding myself here and talking to you. It might take some time for this to soak in."

"I can give you all the time you want, but I'm not sure the other forces at work will be so considerate. I believe it would be in your best interest to stop questioning me and get cracking on your decision. Are you motivated to keep living or not? If you are, you need to return to your body and see if you can bring it back. If you're not, you can just stay here."

"Well pardon me, but this is my first experience with death. I'm not a cat, you know. How can I make an informed decision if I don't know what the consequences are? If I choose to live, what kind of quality of life can I expect to have after my heart attack and surgery? Will I be a drooling vegetable who shuffles around like a zombie, or is there a chance I can make a full recovery? And if I do die, how can I see in advance what it's like? You're asking me to make a decision with very limited data."

"Leroy, Leroy, Leroy. You're not in a business meeting here. You are in a crisis situation with unclear outcomes. The data you want simply are not available and you're going to have to make your decision based on faith, gut, best guess and gobs of unknowns."

"Geez, this is scary, Pickup. The one time in my life I need more counsel than ever before and there's nobody here to help me. Does everybody have to go through this?"

"Nope. Some aren't given the opportunity. Although you may feel an unfair pressure to make up your mind, many people don't get even that. Some of them die instantly in accidents, some are crime victims, some develop terminal illnesses and some just get old and fade away. So I would urge you to count your blessings, sparse as they might seem at the moment, and get on with it."

"Thanks, Pickup. You're wiser than you look. You mentioned that my other cars might have some opinions. Should I get their input, and if so, how do I find them? Just listen to me. I'm seriously asking a pickup how to communicate with other cars I've owned. I think I must have gone over the edge."

"I'll ignore that remark. If you want to speak with any of your cars, just call out for them. It's that simple here. Don't try this on Earth because it won't work and people will give you very wide berth while you're doing it. Want to give it a shot? What car would you like to talk with first?"

"I guess the logical one would be that old Model A Ford that was my very first car. Seems to me a car that old would have the most experience and, I would hope, wisdom. So how do I get in touch with it?"

"Him. Not it."

"Beg pardon?"

"We all use the male designation, not that it makes any difference, since we don't court, date, marry or reproduce. We're neither heterosexual nor homosexual. We're asexual. But since most of us are greasy, smelly, dirty and occasionally aggressive, we think of ourselves as more like human males than females, who tend to smell nice and have cleaner parts than males do. So we refer to each other as 'he' or 'him'. It's easier that way."

"Well, I doubt anybody would ever mistake you for a female. I've owned a few other vehicles that might be viewed as such, but now that you've explained it, I see the logic. But we digress. You said all I have to do is call out to the Model A?"

"Yep, it's as easy as shifting into high on a flat road on a hot summer's day. Go ahead. Call him."

"This is getting weirder by the minute but I guess I can play along until I return from whatever kind of whacko dimension I'm in. Hey, Model A, are you there?!"

"Dagnabbit, Leroy, you don't have to holler. I'm right close and I ain't deef. Why do humans assume that just because things is old they must be broke down, blind, short on memory and hard of hearing?"

"Wow, sorry, Model A. I'm new at this whole thing of talking to spirits so I'm still sort of groping. I didn't mean to offend you."

"I ain't so much offended as annoyed. I don't have much tolerance for people who make assumptions without thinkin' 'em through, and believe you me, I've put up with a passel of them in my life. I'm dang near 80 years old and I've done earned my right to be a might crotchety if I've a mind to. I remember you. You was that kid with the big feet who told the butcher you knowed how to drive when you took me out into that snowstorm. You dang near wrecked me. That wasn't the first time I was nearly killed, nor the last, but each of them made an impression on me. That there was a little pun but you get the point."

"Yes, I do, Model A, and I want you to know that I felt bad about that little episode with the snow bank. You were my first car and I have nothing but fond memories of driving you. I'm especially appreciative because I was a teenager and teenagers are not known for having well developed brains."

"Well, you wasn't no worse than a lot of folks who drove me. If I had my druthers, though, I wouldn't be owned by any of them again. All them hormones and no experience is a recipe for disaster. You was green as a new born toad but a fast learner, and you didn't do no serious damage to me."

"That's good to hear, I think. I wish we could talk longer, Model A, but I don't know how much time we have. I was talking with my '68 Chevy pickup about how I got here to the spirit world and how I should know if I'm ready to return or move on. He advised me to seize the rare opportunity to ask some of my cars what they think. I suppose I could try to find some humans but how often does a guy get to seek the counsel of his cars? For all I know, you're smarter than people anyhow."

"We are, Leroy. Leastways most of us are. Well, maybe not so much smarter as wiser. I've done spent my entire life working and observing. I've spoke on occasion to a human or two but they ain't real good at listening. So even if we ain't got all the answers, you're plumb smart to at least ask us the questions."

"Well, then, I guess my question is whether I should live or not. What do you think?"

"At my age, Leroy, you must know that I've thought about that very question a mess of times. Everbody's mortal. Nobody goes on forever. I dang near have but I'm what they call an exception. You've saw me up there in Chester from time to time and you know that I've been restored. I've got a good life now — a whole lot better than my early days during the Great Depression and even during the '50s when you and other boys cut your driving teeth on me. Most cars a lot younger than me ain't here anymore. I ain't scared of death but I ain't in no particular rush to experience it. When it comes, I'll go peaceful. Meanwhile, I plan to go on observing, showing off in parades, resting in my garage and learning stuff, even at my old age. Sometimes I think it might be fun to see if I can break the world record for car life. That would mean I'd have to live a whole lot longer but why not give it a try? Once you're gone you ain't comin' back."

"So you're advising me to try to live to a ripe old age."

"I ain't advising you one way or the other, Leroy. I'm just telling you my opinion about me. What works for me might not be at all good for you, so you have to make up your own mind. All I can do is try to give you something to gnaw on. I hope I done that. Maybe you ought to get another opinion as long as you're here."

"Hey Plymouth. Are you here?"

"Yep. How's it going, Leroy?"

"Well, normally the stock answer would be 'Fine.' But to tell you the truth, I'm not so sure. I'm floating around wherever I am, having lucid conversations with cars. I think that sort of goes beyond 'fine' but I don't know which direction. I'm sort of confused."

"Humans usually are. I thought you knew that. Cars do."

"Yeah, well, I guess maybe we are. In our defense, though, our lives are a lot more demanding."

"You really believe that, Leroy? What could be more demanding than having no choice but to do whatever the driver wants, to be at his complete disposal with respect to your care and maintenance, and to suffer abuse by idiot teenagers? I'll acknowledge that I have a pretty good life now, but my early years were not easy. I think I had more demands and stress put on me during my first twenty years than most humans suffer in a lifetime. I always had the impression that you had a deeper understanding of cars, and knew that comparing us to humans is right up there with apples and elephants."

"Ouch. You're right, Plymouth. I spoke without thinking. I do realize that comparisons between us are not fair and are usually wrong to boot. I apologize."

"Not needed. Now what can I do for you? If you promise not to shoot a hole in my door or take me down a railroad track I'll try to help."

"Ouch again. I did some things in my youth that I thought were pretty cool at the time, but now I realize how stupid they were. Sorry I had to involve you, Plymouth. I liked you a lot more than my behavior might have indicated. Anyhow, to get to the point, I'd value your opinion on life and death. If you were in my shoes, or should I say tires, and had to make a fast choice whether to live or die, what would you do?"

"Shucks, I don't know. That would depend on how happy or unhappy I was, how seriously I was damaged, how much I liked my owner and what other forces may be influencing my thought process at the moment. If I said 'go ahead and die' today, I would just as likely say 'hang on to life for all you're worth' tomorrow."

"So you're telling me it's situational."

"Well, perhaps I am. There were times in my early years when the crusher would have been a welcome ending. I don't know why, but that never happened. That's probably good, or I wouldn't still be living in Chester today with a shiny body, and fully restored interior and engine. I had no desire to live in the late '40s but now I'm in no hurry to check out. If I'm sold to an abusive owner tomorrow I might change my mind. So yes, I guess it is situational. What do you think?"

"Well, I think I have a pretty good life. I have a devoted wife who I believe loves me as much as I love her. I live on a nice property, we have some good friends, we're still intellectually curious, we want to see more of the world — all in all, no big complaints. On the other hand, I'm here talking with you, which means either that I've lost my mind or I have a traumatic health issue and may not pull through even if I want to. If I do make it through, how will the quality of my life be affected? And what if life on the other side is a hundred times better than the one I'm in now?"

"Valid questions, Leroy, and a cogent analysis for a human. If it were my decision I'd hang on as long as I could. I'll admit that we don't know what death has in store for us. There are some humans who purport to have the answer. Maybe they do, maybe they don't, maybe they're kidding themselves, maybe they're making stuff up, or maybe they really do have irrefutable evidence, although I doubt it. As for me, I don't know what the future holds. Could be good, could be bad. I have all of eternity to be dead, so I might as well stick around and see what happens. But that's just me."

———————

"Hey Leroy, is it my turn to give you my two cents worth yet?"

"Huh? Who are you?"

"I'm your faithful, reliable 1950 Chevrolet, but you can just call me Chevy. It's been a long time since our paths have crossed. I've been eavesdropping so I have a pretty good idea of why you're here in the spirit world."

"Wow, Chevy, I never expected to see you again, let alone talk with you. I always admired you. You were reliable, comfortable (at least after that front seat was replaced) and you always got me where I needed to be. On occasion you even got me to where I shouldn't be but that wasn't your fault. What became of you?"

"After you sold me my life took a downturn, Leroy. I went through a number of owners and each one of them treated me with less respect than the one before. I eventually found myself in an unkempt back yard, up on blocks where I remained for several years. In the late 1970s a kid bought me for next to nothing and towed me to his garage in Chico where, for the next five or so years he tried to restore me. His intentions were honorable, but his skills were even more limited than his financial wherewithal. I didn't care much. At least I was out of the weeds and under a roof. I wouldn't say I was happy, but I was safe and I got a lot of sleep.

"One day I was towed again, this time to a high school auto shop where I became a learning project. My engine was completely disassembled and rebuilt by inexperienced but motivated teenage boys, and my body was subjected to an amateurish attempt at restoration. By the end of that school year I was running again and while I had some odd-looking repairs and patches on my doors, fenders and hood, my rust had been mostly removed or covered. I was back in action, sort of. Eventually I was sold to a guy who lived alone in a modest but clean neighborhood. I stayed there for more than 20 years. My odometer ran up to beyond 350,000 miles. When he had to give up his driver's license I sat in his garage until he died about five years ago. When his family sold his place they had me towed to a junkyard and that was my final resting place. I'm too worn out to restore, so I gradually died there and am now at peace. As I look back on my life I am satisfied that I did what I do best, which is serve my owner. Pardon me for going on so long, but you did ask and it's not every day I get to speak to a human."

"I'm glad you did, Chevy. I have fond memories of my time with you and I've always wondered where you ended up. I think you're telling me that the important thing is what we do with our lives, and that we don't always have control of the outcome. You Chevys have a well-deserved reputation of practicality and I value your opinion."

"That is a fact, Leroy. We aren't the fanciest, fastest, sexiest or costliest cars on the road but we're proud. I think all Chevys, with the possible exception of those elitist Corvettes, would agree that the important thing isn't how we die, but how we live."

"You've given me some valuable counsel, old friend, and I am grateful."

"When you replaced me it was with a 1955 Volkswagen. It's important for you to know that I carry no resentment about that. We cars are accustomed to multiple owners and in fact it makes our lives interesting."

"I appreciate your loyalty now, as I did when we were together, Chevy. Thank you again for sharing your thoughts."

"Hello, Leroy. It has been a long time, nicht wahr?"

"Who's that?"

"I may be out of context, but think back to your first trip to Europe back in 1959. That's where we met. Our time together was short, but a car always remembers its first time on the road. I'm the VW Bus and you and Wayne were my co-drivers."

"I remember you and that trip very well, Bus, from the time we picked up the seven of you at the factory until we parted ways in Barcelona. I've always regretted not completing the adventure with the rest of the group but what's done is done, or more to the point, what wasn't done wasn't done. Nothing we can do about it now."

"That is true. I learned well before my odometer registered six figures that we can influence the future, but we cannot change the past. We can and should learn from it, although not enough cars or people do, in my opinion."

"I can't disagree with that, Bus. I can't set the calendar back and change the outcome of the trip, yet I've never been able to shake this nagging sense of failure. So intellectually I get it. Emotionally, I can't help it if I feel what I feel. Not that I've let the subject rule my life, mind you. It's just one of those regrets that we all carry around when we know we could have done better and did not."

"You're not the only one with a less than perfect past, Leroy. Remember how I was always the slowest bus in the convoy? Well, it may surprise you to learn that my lagging had more to do with my attitude than with my mechanics. I did have a minor compression issue but I could have compensated for it more than I did. I wanted to be either the leader or the last in line. I would not have been satisfied traveling in the middle of the pack. There was one bus that was driven, please excuse the expression, to be in the front. It wasn't worth it to me to challenge him or his petty need, so I opted to be the last one up the hill. I believe it freed us up to enjoy the experience more, to gain some independence and not to keep up just for the sake of convoy etiquette."

"I'm surprised to learn that was intentional, Bus. I have to agree with you, though. My fondest memories of our travels are the times we were separated from the rest of the group and relieved of the pressure to stay in line with regimented photo stops and potty breaks. And while it would be fun to relive those memories with you, I don't have a lot of spare time at the moment."

"I'm aware of your time constraints, Leroy, but the purpose of my rambling is to give you some helpful perspective. After being left in Calais with the other six busses I was sold and returned to Germany. Over the years I was owned by a number of people. The ones I liked I treated well. If an owner was not nice to me, though, I returned the favor by going slow, burning oil, rattling, and doing whatever it took to assert myself. Naturally, the older I got, the less respect I earned, and I found myself in a downward spiral because the more I rebelled, the less satisfied my owners were with me. I was sold several times and each owner seemed worse than the previous one, which made me act up even more. The last time I was sold I found myself owned by a drug dealer who had more cash than intelligence. On just our second trip into Germany from Holland he was arrested at the border and I was impounded. That was the last I saw of him.

"After more than a year in police custody, I was donated to a convent near Munich. The Nuns were nice enough, but not as devoted to my maintenance as they were to their Order. I continued to deteriorate and finally became unable to serve them. As I sat rusting away near a stone fence at the back of the convent, I had plenty of time to reflect on what I might have done differently to have lived a better life. The Nuns had greatly influenced my thinking and I had come to believe in a better afterlife. When I died for good I found myself in spirit world filled with all kinds of cars who had made peace and had taken the final exit from the freeway of life, you should pardon my euphemism, with a clear conscience. I suppose our God is some kind of vehicle, but I have not seen Him. I do hear a mellow rumble every now and then."

"Good story with a happy ending, Bus, but I don't see how that applies to my dilemma."

"Hmm, I thought you'd be a little more enlightened than you were at age 19, Leroy. My point is that we all, cars and people alike, make bad decisions as we go through life. We can't undo them, but we can learn from them and, at least some of us can forgive ourselves and put our faith in a higher power, believing that if He forgives us, we can look forward to a better Eternity than those who never see the Light."

"Ah, now I get it. I have to tell you that I've never been a fan of organized religion, Bus, but that doesn't mean I don't recognize the possibility of an afterlife that will be influenced by the kind of life I lead on Earth. And while I, like you, have made a mistake or two (or a thousand) along the way, I've tried to live an honest, productive life. I hope that will be enough when my time comes, whether it's now or sometime in the future."

"I think that would suffice if you were a car trying to get into a car Heaven, Leroy. I can't say whether human Heaven resembles car Heaven, but my advice to you would be to play the odds, as you appear to have done, and forgive yourself so you can go out with a clear conscience."

"Bus, I have to say that I never imagined in my wildest dream that I would be getting religious instruction from a Volkswagen and what's more, listening to it. But this past few hours has been a strange little journey and I'll accept it. I thank you for your sage advice and I wish you a happy Eternity with no overheating valves."

"Danke, Leroy. Auf Wiedersehen und viel Glück."

"Ach! Is that you, Leroy?!"

"Hi, Bug. Wow, it sure has been a long time, hasn't it?"

"Ya, but time doesn't mean that much to a Volkswagen. We're built to last. I look pretty good for being over 50 though, don't I? After you traded me for that MG I had my doubts. Eggman wasn't very careful with me and I was always covered with chicken feathers."

"That wasn't the smartest trade I ever made, Bug. I was young and immature back then and I thought that MG was a great look-ing car. If I had it to do over, I would have kept you. If we could undo our mistakes, the world would be a pretty great place."

"It is what it is, Leroy. And I came out OK. I've outlived most cars, including old VWs. I was bought by a guy in Chico who completely restored me and now I'm babied. I live in a sparkling clean garage and I'm driven maybe 1,000 miles a year. It's not exactly a trip to Mexico with three giant, smelly human boys, but it's not bad."

"I'm relieved your life turned out OK. Which brings me to the more immediate point of our conversation. As much as I would like to spend a few hours talking with you about the directions our lives have taken since we parted ways, I have a more urgent issue facing me."

"And I bet I know what it is, too, Leroy. Humans and cars don't communicate unless we're all in the spirit world together, so my guess is that you are trying to decide if you should live or die, to put it bluntly."

"You got it, Bug. Any advice?"

"Not really. I've never been dead and I'm not even sure I understand what being dead is. I've been alive my whole life, so far."

"I guess I have too, now that I think about it. But don't you ever wonder what it will be like to be dead? Do VWs believe in God? Do they think there is an afterlife? Do they ever get to the point at which they're so tired and worn out that they just want to unhook their batteries, go to sleep and never wake up?"

"Whoa, Leroy, too many questions at once. But I'll try. Ya, some VWs believe in God, although not all agree about his form, personality or role. Is he a giant, all-knowing Bug? A Porsche? Seems to me he should be a Porsche. Maybe he has no actual form at all, but is just a spirit much the same as we are right now. Others think that when we die the switch just goes off and there's nothingness. Me personally? I don't know. I'll get back to you after I'm dead. That was a joke."

"Ha ha, I guess. Now I'm more confused than ever."

"My point is that nobody knows what being dead is like. Many cars, like people, either think they do or want to convince other people they do. But I don't think we can know until we get there. So the question is not so much what it's like, but whether you're ready to leave the known world behind and check out the unknown."

"That actually makes some sense, Bug. I guess what you're telling me is to think about my life and whether it holds enough promise for me to delay moving on."

"Exactly. You're smarter than you were when you owned me. Now you've got some serious introspection to do and not a lot of time, so you better get started. Before I go, the MG asked if you'd like to speak with him next. At least I think that's what he was saying. I never could understand that Limey accent of his."

"Why not? Maybe he'll think of something we haven't considered. Thanks for the time, Bug. May you live long and happily."

"Hey MG, are you there?"

"Righto, Leroy. I am present. It's been quite a long time, has it not?"

"Yes it has, and I'm sure much asphalt has passed under your tires since we last saw each other."

"Actually, old boy, not all that much, and by the way, I prefer to think of it as macadam. I died fairly young. In fact, it was soon after you sold me back in 1962 to that nice but rather rash young man."

"You know, I can't even remember who that guy was or anything about him. We sold you quickly when I had to go into the military and I didn't pay much attention, given all the other things we had to do. What happened to you?"

"I was grateful for the kind treatment from you, Leroy, despite your large feet. Aside from some occasional issues with my brake and clutch pedals, my life with you was quite nice. Nicer than I realized, actually. The new owner, like so many young men, had more confidence than his skills justified, but he managed not to prang me. I remained with him for two years and he drove me entirely too fast and overconfidently. He, as well as my subsequent owners, seemed to believe I was a true sports car when in fact I was a rather clumsy yet admittedly attractive roadster. But I was not an Austin Healy, and I was not designed to be driven like one. My end was rather violent, occurring in the summer of 1988. Neither my owner nor I survived."

"Yikes, MG, I'm truly sorry. Had I known I was selling you to a frustrated racecar driver I would have chosen another buyer. I hope your demise was quick and painless and moreover, that you will find it in your heart, or is that a poor choice of words, to forgive me."

"Your heart is my carburetor. It was not your fault, Leroy. You had no control over me once the transaction had been documented, nor did you have any responsibility to ensure my subsequent purchasers were careful and competent. So in a word, there is nothing for which to forgive you. As for our deaths, I do not know what his felt like. Mine was painless, as cars have no nerve endings. Sometimes they can be sad, however, particularly if the end is an extended process. In my case it was instantaneous. I was alive, tearing down the road at a speed that was clearly excessive, and we missed the turn, careened off the verge, flipped over several times and came to a smoking, crumpled stop. That was it. I'm telling you all this to make the point that not all of us are given the opportunity to decide whether to live or die."

"MG, I can't tell you how bad I feel for you. In all my years of driving and all the cars I have owned, I have never had a serious accident. Perhaps if I had, I would not be stuck with making the decision I'm now struggling with — my death, like yours, would have taken care of itself."

"Too true, Leroy. Nevertheless, I believe I would have preferred to have a say in the matter. My life on the other side has certainly been nothing at all like it was when I was an actual car, but I can at least opine that if you do opt to move on, there is a possibility that your spirit will live on in some form, as it does with us automobiles. As to whether it's your time, well, that has to be your own decision. I must go now. Did you wish me to summon the 1958 Ford?"

"Yes, please, MG. I thank you for your insight. Perhaps one of these days we will continue our conversation. I wish you well and I want you to know that while I barely fit into your front seat and found it difficult not to push your clutch and brake pedals at the same time, I think we looked pretty good together."

"I concur, Leroy. Pip pip, tally ho."

———————

"Hey Leroy, it is I, the spirit of your 1958 Ford. Tell me, do you still have that annoying dog?"

"Dog? Oh yeah, I recall her, if only vaguely. No, we gave her to a lonely old lady in Nebraska who loved her and was desperate for some company."

"Good riddance. I never did like that worthless cur. Too much hair and slobber to suit me."

"I didn't know you felt that way, Ford. In any case, it's moot now. Actually, I'm a little surprised to hear from you after so many years. I thought you'd be long gone by now."

"Physically, I am indeed. As you may recall, you had me towed to a junkyard after I was unable to perform anymore. I came to terms with my fate and took solace in knowing that many of my parts would be used to give new life to other vehicles and in that way I was living on, if only vicariously. My functional parts have been put to good use, while my body and that unreliable wiring harness have been crushed. But my spirit, like that of the MG and all your other former cars, is intact. Fortunately, we don't take up any space or else it would be more crowded up here than an L.A. freeway at rush hour."

"You've been there for quite a while, Ford. Is it time for me?"

"One thing I have learned over my many years, Leroy, is that wise humans don't need advice and fools don't listen. So I won't tell you what to do, but I can ask you some questions that might help you come to your decision."

"Can't hurt to try, I guess."

"OK, then, first I would have to ask if you're thinking of coming to the spirit world for the right reason, that is, are you escaping something bad or are you happy now but seeking something better?"

"I'd say I have a pretty good life, although I'm not so sure how good it will be after the surgery I'm currently undergoing."

"Yeah, such is life. You can be cruising along smoothly in one instant, thinking you will live forever, and then you blow a tire, crack a block or throw a rod. So you have to realize that anything can happen at any time and that when deciding to live or die, you consider the big picture, not just the moment."

"Makes sense, Ford. I think I also need to consider the effect my decision will have on others, like my wife Liz and my children, Annie and Johnny."

"That was going to be my next question, though I thought your wife's name was Diana. Did you trade her in like you did me?"

"That's a little harsh. It wasn't a trade-in. Let's just say we parted ways and that I remarried. I'm very happy with Liz and I hope Diana has found her own new life. But back to the point, I agree that before we punch out we need to consider the impact on those we leave behind. Naturally, I will, but again, the big unknown at this moment is how much of a burden I will be from now on. If I'm going to be a helpless blob I'd rather let people off the hook and leave quietly."

"Unfortunately, Leroy, you won't have that answer before you have to make your decision. You've got to weigh the risks and choose your course based on that evaluation."

"I get it. I don't like it but I get it. Anything else?"

"Just one thing. As you know, cars are inanimate and we don't have a lot of control over our lives. Oh sure, we can perform better for drivers we like and we can act up when we need to get some attention or make a point, but beyond that we are at the mercy of our owners and how they care for us. When we die we all end up in the same spirit world. Humans, however, do have control over what kind of lives they lead. I suspect that those who die with a clear conscience might live eternally in a happy state. Those who live badly, are mean, dishonest or selfish and have no regard for others, most likely don't have such a good afterlife. Nobody is perfect, nor is anybody totally imperfect, so you won't know where you're going to end up until you get there. You can influence your journey, though, by your actions while you are living. So I would recommend that you ask yourself if there are some things that are undone or not yet atoned that you feel the need to address."

"If I had my life to live over I would do a lot of things differently, Ford. I've tried to live a good, productive, respectable life, but as you say, nobody is perfect. I've made a lot of mistakes and have done some things that embarrass me when I think about them. I can't go back and change what I've done, but I guess I can try to make up for them in some way. That is, if I'm not a vegetable when this little episode is over."

"You've got it, Leroy. I think you know the answers or will figure them out. I wish you well and will put you in touch with my successor, the Mercedes 220S."

———————

"Are you there, Mercedes?"

"Yes I am, Leroy. It's good to hear your voice."

"I would say the same thing, but this is the first time I've heard yours. Actually, it's a little higher than I would have imagined."

"It's the voice they gave me at the factory back in 1959. Maybe they gave all the low ones to the macho speedsters and the tenors were all that were available when I was built. Doesn't really matter, though. What's in a voice?"

"You're right. Before we go on, I do want you to know that of all the cars I've owned in my life, you are the one who most often comes back to me in my dreams. I loved you like a brother and I have wonderful memories or our time together. You were elegant, beautifully designed, reliable and comfortable. I was heartbroken when I had to sell you."

"As was I, Leroy. But a broken piston is a very serious ailment and an expensive repair. I don't hold it against you that you had no choice. Perhaps you'll feel better to know that things ultimately did turn out quite well for me. I am still alive. My engine was repaired and over the years my body and interior have been spruced up as well. I am now deemed a classic, worth $70,000, which is 100 times what you sold me for. I am not driven very much, spending those brief times when out of my garage either in parades or at classic automobile shows. It's a good life for an old car."

"I'm relieved that things turned out so well for you, Mercedes. Have you ever thought about what it would be like if you had not been rescued, but instead had been consigned to the crusher?"

"Of course I have. I'm not an idiot, you know."

"Sorry, no offense intended. I ask because the subject is on the forefront of my mind at the moment. I've got to make a decision and I believe your insight would be helpful."

"None taken. But all cars, like all humans I'd imagine, think about the afterlife and what it would be like to live there. And also like humans, we don't know until we get there, after it's too late to change our minds."

"That's exactly my quandary. If you were in my shoes, what would you do?"

"If I were in your shoes I would look ridiculous. That was a joke. Not my forte. Anyway, the answer is I don't know. I've never been dead. My personal belief is that we only go around once and we have a long time to be dead. I'll acknowledge that I am largely at the mercy of whoever owns me at the time and that at any given moment it could all be over, either as a result of neglect, an accident or a chop shop. But as long as I'm well tended, I want to remain alive. I've seen a lot in my lifetime and if there's one thing I've learned it's that the more I see, the more I realize there is more to see. So in a word, I want to stick around until they drag me away behind the big tow truck in the sky."

"That's pretty succinct, Mercedes. You are living up to your reputation of being a no-nonsense and intelligent car. I would have expected nothing less."

"Happy to help out, Leroy. If you pull through, come down and see me. I spend a lot of time at car shows and I'm easy to spot. I'll give you a high beam when I see you."

———————————

"Are you there, Rambler?"

"Yes, I suppose I am. Good to hear your voice, Leroy. It has been many potholes under the wheels since last we spoke, or more to the point, since last you spoke."

"That's a fact, Rambler. I want you to know that I did feel bad when I traded you in. You had been a reliable car but I believe you would not deny that your days were coming to an end back in, when was it — 1971?"

"Nothing and nobody lasts forever, Leroy. I have no resentment about the end of my life nor reservations about how I lived it. I did my best. I ended up in the junkyard shortly after you traded me in, and when all of my usable parts had been stripped I was consigned to the crusher where I joined a number of other once proud cars. We all ended up eventually in a blast furnace where we were melted down. That confused me at first, as I thought that I had been sent to hell and I couldn't recall any reason why I should be there. Eventually, though, I was recycled into sheet metal and used to form the body of another car. I recall thinking how ironic it would be to come back as a Cadillac and as fate would have it, that's precisely what I did. It wasn't made entirely of me because I had been melded with several other cars in the furnace, but a good percentage of that Caddie's body was formerly a Rambler. I wonder if he knew."

"One man's Rambler is another man's Cadillac, my friend. I have no doubt you did yourself proud in whatever form you came back. Which leads me to my question, I guess. You have just confirmed to me that we live on in some form, even if it might not be the one we are used to. Was that a big adjustment for you? Would you rather have had a say in your future, or maybe not have been recycled at all?"

"Well, Leroy, I had a real aversion to Cadillacs stemming from those visits by your mother-in-law. I tried to ingratiate myself to him, but he was such an insufferable snob that I eventually gave up. That's why I found amusing irony in coming back as part of one. I do my best to persuade his aura to be humble, but I tell you, it's not easy. It's really ingrained. Sure, I would rather have come back in another form, but I resolved to make the best of it. I've even learned to have a little fun teasing the rest of the car when it's parked too close to another one and I yell things like 'Uh oh, we're in for it now. The door in that beat up Honda we're next to is gonna put a major ding in me. There goes my ultra-cool image.' It makes the whole car cringe and it's just a hoot. I guess my point here is that sure, I'd rather have had a say in how I came back but the fact is that I did not, so I adjusted. That's about all we can do."

"I never would have suspected that a Rambler would have a diabolical sense of humor but I have to say that I understand exactly what you're talking about. Given a choice, though, would you have preferred to come back as something entirely different, such as a bike or a toaster? Or maybe nothing at all?"

"Can't say. I've never been a bike and I don't know what a toaster is. As for not coming back at all, that's a tough call as well. I did not know what awaited me after the crusher but I'm thankful that I did get reborn in some fashion, but had I not I guess I wouldn't have known the difference so it really doesn't matter."

"So, Rambler, if I can summarize, I believe you're telling me that we don't have control over our death or what might occur beyond that so we might as well relax and go along with whatever happens."

"Not exactly, Leroy. It is true that I had no control over my death. You, however, can influence your outcome. When you do go is when my philosophy applies, that is, your destiny is out of your hands once you are dead. As long as you are among the living, at least in your current situation, you need to make your own decision whether to hang around or not. Only you can make that call."

"I guess you're right. It sure would be easier just to let go and see what happens."

"Yep, it would. But I advise you to keep in mind that it's a one-shot deal. Once you opt to die, that's it. So I would counsel you not to volunteer to head for the crusher before you're ready."

"Thanks, Rambler. You have given me much to consider. I assure you that whatever decision I make I'll think it over carefully in advance. 'Advance' in this instance isn't all that much time, however. I think I'm getting down to the wire here. I'd better move in case any more of my cars want to weigh in. Thanks for listening — and good luck with those door dings."

"Leroy! Great to see you, sort of. By that I don't mean I actually see you, but I definitely know you're there. Let's not get hung up on technicalities."

"Hey, Bug, it's good to see you, sort of, as well. I trust Johnny is treating you with the respect you deserve."

"He's a thousand percent nicer to me than my original owners were back in 1962. Perspective is important. Had I not experienced those horrible twins I would no doubt complain about Johnny, or even you for that matter."

"You make a good point, Bug. Those guys were pretty rough on you. I suppose we don't appreciate things fully until we experience the good, the bad and the ugly. They were definitely the bad and the ugly."

"That they were. As you probably don't know because conscious humans can't hear us talk, I am a car of few words. If I have something to say, I say it. If I don't I usually go to sleep. I'm not exactly a spring chicken, you know, nor are you now that I think on it."

"I don't need to be reminded. Neither of us is fresh off the assembly line, to put it into terms you can relate to. We've both had our issues with aging. You were restored and I'm sort of undergoing that as we speak."

"That's what I heard. So why are we speaking?"

"Well, Bug, I've come to understand that although I might not have the ultimate say, I do have some influence I can bring to bear on my future if there is to be one. If that's true, I guess I need to make a careful decision whether to live as I was, or to move on to the great unknown and see what it holds in store for me. As a senior citizen, you presumably have absorbed some wisdom along the way, so I'm asking you for your opinion."

"Live."

"That's it? Live? No additional comments?"

"Do you have a gear shift in your ear? I told you I am a car of few words. You asked, I answered."

"Don't get me wrong, Bug. I do value you opinion. But can you give me some rationale for your strong feelings?"

"That's not what you asked for. Since you did, I will. As we both know, I had a rough life in my early years. Things improved after you bought me, but I was not in very good shape and living outside in that salt air of Santa Cruz didn't help my complexion or my top. I was slowly dying and to be honest, I was looking forward to it. I was just tired. Then you had me restored. That gave me a new lease on life, Leroy. With my overhauled engine, new interior, fresh paint and new top I felt like a new Bug. I found my attitude had been restored as well. No longer was I looking forward to the scrap heap. I realized that there is much more to experience once I was up to the challenge. Presumably you are on that operating table undergoing the repairs that, hopefully, will allow you to live instead of die. If the surgery affords you that chance, take it."

"But what if I come out of this as a guy who can no longer take care of himself, can no longer work, can no longer drive or be a productive, independent human being?"

"You won't have that answer by the time you have to make your decision. If you decide now to blow a gasket and call it quits you won't ever know if it was the right decision. Given what you know right now, live."

"Well, I don't know, Bug. I can see now why some people just give up and seek peace on the other side. But you make a good point."

"You're not a fool, Leroy. You're just a human. Your decision will be yours alone. And if you find that you're dead and it turned out to be the wrong one, nobody will be the wiser. I suppose that's some consolation. Think it over carefully."

"I will. Thanks for the time, Bug. Bug? Are you still there?"

"He's not. I am though."

"Which one are you?"

"I'm the Buick Estate Wagon. Remember me?"

"Of course I do, Buick. Our time together was brief but I remember what a sophisticated machine you were. You were roomy, smooth, powerful and quiet. I hated to give you up, but I had no choice. The lawyer said I had to."

"I don't know what a lawyer is or why you had to do what he said, Leroy. Was he bigger than you?"

"Let's just say, Buick, that there are certain advantages to being a car, and lawyers are one of them."

"I can think of a number of other reasons but I gather that is not the reason we are speaking."

"Correct. I assume you know why I am here and what I am grappling with."

"Yes, Leroy, on both accounts. Would you welcome my perspective?"

"I would, Buick. What would you do if you were in my shoes?"

"You're not wearing any at the moment, but I assume you are being metaphorical. Before I render an opinion, I think you should know more about what became of me after you were no longer my driver. It was not a happy time. I also recall that Diana, while she tried to be a careful driver, lacked your innate skills so I was soon living in a constant state of anxiety about my body and its steadily growing number of dings and scratches. Also, I was not well maintained. My service schedule was ignored to the extent that the only attention I received was when the problems became noticeably serious. Within a year of relocating to Chico, my body was dirty and pock marked, my interior was tattered and I was belching blue smoke, leaking oil, overheating and lurching a lot. Rather than make the repairs, Diana sold me to a man who showed me the same disdain she did. He used me for hauling janitorial equipment to his jobs and either he could not afford to repair me or did not realize how sick I really was."

"This is difficult to hear, Buick. When I bought you, you were an elegant, proud car and then, after just two years, you were a janitorial equipment truck."

"I've met other cars who suffered similar fates. The treatment may not have been exactly the same, but the outcome in virtually every case was an abbreviated life. We all ended up being crushed, parted out or up on blocks before we should have. I have to say that I'm enjoying the afterlife a whole lot more than I did the life."

"I'm happy for you that you found some peace, Buick. Sometimes fate can be cruel so when there is a happy ending it mitigates the pain. Do you think it's time for me to end it as well?"

"I wish I had the answer, Leroy, I really do, because you were good to me and I would like to return the favor. Death was the right answer for me. As for you, there are a couple of questions, the answers to which I don't know but are nonetheless germane."

"And those are...?"

"First, do humans have an afterlife? And second, are your days done? To answer the first question, I can assure you that cars have an afterlife. I think humans do as well, but I can't attest to that. I've had no personal interaction with human spirits since I've been a car spirit. As for the second question, my days were done on Earth. I was beyond repair. You are currently undergoing repair, or at least an attempted one, so I can't say if your days are done."

"Neither can I. And I have to say that it would be sorely tempting to just give it up like you did and hope for the best."

"My afterlife is just fine, Leroy, especially when compared to my demise. Personally, I think death is the right answer unless you get a loud and clear message that it's not. But that's just the opinion of a washed up Buick."

"I can respect it, though. Although I do believe there is a risk that my quality of life won't be worth hanging around for, something is tugging at me, trying to tell me not to let go too quickly."

"Well, I'm glad I don't have to make the decision for you, Leroy. I'd love to tell you that everything's going to be fine. My personal opinion is that death isn't that bad so don't fear it."

"I understand, I think. While I still have a little time, maybe I should talk with the next in line. Let me see, which one was that?"

———————————

"That would be me, Leroy, your '72 Bug. You can call me Beetle if you want, in order to avoid confusing me with the '62 you just spoke with."

"Will do, Beetle. So what's your status? Dead or alive?"

"I'm still kickin', as humans would say, and rollin', as we cars would say. I've lasted quite a while and I'm certainly not the flawless VW I once was, but I'm doing well. One of the many advantages of being a VW is our simplicity of design. We don't have a lot of fancy, sophisticated parts and thus there is less to break down. I don't know why car designers feel compelled to create ever more complicated machines unless it's to keep themselves employed. Unfortunately, it also keeps repair shops in business. If VWs were the only cars the world would be a simpler, nicer place."

"I totally agree with you, Beetle. I'd love to spend time discussing your philosophy, but I've got a deadline here and would like to know how you feel about whether I should go on living or not."

"I realize that, Leroy. What I just told you is pertinent, actually. My point is that simple is better. The reason we VWs live so long is that we have fewer parts to go bad. I don't know if humans have that option — if you were to get rid of all your superfluous parts, might you lessen your need for a hospital and thus lengthen your life?"

"Uh, I don't think that's in the cards, Beetle. Humans don't all look alike but we are fundamentally the same when it comes to our construction. With the exception of some enhancements or improvements that might be made by cosmetic surgeons, we all have the same basic organs and parts and we pretty much need all of them except maybe for the appendix. Female parts and male parts have some interesting and important differences but we don't have time to get into all of that. So your idea that we might live longer by simplifying and stripping ourselves down to essentials isn't realistic."

"Yet another reason cars, Volkswagens in particular, are superior to people."

"Could we stay focused here, Beetle? I have an important decision to make and I really don't have time for any sidebar discussions."

"Humph. Fine. So what do you want to know?"

"Shall I try to go on living after my surgery, or just pack it in and move on to the great unknown?"

"Doesn't make any difference to me, Leroy."

"I realize that, Beetle, but it could make a fairly big difference to me."

"Why? You're either alive or dead. What does it matter? Just deal with it."

"So you're advising me to let things develop naturally and the outcome doesn't matter?"

"Yep."

"I'm not so sure I buy into that, Beetle. If we take away our will to live — or not live — we are giving up very important parts of our intellect and motivational forces. I don't believe it would work for humans to think that way."

"How would I know? I'm a car. I can only tell you how I feel. I won't presume to tell you how a human should or does feel. Too complicated and presumptuous."

"I do appreciate your time, Beetle, and you have given me yet something else to think about — I guess. But I better move on. I wish you many more years of happy traveling."

———————

"My turn, amici."

"Amici? You must be the Fiat, right?"

"That I am, Leroy. And believe it or not, I'm still running after all these years. I do have a zillion miles on me by now, and my timing chain has had to be replaced twice, but other than that, I'm doing OK."

"That's good to hear. I lost track of you after I gave you to Annie. I know she drove you while she was in college. What happened to you after she graduated?"

"Pretty much the same thing that happens to all cars when they've experienced college life for a few years, Leroy. I was sold to a teenager, and then to a couple more as time went on. Fortunately, my current owner, while a total nerd, has a friend whose father owns a garage in Chico, so I've had some decent work done on me. And the kid, unlike most teenage boys, drives pretty carefully. I don't know if that's because he's careful or unskilled, but I'll take it."

"Sounds like you were fortunate, Fiat. I'm happy for you. Now I have a question for you."

"I've been listening to your conversations so no need to ask it. I know what it is and I have the answer."

"Oh? And what is that?"

"Que será, será.

"That's it? Que será, será? Have you been listening to Doris Day on your eight-track?"

"Very funny. My point is that what will be will be. You might think you have control over your destiny but I don't really believe that. I think everything is preordained and if you are meant to live to a ripe old age you will. If your time is up, well, it's up and there's nothing you can do about it."

"But Fiat, is it not true that my will to live or die can have an impact on the outcome?"

"Don't believe it. Philosophers like to spout that stuff to give people hope and make them behave themselves. I think it's a bunch of cazzata. I find that life is a lot less stressful when we come to terms with the fact we have no control over it. You just go along living and then, bada bing, you're done."

"Do you really, honestly believe that our death dates are inscribed on some great calendar we can't see? If that's true it makes no difference how we live, does it?"

"The two are not related. Your life span is predetermined, but the way you spend your time among the living is not. You can choose to be a good person or a bad person, a rattletrap or a show car, a star or a dud. But you're going to die anyhow. How you live your life will determine how you are remembered, but not when."

"You sound pretty convinced, Fiat. What makes you so sure you're right?"

"I've thought about this a lot over the years. Most cars and people have their notions about life and death. Some are stubbornly certain they are right and others are constantly beset with doubt. I prefer to hold onto my beliefs because they make the most sense to me. There's always a chance that I'm wrong, but when I find that out I'll already be dead and it won't make any difference one way or the other. So there you have it. You asked my opinion and I gave it to you. Anything else?"

"I guess not, Fiat. I hope you don't take offense if I'm not quite ready to accept your gospel though."

"No problem, Leroy. It's not like I'm one of those born-again evangelical preachers you hear on the radio who purports to have all the answers and will share them with you if you will send your money to him. I don't care if you buy into what I'm saying or not."

"Well, that's pretty straightforward, Fiat. Anything to add?"

"Nope. Que será, será."

"Everybody dies. It's part of life. It doesn't matter much when."

"Huh? Who's that?"

"It is I, Leroy, your former Mercedes 450SL. I hear that you're struggling with finding the answer to your question. Just thought I'd save some time by blurting out my opinion."

"I appreciate that, 450, but I'm not so sure I agree. Sure, we all die eventually. If we didn't, the planet would be pretty crowded. Nevertheless, I think the when matters quite a bit."

"Why? I'll concede that with a possible rare exception most of us aren't ready when our time comes. That sort of goes with the territory of dying. And because nobody's ready, it doesn't much matter when it happens."

"But if I knew that I was about to pack it in, I'd have prepared better. It doesn't seem right to leave so many things undone and to leave Liz, Annie, Johnny and my friends without a little warning."

"Think about it, Leroy. Would your family and friends be happier if you told them in advance that you were going to die? If you knew you were going to depart on a specific date would you really like that? Would you spend all of your final days happily preparing for the big day? On Monday you double-check your will. On

Tuesday you call some old friends to say goodbye. On Wednesday you select your burial suit. On Thursday you prepare the guest list for your wake. On Friday you make certain all the faucet washers have been changed. On Saturday you write your obit. Then you croak on Sunday. That would be the responsible way to spend your final week. But would you want to? Wouldn't you rather just be surprised?"

"Well sure, 450, I don't know of anybody who would enjoy knowing precisely when their time was going to be up. That would be pretty creepy. Isn't there a middle ground? Something between a date certain and total denial?"

"Probably, but then you're already reasonably prepared. You've known for a long time that you're mortal and you've planned for it. You have a will, your assets are in a trust, you and Liz have discussed the inevitability of dying and have agreed that it is OK if the survivor remarries after a suitable a mourning period. Seems to me that's about all you need to do except maybe change those faucet washers. I'm fairly certain that if you told Liz exactly when you were going to shut down for good it would not be well received."

"No, I imagine that would pretty much ruin her day."

"That's why I think there should be some surprise with dying. Maybe not exactly Christmas morning what's in the package surprise, but some reasonable unknown factor."

"Yes those two surprises are very different indeed. You've given me some serious food for thought. I guess if I don't pull through, there's nothing I can do about it. And if I do, I should focus more on living life to the fullest, rather than preparing for death."

"And that, Leroy, is why I believe that because everybody dies, it doesn't matter much when."

"Well thanks, 450. I'm a little rushed at the moment, but I'm curious as to what became of you after we traded you in. How are you doing?"

"Can't complain. The dealer tuned me up, removed all the dents in my body and generally made me pretty spiffy before selling me to a nice elderly woman. I spent my early years in a similar situation so it was no major adjustment for me. I do miss your confident, aggressive technique behind my wheel, but at my age it's probably better to be in my current sedentary existence. Both my owner and I are getting along in years and as I said earlier, we all have to go sometime. I'd rather not know when for either of us."

"Touché, 450. Good talking to you, old friend."

———————————

"Hello? Anybody else here?"

"Huh? Oh, yes. I'm here. Sorry. I was admiring myself in a reflection."

"Who is this? The Porsche?"

"Humph. I rarely am mistaken for one of those low slung, hard riding, overpowered egomaniacs. No, I'm the BMW whom you unceremoniously dumped after my many years of loyal service."

"'Unceremoniously dumped'? I don't recall it that way at all. You were getting along in years and high in mileage, and the dusty vineyard road didn't agree with you. Before Liz and I traded you in we gave it our utmost careful consideration and when we let you go, we did so with regret. If you perceived that as unceremonious or dumping you are mistaken, BMW."

"Yet you kept that lout of a truck who was much older than I and, you must admit, a lot less sophisticated. And ugly to boot."

"C'mon now, aren't you being a little self-centered here? That lout of a truck as you so inaccurately call him, was designed for country living, just as you were designed for urban living, and he has proven himself beyond any doubt that he belongs where he is now. You, on the other hand, had a great deal of trouble adapting to the dusty life in the country and I think if you were honest with yourself you would agree that you are much more in your element in the city. As for his looks, I find them classic, which is a far cry from ugly."

"You never did like me, Leroy. It was obvious to me that I was a chick car to you, and that you could hardly wait to toss me aside for that stuck up Porsche. It was as clear as the poly coat on my finish that you wanted me out of your life."

"I never had a clue you felt this way, BMW. I don't believe you are right, but I can't argue with perceptions. Don't you remember those trips to Chester when we would put your top down and zoom up the mountain road with you hugging the corners? Was I treating you disrespectfully then, or like a chick car?"

"Those were the exceptions, Leroy. Most of the time you didn't like me. I never understood that because I am superior in so many respects."

"Look, BMW, this isn't getting us anywhere and besides, I don't have a lot of time here. Did you want to share with me your opinion as to whether I should awaken from this surgery?"

"Since you ask, I think the most important thing is to look good as you leave and that people express their love for you and cry a lot over your demise."

"Let me see if I understand this, BMW. You're saying that it doesn't matter much if I die so long as I do it prettily and make people sad?"

"Pretty, handsome, dashing — pick your adjective. And if nobody comes to your memorial service to say nice things about you, what's the point? It's not the fact of your death that's important; it's the way you do it and how you're remembered."

"Pardon me, but I find that to be pretty shallow, BMW. What about the feelings of those I leave behind, or the deeds not done, or my influence over my destiny, or the many unknowns about the future, or the fact that life is worth living for as long as we can live it?"

"You're confusing me now, Leroy. I don't like to think about all that stuff. All I want is to be remembered fondly and for people and other cars to cry when they learn that I'm gone. I want a dramatic death and a huge service to follow in which my many positive traits are extolled and there is pervasive sadness that I am gone. That would be just beautiful, wouldn't it?"

"I suppose that having a big crowd of people saying positive things as they recount my life is nice to ponder, but that's just the icing, not the cake. The cake is living a good life. If one lives true to his unvarnished inner self, the service will take care of itself."

"But Leroy, what if nobody recognizes how important you were, or if they do, they don't show up at the service, or if they do, they don't say nice things?"

"I won't care. I'll be dead."

"I can't accept that. I can't bear the thought of being disrespected. That's why to me it's not how you live, but how you die that is key."

"Well, BMW, about all I can say here is that it is obvious that you have thought things through. Not everybody in the universe is on the same road about this subject so I'll respect your opinion and respectfully disagree."

"Fine. Not everybody agreed with Einstein either."

"What does Ein—— oh never mind. I think I have to go now."

––––––––––––

"No so fast, Leroy, although 'not so fast' is an alien concept to me."

"Ah. I'm guessing you are the Porsche."

"Right. I just can't let you go without weighing in on your dilemma. Especially after eavesdropping on your conversation with the BMW. I tell you, he doesn't exactly make me proud to be a German."

"We can't all think alike, Porsche. If we did it would be a drab world indeed. That's not to say I agree with the BMW, mind you, but he's entitled to his opinion even if we think it's a little off to the shoulder."

"I never met one I could trust. I don't know what it is about those guys that makes them all show and no go."

"That's a little harsh, Porsche. They do go, although perhaps not quite as fast as you do. But they do go, particularly when they're behind another car. BMWs do seem to love to tailgate."

"You noticed, huh? The only time I see them going fast is when they want to annoy somebody or get some attention. I have no use for cars like that. I go fast as well, but I don't need an audience. I'm much more centered and self-actualized."

"Good for you. Speaking of going fast, are you feeling better now that you're away from my dusty road?"

"I'm doing fine, Leroy. My new owner is a young man who likes to drive fast, so while I do miss your touch at my controls, I have to say I'm enjoying myself and that I'm running a lot better now that I'm away from the dust."

"Which leads me to my question. At the vineyard you had a taste of not feeling too hot and maybe even contemplating the end that all of us must eventually face. Any words of wisdom for me?"

"You bet. My advice is to forget about death. Concentrate of living life to the max and let death take care of itself. You may not be aware that we Porsches idolize the 1955 silver Porsche Spyder driven by movie actor James Dean on the day of his death in 1955. He was driving it the way Porsches were intended to be driven, that is to say, fast and with abandon. Mr. Dean didn't survive the crash, although his car, affectionately known as 'The Little Bastard' did. He was seriously damaged to be sure, but parts of him were used in other Porsches. These, too met with dramatic ends and before that Porsche's life was over, several more people met their untimely ends due to transplanted parts from The Little Bastard. He was the ultimate Porsche and if I have one regret in my life it's that I didn't have the opportunity to meet him."

"Are you telling me that you hold in reverence a car that was responsible for multiple deaths?"

"Yes I am. I'll acknowledge that it can be traumatic for humans when one of their own dies in a car crash. Not so for a car. That's the way I want to end it when my time is up. Until then, I want to be driven and driven hard. Why do you suppose my speedometer pegs at 180 MPH?"

"I always assumed that was a marketing ploy to sell more cars to guys who could brag about the potential. I never met anybody who actually drove one that fast, and you may recall that I took you up to 110 just once. I could sense that you were enjoying it, but I have to say that I was nervous."

"I do remember, and I've always regretted that you never pushed me harder, Leroy."

"Well, you have more faith in my driving skills than I do, Porsche. Neither U.S. roads nor I were designed for speeds that will please you."

"I can always hope that one of these days somebody will surprise me by taking me to my limit. If we end up in a fiery crash, what a great way to go!"

"That might work for you, but I'm not so sure it's the way I'd like to end my days on Earth. You do make a good point about living life to its fullest. That's something I can agree with. But I think some temperance never hurts."

"Temperance? Not in my vocabulary, Leroy."

"I understand, Porsche. I appreciate your frankness and I wish you happiness. I just hope I don't read about you in the newspaper."

"If you do I hope it's a front page story. Good luck."

"Hey Pickup, are you still here?"

"Yep. Right here, Leroy. I've been listening to all your conversations. What do you think?"

"For starters, I think I've talked about dying more today than I have my entire life. I never knew there could be so many opinions on the subject. Now that I'm at my own decision crossroads I'm suddenly flooded with information and perspectives and I'm a little confused."

"Of course you are. Cars are less emotional about dying than people are and they can be more objective about it. Decisions are easier if you can be more dispassionate."

"How can I be expected to be dispassionate about my own death?"

"I don't expect you to be able to be very objective about this decision. But you do have to come to one, and soon unless you want this whole thing to be taken out of your hands. That's certainly one of the options you've discussed."

"Yes it is, but I don't think I'm ready to cede as long as I can have a say in the matter. I just haven't sorted things out enough yet."

"Maybe I can help, Leroy. Was there a common thread that you picked up in your dialog with your cars?"

"Not really. They all have their opinions and there wasn't very much agreement."

"Maybe they formed different conclusions, but how do you think they got there?"

"This is getting a little deep, Pickup. Keep in mind that I'm anesthetized at the moment. I might not be at my analytical best."

"Oh, all right, I'll give you a little slack given the circumstances. The point I'm trying to lead you to is this: Each of your cars has its own view of death. While the conclusions vary, the common denominator is that their views were all shaped by their lives. Our daily experiences coalesce and lead us to certain conclusions about our existence, its meaning, where we fit in the world, how we view others, and perhaps most important, our attitude about dying. Some dread it, some are fatalistic, some welcome it, some don't care one way or the other, and some are in denial."

"Aha. I'm beginning to understand this. I think you're advising me that my decision will be shaped by my total life experience."

"That's right, Leroy. So your task in, say, the next 60 seconds — your time is getting short — is to think back on your life and based on that reflection, decide whether you with to go on with it or call it a day. This is one of those intensely personal decisions we all have to make, whether we are cars or people. You don't have to share it with me. I'll know."

"Thank you, Pickup. I want you to know how thankful I am for all you have done for me, both on Earth and in this spirit world. That goes for all my other cars as well. Please pass along my heart-felt appreciation to each of them. They all served me well in their special ways. I can only hope they are as grateful for knowing me as I am for knowing them."

"They are, Leroy, they are. In spite of your feet."

ACKNOWLEDGMENTS

If I've learned anything in the course of this project it is the fact that it takes a lot more people to write a book than I ever imagined. I also learned is that it doesn't really need as many commas and participles as I had thought.

Thanks to "El Grupo" — Gary Austin, Jerry Hill and Ted Lopresti — for listening, dusting off faded memories of the past, giving me useful feedback and encouraging me to keep at it; to Roger Evans who has an appreciation for the way cars used to be and truly is one with his stick shift, even though it's on a vintage TR3; to Paul Grist, lifelong friend, valuable cheerleader and former Model A owner; and Dr. Leighton Taylor for his brainstorming and insightful suggestions. Special kudos to Anne Kearney, genius, for her annoying editing. Who'd have thought a refined lady would not only read a book about cars, but actually improve it?! I will be forever indebted to Steve Mitchell — magician, brilliant artist and design guru — who applied his phenomenally creative talents to transform these words into a real book. And above all, heartfelt appreciation to my patient wife Barbara, my copilot on our life's road trip, for her unwavering support, invaluable final editing, wise counsel and love.

Michael Oliver is a native northern Californian
who lives in the Napa Valley with his wife, Barbara.
This is his first attempt at writing
an actual book.